The Prize

Greg Morgan

Adapted from a screenplay by Greg Morgan & Jeanne Morgan.

Original Concept for screenplay by Jeanne Morgan

1

— • —

The Survivor

September

Alex Kelly slept in her clothes. Her shoes sat on the floor beside the bed, laces tied, toes pointed at the door. ready for a quick escape if the day went bad before it even started.

She was up before her alarm. She was always up before her alarm. She made her bed — corners tucked tight enough to bounce a quarter. Wrinkles smoothed flat with the heel of her palm. Then the animals: Elephant first, then Bear, then Penguin, then the nameless rabbit with one ear chewed down to felt, then Dog. Always that order. Always against the pillows. Always facing the door, like they were expecting company.

She touched each one. "Morning. Morning. Morning. Morning. Morning."

Five animals. Five greetings. She didn't know when this had started feeling necessary, only that skipping it now would be like leaving the house without shoes.

Her knees found the cool hardwood beside the bed, and she clasped her hands. She'd never been to church, didn't know the real words, so she borrowed from movies and made up the rest. She prayed to whoever was listening—God, the universe, the crack in the ceiling that looked like a river if you squinted. She prayed that her mother would eat breakfast. She prayed that no one would stare at her head today. She prayed that Chrissy was somewhere good.

When she stood, her fingers went automatically to the gauze wrapped around her skull. Five months since the bombing, and she was still bandaged like a mummy from the neck up. The cast on her arm had come off in June, eight weeks, right on schedule. She'd thought that would be the end of it. But then the headaches got worse in July, and the doctor found the bleed, the 'subdural hematoma' he'd called it, like naming it in Latin made it less terrifying. They'd drilled a hole the size of a nickel and drained the blood that had been slowly pooling against her brain since April.

That was three weeks ago. The stitches itched under the gauze. The wrapping made her look like she'd lost a fight with a lawnmower. She'd begged her mom to let her take it off for the memorial today, just wrap a beanie over the shaved patch, but Donna had said no, the doctor said two more weeks, and for once her mother had been immovable about something that actually mattered.

Alex studied her bedroom walls—every inch covered in her drawings. Not the kind of drawings a thirteen-year-old girl was supposed to make. No horses, no flowers, no anime-style "manga" eyes. Alex drew what other people walked past without seeing. A pair of sneakers dangling from a telephone wire, laces knotted like praying hands. A shopping cart on its side in a ditch, one wheel still spinning. A couch abandoned on a curb with its stuffing erupting through a gash in the cushion, like the furniture was bleeding.

Her backpack hung from the doorknob. She unzipped the front pocket and checked: the ziplock bag was still there, pressed flat between her math notebook and a granola bar she'd been carrying for two weeks. Inside the bag, folded along its original creases, was the newspaper clipping. The photograph.

She didn't take it out. She didn't need to. She'd memorized every pixel, every shadow, every grain of cheap newsprint. The fireman—Ronny Martinez, though she hadn't known his name then—filling the center of the frame, his turnout coat black with soot, his helmet gone, his face caught somewhere between determination and anguish. In his arms, a small boy. Mikey Lowe. Seven years old. First grade. His arm dangling limp, his Spider-Man sneaker half off his foot. And on the right edge of the photograph, a girl stood next to the fireman. Mouth open in a scream. Blood running from her hairline into her left eye, turning half her face into a red mask.

That girl was her.

She hated the photograph. Hated that this was how the world knew her—screaming, bleeding, broken. The first copy she'd taken from the recycling bin the week she came home from the hospital. She'd stared at it so many times the newsprint had gone soft as tissue paper, and then one night she'd fallen asleep holding it and woke to find it torn in half along the fold. The second copy she'd found at the public library, in a week-old Columbus Dispatch someone had left on a table. That one lasted a month before the edges frayed and the image faded to gray from her fingers rubbing across it, like she was trying to reach through the paper and pull herself out.

This third copy she'd sealed in a ziplock bag the moment she got it.

She zipped the pocket shut and slung the backpack over her shoulder.

The kitchen smelled like morning—stale coffee and the faint chemical sweetness that meant her mother had been drinking again. Alex spotted the bottle immediately: Smirnoff, a third empty, standing on the counter next to the toaster like it belonged there. She opened the cupboard above the stove, placed the bottle behind the box of Bisquick where it would be hidden but not gone, and closed the door.

She'd stopped counting the bottles. For a while, she'd kept a tally on the inside cover of her sketchbook—hash marks in groups of five, like a prisoner counting days. She'd gotten to forty-seven. The counting wasn't making her mother drink less. It was only helping Alex measure exactly how much worse things were getting.

Two bowls. Two spoons. Cheerios. Milk. She set her mother's place at the table and sat down across from it, eating in the quiet apartment while the clock above the stove ticked off seconds with a faint click, like a dog's nail on linoleum.

She was on her second bowl when Donna shuffled in, bathrobe cinched tight, hair flat on one side and wild on the other. Her mother had been pretty once. Alex had seen the pictures— Donna at twenty-three, dark-haired and bright-eyed, holding baby Alex on the steps of this same apartment building. Something had dimmed since then. Not all at once. Slowly, like a bulb on its way out, flickering before the dark.

Donna's voice came out rough. "Isn't it Saturday?"

"Yep."

Donna's brow furrowed, then cleared. "The school thing."

"Memorial and orientation. At the new school. They show us classrooms and stuff."

"Right, right, right, right." Donna rubbed her eyes with both palms. "What time?"

"Ten."

"Okay."

"In an hour."

Donna looked at the clock, then at Alex, then at the cereal bowl waiting for her. Her face tightened for half a second. Guilt, maybe. Or the shame of being parented by your own child. She picked up the spoon. Put it down.

"I'm on a diet," she said.

"Mom."

"I'll eat something later. I promise."

Her mother disappeared down the hall toward the bathroom. She listened to the water run. She finished her cereal, washed both bowls—hers and the untouched one—and set them in the rack to dry.

They walked to Whitehall Preparatory School like two people heading to a funeral, which, in a way, they were. Alex matched her mother's pace and navigated the sidewalk with a series of small hops and shortened steps, avoiding every crack. She'd picked up the superstition sometime in the hospital and hadn't been able to shake it. Step on a crack, break your mother's back. She knew it was stupid. She also knew that one hundred and sixty-eight kids and teachers in her school had been alive on a Monday and dead by Tuesday, so maybe the universe operated on dumber rules than anyone wanted to admit.

"It'll be fine," Donna said, reaching for Alex's hand. "New school, new start."

Alex let her mother hold her hand, but didn't squeeze back. A new start. As if they could just leave April behind like a jacket forgotten at a restaurant. As if the bandages on her head and the names of the dead and the photograph in her backpack would all just dissolve with a new address and a different-colored locker.

The school appeared around the corner—a wide, flat building that looked like every other public school in Columbus, all brick and institutional windows, except for the news vans parked along the curb and the police barricades funneling families toward the entrance. Camera crews stood on the sidewalk across the street, lenses aimed at the doors like rifles. Alex pulled her hood up over the gauze, then remembered she wasn't wearing a hood. She ducked her head instead.

They passed through a security checkpoint—metal detector, bag search, a police officer who smiled at Alex with that type of softness adults reserved only for damaged children. She wanted to tell him to stop. She wanted to tell all of them to stop looking at her like she was a bird with a broken wing.

Inside the lobby, Donna spotted someone she knew—another mother from the old school, one of the uninjured parents, the lucky ones—and drifted toward her with a wave that meant, 'go ahead, I'll find you.' Alex didn't argue. She climbed the bleachers in the gym, past the crowded lower rows where parents huddled in tight clusters, past the middle rows where kids sat in stiff, medicated silence, all the way up to the top corner where the air was thinner and nobody would sit next to a girl with her head wrapped in gauze.

The gym was enormous and full of sound that felt like silence—hundreds of people murmuring at once, a white noise of grief that erased any individual word. She scanned the crowd below and cataloged the damage without meaning to. A boy in a wheelchair, his left leg ending above the knee. A girl with burns creeping up her neck like ivy. Two kids on crutches. A boy with a hearing aid who hadn't had one before. These were her people now. The marked ones.

A banner stretched across the far wall: WHITEHALL PREP WELCOMES FOSTER BEGG PREPARATORY SCHOOL STUDENTS. Below it, a second display, longer and quieter: 168 names in alphabetical rows. FOREVER IN OUR HEARTS. Alex read the names from the top of the bleachers, scanning for the ones she knew. She found Chrissy's name third from the left in the D row.

Christine Dawson. Best friend since second grade. The girl who had taught Alex how to French braid and had once eaten an entire jar of pickles on a dare and had been sitting three desks away when the world ended.

Alex's throat closed. She looked away, blinked hard, looked back. Found another name. Michael Lowe. The boy from the photograph. The boy the fireman had been carrying. The boy who had died inches from where she'd been found.

Below, on the lowest bleacher directly across the gym, his mother sat. Jordan Lowe. Alex recognized her from the newspaper stories and from the memorial fund posters that had been stapled to telephone poles all over the South Side. In person, she looked smaller than Alex expected—thin, careful, like someone carrying a glass of water filled to the absolute brim. A line of people waited to speak to her, offering handshakes and embraces that Mrs. Lowe received with a stiff nod each time, her lips moving in what Alex guessed was 'thank you, thank you, thank you,' over and over, a script she'd memorized out of necessity.

Alex wondered what it felt like to be the center of everyone's sympathy. She wondered if it was better or worse than being the girl people looked away from.

The gym doors opened and a column of firefighters entered in dress blues, their uniforms pressed sharp, their faces arranged in the expressions of public sorrow that first responders learned to wear like a second skin. They moved through the crowd and the crowd parted for them—the heroes, the rescuers, the ones who'd run toward the building while everyone else ran away. Alex searched their faces. One of them was Ronny Martinez. The one who'd pulled her out. The one in the photograph. But she'd only seen him in the picture— covered in soot, no helmet, face twisted—and these men all looked the same in their clean uniforms, their hair combed, their jaws set.

The principal took the stage. He talked about resilience. He talked about community. He talked about the counseling services available and the new security measures in place and the school's commitment to healing, the word 'healing' appearing in his speech so many times it stopped sounding like a word and became just a noise, a rhythmic emptiness, like a clock ticking in a vacant room. Alex stopped listening. Below, parents gripped their children. Near the stage, politicians shook hands with the firefighters, posing for photographs that would appear in tomorrow's paper next to words like 'courage' and 'unity.' She thought about how everyone in this room had been assigned a role—victim, hero, mourner, leader—and how none of them had auditioned for the part.

The speeches ended. The crowd began to shift and murmur. Alex descended the bleachers, stepping around bodies and backpacks, and found her mother near the gym floor.

"I need the bathroom," she said.

"Okay, sweetie. I'll wait here."

Alex pushed through the crowd toward the hallway, her head down, the gauze itching, her backpack tight against her spine with the photograph sealed inside it. Near the gym doors she had to turn sideways to pass a group of firefighters, and as she did, her shoulder brushed against one of them—a big man, dark-haired, moving with a slight limp that pulled his weight to the left with each step. Their eyes met. His were brown and tired and held a flicker of something—recognition, maybe, or the ghost of it—but then he blinked and it was gone, and he kept moving toward the exit doors.

That was him. She was almost sure. The jaw, the broad shoulders. That was the fireman from the photograph, the man who'd held Mikey Lowe's body, the man who'd found her screaming in the rubble. And he'd looked right at her—right at her face, her bandaged, scarred, rebuilt face—and hadn't known who she was.

She kept walking.

The hallway was empty and cool after the heat of the gym. Alex found the single-occupancy bathroom, the teacher's bathroom, the private one. She saw it on the way in, during the walk through the lobby — a door marked FACULTY with no line outside it, and she clocked it as she clocked everything worth knowing. She tried the knob. Locked.

"Someone's in there."

Alex turned. A dark-haired girl walked toward her from the far end of the hall. Thin. Wearing a black dress that looked like it had been bought for today and would never be worn again. She recognized her from her old school.

"I had to go to the one down the hall," the girl said, gesturing vaguely behind her. She stopped a few feet away, and her eyes did the thing—the sweep, the assessment, the quick inventory of damage. Gauze. Scar peeking out at the temple. The faded yellow of an old bruise on her jaw.

"I know you," the girl said.

Alex's stomach tightened. "I think I know you, too."

"You were in the photo. With my brother. Alex."

'Yep.' The word sat between them like a stone.

"You're in the grade ahead of me," she added, "Seventh."

"Eighth," Alex corrected. "I'm going into eighth."

"Oh, yeah. I'm seventh now." A pause. "This year."

"I remember you, too," Alex said. "You're Emily. Emily Lowe."

Something shifted in Emily's face—a tightening, a bracing. People probably said her last name to her now, the way they say the name of a disease. With significance. With pity.

"How are you?" Emily asked. Then her eyes went to the gauze again. "How's your head? You still have that on?"

Alex resisted the urge to touch the bandage. "I had another surgery. A few weeks ago. There was a—a bleed. From before. They had to drain it."

"Oh." Emily processed this. "That's gross."

"Yeah."

"I thought you'd be done with all that by now."

"Me too." Alex tried a smile. It felt like putting on a shoe that didn't fit. "Two more weeks, the doctor says. Then I can stop looking like I lost a fight with a ceiling fan."

Emily almost smiled. Almost. It got halfway there and stalled, like a car with a dead battery. "Better than some," she said, and nodded toward the gym.

"Better than some," Alex agreed. The words felt wrong. This girl's brother was one of the 168 on that wall. This girl had every right to scream at her, to ask why

Alex Kelly got to walk around with bandages and a bad joke while Mikey Lowe was in the ground.

They stood in silence. The hallway stretched empty in both directions. The muffled sound of the gym reached them like noise from underwater.

A woman appeared from around the corner. "Are you waiting?" she asked as she walked past.

"Yeah," Alex said.

"There's another bathroom down the hall."

"I'm good. I like this one."

The woman left. The bathroom door opened. A teacher stepped out, saw the two girls, and frowned. "This bathroom is for faculty."

"We're just talking here," Alex said, gesturing between herself and Emily.

The woman adjusted her blouse, decided it wasn't worth a fight, and walked away. Alex caught the door with her fingertip before it closed. She held it open and looked at Emily.

"You can come in. If you want. I don't care."

Emily blinked. "And watch you pee?"

"You don't have to watch. I just figured you didn't want to go back out there yet."

Emily glanced toward the gym. The noise swelled briefly as someone opened a far door, then quieted again. She looked at Alex. "Yeah. Okay."

Alex stepped inside. Emily followed and leaned against the closed door, arms crossed. The bathroom was small—one toilet, one sink, a mirror with a crack in the corner, fluorescent light buzzing the way fluorescent lights always buzzed in places where no one wanted to be.

Alex pulled down her pants and sat. Neither of them spoke for a moment.

"This is weird," Emily said.

"Yep."

"I don't know why I came in here."

"Because the gym is a nightmare and this bathroom has a lock on the door."

Emily looked at her. For a second, something in her expression loosened. "Everyone keeps hugging me. Telling me how sorry they are. Like that's supposed to help."

"Does it?"

"No." Emily picked at a hangnail on her thumb. "Does it help you? When people say stuff?"

"People don't really say stuff to me. They just stare. Or look away real fast, like I'm contagious."

"That sucks."

"Yeah." Alex finished, stood, and pulled up her pants. "The hugging thing sucks too, though."

"Yeah." Emily's mouth twitched. "Pick your poison."

They shuffled around each other in the small space. Alex turned on the faucet. The water was cold and she let it run over her hands longer than she needed to.

"Can I ask you something?" Emily's voice had dropped. "You don't have to answer."

"Okay."

"Do you remember him? My brother. From—" She stopped. The water ran and spiraled down the drain.

"No," Alex replied. "I don't remember much of anything from that day."

Emily nodded. "Doctors say that's normal. Your brain does it on purpose."

"That's what they told me too."

Alex dried her hands on a paper towel, slowly, watching Emily in the mirror. The girl stood with her arms still crossed, shoulders drawn up near her ears, looking less like twelve and more like eight.

"My mom wants to talk to you." Emily's voice was barely a whisper now. "She hasn't said it, but I can tell. She wants to know what happened. What it was like. At the end."

Alex's hands stopped moving. "You could tell her I don't remember," Alex said. "That would be true."

"Or you could. She's not—" Emily searched for the word. "She's having a hard time. Obviously." She picked at the hangnail again, tearing too deep. A bead of blood appeared on her thumb.

"You were there. What happened where you were?" asked Alex.

"I wasn't. I had an ortho appointment."

"That's—" Alex stopped. The word *lucky* sat on her tongue like something sharp. She swallowed it.

Too late. Emily's eyes found hers. "Lucky?" Emily said. "Yeah. That's what people tell me."

The bathroom hummed. The fluorescent light buzzed. Alex wanted to disappear into the tile.

"About my mom," Emily said, letting her off. "I just wanted to warn you. In case she comes up to you or something."

"It's okay. I get it."

Emily stuck her thumb in her mouth, tasting the blood. Tears sat in her eyes, but her jaw held firm — a twelve-year-old girl keeping herself together with nothing but will and habit. "I should go back," Emily said around her thumb. "She gets nervous when I'm gone too long."

"Yeah."

Emily opened the door, then paused, one hand on the frame. She looked at Alex—the gauze, the scar, the tired eyes—and something passed between them that neither of them could have named. Not friendship. Not yet. But a recognition. The understanding that they were standing in the same wreckage, just holding different pieces of it.

"See you around, I guess," Emily said. "Since we go here now."

"Yeah. See you."

Emily slipped out. The door swung shut.

Alex stood alone in the bathroom. She looked at herself in the cracked mirror—the gauze wrapped around her head, the pale skin, the dark circles under her eyes that made her look like a raccoon. She looked like a girl in a hospital, not a girl starting eighth grade. She thought about Jordan Lowe out in that gym, sitting in her folding chair, receiving condolences like a queen receiving subjects, wanting to know what her son's last moments felt like. She thought about not being able to give her that, about having a hole in her memory exactly the shape and size of the worst thing that had ever happened.

She thought about the photograph in her backpack. The ziplock bag. The three of them frozen in that frame—Ronny Martinez, Mikey Lowe, and her. Bound together by a moment none of them had chosen, and by a man with a camera who'd decided that moment belonged to the world.

She turned off the light and left.

Donna was waiting near the gym entrance, talking to the mother from before. "There you are! Did you see the fireman you almost bumped into?"

"When?"

"On your way out to the bathroom. The one with the limp."

"What about him?"

"That was him, sweetie. The fireman that pulled you out."

"I saw him. He didn't recognize me."

"I'm sure he's got a lot on his mind."

"Yeah. Ready for the tour?"

They shuffled through the school with the other families—classrooms with fresh paint and new desks, a cafeteria that smelled like industrial cleaner, hallways lined with lockers in a shade of blue that was probably chosen by a committee to be calming and instead looked like a bruise. The principal led the group and kept saying words like 'safe' and 'supported' and 'community,' and Alex let the words wash over her without sticking, like rain sliding off a window.

Donna chattered the whole walk home. How nice the teachers seemed. How Alex would make friends in no time. How the cafeteria had a salad bar, wasn't that something? How Monday would be great, just great, a fresh start.

Alex's feet found every crack in the sidewalk.

She didn't hop. Didn't shorten her stride. She let her shoes land on every single one—the small ones, the wide ones, the crooked ones that zagged across the concrete like lightning frozen in stone.

She thought about Emily going back to her mother. She thought about Chrissy's name on that banner, third from the left. She thought about the fireman's eyes passing over her face and finding nothing there worth remembering.

Monday. Eighth grade. A new school. She wasn't going.

"Alex? You listening?"

"Yeah, Mom. Sounds great."

2

·

The Hero

The September air hit Ronny Martinez's face like a reprieve. He stood outside the gymnasium entrance of Whitehall Preparatory and breathed it in—sharp, clean, carrying the faint smell of cut grass from the athletic fields—and tried to flush the gym from his lungs. Two hundred people in a room built for basketball, breathing the same recycled grief, and Ronny had stood in the middle of it for an hour in dress blues that fit the same as they always had, while everything inside them had changed.

Behind him, the gym doors were propped open, the murmur of the crowd spilling out into the daylight like heat from an oven. The walkway leading to the entrance was buried under flowers. Teddy bears slumped against the railings like exhausted children. Candles in glass jars, their flames barely visible in the afternoon light. Cards and letters were weighed down with stones. One caught his eye: a crayon drawing of a fire truck taped to the railing, the word HEROS scrawled across the top in red.

The misspelling felt right.

His left knee ached. Five months since the torn meniscus. The doctors said it was healing—six more weeks, maybe eight, and he'd be cleared for full duty. The physical therapist was optimistic. The limp was getting better, they said, and they were right—it was. He could feel it improving, week by week, the hitch in his gait smoothing out, the hot spike of pain dulling to a warm throb. The knee was not the problem. The knee had never been the problem. The knee was just the door

14

he could point to when people asked why he wasn't back at work, and behind that door was a room he couldn't let anyone enter.

Hal stood beside him, lighting a cigarette—a habit he'd quit three years ago and restarted the day after the bombing. The smoke drifted upward, thin and pale against the sky. "You didn't want to talk to the mother?" Hal asked. "She was there on the bleachers."

Ronny shook his head.

Hal let the smoke curl out of his mouth. Didn't push it. That was the thing about Hal—he knew when a man had reached the edge of what he could give, and he respected the edge even when he could see what was on the other side of it.

Ronny had seen her, though. Jordan Lowe. He'd caught a glimpse when the crew entered the gym—front row of the bleachers, close to the door, dressed in black—and he'd looked away before his eyes could settle. He didn't want the details. Didn't want to see her face or her hands or how she held herself, because details made people real, and if she became real he'd have to reckon with what he owed her. So he'd kept his gaze on the back wall, on the banner, on the politicians near the stage—anywhere but the first row.

Her daughter sat next to her. That much he'd caught before turning away.

He'd told himself he would go to her. Had rehearsed it on the engine ride over—*Mrs. Lowe, I'm Ronny Martinez, I'm sorry for your loss*—the words arranged in his head like furniture in a room he'd never enter. Because when the speeches ended and the crowd began to shift and Nate Lowe found him and shook his hand and said *she's right there, first row*, Ronny had looked across the gym at that woman in black and felt something close in his throat like a fist.

He couldn't do it. Couldn't walk across that floor and stand in front of the mother of the boy he'd carried out dead and say words that would sound like comfort but would taste like lies. Not with the truth sitting in his chest the way it sat there every night at three in the morning—the beam, the boy's still legs, the minute in the corridor. He couldn't stand in front of Jordan Lowe and accept her gratitude while carrying that. It would be like accepting a medal for a war you'd lost.

So, he'd stayed near the crew. Shaken hands with the people who approached. Nodded at the principal's speech about resilience without hearing a word of it. Watched the politicians near the stage posing for photographs with firefighters, their faces arranged for cameras.

Then he'd come outside, passed through the security checkpoint, and the air had hit his face. For a moment—just a moment—he could breathe.

The reporters started before Ronny had finished his first full breath. There were fewer than before—the story was fading from the national cycle, settling into the local pages—but the ones who remained were persistent, clustered on the sidewalk across the street with their cameras and microphones, calling out, their voices carrying across the parking lot like dogs that had caught a scent.

"Ronny! When are you planning to return to active duty?"

Left foot, right foot. The limp pulling him slightly off-center with each step, a hitch in his rhythm that he'd learned to compensate for but couldn't hide.

"Have you had a chance to speak with the Lowe family?"

He kept walking. Eyes on the parking lot.

"Ronny! There's talk the photograph is Pulitzer-worthy—any reaction?"

He stopped. The photograph. That photograph existed in Ronny's life as a scar exists on skin—permanently, visibly, impossible to forget. He'd first seen it in the hospital, three days after the bombing, when a nurse had left a newspaper on the table beside his bed. Front page, above the fold, full color. Him. Standing in front of what used to be a school, holding something he couldn't put down. The camera had caught him mid-stride, his face twisted into whatever his face did when his body was moving and his mind had left the building. People kept calling the expression heroic. Ronny thought he looked like a man trying not to drop a child, which was exactly what he'd been.

The world called it beautiful. Ronny thought it was the ugliest thing he'd ever seen.

"Come on." Hal's voice, sharp and commanding. "Back off. Give him room."

The reporters parted. Ronny kept moving. One last voice trailed after him: "Ronny, do you consider yourself a hero?"

He stopped. Turned. "The hero from that day isn't here," he said. His voice came out flat, emptied of everything except the fact. "Andrew Harris. He's the one you should be talking about." He didn't wait for the follow-up before heading toward the fire truck.

Jeannette and Sofia found him in the parking lot. Sofia wore a blue sundress, her dark hair loose around her shoulders, and she slipped under his arm without a word, pressing herself against his side. Twelve years old and still willing to be held by her father in public.

Ronny put his hand on the back of her head and kept it there, feeling the warmth of her, the weight of her, the impossible, terrifying miracle that she was here and whole and breathing.

Jeannette stood a step behind, reading his face. She'd been reading it for five months—searching, calibrating, trying to assess the damage without asking directly. She was good at that. Had been good at it for twenty years of marriage to a firefighter. She knew how to measure the distance between what he said and what he meant, how to hold space for the things he couldn't talk about without making him feel cornered. It was a skill, and she'd never needed it more than she did now, and Ronny loved her for it and felt guilty for making it necessary.

"How'd it go?" she asked. The question was simple. The answer it was really asking for was not.

"Fine."

"You talked to her? Mrs. Lowe?"

"No."

Jeannette waited. He didn't offer more. She nodded—not accepting the boundary so much as marking it, filing it away for later when the kids were asleep and the kitchen was quiet and the questions might find more oxygen.

"We're going to do the tour," she said. "Sofia wants to show me her homeroom, and I told some of the Foster Begg moms I'd walk with them. Help them get the lay of the land." She paused. "A few of them looked pretty lost."

That was Jeannette. Even in the middle of her own family's quiet crisis, she was reaching for the people who had it worse. Making room. Offering to walk alongside someone else's grief because that was how she was built. Steady, generous, a woman who held doors open and remembered names and brought casseroles without being asked.

"That's good," Ronny said. "They could use that."

Sofia shifted under his arm. "Mrs. Patterson said there's a girl in my homeroom from Foster Begg. I figured maybe I should, like, introduce myself or something. Before Monday. So it's not weird."

Ronny looked down at his daughter—already doing the thing most adults in this room were afraid to do, walking toward the damage instead of away from it. He didn't know where she'd learned that. Maybe from Jeannette. Maybe from him, who knows.

"That's a good idea, Sof."

"I know." A crack of a smile. "I have a lot of those."

Jeannette reached for Sofia's hand. "Come on. Let's go find your classroom."

Sofia squeezed Ronny's side once more and then released him, stepping toward her mother. Jeannette caught Ronny's eye over their daughter's head. She didn't say anything. She didn't need to. The look said: We'll talk tonight. And beneath that: I'm here. And beneath that, in the place where words couldn't reach: Come home.

"I'll pick you up at the station in an hour or so," she said. "Take your time."

He nodded, and they turned and walked back inside—Jeannette's hand on Sofia's shoulder, Sofia already scanning the lobby for faces she didn't recognize, already preparing to be brave in the specific, practical way of a girl who had decided that Monday didn't have to be terrible if she got ahead of it.

Ronny had one foot on the bumper when he heard, "Mr. Martinez!" The voice was young and thin and stopped him mid-stride. He turned. A girl walked toward him across the parking lot, moving fast, her ponytail swinging behind her like Sofia's did when she was trying to keep up with adults. She had that same quality—a kid built for running who'd been told to walk.

"I thought you were the fireman," she said. Not a question. "From the photo."

"Yeah."

"I saw you inside. I'm Emily. Emily Lowe."

"I know. I recognized you, too."

"You know my name?"

"Yes," he half lied because he did know her last name. He had seen her inside, sitting next to her mother. She stood with her chin tipped up to look at him, the way small kids do when they're talking to someone tall and refuse to step back to make it easier. A front tooth just barely crooked. Freckles across her nose that the sun had darkened over the summer. She could have been one of Sofia's friends — the same stubborn posture, the same way of planting her feet like she'd decided where she was standing and the earth could adjust.

"My mom wanted to talk to you. Inside. But she couldn't—there were too many people around her and she gets—" Emily stopped. Searched for the word, or decided against it. "She just couldn't."

Ronny looked back at the open gymnasium doors. Jordan Lowe was in there somewhere, and her daughter had walked outside alone to deliver the message she couldn't deliver herself.

"I understand," Ronny said.

"I know she wants to talk to you. For what you did. For bringing him out." Emily said it the way you say something you've been asked to say, practiced words belonging to someone else. But her eyes stayed on his, steady and searching. She wasn't just delivering a message. She was measuring him and deciding whether the man matched the photograph.

Ronny's throat closed. He looked at this girl, this child who had lost her brother and was standing in a parking lot carrying her mother's words because her mother couldn't carry them to the door, and he felt the guilt press against his ribs like a hand.

"You tell your mom—" He stopped. Swallowed. "You tell her I'm sorry I couldn't come over to her. And that... I'm sorry I wasn't at your brother's service. I was in the hospital."

Another lie. He'd been discharged a week before the funeral. Had sat in his living room with the blinds closed, watching the coverage on mute, unable to make himself get dressed and drive to a church and stand in front of a coffin small enough to fit in the back seat of a car.

"It's okay," Emily said. "I'll tell her, but she knows you were hurt, too."

The kindness in it—the easy, unearned forgiveness of a child who didn't know what she was forgiving—was worse than anything the reporters had shouted. Ronny nodded. Couldn't speak.

"Martinez!" Hal's voice from the engine. "We're rolling."

Emily glanced at the truck, then back at Ronny. Something passed across her face—not disappointment, exactly, but the recognition that the conversation was ending before it had reached whatever she'd come out here to reach. She tucked a loose strand of hair behind her ear as Sofia did, an unconscious gesture, her fingers quick and practiced.

"Will you come see her sometime?" she asked. "She'd like that. I think it would help."

I think it would help. The words landed sideways. Not the kind of thing a kid says about a mother who's doing okay. That was a report from the inside—a girl who'd been watching her mother come apart for five months and had learned to measure the damage in language adults would accept.

"Yeah," Ronny said. "I will."

He didn't know if he meant it. He wanted to mean it. Emily looked at him one more time with her dark, assessing eyes, then turned and walked back toward the gym doors, her ponytail swinging with each step, unhurried now, a girl returning to a duty she hadn't asked for.

Ronny climbed into the truck but turned back, looking for her through the window. Emily had vanished into the crowd the way children vanish, quickly and completely, swallowed by the world of adults that kept demanding too much of them.

Ronny put on his headphones and buckled up in the rear-facing jump seat, his usual spot. The seat across from him, Andrew's seat, lay empty. It had been empty for five months. Nobody sat in it. Nobody talked about not sitting in it. Hal had moved to the spot beside it, and the others had shifted accordingly, and the empty seat had become like a missing tooth that everyone's tongue kept finding.

The air brakes hissed. The truck pulled away from the school.

Tom sat two seats down, loosening his collar. Gabe sat beside him, jaw working silently, chewing nothing. Marcus sat nearest the cab, his head tipped back against the bulkhead, eyes closed. Of all of them, Marcus had been the quietest since April. He'd been the one who found Andrew. Had carried him out through the loading dock, through the back of the building, hours after the south wing collapsed. Had refused to let anyone else touch him. Marcus's story hadn't made the front page. Marcus just got the nightmares. And he'd stopped volunteering for interior attack on calls. Took the hydrant now. Worked the exterior. Kept himself outside.

Nobody mentioned that either.

"That girl," Hal said from the front of the compartment using his headset so everyone in the cab could hear. "The one you spoke to out there. That was the Lowe girl?"

"Yeah. The sister." Eyes flashed Ronny's way.

"What'd she want?"

"Her mom wanted to talk to me. Couldn't come outside herself, so she sent her daughter."

Hal pulled on his cigarette and said nothing for a moment before, "You should've gone to her. Inside."

"I know."

"Why didn't you?"

Ronny looked at the floor of the compartment. The question was simple. The answer was a room he couldn't let anyone enter. "I don't know," he said, which was a lie, and Hal knew it was a lie. Everyone on a headset knew it was a lie, but they all kept their mouths shut because that was the deal.

"Did you recognize the other girl?" Hal asked. "The one with the bandages. Gauze around her head. You almost bumped into her as we were leaving."

Ronny looked up. "No. What about her?"

"That was Alex Kelly."

Ronny shrugged his shoulders. He knew the name. He'd seen it a hundred times in the photo's caption written next to his.

"The screaming girl in your photo, Ronny."

"I know who she is," he replied as the engine rumbled beneath him. The city slid past the window—storefronts, traffic lights, a woman pushing a stroller. He thought about the girl in the hallway. The gauze. The backpack. The brown eyes that had searched his face and found—what? A stranger. A man in dress blues who'd looked right at her and seen nothing.

"She recognized you," Hal said. "I saw her face when you almost bumped into her. She knew exactly who you were."

"Anyone would," said Gabe with a grin. "Ronny's a movie star."

As he drove the truck, Tom added, "My wife thinks Ronny's the most handsome at the station. Can you beat that? My wife."

The jokes didn't help. Ronny pressed his palms against his knees and stared at the floor as the cab went silent. Gabe looked to Marcus, and Tom looked to Hal.

Ronny had carried that girl out of a building. Had dug her out of debris with his bare hands while his knee tore and the ceiling groaned above them. Had held her upright while she stumbled through the smoke, her head bleeding, her eyes wide and strange. And today he'd brushed past her and said excuse me and kept walking, and she'd watched him go, and she'd known.

"You saved that girl's life," Hal added without ceremony. The captain, stating a fact as he stated all facts—plainly, without decoration, trusting the weight of the words to do the work. "Whatever else you're carrying, that's real. That happened. She's alive because of you."

Ronny didn't answer. The truck turned onto Broad Street, and the school disappeared behind them.

"Martinez." It was Marcus across from him with his headphones in his lap. His voice was low, almost inaudible over the engine noise. "You think about it?"

Ronny didn't need to ask what it was. "Yeah."

"Every day?"

"Yeah."

Marcus nodded. "Me too."

That was all. Two men in the back of a fire engine, saying out loud what they'd never wanted to admit—that the building was still inside them on fire, that every day they walked through the wreckage all over again, the names on the wall no longer names but faces and voices and how people felt in their hands and all the sounds they would never unhear.

Tom broke the silence with the obliviousness that was either his gift or his survival strategy. "Anybody else starving? There's a Raising Cane's on Fifth. I'll buy."

"You never buy," Gabe said.

"Special occasion. My treat."

"What's the occasion?"

"We survived another memorial without punching a reporter."

Hal snorted. Even Marcus had the ghost of something on his face that wasn't quite a smile but lived in the same neighborhood.

Jeannette's car idled in the station lot when the engine backed in. Ronny climbed down, his knee protesting on the dismount, and crossed the concrete toward her. Danny was in the passenger seat, earbuds in, scrolling his phone. He'd changed out of the button-down already—back in a t-shirt, fourteen years old and done performing solemnity for the day.

Ronny opened his door and moved aside for Danny to get out. "Why do I have to sit in the back?"

Ronny gave him a look, and without further argument, Danny got out and climbed into the back with Sofia. Ronny took his place and shut the door. Jeannette looked at him as she'd been looking at him for five months—love and worry braided together so tight they'd become the same thing.

"How was the tour?" he asked.

"Good. Sofia's classroom is nice. She found the girl from Foster Begg—introduced herself, showed her around. They seemed to hit it off." Jeannette pulled out of the lot. "How was the ride back?"

"Quiet."

They drove in silence for a block. Two. Jeannette glanced at him at a red light. "You didn't talk to the mother."

"No."

"Why not?"

Ronny watched the intersection. A man crossing the street with a dog. A kid on a bike. The ordinary world doing its ordinary business. "I couldn't. Not in front of all those people."

Jeannette didn't say anything. "Her daughter came up to me as I was getting into the truck."

"What did she say?"

Ronny turned to Jeannette for a moment before taking a deep breath with a sigh and looking away to the street. "Nothing," he said.

Jeannette waited two blocks before gently saying, "You should reach out to her, Ronny. When you're ready. She lost her son. You were the last person to hold him. That means something to a mother."

Ronny looked out the window. He thought about Jordan Lowe on the front row of the bleachers—the shape of her he'd caught before looking away, a woman in black he'd refused to bring into focus. He thought about Emily in the parking lot, her chin tipped up, her ponytail swinging, delivering her mother's gratitude because her mother couldn't walk it to the door. He thought about the girl with the gauze—Alex Kelly—whose face he'd looked right through, whose name he'd had to be told by his captain, whose life he'd saved and whose existence he'd erased in the same afternoon.

Hero. The word sat in his head like a stone in a shoe. Every step, there it was. Every time someone said it—the reporters, the parents, the strangers who recognized him at the gas station and the grocery store—he felt it. The wrongness of it. The obscenity. They didn't know what he'd done. They didn't know what had happened in that building. They only knew the photograph, and the photograph was a lie, and the lie had made him famous, and the fame was a prison he couldn't escape because escaping would mean telling the truth, and the truth would destroy everything.

"Ronny?" Jeannette's hand found his on the center console. "You okay?"

"Yeah."

She squeezed his hand. He let her. They drove home through streets he'd known for twenty years, past the same cracked sidewalks and rusting mailboxes, past houses with their last summer's flags still hanging, and Ronny stared out the window and thought about the boy's face—peaceful and still. And behind it, another face. Andrew's. Arms stretched out beneath a collapsed stairwell, reaching toward a door he never opened.

And behind that, the question.

Always the question.

Danny's music leaked through his earbuds in the back seat—a tinny, distant beat, the soundtrack of a boy who'd carried a wreath for a dead man that morning and was already moving on, as do fourteen-year-olds, not because they don't feel it but because their bodies won't let them sit still long enough to drown in it.

Jeannette turned onto their street. The house appeared—the porch, the yard, the fence that needed painting. The swing set Danny and Sofia had outgrown, its chains hanging still. The dead garden that would bloom again in spring.

Ronny got out of the car and stood in the driveway and looked at his house—the house where his children slept and his wife waited and the ceiling above his bed stared back at him every night while he lay awake carrying a minute he couldn't put down and a girl's voice he couldn't stop hearing.

He went inside.

3

The Victim

January

Jordan's slippered feet traced a familiar path along the worn floorboards. The house was still in a way that used to terrify her—those first weeks after, when silence felt like a living thing pressing against her chest, filling the rooms like water, rising to her chin. Now it was just quiet. Early morning quiet, the kind that belonged to her before anyone else woke.

Six-fifteen. She'd been awake since four. The clock in the hallway had ticked her through two hours of darkness, and she'd counted the ticks the same way she counted everything—in groups of five, clusters she could manage, small handfuls of time she could hold without dropping. Five ticks. Five more. Five more. Until the light began to gray the edges of the bedroom curtains and she could justify getting up.

The counting had started in the hospital. The day they told her about Mikey, she'd stood in the corridor while a doctor she'd never seen before said words she'd already stopped hearing, and her eyes had found the floor tiles. She'd counted them from one wall to the other. Thirty-five. Seven groups of five. The number had meant nothing and everything—it gave her mind somewhere to go that wasn't the room where the doctor was still talking, still explaining, still using Mikey's name in past tense. After that, the counting just stayed. Tiles, steps, syllables, heartbeats, the diamonds on Mikey's bedspread, the marshmallows in a bowl of cereal. Groups of five. Always five. The world was chaos and five was the only number she could hold.

She paused at Emily's door and leaned in close. "Morning, Em," she whispered.

Nothing. Jordan pushed the door open. The bed was empty, covers thrown back in careless disarray, and for one sickening instant the floor dropped out from under her. Her hand found the doorframe. Her knees went liquid. She made herself breathe. *She's in the house. She's in the house.*

The fear was instantaneous and total—a trapdoor that opened beneath her feet and dropped her into free fall. It didn't matter that it had been nine months. It didn't matter that the bombing was over, that the school had been rebuilt, that the odds of anything happening to Emily on a Monday night in her own bedroom were statistically zero. Statistics were for people whose children hadn't died at school on a Tuesday morning in April. Jordan's body didn't believe in statistics anymore. Jordan's body believed in the absence of a heartbeat and the weight of a small coffin and the sound she'd made in the hospital when they told her, the sound that had come from somewhere beneath language, beneath thought, beneath anything she recognized as herself.

She checked the bathroom. Empty. The hallway. Empty.

Then her gaze landed on a door she still couldn't look at most days. Mikey's room. It stood slightly ajar. She approached slowly, like approaching the edge of something high, with your weight shifted back, ready to retreat. Her hand trembled as she pushed the door open.

Emily lay curled in Mikey's bed, one arm wrapped around his old Steelers pillow, her breathing slow and even. She wore the oversized Whitehall basketball t-shirt she slept in and a pair of Mikey's Spider-Man socks that she must have found in his drawer, the fabric bunched at her ankles because they were too small for her feet.

Jordan let out a long, shaking breath and stepped inside. Sunlight filtered through the Pittsburgh Steelers curtains, throwing gold bars across the carpet. The room looked the same as it always did—the posters with their curling edges, the shelves lined with action figures and toy cars still in formation, the dusty baseball trophies catching the light. His shoes by the door—not the Spider-Man sneakers, those were gone, but the old ones, the outgrown ones with the lights that no longer worked. His second-favorite jacket on the hook. The handprint turkey he'd made in kindergarten, still taped to the closet door, the construction paper fading from orange to pale peach.

All of it preserved. All of it waiting.

She'd stopped dusting in here months ago. The film on the dresser, on the shelves, on the trophy tops—she'd started to think of it as a kind of sediment. Time settling onto the surfaces of a life that had ended. Disturbing it felt like erasing him. Jordan crossed to the desk beneath the window. The school test still lay there—"Mikey Lowe" in his messy pencil scrawl, the circled B-minus in red ink. He'd been so proud of that B-minus. Had run into the kitchen waving it like a flag: Mom, I got almost a B! And she'd said something like That's great, buddy, while she was loading the dishwasher, not looking up, not stopping what she was doing, because there would be a hundred more tests and a thousand more moments and all the time in the world. She ran her thumb across his name. Set the test back down, lining it carefully with the edge of the desk. Perfectly flush.

She lowered herself onto the bed beside Emily and brushed the hair from her daughter's face. Emily's skin was warm, flushed with sleep. Jordan studied her—the spray of freckles across her nose, the slight furrow between her brows even in dreams, the shape of her mouth, which was Nate's mouth, but the jaw was Jordan's, and the cheekbones were nobody's, they were purely Emily's, and sometimes—in certain light, at certain angles—she looked so much like Mikey that Jordan's chest seized and she had to look away.

Not now. Now she could look.

"Time to get up, Em."

Emily stirred, blinking. Her eyes moved around the room and confusion crossed her face—the slow, disoriented processing of waking up in the wrong bed. "How did I get in here? Did I sleep here last night?"

"Looks like it."

"Huh." Emily rubbed her eyes and sat up. She looked at the Steelers pillow in her arms like she wasn't sure how it had gotten there, then tucked it gently back against the headboard—carefully, the way you set something down that belongs to someone else. "That's weird. I don't remember coming in here."

"It's not weird," Jordan said. "It's okay."

Emily looked at her mother. Those dark, careful eyes doing their daily assessment—the scan, the calibration, the silent question: How bad is it today? Jordan held her gaze and tried to project steadiness. I'm fine. We're fine. It's just a room.

"Ready for breakfast?"

"Yeah. Can we have the good cereal? The one with the marshmallows?"

"Christmas break is over. You know that stuff is pure sugar."

"It's the first day back. That's basically a holiday."

Jordan almost smiled. "Fine. One bowl."

Emily sprang up and padded out, bare feet slapping the hallway floor, the Spider-Man socks making her steps whisper instead of thud. Jordan stayed a beat longer. She let herself look at it all one more time—the trophies, the posters, the test on the desk with his name. The handprint turkey. The shoes by the door.

Only a few months back, she couldn't have sat in this room without shattering. Now she could sit here and only ache. She wasn't sure if that was progress or just a callus forming over something that would never heal.

She pulled the door gently closed behind her and went downstairs to make breakfast.

The kitchen was different now. Not physically—the counters were the same, the appliances, the chipped tile behind the stove that Nate had promised to fix for three years. But the absence had rearranged the room in ways that only someone who lived here would notice. Nate's coffee mug was gone from the hook by the microwave. His newspaper wasn't on the table. The chair at the head—his chair—had been pushed against the wall, and neither Jordan nor Emily had moved it back because moving it back would mean acknowledging that it should be occupied, and leaving it against the wall was easier than looking at the empty seat.

He'd moved out in November. Two months ago. The conversation had been quieter than she'd expected—no shouting, no slamming doors, just two people sitting at this table after Emily was asleep, admitting in low voices that the thing between them had died and neither of them knew when. Maybe April. Maybe before. The bombing hadn't destroyed their marriage. It had just illuminated the cracks that were already there, as a blacklight shows stains you thought you'd cleaned.

Nate had an apartment on the east side now. Emily went there every other weekend. She came back from those visits the same way she left—contained, watchful, careful—and when Jordan asked how it went, Emily said "Fine" — the version that means I don't want to talk about it and I hope you don't push. Jordan didn't push. She had enough battles with her own grief without prying open her daughter's.

She poured two bowls of the marshmallow cereal and set them on the table. Emily came downstairs dressed and backpacked in twelve minutes—a record, even for her. Her hair was in a ponytail so tight it pulled at her temples.

"You do that yourself?"

"YouTube," Emily said through a mouthful of cereal.

"It looks good."

"It took four tries."

They ate in the easy quiet of a routine that had, somehow, through all the wreckage, survived. Jordan counted the marshmallows in her bowl—a reflex, quick, almost unconscious—and then stopped herself. Shook her head slightly. Ate a spoonful without counting it.

Small victories.

Driving east toward Whitehall, Jordan flipped the visor down against the low January sun. She glanced at the rearview mirror. Emily stared out the window, her breath fogging the glass. She'd been home that day. An orthodontist appointment at ten-fifteen that Jordan had almost rescheduled because Mikey had a dentist visit the same week and two appointments felt like too much. She'd kept it. Emily had been sitting in Dr. Regan's chair with a mouth full of rubber bands when the school came down. Sometimes Jordan did the math — if she'd moved the appointment to Thursday, if she'd sent Emily to school that morning instead of driving her across town to get her braces tightened — and the math always ended in the same place, the place where the numbers couldn't help her, the place where one ordinary decision on an ordinary morning had saved one child and couldn't save the other.

The streets were still dressed for a Christmas that had passed. Garlands on the lampposts, a few stubborn light displays still blinking on porches, a deflated inflatable Santa slumped in someone's yard like a man who'd had too much eggnog and given up. The holidays had been terrible. Jordan had anticipated that—had braced for it like bracing for a wave you can see coming. Lily had flown in from Akron, and they'd cooked a ham and opened presents and watched Emily unwrap a pair of ice skates she'd asked for, and everyone had tried very hard not to look at the stocking with Mikey's name on it that Jordan had hung anyway because taking it down felt like agreeing he was really gone.

Her sister, Lily, had gone home on December 28th. Her parting hug had lasted a long time, and she'd whispered, "Call me if you need anything, anytime, I mean it," and Jordan had nodded and said, "I'm fine, I'll be fine," and Lily had looked at her with the expression of a woman who knew exactly how fine her sister wasn't but had a life of her own to get back to.

Jordan didn't blame her. You can only hold someone else's grief for so long before your arms give out.

They pulled up to Whitehall and the world crashed in. Car doors slamming. Kids shouting. Backpacks and lunchboxes and the chaotic energy of a hundred families starting a new semester. Jordan felt her chest tighten as it always did at drop-off—the low hum, the hypervigilance, the animal part of her brain scanning for threats that her rational mind knew weren't there but her body remembered with a fidelity that made reason irrelevant.

The temporary classrooms were visible from the drop-off lane—those white modular units on the playground, their flat roofs dusted with the last of a December snow that hadn't quite melted. They looked permanent now. Part of the landscape. Jordan wondered when that had happened—when the temporary had quietly become the normal, when everything after the bombing had quietly become the normal, when grief itself had become so normal she sometimes forgot what she felt like before it.

She turned to Emily. "See you at three. I love you."

"I love you, Mom." Emily grabbed her backpack and was out of the car in one motion, the door slamming behind her with the decisive force of a girl who did not want to be walked in. She jogged toward a cluster of girls near the entrance, ponytail bouncing, and one of them—Jordan didn't recognize her, a new friend, maybe one of the Foster Begg kids—grabbed Emily's arm and pulled her into the group with the easy, physical intimacy of childhood friendship.

Emily reached the double doors, pulled one open, and was gone. Her hands were tight on the steering wheel. Ten fingers. Five on each side. She loosened them deliberately, one at a time.

She's fine. She'll be fine.

The car behind her honked.

"Fuck off, asshole," Jordan muttered, and put the car in gear.

She drove west on Broad Street without a plan. That was most mornings now—the twenty minutes after drop-off and before home, the gap in the day where she was neither mother nor mourner but just a woman in a car with nowhere to be. Sometimes she drove to the grocery store and walked the aisles without buying anything. Sometimes she sat in the library parking lot and listened to the radio. Sometimes she drove past the site of the old school, now a fenced-off lot of rubble and construction equipment, and sat there until the looking became unbearable and she drove away.

Today she took Broad to Sullivant and turned south, running through the part of the city where the blocks got shorter and the houses got smaller and the convenience stores had bars on the windows. She wasn't going anywhere. She was just moving, because moving was easier than arriving, and arriving meant the empty house and the quiet kitchen and the six hours until three o'clock that stretched ahead of her like a desert.

The photograph found her without warning, without permission. She'd been thinking about groceries, or the electric bill, or nothing at all, and then it was there. The image. A firefighter standing in front of what used to be a school, her son in his arms, a girl screaming beside them, and behind it all the smoke curling upward into an April sky that had no business being that blue.

A man she'd never met had pointed a camera at the worst moment of her existence and the world had decided it was art. Was important. Was beautiful. The photograph had been on the front page of every major newspaper. The cover of Time. Projected on screens at vigils. Printed on posters. Shared so many millions of times online that it had stopped being an image and become a symbol—of tragedy, of resilience, of whatever people needed it to mean on any given day. Someone had made t-shirts. Jordan had heard about that from Nate, and the information had landed in her stomach like a stone and stayed there.

The photographer's name was Demian Ochoa. She'd learned it from the caption. She'd written him a letter in June, sitting at the kitchen table at two in the morning, the words pouring out in a fury so pure it almost felt like relief. You are scum. You saw my son dying and you took a picture. You didn't help him. You didn't save him. You pointed your camera and you stole the worst moment of my life and you sold it and the world applauded.

She hadn't heard back. She hadn't expected to.

She passed Fire Station 17 without registering it. She was a block past when her chest pulled. A tug on a line she hadn't known was attached to her. She hit the brakes. Sat at the intersection, engine idling, staring at nothing. She thought about the firefighter. Ronny Martinez. She'd seen him at the memorial in September—had watched him enter the gym with his crew, had found him immediately among the dress blues, the one with the limp, the broad shoulders, the face she'd memorized from the photograph. She'd sat on the bleacher and waited for him to come to her. He never did. He'd stayed near his crew the entire time, shaking hands with the people who approached him, and Jordan had sat there with her hands folded in her lap, counting the minutes, counting the ceiling tiles, counting the distance between them in floor tiles—forty-two, she'd counted twice—and he had never crossed it.

Emily had gone to him. Had walked outside by herself and found him in the parking lot and delivered the message Jordan couldn't carry to the door. She'd come back and reported it carefully, measuring her mother's reaction. He said he was sorry. He said he was sorry he missed the funeral. He said he'd come see you. Jordan had nodded and said that's nice, sweetheart, and then gone to the bathroom and locked the door and pressed her forehead against the tile wall and counted to one hundred in groups of five.

He hadn't come. Four months since the memorial and he hadn't called, hadn't written, hadn't shown up at the door the way Emily had promised he would. Jordan didn't blame him. She didn't know what she wanted from him. That was the strangest part. She wasn't looking for comfort—she'd had nine months of comfort from strangers and it hadn't helped. She wasn't looking for anything she could name.

It was something else. A pull. A gravity. The irrational, bone-deep sense that this man occupied a space in the story of Mikey's death that no one else could reach—a space between the alive and the gone, between the last breath and the first silence. He had been there. He had held Mikey in his arms. He had carried him out of the building and into the light, and whatever had passed between them in those moments—whatever warmth or weight or stillness Ronny Martinez had felt against his chest—was the closest thing to a final goodbye that Jordan would ever get.

She wanted to be near that. She didn't know why. She didn't examine it. She just turned the car around.

Station 17 was a brick building with two wide bay doors—utilitarian, unremark-able, the sort of place you drove past a thousand times without really seeing. Jordan parked on the street and sat in the car for a full minute, her hands on the wheel, her heart beating in a rhythm she was trying not to count.

This is crazy, she thought. *What are you going to say? Hi, you held my dead son, can we talk?*

She got out of the car before she could talk herself back in.

The bay doors were open. The fire engines stood gleaming in the winter light, enormous and red and somehow alive even at rest, like sleeping animals that might wake at any siren. The bay smelled of diesel and rubber and something metallic she couldn't name—the specific scent of a place where people prepared to enter burning buildings. She thought about Mikey's school. About the smoke and the fire and the sound of the building coming down. About the man who had walked into that and walked out carrying her son.

"Hello?" she called.

Her voice echoed off the concrete walls and came back to her, thin and strange. She walked further in, past the trucks, past a wall of turnout gear—helmets and heavy coats hanging on hooks like the shed skins of larger men, boots lined beneath them in neat pairs. Her gaze drifted up to a banner mounted on the wall above the gear: In Memory of Firefighter Andrew Harris, Who Gave His All in the Line of Duty. Black background, white letters. Formal. Final.

Another name from that day. Another life the bombing had swallowed.

She was still looking at the banner when footsteps approached from a doorway to the right. Hal appeared, wiping his hands on a rag, in uniform pants and a Station 17 t-shirt. He stopped when he saw her, and something moved across his face—recognition, surprise, the quick adjustment of a man who dealt with the public all day and had learned to meet whatever walked through his door.

"Help you, ma'am?"

"Hi. I'm—I was hoping to speak with Ronny Martinez. Is he here today?"

"Ronny's not working right now."

The words landed harder than they should have. She'd driven here on instinct, on something she couldn't explain, and now the instinct had delivered her to an empty destination. She felt foolish. A woman in slippers and an old coat, standing in a firehouse, asking for a man she'd never spoken to.

"Oh," she said. "Okay. Could I—is it possible to leave my number? For him to call me?"

"Of course, of course you can, Mrs. Lowe," Hal said, stepping toward a desk near the wall.

Jordan blinked. "You know who I am?"

He stopped and turned back. His face softened—not pity, exactly, but the gentleness of a man who understood loss from the inside. "Yes, ma'am. From the memorial. At the school. We spoke briefly."

"Oh." Jordan shook her head, embarrassed. "I'm sorry. I don't remember—that day was—"

"You had your hands full. And I'm not a very memorable person anyway." A faint smile. The kind that was meant to put her at ease.

"I don't remember much of that day at all," she said. "The stress."

"That's completely understandable." He picked up a pen. "Give me your number and I'll make sure Ronny gets it."

She recited the digits. He wrote them on a notepad in the neat, careful handwriting of a captain's hand, precise and legible. He tore the sheet off and set it on the desk, then looked at her.

"Is there anything else I can help you with, Mrs. Lowe?"

She almost said no. Almost turned and walked back to her car and drove home and forgot about this strange, impulsive detour. But something in Hal's face—the steadiness, the patience, the way he was looking at her without rushing her—made her stay a moment longer.

"The banner," she said, nodding toward the wall. "Andrew Harris. He was one of yours?"

Hal's expression shifted. The softness remained but something harder moved beneath it. "Yes, ma'am. He was. He died in the building."

"I'm sorry."

"Thank you."

"Were he and Ronny—"

"Partners. Eleven years. Best friends." Hal said it simply, like stating facts that have been stated so many times they've worn smooth. "Andrew was the first one in. Got three kids out before..." He stopped. Cleared his throat. "Well..."

Jordan looked at the banner again. The black background, the white letters. In her mind she saw the memorial wall at Whitehall—168 names in alphabetical rows—and she thought about how every one of those names had a banner somewhere, a framed photograph, a drawer full of clothes that nobody could bring themselves to donate. One hundred and sixty-eight epicenters. One hundred and sixty-eight families sitting in kitchens counting the hours until school pickup.

"Thank you," she said. "For getting him the message."

"Of course."

She walked back through the bay, past the sleeping trucks and the hanging gear and the boots that waited in their pairs. The January sun hit her face as she stepped outside, and she stood on the sidewalk for a moment, blinking, feeling the cold air on her cheeks, feeling the emptiness of having done a thing she didn't fully understand.

She got in the car. Sat there. Didn't start the engine.

What had she come here for? What did she think Ronny Martinez could give her? An answer? A piece of Mikey she hadn't found yet? Some fragment of her son's final moments that would make the absence bearable?

She didn't know. She only knew the pull—the wordless, formless gravity that had turned her car around and brought her to this firehouse and made her write her phone number on a stranger's notepad. It wasn't rational. It wasn't a plan. It was the same instinct that made her sit in Mikey's room and press his shirt to her face and count the diamonds on his bedspread—the instinct to get closer, to reach further into the darkness where he'd gone, as if reaching far enough might let her touch him one more time.

She started the car. Drove home. The house was waiting.

That was how she thought of it now—not as empty but as waiting. Waiting for Emily to come home and fill the hallways with her footsteps. Waiting for the evening, when the television would murmur and the kitchen would smell like whatever Jordan had managed to cook. Waiting for the night, when the counting would resume and the ceiling would stare back at her and the darkness would press in with its questions.

Jordan dropped her keys on the counter. Made coffee on autopilot. While it brewed, she leaned against the counter and turned to the microwave clock. 9:47. Five hours and twelve minutes until pickup. The numbers arranged themselves without her permission—nine and four and seven, twenty, two and zero, two—and she shook her head, pushing them away.

She poured her coffee and sat at the dining table with her laptop. The house was cold—she'd turned the heat down to save money, one of the small, degrading economies of separation that nobody warned you about. Nate's check came on the first and the fifteenth, and it covered the mortgage and Emily's expenses, but the rest—groceries, utilities, gas, the therapist she'd stopped seeing because the copay was forty dollars—came from savings that were running out.

She needed a job. The thought sent a spike of anxiety through her, not because she was afraid of working but because she was afraid of the world. The world outside this house was loud and fast and full of people who hadn't lost anything, people who smiled easily and made plans for the weekend and didn't count the tiles on the floor of every room they entered. The world expected you to function. Jordan wasn't sure she could function. She could survive—she'd been surviving for nine months—but functioning was something else. Functioning meant being present. Being a person. Answering questions and making eye contact and pretending that the low hum of terror beneath everything was not there.

She typed: "Jobs for women over forty Columbus Ohio."

The results stared back at her. Medical office assistant. Practice manager. Teacher's aide. Human resources coordinator. Executive assistant. School bus driver. She read through them twice, waiting for something to catch, some spark of direction or purpose or even mild interest.

Nothing.

She'd been an X-ray technician before Emily. Before Mikey. Before everything. Fluorescent lights, lead aprons, the gray negatives of strangers' bones lined up on screens. Her whole body tightened against the idea of going back. Not because of the work itself but because of who she'd been when she'd done it. That Jordan—the one who wore scrubs and packed lunches for two kids and argued with Nate about whose turn it was to do the dishes—felt like a character in a book she'd read a long time ago. Someone she'd known once. Someone she couldn't get back to.

Her inner voice—the one that had gotten meaner since the bombing, sharper, the voice that counted everything and forgave nothing—offered its assessment: What would make your life just peachy again, Jordan? What's the plan? There is no plan. There's no fixing this. You're just going to sit in this house and count things until you die.

She closed the laptop. The tears were there, right behind her eyes, pressing against the backs of them like water against a dam. She blinked hard. Twice. Three times. Five.

She looked at the coffee cooling on the table. Looked at the stairs. The bed was up there—the covers, the remote, the numbing wash of daytime television where someone else's fake problems could drown out her real ones. She knew what the therapist would say. Don't isolate. Don't retreat to bed. Build structure. Maintain routine. The therapist had a lot of opinions for someone who charged forty dollars to share them.

This is pathetic, she thought. And then: So what if it is. Who's watching?

Jordan left the coffee on the table and climbed the stairs. Fourteen steps. She counted them. She kicked off her shoes, crawled into bed, and pulled the covers up to her chin.

The television flickered to life. A talk show. Two women arguing about something—a man, a lie, a betrayal. A loud, performative conflict that existed in a universe so far from Jordan's that it might as well have been science fiction. She stared at the screen without seeing it.

Five hours and eight minutes until Emily came home.

She pulled the covers tighter. Closed her eyes. The house settled around her—the furnace cycling on, the creak of floorboards adjusting to the cold, the refrigerator humming downstairs in the kitchen where her coffee sat getting cold.

Somewhere across the city, a piece of paper with her phone number on it sat on a desk in a firehouse. A man she'd never spoken to would find it. Would see her name. Would decide whether to call.

She didn't know what she'd say if he did. She didn't know what she wanted. She only knew the pull—the gravity, the formless need to be near the last person who had held her son—and the pull was enough. It was the first thing in nine months that had made her turn the car around instead of driving home. The first thing that felt like reaching toward something instead of retreating from everything.

It wasn't hope. It was too small for that, too fragile, too uncertain. But it was movement. A turn signal. A U-turn on a January morning.

Jordan lay in bed and listened to the house wait, and she waited with it.

4

·

The Observer

The helicopter's shadow chased them across the Afghan plains like something alive, leaping over craters and the burnt-out husks of vehicles that dotted the landscape like the skeleton of a war nobody remembered starting. Demian Ochoa sat beside the open side door, his Nikon D850 braced against his knee, the rotor wash flattening his hair and stinging his eyes with fine grit. He didn't flinch. He'd stopped flinching somewhere around his third embed, years ago, when flinching had started to feel like wasted motion.

They were heading back to base. The LZ behind them had gone hot—Loss of Light—a routine resupply that turned into forty minutes of incoming fire and medics working in the dirt and the chaos that made the recruits go quiet and the veterans go quieter. Demian had shot four hundred frames. His hands still hummed with it.

Corporal Jen Duffy manned the M240 on the opposite door, her hands easy on the weapon, scanning the terrain below with the relaxed attention of someone who'd done this enough times to know when to worry and when not to. Demian had flown with her a dozen times. She was steady. He liked steady.

Beside him sat two reporters—a Reuters correspondent named Walsh who'd been covering Afghanistan longer than some of the soldiers had been alive, and a BBC photographer on her first embed, gripping her seat with both hands, her face a careful mask over obvious terror. Across from them, three recruits: one tapping

41

his foot against the deck, one working a piece of gum like it owed him money, the third leaned back with his eyes closed, either sleeping or praying.

The foot-tapper nodded at Demian. "You CIA or something?" he shouted over the rotors.

Demian looked down at his flak jacket. The word PRESS was velcroed across his chest in letters large enough to read from thirty feet.

The recruit grinned. "Vest says press, but that beard says CIA." The gum-chewer laughed.

Duffy leaned in. "Mr. Ochoa is our platoon photographer."

"That's what they all say," the recruit told his buddy.

Demian shook his head. "Associated Press. I take pictures."

"Don't bother me what you are, long as you're on my side."

Demian sat back against the bulkhead and let it go. His helmet was dusty, his khakis were dusty, everything was dusty. Six months in-country and the dust had become a second skin, working into the creases of his knuckles and the threads of his camera strap and the lines around his eyes that hadn't been there when he'd arrived. He was thirty-four years old and looked forty-five and didn't care.

He lifted the Nikon and scrolled through the day's images on the preview screen, the rotor vibration turning each frame into a small tremor. The transport gunner, frozen mid-burst. A medic's blood-slicked hands pressing gauze into a wound. A dying soldier's face, eyes half-closed, mouth slightly open, as if he'd been about to say something and the words just never arrived.

He'd photographed him from six feet away while the medic worked on him. The medic's head had snapped up. "Delete it."

"I did," Demian had said.

He hadn't. He never deleted anything. The camera captured what it captured. That was the job. He sent everything to his editors and they decided what the world would see. Not him. He was the lens, not the eye. That was what he told himself. That was the same story he'd been telling himself since he was eleven years old, photographing his brother in a hospital bed in Guadalajara, trying to hold onto Miguel one frame at a time while the leukemia took him apart.

Miguel had been ten. Brown eyes, gap-toothed smile, a laugh that sounded like hiccups. He'd liked soccer and comic books and pretending to be a dinosaur, and the chemo had taken his hair and then his appetite and then his energy and then, on a Tuesday morning in March while their mother held his hand and their father stood at the window with his back to the room because he couldn't watch, the rest of him.

Demian had been standing in the corner with a disposable camera he'd bought at the pharmacy across the street. He'd taken eleven pictures that last week. He still had them. The negatives were in a shoebox in his parents' closet in Columbus, Ohio, where his parents, Eduardo and Elena Ochoa, had moved eighteen months after Miguel's death because the house in Guadalajara had become unbearable—every room, every street, every corner store where Miguel had once begged for candy held his ghost, and the only way to survive a ghost was to leave the house it haunted.

Columbus had a Latin community on the west side. Demian's father found work at a meatpacking plant. Elena cleaned offices downtown. Demian enrolled at the high school on Sullivant Avenue with forty words of English and a disposable camera that he'd replaced, by junior year, with a used Minolta his art teacher had given him. He'd photographed everything—the factories, the vacant lots, the faces on the bus. He'd won a scholarship to Ohio State. He'd interned at the Columbus Dispatch. He'd gotten hired by the AP at twenty-five, shipped to his first war zone at twenty-seven, and hadn't stopped moving since.

If he stopped, he'd have to sit with it. With Miguel. With the eleven photographs and the disposable camera and the sound his mother had made when the monitors went flat. Moving was easier. Shooting was easier. Point the camera at someone else's tragedy and it becomes a frame, a composition, a professional problem to solve. Not yours. Never yours.

His thumb hovered over the dying soldier's image on the preview screen. He didn't know the kid's name. Hadn't asked. But he'd seen enough field trauma to read a wound as good as a doctor reads a chart, and the hole in that boy's chest had been a sentence, not a question. The medics would work on him because that's what medics did. They'd pack the wound and call for evac and do everything right and none of it would matter. Demian had named the photo the 'dying soldier' because that's what it was, and the camera didn't have a word for hope. The medic had looked up from the gauze with blood to his elbows and his eyes had said it before his mouth did. Delete it or we'll delete you. The same accusation Demian had heard a hundred times in a hundred forms, from soldiers and civilians and strangers on the internet and editors who should have known better. You watched. You didn't help. You took a picture instead.

The base materialized out of the desert—concrete and canvas, antennas and generators, an outpost of American infrastructure dropped onto Afghan sand. The helicopter touched down hard enough to rattle his teeth. Demian crossed the tarmac to his Sprung structure, a two-person, temporary housing unit provided by the AP. He entered the plywood door and stood in the darkness until his eyes adjusted.

"There he is." Jerry, his bunkmate, lay on his cot scrolling through his phone. "Heard you jumped into a hot LZ."

Demian set down his gear. "News travels."

"The BBC kid was losing her mind. I told her you pull that kind of thing all the time."

"That's what they pay me for." He peeled off the flak jacket. His shirt underneath was soaked through, salt lines dried white across the back.

"Don't get comfortable. George wants to see you."

"About the LZ?"

"Didn't say. But he was amped."

Demian ran a hand through his hair and felt grit between his fingers. His body wanted a cot, a canteen, twelve hours of unconsciousness. "On my way."

Demian put on his sunglasses and crossed to the press building—a long, climate-controlled structure that housed offices for every news outfit in theater. The

AP section was twenty desks deep, reporters and assistants typing and talking, the hum of industry that never paused regardless of what happened outside the walls. A few people glanced at Demian as he passed. Curious. Knowing. He didn't like being looked at. He was the one who looked. That was the arrangement.

George Gelson's private office was in the back. The AP's senior editor for the Middle East—loud, blunt, Brooklyn-born, a newsman who'd been chain-smoking since before it was bad for you and hadn't stopped when it was.

"Ochoa! Get in here!"

Demian sat. George closed the door.

"What's going on?"

George settled into his chair and studied Demian for a moment. A strange energy coming off him that Demian couldn't name. He was savoring something.

"I got off the phone with New York." George leaned forward. "Your photo—the Columbus bombing photo—it's been nominated for the Pulitzer."

Demian heard each word individually but couldn't shape them into a group. "What?"

"Yeah, the Pulitzer Prize. You've been nominated. You're a finalist."

"Finalist? For what photo?" asked Demian.

"The Columbus bombing photo. The one with the fireman and the girl."

Demian shook his head slowly. "Not any of my war work."

"Nope. The Columbus photo," repeated George.

Demian sat back. Tried to process it. The Pulitzer. The thing he'd imagined since he was nineteen, sitting in the Ohio State darkroom, pulling prints from chemical baths, dreaming of the day his work would hang on that wall, in that company, among the photographs that had defined what the world saw and remembered. And it wasn't for Afghanistan or Iraq. It wasn't for the years of dodging bullets and sleeping in dirt and watching men die and turning their deaths into images that editors could evaluate over coffee in Manhattan.

It was for a picture he'd taken while visiting his parents for his father's birthday.

"I was only home for two weeks," Demian said. "My father's sixty-fifth. I happened to be there."

"Fortuitous," George said. "That's what I told New York."

Demian stared at the desk. He'd been in Columbus for six days when the bombing happened. He had been driving to the hardware store to pick up a part for his father's kitchen faucet—his father had asked twice and Demian kept forgetting—when the sound hit. Not an explosion, not from that distance. More like the earth clearing its throat. Then the sirens. Then his hands finding the camera on the passenger seat because his hands always found the camera.

He'd gotten to the school twenty minutes after the blast. The police perimeter wasn't up yet. He'd walked through the gap between two fire trucks and into a scene he'd seen a hundred times in Kabul and Kandahar and Fallujah—the smoke, the rubble, the screaming, the peculiar silence beneath the screaming where the dead were already quiet. His camera had come up. His finger had found the shutter. And his mind had done the thing it always did—the thing it had been trained to do since he was fourteen with a disposable camera watching his brother die—it had stepped back. He framed the shot and found the light.

"Do you have it?" he asked George. "The photo?"

George reached behind him and tossed a newspaper across the desk. The Times Chronicle. Demian picked it up.

He'd seen thousands of his own photographs in print. He knew what his eye did—it found geometry in chaos, and organized destruction into frames that the human brain could process. He'd built a career on that instinct. He'd been praised for it. And now he looked at the Columbus photograph and saw his instinct staring back at him like a mirror.

The composition was clean. Almost too clean. The firefighter slightly left of center, his body angled toward the camera, the turnout coat black with soot, the helmet gone, his face caught in that expression—the one critics had called heroic and haunted and a dozen other words that photographers heard about their best work. In his arms, the boy. Limp. Small. His red t-shirt torn, one Spider-Man sneaker half off his foot, his face turned toward the lens with a peacefulness that the scene didn't earn—as if the boy had fallen asleep and the ruin behind him was just a dream he'd wake from. And on the right edge, the girl. Standing in shock. Mouth open. Blood running from her hairline into her left eye. Her right hand reaching toward the boy.

It was a great photograph. Demian could see that like a carpenter could see a well-built house—structurally, professionally, with the part of his brain that understood composition and light and the geometry of human suffering. The rule of thirds. The diagonal line from the firefighter's face to the boy's dangling arm to the girl's outstretched hand. The smoke behind them diffusing the light into something almost golden. He had taken this photograph on instinct, in seconds, and it was technically as good as anything he'd ever shot.

"I didn't know it had been submitted," he said.

"Mainly New York's decision. They didn't care about the controversy. Pitched it as"—George spread his hands across the air—"a testament to the resilience of the human spirit during tragedy."

Demain's eyes narrowed. "Controversy?"

George's expression shifted. "You haven't heard?"

"I've been here with you for six months, George. Wi-Fi cuts out every other day. Nobody told me anything."

George rubbed his face. "There's been backlash. Significant. Every paper that ran the photo got flooded. Phone calls, letters, emails."

"What were they saying?"

"People don't want to see a dead child, Demian." George said it plainly, as he always did. "We believed it was a significant image. That it described the horror in a way nothing else could. But a lot of readers disagreed. They wanted the heroism. The rescue efforts. The community coming together. Not—" He gestured at the newspaper.

"And the other side?"

"Some people defended it. Said the public needed to see the true cost. But plenty called it exploitative. Said we profited off a dead boy."

Demian stood. Paced the small office. "It's the job, George. The camera documents what's there. I didn't create that scene—I recorded it."

"I know."

"If people don't see it, they forget. They move on. They send thoughts and prayers and change the channel. The photograph forces them to look."

"I know that."

"Then what's the problem?"

"There's no problem. You're nominated for the Pulitzer."

Demian stopped pacing. He looked at the newspaper on the desk. The fire-fighter's face. The boy's still body. The girl's scream, silent and permanent. He thought about the dying soldier in the dirt six hours ago. The medic's head snapping up. Delete it or we'll delete you. The disgust in the medic's eyes. It was the same disgust, wasn't it? The same accusation. You watched. You didn't help. You took a picture instead.

The difference was that in Columbus, Demian hadn't been embedded with anyone. He hadn't been following protocol. He'd been driving to a hardware store and heard a sound and followed it, and when he arrived he'd done the only thing he knew how to do—the thing his hands did automatically, the thing that had kept him sane since Miguel, the thing that turned horror into a frame and put a border around it so it couldn't spread.

He didn't say any of this to George.

"We got a few hundred letters," George added, nodding toward a cardboard box on the floor behind his desk. "They forwarded them from the New York office."

The box sat on the floor like something that might bite. A few hundred people who'd seen his photograph and felt compelled to write. To tell him he'd done something important. Or something unforgivable.

George came around the desk, clapped a hand on Demian's shoulder. "Look, this is good news. A Pulitzer nomination—that's a career-defining moment. Don't let the noise drown it out."

"When do they announce the winner?"

"Few weeks. You'll need to fly back to the States if you win."

"If."

"When." George grinned. "It's a damn good photo, Demian. Whatever anyone says."

Demian folded the newspaper and tucked it under his arm. "Thanks, George."

"Get some sleep. You look like death."

The desert sky had gone dark, stars appearing in the gaps between the floodlights. The air had cooled, the heat of the day radiating upward from the sand like a fever breaking.

In their quarters, Jerry was asleep, his phone still in his hand, its screen casting a pale rectangle of light on the canvas ceiling. Demian sat on his cot and took off his boots. The newspaper was on his lap. He didn't open it.

He thought about the medic's hands on the dying soldier's chest. He thought about his own hands on a disposable camera in a hospital room in Guadalajara, twenty-one years ago, photographing a ten-year-old boy who couldn't hold his head up anymore. He thought about the box of letters sitting in George's office, all those strangers and their opinions, their praise and their fury, their need to tell him what his photograph meant.

He didn't know what it meant. He knew what it looked like. He knew the focal length and the aperture and the shutter speed. He knew the light had been good. He knew the composition was strong. He knew the rule of thirds and the diagonal and how smoke diffused behind the subjects like a scrim.

He lay back on the cot. Stared at the tin ceiling. Listened to Jerry breathe and the generators hum and the distant sound of a helicopter crossing the dark somewhere above him, its rotors beating the air like a pulse. He closed his eyes and saw Miguel. Not the Miguel in the photographs—the thin, bald, fading Miguel of those last weeks—but the real one. The one from before. Gap-toothed. Laughing. Pretending to be a dinosaur in the backyard in Guadalajara, roaring at the neighbor's cat.

He opened his eyes. The tin ceiling was still there.

He reached under his cot, found his phone, and pulled up the Columbus photo on the AP wire. The screen was small but the image was sharp. The firefighter. The boy. The girl. The smoke. The light.

He stared at it for a long time. Then he turned off the phone and lay in the dark and didn't sleep that night.

5

Ronny Martinez pushed through the glass door of Sweetie's Bakery, two vanilla lattes in hand, the little bell above tinkling behind him like a sound from a life that used to be his. The January air hit his face and he welcomed it — cold, clean, anonymous. Nobody on the sidewalk knew who he was. Nobody was staring.

He'd made it six steps before the door burst open behind him. "Excuse me! Excuse me!" He kept walking. Maybe she was talking to someone else. "You're the fireman, right?"

He stopped. She was young — early twenties, brunette, already closing the distance between them with her phone out and her face lit up with that particular excitement he'd come to recognize and dread. "I knew that was you. I was sitting there the whole time like, oh my God, that's him." She was beside him now, phone raised, angling for a selfie before he could respond. "Can I take a picture?"

"Sure," he said. The word was automatic now, a reflex, like blinking.

She pressed herself next to him, held the phone high, snapped twice. Checked the screen. "Thank you so much. My friends are going to freak out."

Ronny managed a smile. It felt like putting on a mask made of wet cement. She turned to walk away, then spun back, still beaming. "Your family must be so proud!" Her voice carried down the block. A few heads turned. A man walking his dog slowed to stare.

"Yeah," Ronny muttered. "Thanks."

He quickened his pace, the limp pulling him off-center with each step. Twenty feet down the sidewalk, the bakery door opened again and Hal appeared, zipping his jacket, looking both ways before spotting Ronny already half a block ahead.

"Hey!" Hal jogged to catch up, falling into step beside him. "The hell happened? I went to grab a napkin and you were gone."

"Had to get out of there."

"Out of a bakery?"

"People stare, Hal. They stare and they whisper and then one of them comes up and wants a photo and tells me my family must be proud and I just —" He shook his head. "I can't sit in a bakery for ten minutes without it turning into a thing."

A small giggle escaped Hal as he matched Ronny's pace. "Everyone's just proud of you."

"I did the same thing you and the rest of us did. Why aren't you guys getting stopped at the bakery?"

"It's been nine months. It'll die down."

"You've been saying that for six months."

"And it has died down. You used to get stopped five times a trip. That was one girl," said Hal as he turned to look at her down the block. "And she was cute too." Hal pulled out his phone, glanced at it, put it back. "You headed home?"

"Yeah."

"Mind if I walk with you? Haven't seen Jeannette in a while."

That should have been the tell. Hal lived in the opposite direction. But Ronny was tired, and the limp was worse in the cold, and he didn't feel like being suspicious. "Sure."

They walked the rest of the way in silence, past the familiar storefronts and bare-limbed trees of the neighborhood Ronny had called home for twenty years. Everything looked the same — same cracked sidewalks, same rusting mailboxes, same houses with their Christmas lights still up because nobody in Columbus took them down before February. But nothing felt the same. Nothing had felt the same since April, when the world cracked open and showed him what was underneath.

Arriving at the house, Ronny had a coffee in each hand. He motioned at the door with his elbow. "You got it."

Hal turned the knob.

The living room was full of firefighters.

Hal sat in the armchair by the window, his captain's authority settled around him like a coat even in civilian clothes — jeans, a flannel shirt, reading glasses pushed up on his forehead. Gabe was on the couch, legs stretched out, his size making the furniture look like it belonged in a dollhouse. Marcus sat in a dining room chair he'd dragged in from the kitchen, hands folded between his knees, quiet as always. Pete leaned against the bookshelf. Kirk — from B-shift, a guy Ronny had trained years ago — had pulled up a stool from the breakfast bar.

Jeannette perched on the arm of the sofa. She looked at Ronny the way she'd been looking at him for nine months — love and worry and something else, something close to exhaustion, the fatigue of a woman who'd been holding a family together while her husband slowly disappeared into himself.

Ronny stopped in the doorway. "What the hell is this?"

"We're here to drag your ass back to work," Gabe said. A smirk, but his eyes weren't smiling.

"Jeannette didn't know anything about this," Kirk said quickly. "We just decided to come by."

"All at the same time?" Ronny turned to Hal. "You knew." Hal found a spot against the wall. Shrugged.

Ronny looked at his wife. Jeannette's face said: I didn't plan this, but I'm not going to stop it either. He handed her the latte. She took it without a word.

He lowered himself into the empty chair they'd obviously left for him — positioned in the center of the room like a witness stand. His knee protested as he sat, the familiar hot spike that had become the background music of his life. He'd accepted that like accepting weather — not happily, but without the energy to argue.

The room was quiet. Everyone was looking at him with that expression — the one that said they'd talked about this beforehand, maybe rehearsed it, and now that the moment had arrived nobody wanted to go first.

Tom leaned forward. "First thing — we're all here because we give a shit about you. I want you to know that."

"I know."

"Good." Tom took off his reading glasses, folded them, set them on the armrest. A deliberate gesture. The captain preparing to be the captain. "So talk to us."

"About what?"

"You haven't been back to work. It's been nine months."

"I'm coming back."

"We want you back," Tom said carefully. "But the department needs a date, Ronny. Not a promise. A date."

"As soon as the knee —"

"The knee." Gabe's voice cut in, not unkind but blunt in the way that Gabe was always blunt. "Ronny, I tore my ACL in '09. I was back in four months. You tore your meniscus nine months ago."

"It's not the same."

"Why not?"

"Because it's not just the meniscus." Ronny's voice tightened. "There's nerve damage. The doctor said —"

"You told me last month the doctor cleared you for light duty," Hal said from his spot against the wall.

Silence. Jeannette's hand found Ronny's shoulder. He could feel the warmth of her palm through his jacket but couldn't make himself lean into it.

"There's something else, isn't there?" Hal said. Not an accusation. A question from a man who'd been reading firefighters for thirty years and knew what guilt looked like from across a room. "Something you're not talking about."

"I'm fine."

"You're not fine. None of us are fine. That's why we're here."

Marcus spoke for the first time. His voice was low, almost inaudible, the voice of a man who'd been quiet for nine months and had only just decided to use his words. "It's about Andrew."

The name landed in the room like a dropped glass. Everyone heard it shatter. Ronny's jaw tightened. "What about Andrew?"

"He was a brother to all of us," Gabe said. "Not just you."

"We all lost him," Hal continued. "We all carry that. But you and Andrew — you were partners. Eleven years. We know what that means."

Ronny could feel the walls closing in. Seven pairs of eyes searching for cracks, trying to pry open a door he'd spent nine months keeping bolted shut.

"Andrew's not the reason I'm not back," he said. "The knee —"

"The knee is cleared," Tom repeated. Quietly. Without malice. Just the fact, sitting in the room like a stone.

"Listen." Ronny's voice hardened. "I already have a department psych. I don't need seven more." The room went still. Hal let the silence hold for a long moment — the captain's trick, giving a man enough rope to hang himself or pull himself to shore.

"Nobody's trying to shrink you," Hal said. "We're trying to bring you home. That's all this is. You're part of this house. You're part of us. We all carry that day — every one of us. But we carry it together. That's how this works. That's how it's always worked."

"Andrew died doing the job," Pete said. It was the first time he'd spoken. "He died getting kids out. Three kids are alive because of him."

"I know," Ronny said. The word was hollow, a shell with nothing inside it. Because they didn't understand. They thought his guilt was simple — survivor's guilt, the textbook kind, the kind the department counselor had a pamphlet for. They thought he felt bad because Andrew died and he didn't. And that was true, as far as it went. But it didn't go far enough. It didn't reach the thing that actually lived inside him — the minute, the hallway, the choice — the thing he'd told no one.

"I hear you," Ronny said. "I appreciate you guys coming. I do. But I'm just not ready yet. That's all it is. I'll come back when I'm ready."

He said it with enough finality to close the conversation. Hal looked at him for a long moment — the look of a captain who knew he was being managed and was choosing, for now, to let it happen.

"Alright," Hal said. "But the door's open. Whenever you're ready, the door's open."

The men began to rise. Handshakes. Shoulders clapped. The too-firm grip that firefighters used on each other when words ran dry. Gabe pulled Ronny into a hug that lasted two seconds longer than regulation, and Ronny let him, because Gabe was the type who hugged you whether you wanted it or not and was usually right about your needing it.

Marcus was the last of the group to pass. He stopped in front of Ronny, and for a moment neither of them spoke. Marcus's eyes were flat, controlled, holding something behind them that Ronny recognized because he carried it too.

"You're not the only one," Marcus said. Low. Just for Ronny.

"I know."

"But you think you are. That's the problem."

Marcus walked out. Tom followed, pausing at the threshold. "Take care of yourself," he said.

"Yeah."

The door clicked shut, and the house sank into a silence so deep it felt immense. Danny was at a friend's house. Sofia was at basketball practice. Just Ronny and Jeannette and the echo of seven men's concern hanging in the air like cigarette smoke.

Jeannette gathered the coffee cups. Her movements were careful, deliberate, the choreography of a woman who'd learned that the minutes after a hard conversation required space, not words. She carried the cups to the kitchen. He heard the water run. The clink of ceramic in the sink. He sat in the empty chair and stared at the carpet and felt the weight of everything he hadn't said pressing on his chest like a hand.

An hour later, the sound of a truck in the driveway.

Ronny watched from the window as Hal climbed out — alone this time, no ambush, no formation. Just the captain in his flannel shirt, hands in his jacket pockets, breath clouding in the cold. He walked back toward the house.

Ronny opened the door before he knocked. "Forgot something?"

"Yeah." Hal met his eyes. "You."

They sat on the back porch in the January dark, two beers sweating despite the cold, the yard stretching out in shadows. Jeannette's garden was dead for the winter — brown stalks and frozen mulch. The swing set Danny and Sofia had outgrown years ago stood against the fence, its chains hanging still. The fence needed painting. It had needed painting since before the bombing. Ronny kept meaning to get to it. He kept meaning to get to a lot of things.

Neither spoke for a long time. They'd known each other long enough that silence didn't need filling.

"They mean well," Hal finally said. "The guys."

"I know."

"They just don't know how to say it."

"Neither do I."

Hal took a drink. Set the bottle on the railing. "So say it badly. Nobody's grading you."

Ronny stared at the yard. The swing set. The dead garden. The fence. He could hear the furnace running inside the house, a low mechanical hum that meant Jeannette was in there, waiting, giving him room.

"Andrew and I were paired up," he said. "Protocol. We went in together." Hal waited.

"He pushed ahead. You know how he was — always first through the door. I called out to him. He didn't stop. Or didn't hear. The building was —" Ronny stopped. Took a breath. "He was gone. Into the smoke. One second he was there, the next he wasn't."

"And then you heard the kids," Hal said. Not a question. He'd read the reports. He knew the shape of the story, if not its interior.

"I heard the kids. The screaming. I went toward them. Found the girl — the one in the photo. She was pinned."

He stopped there. Took a long pull from his beer. The cold burned his throat. He could feel the rest of it pressing behind his teeth — the beam, the minute, the hallway, Andrew's name echoing off smoke-filled walls, the boy's still face — and he clamped down on it. He'd opened the door an inch. That was enough. That was more than he'd given anyone.

Hal waited for more. Ronny shook his head. "That's all I got right now."

Hal nodded. He didn't push. That was the thing about Hal — he knew when a man had reached the edge of what he could give, and he respected the edge even when he could see what was on the other side of it.

"Okay," Hal said. "That's enough for tonight."

They drank in silence. The yard darkened further. A dog barked somewhere down the block — twice, then quiet.

"Come back to work," Hal said. "Light duty. Start there. Ride the truck. Answer calls. Remember what it feels like."

"I can't."

"Can't or won't?"

Ronny didn't answer. The distinction felt like a luxury he couldn't afford — the kind of question therapists asked because they had the distance to parse it. From where Ronny sat, can't and won't lived in the same house and slept in the same bed and he couldn't tell them apart in the dark.

"Andrew would want you back," Hal said.

"Don't do that."

"It's true."

"I know it's true. That doesn't make it useful."

Hal finished his beer. Set the empty on the railing. He sat for another minute, looking at the yard, then stood. Gripped Ronny's shoulder — one squeeze, firm, brief.

"The door's open," he said again. "Whenever."

"Yeah."

Hal walked back through the house. Ronny heard him say goodnight to Jeannette. Heard the front door open and close. Heard the truck start in the driveway, the headlights sweeping across the yard as Hal backed out.

Then quiet.

He sat on the porch for a long time after that. The cold settled into his bad knee and made it ache in a way that felt almost good — a clean, physical pain, simple and honest, so different from the other thing he carried that he almost welcomed it. The dark yard stretched before him with the dead garden, the still swing set, the fence that needed painting, and he thought about the minute in the hallway, and he thought about Andrew, and he didn't think about going back to work because going back to work meant being the hero again, wearing the uniform, answering the questions, accepting the handshakes and the gratitude and the word — hero, hero, hero — that landed on him like a weight every time someone said it, and he couldn't carry that weight and the other weight at the same time. One of them would break him. He wasn't sure which.

The back door opened. Jeannette stepped out, wrapped in a blanket, and sat beside him without saying a word. She didn't ask how it went. Didn't ask what he'd told Hal. She just sat close enough that their shoulders touched and breathed the cold air and waited.

After a while, Ronny said, "I'm not going back yet."

"Okay."

"I know you want me to."

"I want you to do what you need to do."

"What if I don't know what that is?"

Quiet for only a moment, Jeannette said, "Then we figure it out. But not tonight."

She leaned into his shoulder. He let her. They sat together in the cold, and Ronny felt the specific loneliness of a man surrounded by people who loved him and couldn't reach him — a man locked inside a room whose door opened only from the inside, and who'd lost the key somewhere in a burning building nine months ago and hadn't found it yet.

Inside, the furnace hummed. The clock in the hallway ticked. The house waited for the children to come home.

Ronny stared at the fence that needed painting, and the dead garden that would bloom again in spring, and the swing set that nobody used anymore, and he wondered how long a person could sit still before the stillness became permanent — before the not-moving calcified into something structural, something load-bearing, something he couldn't remove without the whole thing coming down.

He didn't know. He finished his beer and went inside. The stairs were dark. He climbed them slowly, one at a time, his knee complaining on every other step, Jeannette's hand light on his back.

At the top, the hallway stretched toward their bedroom, and toward the bathroom, and toward the kids' rooms where Danny's music would start thumping through the wall when he got home, and toward the long night ahead where Ronny would lie on his side of the bed, awake, staring at the ceiling, carrying a minute he couldn't put down and a name he couldn't stop hearing and a question he couldn't answer.

What if. Always what if.

6

Alex's fingers traced the spine of each textbook, a ritual as familiar as breathing. Algebra II settled into the bottom of the backpack first, facing front — always facing front, always the heaviest book first, always in the same order. American History next. Then Earth Science. Then the three notebooks, their covers dense with doodles she'd drawn during the months she'd actually attended class, back when attending class was something she did. The sketchpad went in last, slid into the pocket behind everything else, protected.

She wouldn't open the textbooks until she got to the library. The sketchpad she'd open on the roof.

Alex zipped the backpack and hoisted it onto her shoulders. The straps dug in — twenty-two pounds, she'd weighed it once on the bathroom scale, curious — and she caught her reflection in the mirror on the back of her bedroom door. A girl in jeans and a hoodie with a backpack full of books she was carrying to a school she had no intention of entering. The costume of a dutiful student. The uniform of a con artist.

She was getting good at it. Four months now. Every school day since the second week of September, when she'd walked through Whitehall's front doors for the last time, sat through forty minutes of a history class where the teacher spoke to her in the slow, gentle voice people used on damaged things, and decided — not dramatically, not with tears or rage, just with the quiet clarity of a girl who'd already survived the worst thing that could happen — that she was done.

She wasn't done with learning. She was done with school. There was a difference, and the difference was everything.

From the kitchen, Donna's voice: "Alex! It's seven-thirty!"

"Coming!"

Alex checked the backpack one more time. Books, notebooks, sketchpad, two pencils, a charcoal stick she'd stolen from the art supply store on High Street (she'd pay them back someday), her phone, a peanut butter sandwich in a plastic bag, and the ziplock with the photograph. Always the ziplock. Fourth copy now — the third had started to go soft at the creases from too much handling, so she'd printed a new one at the library from the newspaper's website, trimming it carefully with scissors to match the dimensions of the original.

Donna was in the kitchen, dressed for work — or dressed for the attempt at work, which was the more accurate description. She'd gotten a job at a dry cleaner's on Parsons Avenue in October, four shifts a week, and had managed to keep it so far, which was a record. The vodka bottles had slowed from daily to every few days, a reduction that Alex tracked with the precision of a scientist monitoring a variable. Forty-seven empties in the first five months after the bombing. Fourteen in the four months since. Progress. Maybe.

"I made your lunch," Donna said, holding up a brown paper bag.

"I already made mine. Last night."

Donna looked at the bag in her hand. Something crossed her face — the flash of shame that appeared whenever Alex demonstrated competence that highlighted Donna's absence of it. She set the bag on the counter. "Well, now you have two."

"I'll take both." Alex took the bag because leaving it would be crueler than carrying extra weight. She tucked it into the backpack's side pocket. "Mom, remember to leave early. There's construction on Broad Street and the buses are getting rerouted."

"How do you even know that?"

"I read the news."

Donna's mouth twitched. "Thank you... Mom."

Alex didn't rise to it. "You don't want to be late. You were late Tuesday."

"I wasn't late Tuesday."

"You told me you clocked in at two-twelve. Your shift starts at two."

Donna stared at her. The expression on her face was complicated — love, exasperation, guilt, and the discomfort of a parent who knows she's being managed by her child and can't figure out how to reverse it.

"Let's go," Alex said.

They walked to Whitehall together, the way they did every morning — two figures on the sidewalk, matching stride, the January air cold enough to make their breath visible. Alex navigated around the sidewalk cracks. She'd tried to stop, had told herself it was stupid, had deliberately stepped on three cracks one morning in November and then spent the rest of the day in a state of low-grade panic that didn't ease until Donna came home from work alive. So she kept doing it. The universe operated on stupid rules. She'd learned that in April.

They stopped at the side gate to the playground, their usual spot. Alex preferred this entrance — it faced the athletic fields, not the main lot where parents clustered and teachers stood with their coffee cups and everyone wanted to make eye contact and ask how you were doing. The side gate was quiet. The side gate didn't require a performance.

Donna stepped in front of her and took Alex's head in both hands. "Three lucky kisses," she said, and bent down to press her lips to Alex's forehead. One. Two. Three. "I love you, I love you, I love you." It was Donna's superstition, acquired after the bombing — she'd convinced herself she'd done this the morning of, that the three kisses had been a talisman that kept Alex alive. Alex didn't remember her mother walking her to school that day at all. But the kisses had become a fixed point in their morning, a thing Donna needed to do, and Alex let her do it because the things that kept Donna from drinking were the things Alex protected.

"I love you too, Mom."

"Have a good day."

"I will."

"Learn something."

"Always do."

Donna turned and walked away, joining the stream of parents heading back toward the street. Alex watched her until she rounded the corner — the slight hunch of her shoulders, the purse clutched too tight, the walk of a woman trying very hard to be a person — and felt the familiar tug of guilt and love and exhaustion that was the Alex Kelly Special, available daily, no substitutions.

She waited thirty seconds. Scanned the schoolyard. Two teachers by the main entrance, backs turned. A crossing guard on the far corner, focused on the intersection. Kids streaming through the front doors in that chaotic first-bell rush that made individuals invisible.

Alex turned away from the gate, slung her backpack onto both shoulders, and walked in the opposite direction. Four months. Sixty-three school days skipped. Not that she was counting. She was absolutely counting.

The first library had been the Parsons branch, eight blocks from school. She'd lasted six weeks there before a volunteer started recognizing her and asking friendly questions — Homeschooled? What grade are you in? — and Alex had known it was time to move. The second was the Driving Park branch, farther south, where she'd found a table in the back corner near the large-print romance novels that nobody under seventy visited. That had lasted almost two months before a different librarian — younger, sharper — had asked her directly why she wasn't in school.

"I'm doing an independent study," Alex had said, gesturing at the textbooks spread across the table. "My school approved it." The librarian had looked skeptical but hadn't pushed. Alex had given it one more week and then stopped going. Now she was at the Hilltop branch, on the west side, a forty-minute bus ride from school.

It was bigger, busier, and the staff rotated enough that she could blend in. She'd been coming here since early December — five weeks — and had established herself as a quiet, studious girl who occupied the same table every morning, worked through textbooks in silence, and never caused problems.

But yesterday, a woman behind the reference desk — mid-fifties, kind face, reading glasses on a chain — had watched Alex walk in and said, "Back again? You must really love this library."

"I do," Alex had said, smiling, and sat down at her table with a new knot in her stomach. It was starting. The noticing. The friendly curiosity that preceded the harder questions.

She'd have to find another branch soon. The Columbus Metropolitan Library system had twenty- three locations. She'd burned through three in four months. At this rate, she'd run out by junior year.

She got off the bus at Hilltop and walked the two blocks to the library, head down, hood up. Inside, the warm air hit her like a blanket. The reference desk woman wasn't there today — someone else, a young guy with headphones around his neck who barely glanced at her. Alex exhaled.

She set up at her table. Books out. Notebook open. Phone face-down beside her, ringer off. The phone was the masterpiece of the con. On the second day of school in September, when they'd handed out the emergency contact forms, Alex had filled in her own cell number as the primary contact and Donna's as the secondary. A small, deliberate inversion. Every automated attendance call, every voicemail about missed assignments, every message from the guidance counselor's office — they all went to Alex's phone first. She deleted them as they came in, usually before lunch. If anyone at Whitehall had tried to reach Donna directly, Alex didn't know about it, which meant either they hadn't tried or the school was too overwhelmed with the influx of Foster Begg students to follow up on one quiet girl who'd stopped showing up. She suspected the latter. Whitehall had absorbed two hundred new students in September. The administration was drowning. The counselors were overloaded. And Alex had been careful — she'd attended enough days in the first two weeks to establish herself as a face, had been polite and cooperative during that time, and had then simply... evaporated. In a school that was tracking kids with missing limbs and PTSD and parents who called daily in tears, one girl who quietly disappeared barely registered.

The mail was the other piece. Alex got home before Donna every afternoon, and the mailbox was the first thing she checked. Any letter from Whitehall — attendance reports, progress notices, the mid-semester warning that had arrived in November — went directly into Alex's backpack and from there into a dumpster behind the CVS on the walk home. Three letters so far. She'd read each one carefully before discarding it.

The November warning had been the most alarming: We have been unable to reach you by phone regarding Alex's continued absences. Please contact the attendance office at your earliest convenience.

Alex had contacted the attendance office the next morning, from the bus, using her best impression of Donna's voice — higher than her own, slightly breathless, with the faint apology that lived permanently in her mother's tone. "I'm so sorry, Alex has been having some health issues related to her injuries. We're working with her doctors. She should be back soon." The woman on the phone had been sympathetic. Had said she understood. Had said to take all the time she needed.

That had bought her another two months. But the clock was ticking. Eventually someone would cross-reference records, or send a certified letter, or show up at the apartment. Eventually the con would collapse. Alex knew this. She knew the sidewalk cracks were just concrete — rationally, clearly, with the part of her brain that understood consequences and probability. She just couldn't make herself care enough to stop.

School was unbearable. The empty desks. The teachers' careful voices. The new security guards who stood in the hallways like soldiers. The counselor who'd pulled her aside on Day Three and asked how she was really doing, with that tilted-head expression that made Alex want to scream. The memorial wall in the gym where Chrissy Dawson's name sat third from the left in the D row, and where Alex had stood one morning before first bell, staring at those eleven letters — C-H-R-I-S-T-I-N-E D-A-W-S-O-N — and felt something close in her chest like a fist, and walked out the side door and not come back.

She couldn't be there. She couldn't explain why in any way that would satisfy adults who wanted to help. She just couldn't be there.

So she was here. Hilltop branch. Table in the back. Algebra II open to Chapter 9: Polynomial Functions.

She worked through the problem sets with the grim efficiency of a girl who'd decided that if she was going to skip school, she was going to be smarter than the school she was skipping. It was a point of pride. She did every assignment

— figured out the schedule from the syllabus she'd kept from the first week, cross-referenced it with the textbook, and taught herself what the teachers would have taught her. She was better at it than they were. She could move at her own pace, reread what she didn't understand, skip what she already knew. Her test scores — the ones she took from the practice sections at the end of each chapter — were higher than they'd ever been.

She just couldn't turn them in.

By eleven she'd finished the math and started on American History — the Reconstruction Era, which was dense and depressing but at least had the virtue of being about a country trying to rebuild after catastrophic destruction, which felt relevant. She took notes in her small, precise handwriting, filling pages with dates and names and connections, because the structure of note-taking calmed her.

At eleven-thirty, she packed up. Ate the peanut butter sandwich on a bench outside the library. Ate half of Donna's lunch too — a bruised apple and a granola bar that was probably expired. Threw the rest away.

Then she caught the bus south.

The building was on Harrisburg Pike, an old two-story commercial space that had been vacant for as long as Alex could remember. The ground floor had plywood over the windows and a faded FOR LEASE sign that nobody had responded to. The alley on the south side had a fire escape — rusted, questionable, but functional — and at the top of the fire escape was a roof ladder bolted to the brick wall, eight rungs that led to the flat tar-and-gravel roof.

She'd found it in October, during the first week of the con, when she'd been wandering the neighborhood looking for a place to sit that wasn't the library and wasn't a park bench where someone might notice a girl alone during school hours. She'd spotted the fire escape from the alley, climbed it on a dare to herself, reached the roof, and known immediately that this was her place.

The roof was flat, roughly forty feet by sixty, bordered by a low parapet wall. No one came up here. There was nothing to come up for — no equipment, no antenna, just the tar surface and the gravel and the sky. From the south edge, she could see the tops of the trees in the Scioto Audubon park. From the north, the downtown skyline, the buildings catching whatever light the day offered. On clear days, the view was enormous — the whole city laid out beneath her, small and manageable, how the world looked from an airplane, where everything that was complicated on the ground became simple geometry from above.

Alex sat with her back against the parapet wall, the gravel rough through her jeans, and pulled out the sketchpad.

This was the real work. The textbooks were maintenance — keeping the engine running, making sure she didn't fall behind, preserving the possibility of a future where she went to college and became something. But the sketchpad was the thing itself. The thing she was, underneath the con and the backpack and the sidewalk cracks and the ziplock bag with its photograph. She was a girl who drew.

She drew constantly. Filled pages. The view from the roof in different seasons — October's golds and reds, November's gray, December's skeletal trees, January's flat white sky.

The people on the bus, captured in quick gestural sketches — the woman who always carried two grocery bags and talked to herself, the old man who fell asleep with his mouth open, the teenager with the neck tattoo who once caught Alex drawing him and said, "That's dope," and went back to his phone. The librarians at their desks. The pigeons on the parapet.

And the photograph.

She drew the photograph — compulsively, repeatedly, the same image rendered over and over in pencil and charcoal until the pages curled with the weight of the graphite. She'd drawn it thirty-one times. She knew because she'd numbered each one in the bottom corner, the way real artists numbered prints.

Version one had been crude — a rough copy, proportions wrong, the smoke behind the figures looking more like cotton balls than destruction. Version twelve had been the first one that looked like art. Version twenty had been so accurate that she'd stared at it for twenty minutes, heart pounding, because she'd drawn her own face screaming and the face had looked back at her with an expression she didn't recognize from the inside — wild, feral, desperate. Not her, someone she didn't know. Someone she'd been for one second, in one frame, and then stopped being. But the photograph had kept her there. The photograph had frozen her in the worst moment of her life and shown it to the world, and the world had decided that was who she was.

She was drawing version thirty-two now. This time, she was changing things.

She kept Ronny the same — the soot-covered turnout coat, the missing helmet, the expression between determination and horror. She kept Mikey the same — the limp body, the torn red shirt, the Spider-Man sneaker half off his foot, the peaceful face that didn't match the ruin behind it. But the girl on the right edge — herself — she changed. Instead of screaming,

Alex drew her standing proudly. Looking directly at the camera. Not reaching for Mikey. Just standing in the rubble, blood on her face, eyes open, staring straight out.

She didn't know what it meant. She just knew the original was wrong. The original showed her breaking. She wanted to see what she looked like whole.

The charcoal was soft in her fingers, responsive, leaving black smudges on the side of her hand and the knee of her jeans. She worked in silence. The city hummed below her — traffic, sirens, the faint bass of someone's car stereo — and the sounds rose up the walls of the building and dissolved before they reached her, leaving the roof quiet enough for her to hear her own breathing.

She drew for two hours. Lost in it. The good kind of lost, where time doesn't disappear but stretches, where every minute is full and present and accounted for. She shaded the smoke behind the figures, blending it with her thumb, building layers of gray that deepened into black at the edges. She worked Ronny's face with fine lines — the creases around his eyes, the set of his jaw, with his mouth caught between open and closed, trying to breathe or trying not to cry. She drew Mikey with the tenderness she'd learned to bring to things that were fragile, each line placed carefully, the small details — the laces on the remaining sneaker, the collar of the torn shirt, the eyelashes resting on his cheeks — rendered with a precision that hurt.

And herself. Standing. Eyes forward. Bleeding but upright. She held the sketchpad at arm's length and looked at it. It was the best one yet. Thirty-two versions and this was the first one that felt true — not true to the photograph, but true to something deeper than the photograph, something the camera hadn't seen because cameras only captured surfaces and the truth was underneath.

She closed the sketchpad. Leaned back against the parapet. Watched the sky. Her phone buzzed. She checked it — a voicemail from Whitehall, the automated system. *This is a message for the parent or guardian of Alex Kelly. Your student was absent today, January 6th. If this absence is excused, please contact the attendance office.*

She deleted it. Sixty-four.

The bus home dropped her three blocks from the apartment at 2:48 — twelve minutes before Donna expected her. She walked the route she'd walk if she were coming from Whitehall, approaching from the east instead of the west, so that if Donna happened to be looking out the window, the direction would be right.

She checked the mailbox first. Junk, junk, electric bill, and a white envelope with the Whitehall Preparatory logo in the corner. She slid the school envelope into her backpack without opening it. She'd read it later, in the bathroom, with the door locked and the fan on, and then she'd walk it to the CVS dumpster tomorrow morning.

Upstairs, the apartment was quiet. Donna wouldn't be home until six. Alex dropped her backpack on her bed, washed the charcoal off her hands, and stood at the bathroom mirror looking at her face.

The scar was fading. The line along her hairline where the debris had split the skin — the wound that had bled into her left eye in the photograph, the wound that had required the second surgery for the subdural hematoma — was now a thin pink thread, barely visible unless you knew where to look. The bandages were long gone. Her hair had grown back over the surgical site. She looked, to anyone who didn't know, like a normal thirteen-year-old girl.

She didn't feel like one. But she looked like one. And looking like one was its own kind of camouflage, its own con — the appearance of normalcy stretched over a frame that didn't fit anymore.

She went to her room and unpacked the school envelope. Tore it open.

Dear Parent or Guardian,

This letter is to inform you that Alex Kelly has accumulated 47 unexcused absences in the current semester. Ohio state law requires students between the ages of six and eighteen to attend school regularly. After 30 unexcused absences, the school is required by law to file a referral with the county truancy intervention program.

We have made multiple attempts to contact you by phone and mail regarding this matter. Please contact the Whitehall Preparatory attendance office immediately to schedule a conference.

Failure to respond within 10 business days may result in a referral to Franklin County Children Services.

Alex read it twice. Then a third time. She sat on her bed and stared at the wall and felt the machinery of her con grinding against something harder than she'd planned for.

Children Services. That was new. The previous letters had been concerned, gentle, administrative. This one had teeth.

She could call again. Do the Donna voice. But forty-seven absences was a number that wouldn't be soothed by a phone call. Someone would want a meeting. A face. Documentation. They'd want to see Donna sitting in a chair across from a principal, explaining where her daughter had been for four months, and Donna would have nothing to say because Donna didn't know, because Alex had made sure Donna didn't know, because knowing would break the fragile scaffolding that was keeping Donna upright — the four shifts a week, the fewer bottles, the three kisses at the gate every morning.

If Donna found out, everything would unravel. The guilt would swallow her. She'd blame herself — for the drinking, for the not-noticing, for being a mother whose daughter could disappear for four months without her knowing. And the drinking would get worse, not better, and the dry cleaner job would go like every other job, and the bills would pile up, and the calls to creditors would start again, and Alex would be back where she started, except now with a truancy referral and a social worker and the state of Ohio looking over both their shoulders.

Alex folded the letter carefully along its creases. Slid it back into the envelope. Put the envelope in the bottom of her backpack, beneath the textbooks, where it would sit beside the photograph in its ziplock bag.

Two secrets in a backpack. Both getting heavier.

She went to the kitchen and started dinner — spaghetti, Donna's favorite, the one meal Alex could make well enough that her mother would eat a full plate. She boiled the water and measured the pasta and opened the jar of sauce and set the table for two, and when Donna came home at six-fifteen, smelling of dry cleaning chemicals and winter air, Alex was sitting at the table with her homework spread out in front of her — the real homework, the work she'd done at the library that morning — looking exactly like a girl who'd had a normal day at school.

"How was your day?" Donna asked, dropping her purse on the counter.

"Good. Boring. We started polynomial functions in math."

"Is that hard?"

"Not really."

Donna smiled. A real smile, tired but real. "That's my girl."

Alex smiled back. Hers was real, too, or close enough. The con required it. The love required it. The difference between those two requirements had become so thin she could no longer see the seam.

They ate dinner. Alex washed the dishes. Donna fell asleep on the couch watching a cooking show. Alex covered her with a blanket, turned off the television, and went to her room.

She sat on her bed with the sketchpad open to version thirty-two. The girl standing in the rubble, bleeding but upright, eyes forward. She looked at that girl for a long time. Then she turned to a fresh page and started version thirty-three.

7

A thin film of dust coated the window of the tent, turning the Afghan sunlight the color of old paper. Demian sat on his cot with his Nikon in his lap, working a blower across the lens mount, chasing the grit that crept into everything out here — into the camera, into his clothes, into the folds of his ears and the gaps between his teeth. The desert wanted to own everything. His job was to not let it own this.

Jerry pushed through the tent flap, phone in hand, a look on his face that Demian couldn't immediately read. "You care for that thing like it's a baby."

"It costs more than a baby." Demian held the lens up to the light, checking for scratches. Clean. "What's up?"

"Saw something in the mess hall. On the TV." Jerry dropped onto his cot, tossing his phone onto the blanket. "Someone talking about you."

Demian looked up. "About me?"

"CNN was running a segment on the Pulitzer nominations. They pulled up an old clip — the fireman from your Columbus photo. Doing an interview."

"The fireman?"

"Yeah. The clip's from right after the bombing, but they're replaying it because of the nomination. It's on YouTube." Jerry paused. "He says he wants to kick your ass."

Demian set the camera down. "What?"

"His words. Check it out."

Demian picked up his phone and searched. Multiple tags — Ronny Martinez interview, Columbus bombing firefighter, Pulitzer photo controversy. A thumbnail appeared: Ronny. He stood in the driveway of a house as reporters clustered in front of him, a fellow firefighter beside him. The video had been posted in May, three weeks after the bombing. Demian clicked.

Ronny limped down the driveway toward the cameras, favoring his left leg badly, each step a visible negotiation with pain. He wore his dress blues, the formal black uniform pressed sharp, but the limp made the formality look wrong — like a soldier in parade dress dragging a wound across the parade ground. His face was drawn, thinner than the photograph had shown, dark circles under his eyes.

"Ronny, come talk to us!" someone shouted.

Ronny hobbled over, the other firefighters flanking him. "Just a few questions. I want to watch the game."

"It's halftime, Ronny."

"Then I'm missing the cheerleaders." The reporters laughed. Ronny didn't.

"Was your engine the first to arrive at the school?"

"I think we were the second. But it was chaos. We assessed the situation as fast as we could, and since there wasn't much fire on our side, we just went into rescue mode."

"I want to give my condolences for your station having lost one of your own. Did you know Lieutenant Harris was in the building with you?"

Ronny's face changed. The easy deflection dropped away and something harder moved underneath. "I don't want to discuss Andrew."

The firefighter beside him stepped forward. "Talking about Andrew is too fresh for any of us from the station. Please respect that."

A pause. Then another reporter: "How many did you save, Ronny? How many did you pull out?"

Ronny looked at the ground. When he spoke, his voice was quieter. "It's how many I didn't save that bothers me."

"Ronny, how does it feel to be called a hero?"

Ronny's jaw tightened. "How am I a hero? Just because I'm in that stupid photo?"

Demian's stomach turned.

"You're referring to the photo by Demian Ochoa? How do you feel about how you were depicted?"

"The photo sucks." Ronny said it flatly, without heat, which made it worse. "It was pretty messed up to take a photo at a time like that." He turned to walk away.

"That's enough questions."

He made it a few steps before turning back. His face had changed again — not anger, exactly, but something rawer, something that had broken through the surface despite his efforts to keep it down. "And if I ever see that photographer — Demian, whatever — I'll beat his ass. Let him know that."

The video ended. Demian set the phone down.

"He's gonna beat your ass, Demian," Jerry teased from his cot.

Demian didn't respond. He was staring at the blank screen, replaying Ronny's face in his mind. Not the threat — the threat was nothing, the bluster of a man performing for cameras. It was the other moment. The one before. *It's how many I didn't save that bothers me.* The way his voice had dropped and he'd looked at the ground and the word hero had landed on him like something heavy and unwanted, and the way he'd turned it back on the photograph — on Demian's photograph — as if the image itself were the source of the weight.

The photo sucks.

Demian had been called a lot of things by a lot of people. Editors had torn his work apart. Critics had dismissed entire portfolios. A colonel in Helmand Province had once called him a vulture to his face. None of it had stuck the way those three words stuck. Because Ronny wasn't a critic or a colonel or a stranger writing a letter. Ronny was in the photograph.

Ronny had been standing in the rubble holding a dead child when Demian raised his camera and pressed the shutter. Ronny had a claim to that image that no one else on earth had — not the editors, not the public, not even the boy's mother — because Martinez was there, in the frame, caught forever in the worst moment of his life, and he was looking at Demian's work and calling it what it was. Stupid. Messed up. Something that shouldn't have been taken.

Demian stood and walked to the shared computer on the desk near the tent entrance. His fingers moved over the keyboard, searching — Columbus bombing photo controversy, Ochoa photograph backlash, Pulitzer nomination criticism. The Wi-Fi was crawling, the spinning wheel turning like a clock running out of battery.

"I just don't get all this," Demian said, half to himself. Jerry rolled onto his side. "Don't go down that rabbit hole."

"Have you heard anything? About the backlash?"

"We live in a tent in Afghanistan, Demian. I hear mortar fire and your snoring."

The Wi-Fi died. Demian slapped the desk. "Damn it." He grabbed his sunglasses and walked out of the tent, crossing the compound to the press building.

George was in his office, phone to his ear, waving Demian into a chair. He finished the call and hung up. "What's up?"

"I need to know more about the controversy around my photo."

George leaned back. "Why?"

"Because I just watched the firefighter in my photo call it stupid and say he wants to kick my ass on national television."

"That clip is months old. CNN dragged it up because of the nomination."

"I don't care when it was filmed. He said it."

George studied him. "So what? He's angry. He's in pain. He's a guy who went through hell and somebody took his picture while he was in it. Of course he's angry."

"That's my point. I need to understand what people are saying. I need to read the letters."

"No, you don't."

"George —"

"What you need is to focus on your work. The controversy has died down. The nomination is moving forward. You're going to win this thing, and when you do, nobody's going to remember the angry letters. They're going to remember the photo."

"The fireman remembers."

George was quiet for a moment. He looked at Demian the same way he looked at all his photographers when they were about to do something he couldn't stop — with resignation, combined with preemptive sympathy. "The letters are right here in the box," George said as he gestured his head to the left behind him. "Where they've been since October."

"I want them."

"I know you do." George stood, picked up the cardboard box, and set it on the desk between them. It was heavier than it looked. "Throw it away when you're done. I don't need it back."

Demian reached for it. "Demian." George's voice stopped him. "You should know — there's one from the boy's mother. From Mrs. Lowe. It's not gentle."

"I figured."

"You can't please everyone. If you're not pissing somebody off, you're probably not doing your job." George sat back down. "But some of these people aren't pissed off. They're in pain. There's a difference. Don't confuse the two."

Demian picked up the box and carried it back to the tent. He started with the strangers. He sat on his cot with the box between his feet and opened them one at a time, reading each letter completely before setting it on the floor and reaching for the next. Jerry lay on his cot pretending to read a magazine, but Demian could feel him watching.

The first ten were what he'd expected — outrage, indignation, the fury of people who believed they'd been assaulted by an image they hadn't asked to see. Some were articulate. Some were barely literate. All of them were certain.

...callously disregards the sanctity of grief...

...you perpetuate a culture of voyeurism...

...your publication has chosen a path that fans the flames of pain and anguish...

...that child's memory deserves more than to be reduced to a shocking image in a newspaper...

He read twenty. Thirty. The letters blurred together, a chorus of voices saying variations of the same thing: You shouldn't have taken this photo. You shouldn't have published this photo. This photo causes pain. And beneath the anger, in every letter, the thing they weren't quite saying but that Demian could hear anyway: I saw a dead child and I didn't want to see a dead child and I'm angry at you for making me see what I didn't want to see.

He understood that. He did. He'd been making people see things they didn't want to see for his entire career. That was the job. The camera was a witness. The shutter was a verdict. You don't look away. You don't delete. You capture the truth and you send it out into the world, and you let the world decide what to do with it.

Except.

He thought about the dying soldier. The medic's head snapping up. Delete it or we'll delete you. He thought about the photograph on his camera — the one he'd told the medic he'd deleted and hadn't. The one that was still on the memory card in his bag, right now, ten feet away.

He'd never deleted anything. That was the principle. That was the code. The camera captures what it captures. Not his decision. The editors decide. The world decides.

But the firefighter's voice was in his head now. The photo sucks. It was pretty messed up to take a photo at a time like that. And the medic's voice. He didn't make it. And this asshole took his picture. And thirty letters on the floor of a tent in Afghanistan, thirty strangers telling him the same thing in thirty different ways.

Demian set down the letter in his hand. Reached for his camera bag. Found the Nikon. Turned it on.

He scrolled back through the images — weeks of work, hundreds of frames — until he found it. The dying soldier. The young private's face, slack, half-lidded, mouth slightly open. The medic's bloody hands on his chest. The light from the blown-out window falling across them both. He looked at it for a long time.

It was a good photograph. Technically excellent. The composition, the light, the emotional clarity — everything he'd trained himself to see was there, captured in a fraction of a second by hands that moved faster than his conscience.

He pressed delete. The camera asked him to confirm. He confirmed. The image disappeared. The screen showed the frame before it — a wall, a doorway, nothing — and the frame after — the sergeant shouting orders, mouth open, spit frozen in the light. The dying soldier was gone. Erased from the record. As if Demian had never been in that room, had never raised his camera, had never pressed the shutter while a man died three feet away.

He scrolled further. Found the other ones — the frames he'd shot on other days, other operations, moments when his lens had found the dying and the dead and captured them with the same reflexive precision. A Marine with a chest wound, staring at the sky. A translator curled on his side in a ditch, one hand reaching for nothing. A woman in a doorway holding a child who wasn't moving.

He deleted them. One by one. Frame by frame. Each deletion a small, irreversible act that went against everything he'd believed about his work and his purpose and the code he'd built his career on.

He didn't delete everything. He kept the combat shots — the muzzle flashes, the sprinting soldiers, the helicopters, the ruins. He kept the landscapes. He kept the portraits of the living. He deleted only the dead. Only the ones who hadn't asked to be photographed. Only the ones who couldn't say no.

When he was done, he turned off the camera and set it on the cot beside him. Jerry lowered his magazine. "You okay?"

"Yeah."

"You just deleted photos."

"Yeah."

"You never delete photos."

"I know."

Jerry looked at him for a moment. Then he went back to his magazine, and the tent was quiet except for the wind outside and the hum of the generators and the sound of Demian breathing.

The letter was at the bottom of the box.

He'd known it would be. He'd been working his way down to it the way you work your way down to the thing you're most afraid of — methodically, deliberately, reading every letter above it as a preparation, a series of smaller blows to ready himself for the big one.

The envelope was plain white. The return address, handwritten in blue ink: Jordan Lowe. No embellishment. No title. Just a name that Demian had seen in newspapers and on television and in the caption beneath his own photograph: Mikey Lowe, 7, held by Firefighter Ronny Martinez.

He opened it. The paper inside was a single sheet, college-ruled, torn from a notebook. The handwriting was careful but unsteady — the penmanship of a person trying to hold something together while putting words on a page.

To The Associated Press,

The photograph depicting a fireman holding the lifeless body of my seven-year-old son was published without my knowledge or consent. It is inconceivable to me that anyone could be so callous as to capture such a devastating moment, let alone distribute it for the world to see. I am stunned by the audacity displayed by every paper that chose to run this image.

I am aware of the role media plays in informing the public. However, the decision to publish an image so deeply personal and traumatic is an affront to common decency. It reveals a disturbing lack of empathy for the very real, very human lives shattered by the tragedies you put on display.

My anger is not just directed at your photographer, Demian Ochoa, who saw fit to invade my worst moment, but at you for your failure to exercise basic ethical judgment. This photograph has not only disrespected the memory of my child but disregarded my family's need to mourn in private.

Please pass this letter to Mr. Ochoa. Tell him it is my dream that he someday feels the nightmare I endure.

Sincerely, Jordan Lowe Mother of Mikey Lowe

Demian read it five times.

The first time, the words hit him one by one, like stones thrown from a distance — each one landing, each one leaving a mark. Callous. Devastating. Audacity. Affront. The vocabulary of a woman who had taken the time to choose her words carefully, who had sat down at a table or a desk and organized her grief into sentences and her fury into paragraphs, and who had done it not for herself but for her son, because her son could no longer speak and she was speaking for him.

The second time, he noticed the handwriting. The slight tremor in the letters and how certain words pressed harder into the page — lifeless, worst moment, nightmare — as if the pen had been bearing down under the weight of what it was writing.

The third time, he heard her voice. He didn't know what Jordan Lowe sounded like, but he heard her anyway — the voice of a mother who had picked up a newspaper and seen her dead child in a stranger's arms, in color, above the fold, and understood that this image would follow her for the rest of her life. That strangers would see it. That it would be discussed and debated and nominated for prizes. That her son's death had been turned into a composition.

The fourth time, he stopped on a single phrase: my worst moment. Not the city's worst moment. Not the nation's. Hers. The photograph belonged to her in a way it would never belong to the editors or the public or the Pulitzer committee. It was her son. Her grief. Her worst moment. And Demian had been standing thirty feet away with a camera, and his hands had done what they always did, and now her worst moment was famous.

The fifth time, he folded the letter along its creases and held it against his chest and stared at the canvas ceiling and thought about his brother Miguel in a hospital bed in Guadalajara, and what he would have done if a stranger with a camera had walked into that room and photographed his brother dying and published it in a newspaper for the world to see. He knew exactly what he would have done. He would have written a letter just like this one.

"Stop reading those," Jerry said from across the tent. "It's an excellent photo. One of your best."

Demian didn't respond. He held the letter against his chest. The tent was dim. The wind pressed against the canvas walls. Somewhere outside, a helicopter crossed the sky, its rotors beating the air like a pulse that nobody had asked for and nobody could stop.

He read it a sixth time.

It didn't kill him. But it changed him. He could feel it happening — a shift in the architecture of something he'd built inside himself, some wall between the camera and the conscience, between the instinct and the cost. The wall didn't fall. It cracked. A fissure, thin as a hair, running from top to bottom.

He put the letter back in its envelope. Put the envelope in the breast pocket of his shirt, against his heart, where it would stay for the rest of his tour and the flight home and the ceremony where they would hand him a prize for the photograph that a dead boy's mother had called an affront to common decency.

He lay on his cot. Closed his eyes. He couldn't read it a seventh time. A seventh time would've killed him.

8

Ronny and Jeannette lay side by side in the quiet of the bedroom, the afternoon sun slanting through the half-drawn curtains and throwing a bright stripe across the rumpled sheets. From outside, the neighbor's sprinkler ticked back and forth, a lazy metronome counting off seconds that neither of them wanted to fill.

Ronny dragged his hands down his face. His stubble rasped against his palms. "Ronny." Jeannette bit the word off short. "What?"

"I don't know, Jeannette," he pleaded.

She propped herself up on one elbow. Her hair fell in tangled waves around her face, and her expression was the careful, controlled version of the frustration she actually felt. "You said you can't when the kids are home. So, I came home on my lunch break. Kids are at school. House is empty."

"I know."

"And nothing. Again."

"I know."

The bed creaked as Ronny swung his legs over the edge and reached for his jeans on the floor. He pulled them on without standing, his bad knee protesting as he bent it. He sat on the edge of the mattress, elbows on his knees, staring at the carpet. He could feel her eyes on his back — the weight of her patience, the weight of her hurt, the weight of everything she wasn't saying because she'd already said it three times this month and it hadn't changed anything.

"Is it me?" Jeannette asked.

"Of course not."

"Are you bored of me?"

"Stop."

"Because if you're bored of me, just say it. I'm a big girl."

"I'm not bored of you." He turned to look at her. She was sitting up now, the sheet pooled around her waist, and the expression on her face was the one he hated most. She was studying him. Trying to read a language she used to be fluent in. "Nine months, Ronny." Quieter now. Harder. "Nine months and it's the same thing every time. It's Andrew or it's the photograph or it's whatever happened in that building that you won't talk about. It follows you in here. Into our bed. And I can't compete with it."

She threw the covers off and swung her feet to the floor. Her movements were sharp — pulling on her pants, stepping into her shoes, crossing to the dresser mirror to fix her hair. She looked at his reflection in the glass. "We need to talk about what's going on."

"Nothing's going on."

The lie sat in the room like a third person. Jeannette's eyes in the mirror said she could see it. "Something is going on," she said. "And we both know it," she added as she walked out. Ronny pulled his shirt over his head and followed her to the kitchen. She was at the sink, running water over dishes that were already clean — the thing she did when she needed her hands busy and her back turned.

"You went in there," she said, her tone shifting to something more measured, more deliberate. The voice she used when she'd been thinking about something for a long time and had finally decided to say it. "You pulled people out. Kids. Teachers. You were in the news. You're still famous."

"That's the problem. I'm famous for carrying a dead kid out of a building."

"You're also famous for pulling the girl out. And a dozen others who never made the papers."

Ronny said nothing. Jeannette turned off the water. "I think it's time you went back to that therapist," she said.

"He doesn't do anything. I sit there for an hour and he writes in his notebook and nods. He's never once made a suggestion. Not one. I don't need someone to nod at me, Jeannette. I need someone to tell me what to do."

"Maybe that's not how it works."

"Well, it doesn't work the way it works, either."

She turned around, dish towel over her shoulder, leaning against the counter. "Then go back to work. Hal and the guys — you heard them. They want you there."

"I'm still on disability."

"That's a choice you're making." She let the word choice land. He felt it. "And you haven't played with the kids in weeks. Danny asked me yesterday if you were mad at him. Your fourteen-year-old son thinks his father is mad at him."

Ronny flinched.

"Play with your kids," Jeannette said, softer now. "Throw a ball with Danny. Take Sofia to the park. I don't care what it is. Just do something. Stop sitting in this house."

She turned back to the sink. Ronny stood in the middle of the kitchen, the linoleum cold under his bare feet.

"I made a choice that day," he said. The water stopped. Jeannette didn't turn around. "In the building. I made a choice. And I've been carrying it for nine months and I can't put it down."

She turned with the dish towel on her shoulder. Her face had gone still, the way a person goes still when they know what's coming and can't stop it. "Tell me," she said.

He told her leaning against the refrigerator. Standing, not sitting, because sitting down would give it too much ceremony. "Andrew and I went in together. Protocol. Always in pairs. East corridor, ground floor. The ceiling had come down in sections — concrete, rebar, everything at wrong angles. The dust was so thick you had to chew it before you could breathe it."

Jeannette stood at the counter. She didn't sit. Didn't move.

"Andrew pushed ahead. You know how he was. Always first through the door. I called out — stay together. He didn't stop. He'd heard kids screaming somewhere deeper in, I could hear them too, but I also heard a scream to my right. Andrew didn't wait for anything when it came to kids. He went left, toward the south wing. I went right, toward the scream I heard." He closed his eyes. The kitchen disappeared. "Found a classroom. The ceiling had pancaked onto the desks. I had to crawl in. The girl was pinned under a beam. Concrete-core, rebar on one end. She was conscious, screaming, her head bleeding. And near her — maybe eight feet away — a pair of little legs – the Lowe boy. A concrete slab had come down on him at an angle. On his upper body. His chest. All I could see were his tiny legs. His feet. Spider-Man sneakers."

He opened his eyes. Jeannette was watching him with an expression he'd never seen — not the studying look, not the angry look. Something even more raw. Something open.

"I didn't check him." The sentence sat in the kitchen like something dropped from above. "I looked at a concrete slab on a seven-year-old's chest and I made the call. I didn't kneel down. I didn't check for a pulse. I didn't put my hand on his ankle—"

"You didn't have time—"

"I saw the slab and I saw the legs weren't moving and I made the call — the boy is gone, the girl is alive, go to the girl."

"That's triage," Jeannette said. "That's what you're trained—"

"I know what I'm trained to do. I'm telling you what I did. I looked at that boy and I didn't check." The flat voice of a man reciting something he'd gone over in his head so many times it had worn smooth.

"I went straight to the girl. Dug her out of debris as much as I could, tried to move the beam. Couldn't do it alone. Too heavy. Needed a second set of hands." He paused. "I got on the walkie. Called Andrew. Nothing. Called again. Static. The building was groaning — steel, pipes, the whole structure shifting overhead. So, I went into the corridor. On foot. Looking for him."

"How long?"

"A minute. Maybe ninety seconds. Not long. Calling his name into the smoke. Couldn't see past my own hands. Nothing came back and I had to get back to the girl. She was screaming." He stopped. Swallowed.

"I went back to the classroom. The girl was there, still pinned. But she stopped screaming. With all that pain, she stopped screaming. Her head was turned — away from me, toward the boy. Toward his legs, his feet. She was just staring. This odd, far-off stare. "I moved the beam off her. Something in my knee tore — felt it pop. Didn't matter. Freed her somehow, I have no idea how…And she could almost stand up because of the pancaked ceiling, and when she did, she casually dusted herself off, turned her head, and she looked at me, and as she pointed to the Loew boy's tiny legs… and she said—" His voice cracked for the first time. "She said, 'I think it moved.'"

Jeannette's hand went to her mouth.

"His foot. She said she saw the boy's foot move. While I was gone. While I was in the corridor calling Andrew's name."

"Ronny—"

"I looked at it. Looked the same to me. Same sneaker, same angle, same dust settling on it. And she had a head wound — bleeding bad, ended up needing brain surgery weeks later. She was in shock. Pinned under a beam. She could have been seeing things."

"She was seeing things," Jeannette said. "Ronny, she's a little girl with a traumatic brain injury—"

"Maybe. Probably." He dropped his head. "That's what I tell myself every night at three in the morning. But I wasn't there, Jeannette. I was in the corridor chasing a name through the smoke, and she was lying there pinned, staring at that boy's foot for a minute, maybe ninety seconds, and she said it moved. And I never checked him. I never put a hand on him. I saw concrete on his chest and decided he was dead without touching him."

The kitchen went silent. The sprinkler outside had stopped. The house held its breath. "Then I got the debris off the boy."

"And?"

"Nothing." Ronny's jaw tightened. "No pulse. No breath. His face was peaceful. Like he was sleeping. He was gone."

"So he was—"

"He was dead, Jeannette. He was dead when I pulled him out. But was he dead when I first walked into that classroom and didn't check? Was he dead during the minute I was gone? I don't know. I'll never know. Because I didn't check." He pressed the heels of his hands against his eyes. "I had to get them out of there.

The building was collapsing. The girl was walking but barely — stumbling. I had the boy in my arms. We came through the east exit, I was looking for triage when a man with a camera standing thirty feet away took his pretty little photo." He dropped his hands. "That was the photograph. The hero carrying the dead child into the light."

"Ronny—"

"I was at triage two minutes. Maybe three. Catching my breath. Trying to get my knee to hold weight. And then the building came down."

Jeannette went pale.

"Not all of it. The south wing. Andrew's section. It collapsed — a roar like a freight train, and then this wall of dust came rolling out of every opening like a wave. I tried to go back in. Couldn't. The entrance was gone. Sealed. Concrete and steel floor to ceiling." His voice was barely a whisper now. "I was standing outside. In the light. Having my photograph taken. And the building was killing my best friend."

"You didn't know—"

"Marcus found him hours later. Came in from the back of the building, through the loading dock. Andrew was under a collapsed stairwell. His arms were stretched out, reaching toward a door he never opened."

Tears ran down Jeannette's face. She didn't wipe them. Didn't blink. Just stood there letting them fall, as if acknowledging them would mean acknowledging everything he'd just told her.

"So that's it," Ronny said. "I saw a slab of concrete on a seven-year-old boy and didn't check if he was alive. I went looking for Andrew for a minute while a girl with a brain injury watched that boy's foot and says she saw it move. I carried the boy out dead. And while I was standing outside at triage — while I was being photographed — the building collapsed and killed Andrew." He looked at the ceiling. "I didn't check the boy. I left him to find Andrew. And I was outside getting famous while the building killed my best friend."

The clock in the hallway ticked into the silence, each second landing in the kitchen like a dropped coin.

Jeannette crossed the kitchen. She put her hands on his face and made him look at her. "Listen to me." Her voice was steady and fierce and cracking at the edges, all at once. "You did everything you could. Under impossible conditions. With no time and no information and a building coming apart around you. You saved that girl. You tried to save your partner. You carried that boy out when you could have left him."

"But the minute—"

"That minute wouldn't have mattered. He wasn't moving. Pinned under concrete. Even if there was some involuntary twitch in his foot — Ronny, the kind of trauma that child had—"

"You don't know that."

"Neither do you. And that's the point. You will never know, and you cannot build a life on a maybe."

"Almost," Ronny said. "Almost certainly means there's a window."

"That window is going to eat you alive if you let it."

He knew she was right. Rationally. The part of his brain that dealt in evidence had already ruled. But his chest didn't deal in evidence. It ran on something else — the thing that woke him at three in the morning, the thing that had lived in the kitchen of a burning building for nine months, the thing that only heard a girl's flat, calm voice saying five words that would follow him for the rest of his life. He pressed his heel against the cold linoleum. It didn't help.

Jeannette pulled him down and held him. His forehead against the top of her head. His chest loosened. Not all the way. Not enough. But enough to breathe. "Thank you," he said into her hair. "For listening."

"That's what I've been trying to do for nine months, you stubborn bastard."

He almost laughed. It came out as something closer to a cough, but it was there — the ghost of a sound that belonged to the man he used to be. They stood in the kitchen holding each other. The refrigerator hummed. The clock ticked.

"I think about her sometimes," Ronny said. "The girl."

"What about her?"

"She's the only other person who was there. The only one who saw what I saw — who was lying there staring at that boy's feet while I was gone." He paused. "If

I could talk to her someday. Hear what she actually remembers. Maybe it would put it to rest."

"Or make it worse."

"Yeah."

Jeannette pulled back and looked at his face. "She's a kid, Ronny."

"I know. I'm not going to show up at her door. It's just in my head. The idea that she might know something."

Jeannette studied him for a long moment. "Let's put that away for now," she said, but her voice had lost its edge. "For now — you need to get off the couch. Play with your kids. Start living again. Even if you have to fake it."

"Fake it."

"That's what the rest of us are doing." She glanced at him. "You think going to work and making lunches and pretending everything's normal doesn't take everything I've got some days? But I do it. Because Danny and Sofia need me to. And they need you to."

Ronny nodded. Before he could respond, his phone buzzed in his pocket. "Hello?"

"Ronny. It's Hal."

"Hey, Cap."

"Got a minute? Jordan Lowe came by the station today. She was looking for you." Ronny went still. The kitchen, the conversation, the loosened thing in his chest — everything paused.

"She did?"

"Yeah. Seemed a little nervous. Left her number. Wants you to call her."

He stood at the edge of a door he'd been circling for nine months, and someone on the other side was knocking. "Can you text it to me?"

"Will do. She seemed okay. But, you know."

"Yeah. I know. Thanks, Hal."

"Take care."

Ronny clicked off. Stood in the kitchen holding the phone, staring at its dark screen. "Who was that?" Jeannette asked.

"Hal."

"What did he want?"

Ronny looked at her. Despite everything — despite the weight of what he'd just told her, the heaviness sitting on both of them — the set of his face changed. Not a smile. An opening.

"Speak of the devil," he said. "The Lowe boy. His mother came to the firehouse today. She wants me to call her."

Jeannette dried her hands on the dish towel. Looked at him for a long moment. "So call her."

9

— · —

Dust blew in from under the tent door, the half-inch plywood walls shuddering with the weight of the windstorm. Demian sat on his cot with Jordan Lowe's letter in one hand and the Columbus photograph in the other, holding them side by side like evidence in a trial he was losing.

The letter he'd read six times. The photograph he'd looked at ten thousand times. But tonight — with the wind pressing against the barracks and Jerry asleep three feet away, his breathing steady and oblivious — the two objects seemed to be having a conversation that didn't include him. The letter accused. The photograph sat there, glossy and indifferent, refusing to defend itself.

He set the photograph down and reached into his file case, pushing past contact sheets and negatives until his fingers found what they always found when he went deep enough — the fragment of newsprint, brown and brittle, curling at the edges. He didn't need to look at it. He knew every line. But he looked anyway.

The article was from a Guadalajara newspaper, the Spanish text faded but legible. A grainy photograph of a boy in a hospital bed, tubes running from his arms, his head bare from chemotherapy, his eyes half-closed. Miguel Ochoa, age 10. The article was about the hospital's pediatric wing, a human-interest piece about the children there. Miguel had been one of three kids featured. He'd died two weeks after it was published.

Demian remembered the photographer who'd taken it — a woman with a press badge and a kind smile who'd asked Elena's permission before shooting. His mother had said yes because she'd wanted people to know Miguel existed. Because the world should see her son, even like this. Even dying.

And fourteen-year-old Demian had stood in the corner of that hospital room with a disposable camera from the pharmacy down the street, and he'd taken his own photographs — eleven pictures in Miguel's final week. The last one was Miguel asleep, his hand curled around their mother's fingers, the light from the window making the IV bag glow like something holy. Demian had taken it because he'd known, with the clarity of a boy watching his brother disappear, that soon there would be nothing left to look at. The camera was a way to keep him. To hold the image still when everything else was moving toward gone.

That was where it started. Not with journalism school. Not with the AP. With a disposable camera and a dying brother and the need to stop time from taking everything.

He held the newsprint clipping beside the Columbus photograph. Two children. Miguel in a hospital bed. Mikey in a firefighter's arms. Both still. Both beyond help. Both captured by a camera that couldn't save them and couldn't look away.

Demian set the clipping back in the case. He picked up his phone.

The number for Station 17 was on the Columbus Fire Department website. Demian dialed, his thumb hesitating over the last digit before pressing it.

"Station 17."

"Yes. May I speak to Ronny Martinez, please?"

"He's not working today."

"Will he be in tomorrow?"

"No, he's out on disability for a while. Can I take a message?"

"Would you have his home number?"

"Can't give that out. I can take a message. What's this regarding?"

"My name is Demian Ochoa."

A pause. Then a decision. "And what is this regarding?"

"I'm a photojournalist—"

"Yeah, I know who you are." The voice had changed. Flatter. Colder. "I can tell you right now he's not going to talk to you."

"If you could just take my information—"

"I'll take it and pass it along, but don't hold your breath. According to him, that photo destroyed his life."

The words landed in Demian's chest like something heavy dropped from a shelf. "Well. My number is 555-435-5858."

"Got it."

The line went dead. Demian sat on his cot, the phone in his lap, staring at the canvas wall. That photo destroyed his life.

He thought about the interview — Martinez on crutches in his driveway, telling the reporters that the photo sucked, that it was messed up to take a picture at a time like that. He'd assumed that was performance. Bluster for the cameras. But the man on the phone — the firefighter at the station, whoever he was — hadn't been performing. He was stating a fact like stating the weather.

Demian picked up Jordan Lowe's letter from the cot. Read the last line again: *Tell him it is my dream that he someday feels the nightmare I endure.*

He dialed George's office. "George Gelson's office, this is Rachel."

"Rachel, it's Demian. Is George in?"

"Hey, Demian. Hold on."

A click. Then George: "Where are you?"

"In my hut."

"Why can't you walk over here and talk to me?"

"I'm lazy. Listen — do you have Jordan Lowe's number? The mother—"

"Demian. Don't."

"I think I need to."

"Did you read the letter?"

"I need to talk to her, George."

A long breath on the other end. "It's a mistake. She's in the middle of it. Let her be."

"You going to give it to me, or do I find it myself?"

"Hold on." The line clicked to hold. Demian stood and paced the tent, five steps one way, five steps back. The wind pressed against the walls.

Rachel picked up. "You wanted Jordan Lowe's number?"

Yeah."

"316-555-8823."

"Thanks."

"Good luck."

He paced the tent for another three minutes after hanging up, each step kicking up small clouds of dust. Then he dialed.

The phone rang four times. Five. He was about to hang up when a voice answered — a woman's voice, flat with the weariness of someone who answered the phone expecting nothing good to come from it.

"Hello?"

"Hello, Ms. Lowe. My name is Demian Ochoa—"

Silence. Total. As if the line had died. Demian pulled the phone from his ear, checked the screen — still connected — and brought it back.

"I'm the photographer who—"

"Did you read my letter?" The question cut through everything — the static, the wind, the distance between a tent in Afghanistan and wherever she was sitting in Columbus. Her voice wasn't loud. It was precise. A scalpel, not a hammer.

"I did. And that's why I'm calling—"

"Then you didn't read it closely enough. I specifically said I didn't want to hear from you."

"Ms. Lowe—"

"It's not Mrs. Lowe anymore, by the way. It's Ms." The words were clipped. Sharp. "I'm not with my husband anymore, Mr. Ochoa. That's one of the things that's happened since your photograph." A tremor ran under her voice, a fault line threatening to give. "Do you have the photo there with you?" Demian looked at the photograph lying face-up on his cot. He couldn't speak. "Of course you do," she continued. "You see that little boy the fireman is holding? That's my son. That's the last image of my son. Your photograph is the last recorded picture of my little boy on this earth."

Her voice rose, not in volume but in pressure — the sound of something being compressed past its tolerance.

"That photo is everywhere. Do you understand what that means? I see my dead son everywhere. In newspapers. On television. On the internet. I can't go to the grocery store without seeing his face on the magazine rack. I can't turn on the news. My daughter can't go to school without some kid showing her a picture of her dead brother on their phone. That's what your photograph did."

Demian's mouth opened. No sound came out.

"You stood outside the building," she said, and now her voice dropped to something low and raw and barely held together. "You stood outside the horror of it all with your camera, and you took a picture of my son's body, and you made yourself famous. Now go look at your photograph, Mr. Ochoa. Look at that limp, helpless body. And remember that I never — never — want to hear from you again." The line went dead.

Demian's phone slipped from his fingers and clattered to the floor. He sat on the cot, his hands hanging between his knees, and stared at the photograph lying beside him. The firefighter's face. The boy's still body. The girl's scream. The smoke diffusing the light into something almost golden.

He'd taken this photograph in less than a second. A fraction of a moment. The shutter had opened and closed, and in that sliver of time he'd captured something that had won him a nomination for the highest prize in journalism and made a mother unable to buy groceries without seeing her dead son's face. From across the tent, Jerry's voice, groggy: "You alright?"

"Go back to sleep."

"Were you on the phone?"

"Go back to sleep, Jerry." Jerry rolled over.

Demian reached down to the footlocker at the end of his cot. Dug through clothes and equipment until his fingers found the cool glass of a tequila bottle. He pulled the cork with his teeth. Drank. His hands shook badly enough that it took both of them to keep the bottle steady. He drank until Jordan Lowe's voice stopped echoing in his head. Then he drank until it started again. Then he drank until it didn't matter.

Morning arrived like a punishment. Demian lay on the cot with the sunlight cutting through the dust-filmed window and into his skull. His mouth tasted like something had died in it. The tequila bottle lay on its side on the floor, empty, a thin brown line of residue trailing from its mouth across the plywood.

He sat up. The tent tilted. He waited for it to stop, then swung his legs off the cot and stood, and the tent tilted again, and he held onto the cot frame until the world agreed to be horizontal.

He threw on his sunglasses and walked across the base to the press building, the sun hammering the back of his neck. His head pounded with each step. His stomach was a fist. But beneath the hangover, something else — a clarity that hadn't been there the night before. Not a good clarity. The kind that comes after you've hit something and stopped falling and can finally see where you landed.

George saw him coming the moment he walked in. "I thought you were too lazy to come over here?"

Demian stopped in front of his desk. George leaned back and waved a hand in front of his nose. "You smell like a distillery. Phone call didn't go well?"

"No."

"Warned you." George studied him. "So what's up?"

Demian sat down. The chair creaked. "George, I want to talk about the nomination."

"What about it?"

"I don't want it."

George's face went still. "You don't want the Pulitzer nomination."

"Not with this photo. I want to withdraw."

"Why?"

"Because it's causing harm. The firefighter won't speak to me. The mother can barely say my name without—" He stopped. Rubbed his face. "It's not right."

George leaned forward, elbows on the desk. "Demian. The Pulitzer committee nominated that photograph because it is one of the most significant images taken this year. It is powerful. It is important. It is exactly the kind of work this prize exists to recognize."

"The people in the photograph don't think it's important. They think it destroyed their lives."

"That's not the same thing."

"It feels the same."

George picked up his coffee, took a sip, grimaced, set it back down. "Every significant photograph in the history of this profession has caused someone pain. That's what significant photographs do. They show people what they don't want to see. The fact that it hurts doesn't mean it shouldn't exist."

"I'm not saying it shouldn't exist. I'm saying I don't want a prize for it."

"Too bad. The nomination stands. The AP submitted it. The AP supports it."

Demian stared at him. "It's my photograph."

"You work for the Associated Press. You took the photograph for the Associated Press. The copyright and ownership belong to the AP — it's in your employment agreement. We have the right to use, distribute, and license it as we see fit. And this nomination is an honor for the organization, not just for you."

"I didn't take it for the AP. I was visiting my parents. I wasn't even on assignment."

"You submitted it. If it was personal, why did you submit? You used AP equipment. You filed it through AP channels. It's ours." George's voice softened, but the message didn't. "I know this is hard. But you need to separate what you're feeling from what this photograph means to the profession. Twenty years from now, you'll see it differently."

Demian sat in the chair and felt the walls close in — the building walls, the contract walls, the walls of a decision he'd made in a fraction of a second with a camera he couldn't put down. "Fine," he said.

"Fine?" probed George.

"The nomination stands. I won't fight it." He paused. "But I need something from you."

George closed his eyes. "Here we go."

"I want to go to Columbus. I want to talk to the girl from the photograph. Alex Kelly." George opened his eyes. "The kid?"

"She's the only person in that photograph who might actually talk to me. Martinez wants to break my jaw. The mother told me to never call again. But the girl — she's done interviews. She's talked about the bombing publicly. She doesn't hate the photograph."

"She's a little girl, Demian. She's been through enough."

"I'm not going to ambush her. I want to tell her story. Give her a platform. An interview — her perspective, her words."

It sounded thin, and he knew it. George knew it too — he could see it in the way George was looking at him. His eyes narrowed. He leaned back in his chair — the calibrating stillness of a man measuring the distance between what someone was saying and what they actually meant.

"What's this really about?" George asked.

Demian didn't answer right away. He looked at his hands — the hands that had held the camera, that had pressed the shutter, that had developed and filed and distributed an image of a dead boy in a firefighter's arms. What was it really about? He didn't have the words for it. He just knew that the girl in the photograph was the one door that hadn't been slammed in his face, and he needed to walk through it before it closed too.

"I need to do this," he said. "For me."

George studied him for a long time. The fluorescent lights hummed. "Your own leave time," George said. "Your own money. We're not paying for this."

"Fine."

"And if the nomination goes through — when it goes through — you go to the luncheon. You accept the prize. You make a speech. A good speech. One that makes the AP look like what it is." Demian turned his head toward the ceiling. "That's the deal," George said. "Columbus for the luncheon. Take it or leave it."

Demian's jaw worked. He looked at the ceiling for another moment, then back at George. "Alright."

"How long?"

"Four weeks should do it. I want to see my parents while I'm there."

"I'll have Rachel set it up. When do you want to leave?"

"As soon as possible."

George nodded. "I'll let you know if there are problems." He paused as Demian stood from the chair. "Demian." Demian turned. George's eyes held a worry Demian rarely saw in them. "Stay safe."

"You never say that when I go to a battlefield."

"Because that's where you know what you're doing." George held his gaze. "You're going to a different kind of battlefield now. One you don't know your way around."

10

Ronny stepped into the backyard with the phone in his hand. The grass needed cutting — it had needed cutting since October — and the cold had turned it brown at the tips, giving the whole yard the look of something that had stopped trying. He'd been staring at the number Hal had texted him for twenty minutes — ten digits on a screen that felt like a door he wasn't sure he should open.

He paced the cracked concrete path along the fence. A football hid in the bushes near the patio — Danny's, left there weeks ago, maybe longer. Ronny couldn't remember the last time he'd thrown a ball with his son. Couldn't remember the last time Danny had asked.

He pressed dial. It rang twice. "Hello?"

"Mrs. Lowe? It's Ronny Martinez. From Station 17. You came by earlier today." "Ronny." His name left her mouth like she'd been holding it. "Yes. Thank you for calling me back."

"Of course."

A pause. He could hear her breathing — the slightly too-fast rhythm of a woman who'd rehearsed this call in her head and was now discovering that rehearsal didn't help. "Would it be possible for us to meet?" she asked. "I'd like to speak with you. In person."

Ronny picked up the football and tossed it onto the patio. "Sure. Could we have coffee? There's that place on Fortieth—"

"Actually — I really don't like to go out much these days. Would it be okay if you came here? To the house? I'll make coffee. Or tea, if you prefer."

Ronny's fingers drummed against his thigh. He could hear what it had cost her to ask — the slight breathlessness in it, the way she'd corrected herself mid-sentence, steering away from the public coffee shop toward the safety of her own walls. This was a woman who had shrunk her world down to the rooms she could control.

"Coffee's fine, Jordan. When would you like—"

"Can you come now?"

The urgency in it surprised him. Not desperate — just exposed. Like she'd used up all her courage making the call and couldn't afford to spend more of it waiting. He glanced at his watch. "Give me thirty minutes."

"Perfect. I'll text you my address."

"Sounds good. See you soon."

The call ended. Ronny stood in the backyard, staring at his dark screen, the football lying on the patio behind him. The oak tree shifted in the wind. He didn't know what he was walking toward. He only knew that a woman who'd lost her son had asked him to come, and that the son she'd lost was the boy whose still face he saw every night at three in the morning. He went inside, grabbed his keys, and left.

The house sat on a quiet street in a neighborhood that looked like every other neighborhood in this part of Columbus — small lots, chain-link fences, cars in driveways that were one repair away from the junkyard. Jordan's house was tidy from the outside. The lawn was mowed. A planter by the front steps held dead flowers that had been alive in some other season.

Ronny parked on the street and sat in his truck for a moment. His knee ached from the drive — it always ached in the cold — and he took the time to straighten it, pressing his palm against the kneecap the way the physical therapist had shown him.

He walked to the door and rang the bell. It opened almost immediately. She'd been waiting on the other side. He could tell by how fast it happened, by the way she was already composed when the door swung back, her face arranged into the expression of a woman who was holding herself together through sheer force of will. "Hey. Come in."

"Hey."

She led him through a small living room — clean, sparse, a couch and an armchair and a television and nothing on the walls except a single framed photograph that he didn't look at closely because looking at photographs closely was something he'd stopped doing in April — and into the dining area off the kitchen. Sunlight came through the windows and lit the table, catching dust motes in the air.

"Sit. Please." She gestured at a chair. "How do you take your coffee? I have creamer."

"Creamer's good."

She went to the kitchen. Ronny sat down and looked at the table with its scratched, wooden surface. A table where a family had eaten thousands of meals. Two place settings were stacked at one end. A bowl of fruit that looked like it hadn't been touched in days. A stack of mail, rubber-banded. He could hear her in the kitchen — the pour of coffee, the clink of a spoon, the small sounds of a woman doing something with her hands so her hands would stop shaking. When she came back with two mugs, her fingers grazed his as she set one down in front of him. She pulled her hand back quickly, as if the contact had been electric, and sat down across from him.

She looked at him. He looked at her. The silence between them filled the room. "So," Ronny said, "How have you been?"

"How have I been." She said it flat, not as a question. She wrapped both hands around her mug. "Existing, I suppose. That's the word I use now. Existing."

The honesty of it caught him off guard. "I'm sorry."

"How about you?"

"Truth is — about the same." He caught himself. "I mean, not the same as you. I didn't lose—"

"Don't do that," Jordan said. "Don't rank it. Your grief is yours. Mine is mine. They're different worlds."

Ronny looked at her. She'd said it without bitterness — just a statement, clean and direct, from a woman who'd had enough people measure their pain against hers and come up short on purpose. He nodded.

"Andrew Harris," she said. "Your partner. I saw the banner at the fire station."

"My best friend. Since middle school." Ronny turned the coffee mug in his hands. "We were in there together. He didn't come out."

"I'm sorry."

"Tough to get past. I shouldn't say get past — there's no getting past. Getting through, maybe."

Jordan nodded. She understood the distinction. "I know what you mean."

They talked. Carefully at first — circling the thing between them, testing the edges, finding the places where it was safe to step. Jordan asked about his kids.

"Two," Ronny said. "Danny's fourteen. Sofia's twelve."

"Sports?"

He almost smiled. "Everything. Volleyball, soccer, baseball. Keeps us busy."

"Busy is good." Her eyes softened. "Mikey played baseball. Riverside Little League."

"No kidding. I coach Danny's team there."

The lines around her mouth eased. Not quite a smile, but a loosening, a small release. "Steelers fan too. You should see his room."

"Me too. Since I was a kid."

"You should see his room," she said again, quieter this time, and Ronny understood that she wasn't repeating herself — she was offering something — An invitation. A door he could walk through.

He didn't walk through it.

"How's your daughter?" he asked. "Emily."

"Yes. She handling okay?"

Jordan sighed. "She doesn't talk about it much. Seems normal — or what passes for normal. She's back at school."

"Kids are resilient. They find their own ways."

"That's what everyone says. But sometimes I think her way of coping is just burying everything so deep it'll take years to find it."

Ronny nodded. He thought about Sofia — quiet since April, careful around him, reading the house the way animals read weather. Kids were resilient. Kids also absorbed everything the adults around them were radiating, and what Ronny had been radiating for nine months was damage.

"Are you back at work?" Jordan asked.

"No. Still on disability. The knee." He tapped his left leg. "From the building."

"I remember. From the school thing — the memorial. You were limping."

"Still am. Probably always will."

Jordan opened her mouth to say something else. The color drained from her face — not a blush but its opposite, the blood pulling back from the surface. Beads of sweat appeared on her forehead. Her hand went flat on the table.

"Jordan?"

Her breathing went shallow — fast, short pulls of air that weren't reaching her lungs. Her eyes widened and her jaw clenched and Ronny recognized it immediately because he'd seen it a hundred times on the job — in victims pulled from car wrecks, in bystanders at house fires, in anyone whose body decided to relive a trauma that the conscious mind thought it had filed away.

"Jordan, you're okay. I think you're having a panic attack."

She shoved back from the table and lunged for the kitchen sink. He heard the water turn on, heard her gasping — "I'll be fine, I'll be fine" — and he followed her, keeping his distance but close enough to reach her. She splashed water on her face, her hands gripped the edge of the sink, her shoulders heaved. "This is so embarrassing. I don't know what—"

"Don't be embarrassed. This happens. It's your body, not you." He stepped closer. "Can I take your pulse?"

She nodded without looking at him. He placed two fingers gently on the inside of her wrist. Her pulse was racing — a hundred and twenty, maybe more, a hummingbird's heart trapped in a woman's body.

"Okay. We're going to breathe together. Inhale for four counts. Hold for four. Exhale for eight. Match me."

He breathed in. Held. Let it out slow. Her eyes locked on his face like he was the only fixed point in a room that was spinning. In through the nose. Hold. Out through the mouth. Four and four and eight. Again. Again.

Her pulse slowed under his fingers. Her shoulders dropped. The color came back to her face in uneven patches, like a tide returning to shore. "Better?"

"Y-yes." She wiped her eyes with the back of her hand. "I'm sorry. That hasn't happened in—"

"Don't apologize."

She was still gripping the edge of the sink with one hand. Her other wrist was in his fingers. They stood in the kitchen, three feet apart, and the quiet was different now — not the stiff silence of two strangers at a table but something closer, something with the intimacy of a moment where one person has been seen at their worst and the other person hasn't looked away.

Jordan let go of the sink. Without a word, she stepped forward and put her arms around him. Ronny went still. His hands hung at his sides for a moment — one beat, two — and then he put them on her back, lightly, the way you hold something you're not sure you're allowed to touch. She pressed her face into his chest. He could feel her breathing against his shirt, could feel the small tremors still running through her body, could feel the desperation of a woman holding onto another human being because letting go meant being alone again in a house full of silence.

"I'm sorry," she whispered into his shirt. "I'm not — this isn't—"

"I know."

"Your hands." Her voice broke. "Your hands were the last ones to hold my little boy." Ronny closed his eyes. "I just need to be near that," she said. "I know it doesn't make sense. I just need to."

"It makes sense," he said. And it did — not logically, not in any way he could explain, but in the part of him that had carried Mikey's weight in his arms and still felt it there, a phantom heaviness that lived in his chest and shoulders. He understood the pull. He was standing in the middle of it.

They held each other in the kitchen for a long time. Not moving or speaking. The light shifted in the windows. Ronny stepped back. Gently. His hands on her shoulders for a moment before dropping to his sides. "You alright?"

"Yes, yes. I feel better."

"Maybe you should take a seat."

"I'm better. I, I feel better."

They stood there, appraising each other before he said, "I should go." with a hoarse voice. Jordan nodded. She wiped her face with both hands, pressing her palms against her cheeks as if she could push the emotion back inside. "Thank you," she said. "For coming."

"Of course."

She walked him to the door. He stepped out onto the porch and turned back. She stood in the doorway, backlit by the light from the living room, her arms crossed over her chest. She looked smaller than she had when she'd opened the door an hour ago. Or maybe she looked the same and he was seeing her differently now — not as the mother of the boy in the photograph, but as a woman standing alone in a house that was too quiet, holding onto the edges of a life that had been rearranged by the same explosion that had rearranged his.

"Call me," he said. "If you need to talk. Anytime."

She nodded. He walked to his truck. Started the engine. Pulled away from the curb. In the rearview mirror, her door closed.

Jeannette was at her car in the driveway when he pulled in, sliding her keys from her pocket. She paused, watching him climb out of the truck. "How'd it go?"

Ronny stood in the driveway, the evening air cold on his face. "It was something."

"Good something? Bad something?"

"I don't know. Heavy."

She studied him, looking for the thing beneath the thing. "Come to the store with me. You can tell me on the way."

"I should probably—"

"You're not doing anything. Come on." The leather seats of Jeannette's car creaked as he settled in. She backed out of the driveway, the last of the evening sun painting the houses amber. At the stop sign, she glanced his way. "So? What happened?"

The houses slid past the window. "She's not okay, Jeannette."

"Not okay how?"

"Lost. Hurting." His fingers traced the seam of the armrest. "She grabbed my hand at one point. Said it was the last one to hold her son." Jeannette's knuckles whitened on the steering wheel. "She had a panic attack while we were talking. A real one — heart racing, couldn't breathe. I talked her through it."

"Poor woman."

"She's alone in that house all day. Her husband left. Her daughter's at school. She's just — sitting there."

Jeannette sat quietly as she made the turn into the supermarket lot, the signal clicking steadily. She parked and turned off the engine, but didn't move to get out. "We could have her over for dinner," she said. "Or I could reach out. Woman to woman."

The offer landed in Ronny's chest like something he didn't deserve. Jeannette — who had been holding their family together while he disappeared into himself — was offering to bring this woman into their home. To share her table. To extend the same generosity she'd been extending to him, despite everything he'd failed to give her in return. "Maybe," he said. "Let's see if she calls again. I don't want to push."

Jeannette looked at him. Her eyes were steady, and somewhere behind them was a question she hadn't asked yet. One she might not have formed. Or had formed and decided not to voice. She held his gaze for a moment, then opened her door. "Come on. I need garlic and bread."

Ronny followed her into the store, walking beside her through the bright aisles, the fluorescent lights humming overhead, the ordinary world of shopping carts and produce displays and a woman checking a list on her phone. He pushed the cart. She picked out tomatoes. They moved through the store like a thousand stores before — in tandem, in routine, in the comfortable choreography of a marriage that had lasted twenty years.

Something had shifted in the hour he'd spent in Jordan Lowe's kitchen. He could feel it the way you feel a crack in a foundation before you can see it — not in the structure yet, but in the ground. It was going to move a lot more before it was done.

At the checkout, Jeannette put her hand on his arm. "You did a good thing today," she said. "Going to see her."

Ronny nodded. He loaded the bags into the car. He drove home with his wife. He helped unpack the groceries and started dinner and called Sofia down from her room and listened to Danny talk about basketball practice and sat at the table with his family and ate and smiled and said the right things in the right order.

And underneath all of it — beneath the garlic and the bread and the bright aisles and the twenty-year marriage — he could still feel Jordan Lowe's arms around him, and her face pressed against his chest, and her voice saying the words that had cracked something open inside him that he didn't know how to close.

Your hands were the last ones to hold my little boy.

He washed the dishes. He climbed the stairs. He lay in bed beside Jeannette and stared at the ceiling. The crack widened, millimeter by millimeter, in a direction he couldn't stop.

11

The wipers on his father's truck swept rain from the windshield in lazy arcs. Demian navigated streets he'd known since high school — Sullivant Avenue, where the signs were half in Spanish, where the tiendas and panaderías still had the same awnings, where his father had driven this same 1972 Chevy to the meatpacking plant six days a week for twenty years. The truck smelled like it always had — old leather, motor oil, and the faintest trace of his father's aftershave, baked into the seats over decades.

Demian had been home four days. Four days of his mother's cooking and his father's quiet pride and the old bedroom with the twin mattress and the shelf where Miguel's baseball glove still sat, cracked and stiff, next to a framed school photo of a gap-toothed boy who would never turn eleven. Four days of sleeping in a bed that didn't vibrate with artillery, in a house where the only explosions were his mother burning toast.

He hadn't told his parents why he was really here. Visiting, he'd said. Taking a break. His mother had looked at him over the dinner table with the expression she reserved for lies she chose not to challenge and passed him more rice.

The coffee shop was on High Street — a small place with exposed brick and chalkboard menus and the intentional coziness that made Demian, who'd spent the last year in tents, feel like he was trespassing in someone's living room. He arrived twenty minutes early, set his camera bag on the floor beside a table by the window, and ordered a black coffee he didn't want.

Rachel had arranged everything. She'd contacted Alex Kelly's mother — Donna — through the AP's media liaison, identifying Demian as an AP journalist in-

110

terested in a follow-up profile on the bombing survivors. Rachel had been careful, per Demian's instructions: she hadn't mentioned the photograph. Hadn't said Demian's full name. Just "a reporter from the Associated Press." The mother had agreed eagerly. Proudly, Rachel had said on the phone. She seemed really proud of her daughter.

That word — proud — sat in Demian's chest like a stone. Proud. This woman was proud that her daughter had survived a bombing and been photographed in the worst moment of her life, and she was sending her to a coffee shop to talk about it with the man who had taken the picture. And she didn't know. And Alex didn't know. And Demian was sitting here with a black coffee and a glossy print of the photograph in his bag, waiting for a thirteen-year-old girl to walk through the door so he could — what? Apologize? Explain? Understand something about himself that he couldn't reach alone?

He didn't know. George was right. This was a battlefield he didn't know his way around. The bell above the door chimed.

A woman entered first — mid-thirties, thin, with the thinness of someone who'd stopped eating regularly and hadn't noticed. She wore a coat that didn't fit quite right and carried herself with the careful posture of a person trying to take up as little space as possible. Behind her, a young girl. Short chestnut hair under a hoodie, jeans, a backpack slung over one shoulder. She moved differently than her mother — shoulders set, chin level, eyes scanning the room with the quick, cataloguing attention of someone who assessed every space she entered.

The girl's gaze found Demian and held. No smile. No wave. Just a look — direct, measuring — and then a small nod, as if confirming something she'd already decided. Demian stood. "Alex?"

"Yeah."

He extended his hand. She shook it with a grip that was firmer than he expected. "Demian. Thanks for meeting with me."

"Sure." She glanced back at her mother, who had settled at a table near the entrance, close enough to see them, far enough to give the conversation room. Donna caught Demian's eye and offered a small, nervous smile — the smile of a mother who wanted this to go well, who believed her daughter was brave for doing this, who had no idea what she'd actually agreed to.

Alex slid into the chair across from him. She set her backpack on the floor between her feet and looked at him the way she might look at a substitute teacher — willing to cooperate, not yet willing to trust.

"Can I get you something?" Demian asked.

"Vanilla steamer."

"Coming up."

He went to the counter, ordered, and came back with the drinks. Alex was sitting exactly as he'd left her — hands in her lap, eyes tracking the room. She hadn't taken out her phone. Hadn't fidgeted. She was still.

"So," Demian said, setting the steamer in front of her. "Thanks again for doing this. I know interviews can be—"

"It's fine. My mom wanted me to do it." The honesty was disarming. Not rude — just clean. She wasn't going to pretend she was excited to be here.

"Fair enough," Demian said. "Mind if I record on my phone? Just for accuracy."

"Go ahead."

He set the phone on the table between them. "Let's start simple. How are you doing? How's school?"

"Fine." A pause. "Normal."

"Back at Whitehall?"

"Yeah."

"And you're — what, eighth grade?"

"Yep."

"How are you handling everything? After the bombing."

Alex took a sip of her steamer. Set it down. Looked at him with those steady, assessing eyes. "Are you going to ask me real questions, or are we doing the 'how do you feel' thing? Because I've done a lot of these, and the 'how do you feel' ones are boring."

Demian almost laughed. "Fair. Let me ask you something real, then." He leaned back. "Tell me about the day of the bombing. Whatever you remember."

"I don't remember much." She said it without apology or self-pity. A fact. "I know I was in class. Fifth period. Then I wasn't. I woke up in the dark. I didn't know what had happened — I thought maybe the lights went out, or I'd fallen asleep. Then I felt the pain in my head, and I couldn't move, and I realized something was on top of me."

"The beam."

"Yeah. Concrete. I could see a little — like a crack of light. Then the light got bigger, and I could see a face. The fireman."

"Ronny Martinez."

"Yeah. He pulled stuff off me until I could move." She paused. Took another sip. "After that, it's patchy. I remember standing up. I remember seeing—" She stopped. Her jaw tightened almost imperceptibly. "I remember seeing Mikey. The boy from the photo. He was near me. I didn't know he was there until the fireman cleared the debris."

"Did you know Mikey?"

"He was a couple grades below me. I knew who he was but we weren't friends or anything. I don't understand how he ended up near me. His classroom wasn't even close to mine."

Demian studied her. She was composed — remarkably so. But he could see the effort behind the composure, like a tightrope walker looking calm from the ground but making a thousand adjustments per second.

"This doesn't bother you? Talking about it?"

"No." She held his gaze. "I like talking about it."

Demian's pen stopped. "Like it?"

"Yeah." She seemed to hear how it sounded and almost smiled. "That's weird, right? People think it's weird."

"I'm not here to judge what's weird."

Alex wrapped both hands around her steamer. The warmth seemed to settle her. "When I first started doing interviews — after the bombing, when the reporters came — I didn't want to. My mom made me do a couple. But then I started to... I don't know. It felt like something. Like picking a scab."

"What do you mean?"

"You know how when you have a scab on your knee, and you know you shouldn't pick at it, but you do anyway? And it's gross and it hurts but there's also this weird satisfaction in it? Like you need to do it even though it makes it worse?"

"Yeah."

"Talking about the bombing is like that. It hurts. But I need to do it. Not because it makes me feel better. It doesn't. It just — I need to." She paused. "But talking about it isn't the real thing. The real thing is the photo."

Demian's stomach tightened.

"The photo of me," Alex said. "Me and the fireman and Mikey." She was looking at the table now, tracing the grain of the wood with her fingertip. "When it first came out, I cried. It scared me. I couldn't believe that kid was me — screaming, covered in blood, standing there like a zombie. My mom threw it away. The newspaper, the whole thing. Put it right in the trash." She looked up at him. "I pulled it out after she went to bed."

The coffee shop hummed around them. Donna sat at her table near the door, checking her phone, oblivious.

"I started looking at it. Not a lot at first. Just sometimes, when I felt bad, I'd pull it out and stare at it. I hated myself in it — hated the screaming, the blood, the way I looked like I was falling apart. And Mikey—" She swallowed. "Seeing Mikey in it made me sick. But I kept looking. I couldn't stop. It was like — the more disgusting it was, the more I needed to see it. Like the scab. You pick and pick and it bleeds and you know you should stop but you don't."

Demian glanced toward Donna. She was stirring her coffee, reading something on her phone. She had no idea what her daughter was saying fifteen feet away. "I looked at it so much the newspaper fell apart," Alex said. "The ink smeared, the paper went soft from me holding it. It basically disintegrated. I think I cried on it too many times. After that, I'd look for it in stores. In magazines, in newspapers that still had it. I'd find copies and take them."

"Take them."

"Yeah. And my mom would find them and throw them out. Every time. She'd go through my room and if she found a copy, it went in the trash. She never said anything about it. I never said anything about it. It was just this thing we did."

Demian looked at Donna again. She was still on her phone. Alex was watching him look — watching him understand the secret she was handing him, the private war between a mother who wanted to protect her daughter from an image and a daughter who needed the image the way a body needs a wound it can't stop reopening. "That's why I wanted your copy," Alex said.

Demian blinked. "What?"

"You have one, right? A copy of the photo?"

"I — yes."

"Can I have it?"

He reached into his camera bag and pulled out the glossy print — the same print he'd been carrying since Afghanistan, the one he'd held beside Jordan Lowe's letter, beside the clipping of Miguel. He handed it to Alex.

She didn't look at it. She slid it directly into her backpack, zipping the pocket shut with a quick, practiced motion. The way someone pockets a pill or hides a bottle.

"You're not going to look at it?" he asked.

"Not here."

"You just wanted a copy."

"Mine got old. My mom found the last one. One reason I came is because I thought you'd have one."

Demian sat with that as she calmly zipped his photograph into her backpack, and he thought about the dying soldier and the medic's fury and the letters in the box and Jordan Lowe's voice on the phone: *Your photograph is the last recorded image of my precious little boy.*

Every person who'd encountered this image had been damaged by it. Every person except, possibly, this girl — who had been damaged by the bombing itself and had turned the photograph into something else entirely. Not a wound. Not an accusation. A scab she needed to pick. A drug she needed to take. The one object in the world that let her touch the worst day of her life on her own terms, in her own time, in private.

He didn't know what to do with that. He didn't know what it meant about his work, or about her, or about the distance between taking a photograph and understanding what it became. "There's something I should tell you," Demian said.

Alex looked at him. Those steady eyes. He opened his mouth. The words were right there

— I took that photo, I'm the one who took it, I was standing thirty feet away with a camera — and they wouldn't come. Because she was thirteen. Because she'd just handed him a piece of herself that she'd never given anyone. Because telling her now, in this coffee shop, with her mother twenty feet away, would turn this conversation into something else entirely, and he wasn't ready for what it would become.

"Never mind," he said. "It can wait."

Alex studied him for a moment. Then she shrugged and took another sip of her steamer.

From across the room, Donna stood and walked toward them, her coat over her arm, her smile apologetic. "I'm sorry to interrupt, but we've got to get going, sweetheart. School." Alex nodded.

"Can I talk to you again?" Demian asked. "There's more I'd like to discuss."

"Sure. I get home at three. My mom can text you the address."

"I'd like that."

She stood, pulled her backpack onto both shoulders — the backpack that now held twenty-two pounds of textbooks she'd study at a library she shouldn't be at, a sketchpad she'd fill on a rooftop she shouldn't be on, and a glossy photograph from a man whose name she didn't yet understand — and looked at Demian.

"Thanks for the steamer," she said.

"Thanks for talking to me."

She turned and followed her mother out. The bell chimed. Through the window, Demian watched Donna put her arm around Alex's shoulders as they walked to the car. Alex let her. It was a small thing. A girl letting her mother hold her. It broke Demian in a place he hadn't known was still whole. He sat at the table for a long time after they left. His coffee was cold. His phone was still recording. He turned it off.

The rain had stopped by the time he pulled his father's truck onto the street where Station 17 sat — a brick building with two bay doors, the same unremarkable firehouse that existed in every neighborhood in Columbus. Demian parked across the street and sat for a moment, watching two firefighters wash the side of an engine, their movements easy and practiced, the spray of the hose catching the light.

He got out and crossed the street. The bay doors were open. The smell of diesel and rubber and the metallic tang of the trucks hit him as he stepped inside.

"Morning," he said.

The two firefighters turned. The bigger one — stocky, broad-shouldered, his turnout pants held up by suspenders over a Station 17 t-shirt — straightened and wiped his hands on a rag. The name on his shirt read GABE.

"Help you?"

"I'm looking for Ronny Martinez."

The other man — leaner, older, with the calm authority of someone who'd been in charge for a long time — set down the hose and studied Demian.

"You press?" Hal asked.

"How could you tell?"

Gabe grinned. "You got that look. We get a lot asking for Ronny."

Hal didn't grin. "Ronny's not here. He's been on disability since the bombing."

"I was hoping to speak with him. My name is Demian Ochoa." The name landed between them like a change in the weather. Gabe's grin disappeared. Hal's expression didn't change, but a door closed behind it.

From the far side of the truck, a third firefighter appeared, wiping his hands on a towel. Tom. He looked at Demian and recognition crossed his face — not of the man, but of the name. "Mr. Ochoa," Tom said. "I told you on the phone. He doesn't want to talk to you."

"I understand that. I was hoping — if I could just—"

"I gave him your number. He didn't call. That's your answer." Tom's voice wasn't hostile.

It was the flat, final tone of a man delivering information that wasn't going to change. "I'd like to apologize to him," Demian said. "That's all. In person."

Tom looked at Hal. Hal looked at Demian. The quiet stretched. "That's a nice thought," Hal said. His voice was measured — the captain's voice, careful and precise. "But Ronny's dealing with a lot right now. Your photograph is part of what he's dealing with. Showing up at his door isn't going to help him."

"I don't have his address."

"And we're not going to give it to you." Hal said it without malice. A fact, like the weather. "If Ronny wants to talk to you, he knows how to find you. That's where it stands."

Demian looked at the three of them — Gabe with his arms crossed, Tom with the towel over his shoulder, Hal with his steady, unreadable captain's eyes. Three men standing between him and the firefighter in his photograph, and not one of them was going to move.

"Okay," Demian said. "Thank you." He turned and walked back to the truck. Behind him, he heard Tom say something low to Hal — too quiet to catch — and Hal's response, equally low. He didn't look back.

He climbed into the truck, its old leather creaking under him. Through the windshield, the firefighters had already returned to washing the engine, their movements easy and unhurried, as if he'd never been there at all.

Demian sat in the truck and thought about Alex Kelly zipping his photograph into her backpack without looking at it. He thought about Jordan Lowe's voice on the phone: Never want to hear from you again. He thought about Ronny Martinez's face on the YouTube video: The photo sucks. Three people in one photograph. Three completely different relationships with the image he'd made.

One couldn't stop looking at it. One couldn't bear to see it. One wanted it to never have existed.

And Demian — the fourth person, the one who'd pressed the shutter — didn't know which of them he agreed with. He started the truck and drove back to his parents' house, the wipers off now, the streets still wet, the city he'd grown up in looking like something he recognized but couldn't quite reach.

12

Ronny stood under the hatch of his wife's SUV in the supermarket parking lot, loading bags into the back while the rain hammered the asphalt around him. His phone buzzed in his pocket. He pulled it out, wiped the screen with his thumb. Jordan Lowe.

He put it to his ear. "Hey — can I call you right back? I'm loading groceries in a rainstorm."

"Sure."

He got the last bag in, slammed the hatch, and jogged to the driver's seat. The rain pinged against the roof in heavy, irregular drumbeats. He sat there for a moment, wiping the phone dry on his jeans, looking at her name on the screen.

He called her back. "Hey. Sorry about that. How are you?"

"Good. Good." A pause — the hesitation of someone rehearsing an apology and finding that the rehearsal didn't survive contact with the actual conversation. "I wanted to say I'm sorry. About yesterday."

"No — I wanted to apologize."

"You didn't do anything wrong."

"I shouldn't have left like that. You were upset and I just walked out."

"You didn't walk out. You were being kind. I was the one who —" She stopped. He could hear her breathing. "I grabbed you like a crazy person and had a panic attack in my own kitchen. That's not exactly a normal first impression."

"Jordan, you had an anxiety attack. I see those all the time. There's nothing to apologize for."

"Still."

"Still nothing." A silence. Then Jordan let out a small breath through her nose — not quite a laugh, but close. "Well. First time for both of us, I guess."

"Yeah."

Another pause. The rain filled it, drumming on the roof, streaming down the windshield. "Can I make it up to you?" she asked. "Will you come by again?"

Ronny sat in the parking lot with the engine off and the rain closing in around the car like a curtain, and he thought about Jeannette at the supermarket last night saying we could have her over for dinner, and he thought about Jordan's arms around him in the kitchen, and he thought about the weight of a boy's body in his arms and the girl's voice saying I think it moved, and he knew he should say no. "Sure," he said.

"I got a new creamer. Irish coffee flavor."

"Sounds good."

"Whenever you can. No rush."

"I'll drop these groceries off and come by."

"Really?"

"Yeah. Give me thirty minutes."

He drove home. Unloaded the bags. Put the cold stuff in the fridge, left the rest on the counter. Jeannette was at work. Danny was at school. Sofia was at school. The house was empty and quiet and he stood in the kitchen for a moment, his keys still in his hand, and felt the pull — the same gravity that had turned Jordan's car around at the firehouse, though he didn't know that, would never know that they were both orbiting the same unnamed thing. He drove to Jordan's house.

The door opened before he made it up the porch steps. Jordan stood in the doorway, and the first thing he noticed was that she looked different — not better, exactly, but more present. She'd brushed her hair. Changed her clothes. Small things, but they registered, the way small changes in a patient's condition register to someone trained to notice.

"Hey," she said.

"Hey."

"Come in."

The house looked the same — the sparse living room, the dining table, the stack of mail. But the curtains were open today, and the sunlight made the rooms feel less like a place where someone was hiding and more like a place where someone was trying.

He sat in the same chair. She brought coffee — two mugs, the Irish coffee creamer, a small plate of cookies that looked store-bought and recently opened, as if she'd gone out specifically for this visit. She set everything down and sat across from him.

"So," she said. "How's your day?"

"Groceries. Rain. The usual excitement of a man on disability."

She smiled. It was small but real. "I know the feeling. My biggest achievement today was getting dressed before noon."

"That counts."

"Does it?"

"On Tuesdays and Thursdays it counts."

She laughed. "Lucky it's a Thursday, I guess."

They drank their coffee. The conversation moved easier than the day before — not easy, but easier. The way a second meeting smooths the rough edges of a first. They talked about the rain. About the neighborhood. About the Steelers' chances next season, which led to a debate about whether the offensive line was the problem or the coaching, which led to Jordan laughing — a real laugh, sudden and surprised, as if she'd startled herself by making the sound.

Ronny watched it happen. Watched the laugh move through her face and change it — the lines around her eyes shifting from grief to something lighter, just for a second, before the gravity pulled them back. He thought: She used to laugh like this all the time. Before.

"You mentioned yesterday," Jordan said, and the temperature in the room dropped a degree. "You were a Steelers fan, too. Would you like to see Mikey's room?"

Ronny set his mug down. She'd asked three times now. Twice yesterday, once today. He understood what that meant. "You sure?"

"I'm sure."

She led him down the hallway to a closed door. Her hand found the knob and turned it slowly, carefully. The door swung in. The room was a museum. The bed was made — neatly, precisely, the covers tucked with the care that suggested they hadn't been disturbed since the last time someone smoothed them. The walls were covered in Pittsburgh Steelers posters and pennants, their edges curling. Shelves held action figures and toy cars lined up in formation, and a row of baseball trophies caught the light from the window, their cheap gold surfaces dulled by dust. Everything was dusty. A fine, undisturbed film covered every surface — the desk, the shelves, the dresser. Time settling onto a life that had ended.

"Sorry about the dust," Jordan said. She traced a line through it on the desk with her fingertip.

"I'm not allergic," Ronny said, and was grateful when she almost smiled.

He moved through the room slowly, giving everything the attention it deserved. The trophies — little gold figures frozen mid-swing, the kind every kid in Little League got. He pointed to one. "Danny did that league when he was younger. I've got a hundred stories about seven-year-olds in the outfield picking dandelions instead of catching fly balls."

"Mikey was the dandelion picker," Jordan said.

Ronny moved to the bulletin board above the desk. School artwork — a crayon drawing of a house, a watercolor that might have been a dog or might have been a horse. A spelling test with a gold star. A certificate: Most Improved Reader.

"Smart kid," Ronny said.

"Smartest in his class." Her voice had thickened.

He looked at the desk. A test paper — "Mikey Lowe" in messy pencil, a circled B-minus. The Spider-Man pencil case beside it, still holding pencils that would never be sharpened again.

Ronny tucked his hands into his pockets. He did it without thinking — a reflexive withdrawal, the body protecting itself from touching things that belonged to a boy it had carried out of a building. But Jordan noticed. He saw her notice — saw her eyes track his hands as they disappeared into his jeans. Her face changed — not grief exactly, a private thing he'd walked into by accident.

"A few days ago was the first time I'd been in here since everything," she said. She was sitting on the edge of the bed now, her hands flat on the mattress.

"What brought you in?"

"Emily. I found her sleeping in here one morning. She didn't know how she'd gotten in. Must have been sleepwalking."

Ronny nodded. He looked at the Steelers curtains, the gold light they threw. He looked at the shoes by the door — small, outgrown, the lights in the soles dead. He looked at the handprint turkey on the closet door, its construction paper fading.

"We should get out of here," he said gently. "It's a lot."

Jordan nodded. She stood up from the bed, pressing her hands against her thighs to push herself up. Her eyes swept the room one more time — the inventory of a mother making sure everything was still where her son had left it.

They walked back to the kitchen. Jordan leaned against the counter and pressed her fingers against her eyes. She wasn't crying — not yet — but she was close, holding it back like holding back a sneeze, with pressure and concentration and the knowledge that it was coming anyway.

"Thank you," she said. "For looking at his room. For seeing it."

"Thank you for showing me."

She dropped her hands. Her eyes were wet but steady. She studied him. Not the polite glances of conversation but the direct, unguarded gaze of a woman who had nothing left to hide and no energy to pretend. "Can I—" She stopped. Started again. "Your hands."

Ronny took his hands out of his pockets. Jordan reached for them. She took both of his hands in both of hers and brought them up — slowly, deliberately — to her face. She pressed his palms against her cheeks. His fingers curved along her temples. She closed her eyes.

Ronny stood perfectly still. He could feel her skin under his palms — warm, damp at the edges of her eyes, alive. He could feel the bones of her face, the jaw, the cheekbones, the architecture of a woman who had been beautiful before grief had carved new lines into her. She moved his hands — across her eyes, along her forehead, down to her mouth. She held them there, against her lips, and breathed.

He understood what she was doing. These hands had held Mikey. These hands had lifted a boy from the rubble and carried him into the light. She pressed them against her own face the way you press a letter from someone who's passed on against your chest — trying to absorb whatever trace of him might remain. Trying to touch her son through the last hands that had touched him.

She opened her eyes. They were inches apart. His hands were still on her face. He watched the need change shape in her eyes — sliding from grief into something warmer, something that frightened them both. Her gaze dropped to his mouth and came back to his eyes, and in that fraction of a second, the air between them compressed into something dense and charged and inevitable.

Jordan leaned forward and kissed him.

Ronny froze. His hands were still on her face. Her lips were on his — soft, tentative, tasting like coffee and salt from the tears she was still holding back. His body went rigid, every muscle locked, his brain sending two signals simultaneously: pull away and don't move and the signals canceled each other out and he stood there, paralyzed, while a woman kissed him in a kitchen that smelled like Irish coffee creamer, three doors down from her dead son's room.

Then — for a moment, for no more than three or four seconds that would expand in his memory to fill hours — he kissed her back. His hands slid from her face to the sides of her neck and he leaned into her and felt something open in his chest that had been sealed shut for months, something that wasn't desire exactly but wasn't not desire, something that lived in the space between guilt and need and loneliness and the alchemy of two broken people standing too close to each other in a quiet house on a rainy afternoon.

He pulled back. His hands dropped to his sides. He took a step backward. The kitchen expanded between them — three feet, then four, the distance of a decision made too late.

Jordan's fingers went to her mouth. Her eyes were wide, horrified, searching his face for the damage she'd just done. "I'm sorry," she whispered. "Ronny, I'm so sorry. I don't know why I—"

"It's okay."

"It's not okay. You're married. You have a family. I don't know what I—"

"Jordan. It's okay." His voice was steadier than he felt. "Grief makes us do things."

"That wasn't grief. I don't know what that was."

Ronny looked at her — this woman standing in her kitchen with her fingers on her lips and her son's room down the hall and her husband gone and her daughter at school and the whole enormous emptiness of her life pressing in from every side. He looked at her and he felt the pull and he knew, with the clarity of a man who had spent months lying awake at three in the morning, that if he didn't leave now he wasn't going to leave at all. "I should go," he said.

"I know."

"Are you going to be alright?"

She nodded. But she wasn't going to be alright. They both knew it. He walked to the door. She followed him but stopped in the hallway, leaning against the wall, her arms crossed over her chest.

He turned on the porch. "Jordan."

"Yeah."

"Don't apologize for that. Don't carry it around. It happened. It's okay."

She nodded again. Her eyes were bright and wet and she was biting the inside of her cheek and he could see the effort it was taking her not to cry.

He got in the truck. Sat there. The rain had started again — lighter now, a steady drizzle that blurred the windshield. He gripped the steering wheel with both hands, stared at the house through the water on the glass, and felt the crack that had opened in his chest last night widen by another inch.

He pressed his forehead against the steering wheel and closed his eyes. Three seconds. He'd kissed her back for three seconds. And in those three seconds he'd felt more alive — more present, more connected to another human being — than he had in months of lying beside his wife in the dark.

That was the thing he couldn't tell anyone. Not that she'd kissed him. Not that he'd been in her house. But that for three seconds, in a kitchen that smelled like Irish coffee, he'd felt something other than guilt, and the feeling had been so overwhelming and so wrong and so desperately needed that his body had responded before his conscience could intervene.

He drove home. Jeannette was making dinner when he walked in. Sofia was at the table doing homework.

Danny was somewhere upstairs, his music a low thump through the ceiling. "Where've you been?" Jeannette asked. Not suspicious. Just asking. "Dropped the groceries off and went to see Jordan."

Jeannette turned from the stove. "How is she?"

"The same. Struggling."

"Did she have another panic attack?"

"No. We just talked. She showed me Mikey's room."

"That must have been hard."

"It was."

Jeannette studied him for a moment — the automatic scan, the read. He met her eyes and held them, and the holding was its own kind of lie, because meeting your wife's eyes after kissing another woman requires a performance of normalcy that is itself a betrayal, and Ronny delivered it with the same steady competence he brought to everything, and hated himself for how easy it was.

"Dinner's in twenty," Jeannette said, and turned back to the stove. Ronny went to the bathroom. Closed the door. Ran the water. Looked at his face in the mirror — the same face, the same eyes, the same man who had walked out of this house two hours ago, except not the same at all, not anymore, because the man in the mirror had kissed a woman in a dead boy's kitchen and felt something crack open and hadn't told his wife.

He washed his hands. Dried them on the towel. Went back to the kitchen and sat at the table and asked Sofia about her homework and told Danny to turn the music down and ate the dinner Jeannette made and did the dishes and climbed the stairs and brushed his teeth and lay in bed beside the woman he'd been married to for eighteen years.

Jeannette read for a while. Turned off her light. Said goodnight. Ronny said goodnight.

He stared at the ceiling. The house settled around him — the creak of pipes, the hum of the furnace, the distant sound of Danny's music finally going silent.

He could still feel Jordan's lips on his. Could still feel the warmth of her face under his palms. Could still feel those three seconds expanding in his chest like a breath he couldn't exhale.

The ceiling stared back.

He didn't sleep.

13

D emian parked his father's truck across from the apartment building — a two-story rectangle of brick and iron from the seventies, twenty units arranged around an open courtyard, ten up, ten down, with iron staircases on either side. This building existed in every working-class neighborhood in Columbus — functional, unremarkable, holding its residents without pretending to impress them.

He checked the address Alex's mother had texted and climbed the stairs to the second floor. Unit 203. His boots echoed on the metal walkway. Through the railing, the courtyard below was empty — a patch of concrete with a rusted bike rack and a single tree dropping the last of its leaves onto the pavement.

He knocked on the security door. The main door behind it opened, and a shadow appeared behind the metal screen. "Hello?"

"Alex?"

The security door swung toward him. Alex stood in the doorway in a hoodie and jeans, backpack on the floor behind her, her face carrying the same watchful, assessing expression he remembered from the coffee shop.

"Yeah, come in. Just got home."

Demian stepped inside. The apartment was small — a kitchen to the right, a living room straight ahead, a hallway to the left leading to what he assumed were the bedrooms. Clean, but spare. The furniture had the look of things acquired over time from different sources — a couch that didn't match the chair, a coffee table with a ring stain, curtains that were a different era than the carpet. A home held together by effort, not money.

Alex moved into the kitchen. As she passed the counter, her hand shot out and swept a bottle off the surface — quick, practiced, a gesture so fast Demian almost missed it. She tucked it into the cabinet beneath the sink and shut the door in one motion. The label had been visible for half a second. Vodka.

Demian turned his head sharply, studying the living room wall as if something there had caught his attention. He said nothing. But he filed it — the speed of the movement, the muscle memory in it. She'd hidden bottles of vodka before.

"I'm going to have a bowl of cereal," Alex said, pulling a box from the cabinet. "Want one? Or anything?"

"No, I'm fine. Thank you."

He looked down the hallway. "Is your mom home?"

"She's at work."

"Got it." Demian nodded, still taking in the apartment. A stack of mail on the counter. A calendar on the wall with shifts written in blue ink. A single framed photo on the bookshelf — Alex and another girl, younger, both grinning, arms around each other, a birthday cake between them.

"Hey," Demian said, "I have a meeting tomorrow morning with your school. The principal."

Alex's spoon stopped halfway to her mouth. Her eyes cut to him — a quick, sharp look, the watchfulness dialing up several notches. "What for?"

"Background for the story. Context about the school, the students, the recovery."

Alex resumed eating, but her posture tightened. "If she says anything about me, keep it to yourself."

"What do you mean? What would she say?"

"I don't know. Just — don't go telling my mom stuff." She said it casually, but her eyes weren't casual. They were the eyes of someone protecting a perimeter.

"Okay," Demian said. He let it go, but filed that too.

Alex carried her cereal to the couch and settled in, legs crossed, the bowl balanced on her knee. "You can sit," she said, nodding at the chair opposite.

Demian sat. Took out his phone. "Mind if I record again?"

"Go ahead." She took a spoonful. "You going to ask me the special question now? The one you chickened out on last time?"

Demian laughed — caught off guard by her directness. "Not yet. I want to ask you something else first. How well do you know the firefighter in the photo? Ronny Martinez."

"I saw him at the thing at the school. Some thing they had the weekend before school started. All the firefighters were there. I walked right past him, and he didn't recognize me." She shrugged. "He used to be on TV all the time. I don't see him anymore."

"I went to his station. They said he's still on disability."

"He had a limp when I saw him. A bad one. But that was months ago." Another spoonful. "You want to interview him, too?"

"I'd like to." Demian paused. "What about Mikey Lowe's mother? Do you know her?"

"I know her daughter, Emily. Saw her at the school thing too. She's a grade below me."

Alex set the bowl on the coffee table. "Hey, you want to see my room?"

"I'd like that."

She led him down the hallway. The door to her bedroom was open, and when Demian stepped inside, he stopped. The room was immaculate. Not clean in the way a teenager's room is clean when company is coming — clean in a way that suggested a permanent, structural need for order. The bed was made with military precision, the covers pulled tight, the pillows arranged symmetrically. Clothes were folded and stacked on shelves with the edges aligned. Books stood upright on a small bookcase, organized by size. A desk beneath the window held a neat row of pencils, a cup of pens, and a closed sketchpad positioned exactly parallel to the desk's edge.

And on the walls — drawings. Everywhere. Taped in rows, overlapping at the edges, covering nearly every surface. Demian moved closer. They weren't what he'd expected. No flowers, no rainbows, no teenage abstraction. These were observational — precise, technical, rendered with a skill that had no business belonging to someone her age. A city skyline seen from above, the buildings rendered in fine graphite lines with the shadows falling at a consistent angle. A woman on a bus, her head tilted against the window, her grocery bags sagging on the seat beside her. An old man asleep with his mouth open, every wrinkle mapped. A row of pigeons on a ledge, each one distinct, each one alive.

"These are yours?" Demian asked, though he already knew.

"Yeah."

"Alex, these are—" He moved from drawing to drawing, stunned. "These are highly technical. Have you had lessons?"

"No. Just me."

"The perspective work alone — this skyline, is this from a photograph?"

"From a roof."

He looked at her. She was sitting on the edge of the bed, watching him look at her work. For the first time since he'd met her, the guardedness was gone. What was left was the exposure of an artist letting someone see the thing they actually care about.

"You have a serious gift," Demian said. "I mean that."

"Thanks." A change of color in her cheeks. Then the guard came back up, quick as a blink. "I have more. You want to see?"

"Absolutely."

"They're in a secret spot."

"A secret spot?"

Her eyes flashed — the first time he'd seen anything close to excitement in them. "I've got a key." She said it as if she were sharing classified intelligence.

Demian raised his eyebrows. "Lead the way."

She took a key from her desk drawer and led him out of the apartment, down the walkway, down one staircase, and up the other to the far side of the building. Unit 210. The door was plain, identical to every other door on the walkway, but the window beside it was dark. Alex fumbled with the key — her hands shaking slightly, not from fear but from the adrenaline of sharing a secret. She grinned at him, a real grin, the first one he'd seen, and unlocked the door. "Welcome," she said, and pushed it open.

The apartment was empty. Completely, utterly vacant — no furniture, no curtains, no signs of habitation except the faint smell of disinfectant and a thin layer of dust on the hardwood floor, disturbed only by footprints. Alex's footprints. Many of them, in different patterns, tracking back and forth from the door to a hallway. She'd been here often.

"My best friend Chrissy used to live here," Alex said. She walked ahead of him, her voice matter-of-fact. "Her parents gave me a key so I could come here after school. My mom was always working, so I'd let myself in and hang out with Chrissy until dinner."

"Where did her family move to?"

"Her parents moved after Chrissy died in the bombing." She said it without drama. A fact. But Demian heard the weight beneath the flatness — the same controlled delivery he'd heard from soldiers reporting casualties. The voice of someone who'd said a thing so many times the words had worn smooth, the sharp edges rubbed off by repetition, the pain pushed down beneath the surface where it could be carried without being felt.

"She was your best friend?" Demian asked.

"Since we were seven."

Alex led him down the hallway to a bedroom — Chrissy's bedroom, Demian understood. The room was empty like the rest, the walls bare, the closet doors slightly ajar. Alex slid down the wall and sat on the dusty floor, her back against the cool surface, her knees pulled up. "Look in the closet," she said.

Demian stepped forward and opened the doors. The inside of the closet was covered in drawings. Floor to ceiling, taped and layered, some overlapping, some arranged in careful rows — dozens of them, maybe fifty or more, filling every inch of the closet's interior walls. They were Alex's work — he recognized the style immediately, the same precise linework, the same observational eye. But these were different from the ones in her bedroom. These were more personal. A sketch of two girls sitting on a staircase, heads together, laughing. A pair of hands braiding hair. A birthday cake with crooked candles. A view through a window — this window, next to him, looking at the same courtyard below, with two figures in the courtyard, small and distant, throwing a ball.

"These are yours too?" he asked, though his throat had tightened.

"Yeah. Chrissy used to tape my drawings up in here. I'd give them to her, and she'd put them on the walls. By the time they moved, this closet was full. Her parents packed them all up and took them."

"So these are new ones."

"I keep putting them up. New ones, whenever I come." She was tracing a crack in the floorboard with her fingertip, not looking at him. "It's like — by putting drawings up in here, I'm still having a conversation with her. Even though she's gone, I like to think she'd want me to. Eventually, I'll fill the closet again. That's what I want to do."

Demian stood in the closet doorway, looking at the drawings, and felt something give way in his chest. He thought about his brother Miguel — about the photographs he'd taken with a disposable camera in a hospital room in Guadalajara, eleven pictures in the last week of a ten- year-old's life. He'd kept the negatives in a shoebox at his parents' house, two miles from where he was standing right now. He'd never shown them to anyone. They were his conversation with Miguel — private, ongoing, kept in a box the way Alex kept hers in a closet.

"Sometimes we need something tangible," Demian said. He had to clear his throat to get the words out. "A bridge between memory and the present. You've found a way to build that."

"I guess." Alex looked up at him. "Drawing helps me make sense of things. Like taking all the chaos in my head and giving it a shape I can understand."

"Like photography," Demian said, before he could stop himself.

Alex tilted her head. "Oh, you do photography too?"

His pulse spiked. "Both. I'm a journalist, but I do some photography as well."

"That's cool. I'd love to learn photography. Some things I see, I can't get right in a drawing."

"Your drawings get a lot right." He steered away from the edge he'd almost walked over and back to safe ground. "This work is exceptional, Alex. You should be showing it. Galleries. Competitions."

"Maybe." She looked at him from the floor, those steady eyes doing their assessment. "You're different from the other reporters."

"How so?"

"You look at things. Like, really look. The others just asked questions and wrote stuff down. You actually see stuff."

The words landed in Demian's chest and sat there, warm and unbearable, because she was describing what a photographer does — what he does — and she was telling him she trusted him, and the trust was built on a lie he'd been carrying since the coffee shop. He was standing in a room where a girl came to have honest conversations with her dead best friend, surrounded by drawings that were the purest form of truth he'd ever seen, and he was hiding the one thing about himself that mattered most.

He couldn't do it anymore. Not here. Not in this room.

"Alex." His voice came out different — lower, stripped of the journalist's practiced ease. "There's something I need to tell you. The thing I couldn't say at the coffee shop."

She looked at him. The assessment sharpened. Demian sat down on the floor across from her, his back against the opposite wall, so they were at the same level. Eye to eye. He owed her that.

"My name is Demian Ochoa," he said. "I'm not just a journalist. I'm a photojournalist. I work for the Associated Press." He paused. The dust floated in the light from the window. "I'm the one who took the photograph. Your photograph. The one of you and Ronny Martinez and Mikey Lowe."

Alex didn't move. Her face didn't change. She sat with her knees pulled up and her back against the wall and looked at him the way she'd been looking at him since the coffee shop — steady, measuring — except now the thing she was measuring had changed shape entirely. The silence lasted five seconds. Ten. Long enough for Demian to feel the sweat on his palms and the dust in his throat and the full weight of what he'd just done.

A smile grew on her face. "I know," Alex said.

Demian blinked. "You know?"

"I Googled you before the coffee shop. Demian Ochoa, Associated Press. Your photo came up. Like, immediately." She said it matter-of-factly, the way she said everything — clean, direct, no decoration. "Why do you think I asked for a copy of the photo? I knew you'd have one."

Demian stared at her. The confession he'd been dreading — the reveal he'd rehearsed and chickened out of and finally forced himself to deliver in a dead girl's bedroom — and she'd known the whole time. She'd walked him through her apartment, shown him her drawings, led him to Chrissy's closet, handed him the most private thing in her life, knowing exactly who he was.

"Why didn't you say anything?" he asked.

Alex shrugged. One shoulder, the way she did. "I wanted to see what you'd do. If you'd tell me or keep hiding it."

"And if I'd kept hiding it?"

With a half grin, Alex shrugged. "I guess I have some secrets I keep to myself as well."

Demian let that settle. She'd led him here knowing who he was, and she'd waited to see if he'd be honest, but it didn't matter if he wasn't; she'd still let him in. Thirteen years old. This girl was thirteen years old.

"Are you angry?" he asked.

"About what?"

"The photograph. That I took it."

Alex was quiet for a moment. She pulled at a thread on the knee of her jeans, winding it around her finger, unwinding it. "You want to know something weird?" she asked.

"Yeah."

"When I found out it was you — when I Googled you and saw your face — I wasn't angry. I was—" She stopped. Searched for the word. "Relieved."

"Relieved?"

"Because I've been looking at that photo every day. I've drawn it thirty-something times. I carry a copy in my backpack. My mom takes them away, and I like to get new ones. It's like—" She gestured vaguely, frustrated with the limits of language. "It's the most important thing in my life and I don't know why. And then you showed up. The person who made it. And I thought — maybe you know. Maybe you can tell me why I can't stop looking at it."

Demian felt the floor shift beneath him. Every person who'd encountered his photograph had told him what it had taken from them. The firefighter's dignity. The mother's privacy. The public's comfort. Everyone had told him what the photo had cost. And here was a sweet, young girl sitting on the dusty floor of her dead friend's empty bedroom, asking him not what it had taken, but what it meant.

"I don't know," Demian said. It was the most honest thing he'd said in months. "I don't know why you can't stop looking at it. I don't know why I can't stop looking at it either."

"You look at it too?"

"Every day."

Alex studied him. Her expression shifted — not softening, exactly, but recognizing. The way two people recognize each other when they share a thing they can't explain to anyone else.

"You get it," she said. "The scab thing."

"Yeah, I get it."

"Looking at it became like — like breathing. Something I just have to do."

"Your mom doesn't understand that?"

"Nobody understands that. Nobody would." She looked at him. "Except you."

Demian thought about the medic in Afghanistan — Did you just take a photo? He thought about George telling him it was brilliant. He thought about Jordan Lowe's voice: Your photograph is the last recorded image of my precious little boy. He thought about the six times he'd read her letter. He thought about deleting the soldier's photo and the dead in his camera, one frame at a time. "I think I do," he said.

They sat on the floor of Chrissy's empty room, the photographer and the girl in his photograph, the dust floating between them in the afternoon light, and for the first time since Demian had pressed the shutter in front of a bombed school in Columbus, Ohio, he felt something other than guilt when he thought about what he'd made. Not pride. Not absolution. Just the strange, fragile recognition that the thing he'd created — the thing that had caused so much pain — had also, for one person, become a way to survive. He didn't know what to do with that. He didn't know if it made things better or worse.

"Come on," Alex said, standing, brushing the dust from her jeans. "Let's go back."

Demian followed her out of the bedroom. At the doorway, he stopped. Penciled on the door jamb — faint, in a child's handwriting — were height measurements. A series of horizontal lines with dates beside them, the handwriting getting slightly larger and more confident as the lines climbed. The final measurement of a girl who would never grow taller read 4'10" — Age 12.

14

The seventh time Ronny came over, Jordan made coffee she knew neither of them would finish. She'd stopped counting the visits by number — that was a lie. She counted everything.

She counted the minutes between his truck pulling up and the doorbell ringing (usually four — he sat in the cab first, she'd learned, gathering himself). She counted the seconds his hands stayed in her grasp before he gently pulled them back (longer each time, twelve the first visit, forty the third, last Tuesday she'd held them for the entire length of a conversation about Emily's science project and he hadn't pulled away at all). She counted the hours after he left, the way they stacked up like bricks in a wall between his departure and the next time she'd see him.

It was Tuesday again. Emily was at school. The house was clean — cleaner than it had been in months, because somewhere around the fourth visit, Jordan had started noticing things. The water stain on the kitchen ceiling. The scuff marks on the baseboards. The way the living room looked when the afternoon light came through the curtains she'd finally washed. She'd started noticing because he was going to see it, and she wanted it to look — she didn't finish the thought. She never finished the thought.

The coffee was ready. The Irish coffee creamer was on the table — she bought it now specifically, a bottle a week, the same brand, because he'd said he liked it and she'd held onto that the way she held onto everything: tightly, precisely, with the desperate attention of a woman who had learned that the things you failed to notice were the things that disappeared.

The doorbell rang.

She smoothed her shirt. Checked her reflection in the microwave door — a habit she'd developed around the fifth visit and refused to examine. She opened the door.

"Hey," Ronny said.

"Hey. Come in."

He walked past her and she caught it — the soap, the detergent, something underneath that was just him, a warmth that didn't have a name. She'd started noticing that as well. Around the fourth visit. She closed the door and followed him to the kitchen.

He sat in his chair. She sat in hers. The table between them, the mugs, the creamer. The ritual of it had become something she depended on. The sameness. That was the thing.

Every Tuesday at two o'clock, Ronny Martinez sat at her dining table and drank coffee with Irish coffee creamer and talked to her, and for two hours the house wasn't empty and the silence wasn't total and she wasn't alone with the sound of the clock and the dust settling on Mikey's trophies and the slow, grinding machinery of grief that ran day and night without an off switch.

"How's your week?" he asked.

"Same. Emily had a thing at school — a science fair. She built a volcano."

"Baking soda and vinegar?"

"The whole kitchen smelled like a salad for two days."

He laughed. When he laughed, the lines around his eyes deepened and his shoulders dropped — for half a second, the look of a man who wasn't carrying anything. She'd started collecting these moments — adding them to the inventory of small things that got her from one Tuesday to the next.

They talked. About Emily. About Danny's basketball season. About a show Jeannette had made him watch that he pretended to hate but actually liked. He mentioned Jeannette casually, the way he always did — not avoiding her name, not emphasizing it, just the natural mention of a wife in a married man's conversation — and every time he said it Jordan felt the word land in her chest like a small, precise stone. Jeannette. She existed. She was real. She was home right now, or at work, or wherever wives were when their husbands were sitting in other women's kitchens on Tuesday afternoons.

Jordan knew what she was doing. She wasn't stupid, and she wasn't delusional, and she wasn't a woman who pretended not to see the thing she was walking toward. She saw it. She saw it every Tuesday at two o'clock when she opened the door and felt the relief flood through her like a drug hitting a vein — the instant, full-body release of, 'he came back, he's here, I'm not alone.' She saw it when she reached for his hands and felt the current run through her, the warmth, the aliveness that she couldn't get from anything else — not from Emily, not from her sister, not from the therapist she'd stopped seeing, not from the pills the doctor had prescribed that she took every night and that dulled the edges but never touched the center.

Ronny's hands were the center.

It had started as grief. She knew that. The first time she'd grabbed his hand at the table — the first visit, the day of the panic attack — it had been about Mikey. His hands held my son. His hands were the last to touch my boy. She'd needed to touch the thing that had touched Mikey, like pressing a dead person's shirt to your face to catch the last of their smell. A bridge. A reaching.

But the bridge had become something else. She didn't know when — the third visit, the fourth, the moment she'd taken his hands and pressed them to her face in Mikey's room and felt his palms against her cheeks and closed her eyes and felt, for the first time since the bombing, that she existed inside her own skin. That she was a body, not just a wound. That she was warm, not just grieving. That she was a woman being touched by a man's hands, and the feeling was so foreign and so necessary that it had rearranged something fundamental in her, the way a broken bone heals at a new angle and you can never go back to the old shape.

That was the truth she circled and never landed on. She needed his hands the way she needed the pills at night. The pills stopped being enough. The hand-holding was no longer enough. The first dose of anything eventually stopped doing what it did.

"Jordan?"

She blinked. Ronny was looking at her. She'd gone somewhere — drifted, lost the thread of whatever he'd been saying about Danny's free-throw percentage.

"Sorry. I zoned out."

"You okay?"

"Yeah. Just tired."

He studied her. The fireman's read — she'd come to recognize it. His eyes scanned her face the way they might scan a building for structural weakness. Assessing. Professional. Kind. "You sleeping?"

"Some. The pills help. Mostly I lie there and count."

"Count what?"

"Anything. Tiles on the ceiling. Seconds between the furnace cycling on and off. The number of times the clock ticks in a minute." She smiled. It felt thin. "My therapist says it's a coping mechanism. I say it's insomnia."

Ronny reached across the table and put his hand over hers. He did it — not her. He'd started doing that around the fifth visit, meeting her halfway, offering instead of just allowing. The shift had been small but seismic. The first time he'd reached for her hand instead of waiting for her to reach for his, Jordan had felt something crack open in her chest that she'd spent months trying to keep sealed.

She turned her hand over and laced her fingers through his. Held. The warmth moved through her palm and up her wrist and into her arm and she closed her eyes and breathed and let it do what it always did — the thing the pills couldn't do, the thing the therapist couldn't do, the thing no amount of counting could accomplish. It made the silence bearable. It made the house feel like a house instead of a tomb.

But today it wasn't enough.

She could feel it — the insufficiency, the gap between what the hand-holding gave her and what she needed. The dose wasn't working. She held his hand and felt the warmth and the connection and the relief, and underneath it all, the ache persisted, untouched, unbothered, patient.

They talked for another hour. Ronny told a story about Sofia's volleyball game — a serve that went sideways and hit the referee — and Jordan laughed and held his hand and felt the ache and smiled and hated herself for wanting more and couldn't stop wanting it.

At three-thirty, Ronny stood. "I should get going before the kids get home."

"Of course."

"I'll hit the bathroom first, if that's okay."

"You know where it is."

She listened to his footsteps on the hardwood. The bathroom door closed. The fan came on — a low hum that filled the hallway. She stood at the kitchen counter, her hands flat on the surface, her head down, and felt the Tuesday afternoon stretching out ahead of her like a sentence she'd have to serve — the hours between now and Emily's return, the evening of homework and dinner and television and the mechanical performance of normalcy that she executed every night.

She walked to the hallway.

She didn't decide to do it. That was what she'd tell herself later — that there was no decision, no moment of choosing, just a body moving through a house toward a thing it needed. Like gravity. Like water finding its level. She walked to the hallway and stood outside the bathroom door, and her bedroom door was right there, two feet to the right, open, the bed visible, the afternoon light coming through the window and falling across the comforter.

The toilet flushed. The water ran. The fan hummed. The door opened.

Ronny stepped out and she was there — right there, close enough to feel his breath, close enough to see the surprise in his eyes, the quick recalculation, the understanding arriving on his face like weather. The hallway was narrow. His body filled it. She didn't step back.

"Jordan—"

She took his hands. Both of them. Brought them up to her face the way she always did — pressed them against her cheeks, his palms warm, his fingers curving along her temples. She closed her eyes. Breathed.

"I'm sorry," she whispered. "I need—" She couldn't say it. The word wouldn't come — not because she didn't know what it was, but because saying it would make it real, would make it a thing she was choosing instead of a thing that was happening to her, and she wasn't ready for that, couldn't carry the weight of choosing this on top of everything else she was carrying.

She turned her face into his palm and pressed her lips against the center of it. Not a kiss — or not only a kiss. Something more desperate. Something that lived in the space between worship and need. His hand tensed under hers. The muscles in his fingers tightened — the married man, the father, the firefighter, all of those men pulling back at once.

She opened her eyes and looked at him. The hallway was narrow and her bedroom door was open and the light was coming through and they were so close she could hear his heartbeat — or maybe it was hers, she couldn't tell anymore, they were that close. "Please," she said.

One word. She put everything into it — every empty Tuesday, every silent night, every morning she'd woken up in a house that felt like a coffin, every time she'd held his hands and felt the warmth drain away the moment he let go. She put Mikey into it, and Nate's absence, and Emily's sleepwalking, and the pills that didn't work and the counting that never reached zero. She put months of being untouched and unloved and alone into a single syllable and offered it to the only person in the world who might understand what it meant.

Ronny looked at her. His hands were still on her face. His jaw was tight. She could see the war behind his eyes — duty and desire, guilt and need, the man he was supposed to be fighting the man who was standing in a narrow hallway with a woman who was asking him for the one thing he shouldn't give.

He didn't say anything. He didn't move toward her and he didn't move away. He stood there, his hands on her face, and the choice hung between them like a held breath.

Jordan stepped backward through her bedroom door. She didn't pull him. She didn't take his hand. She just stepped back, into the light, and looked at him. Ronny stood in the hallway for a long moment. The bathroom fan hummed behind him.

He stepped forward.

The door closed behind them with a soft click — the sound of a line being crossed, quiet and ordinary and irreversible, like a crack forming in a foundation that would never be repaired.

Afterward, Jordan lay on her side, facing the window. The afternoon light had shifted — lower now, amber, falling across the tangled sheets in long bars. She could feel him behind her, the warmth of his body, the rise and fall of his breathing. Neither of them had spoken.

Her face was wet. She'd cried — not during, not exactly, but at some point the boundary between what her body was feeling and what her grief was doing had dissolved, and the tears had come, and she hadn't tried to stop them, and he hadn't tried to stop them either. He'd just held her. That was the thing she'd remember later. Not the sex itself but the holding — his arms around her, his chest against her back, his hands steady and warm. He'd stayed. He hadn't pulled away — the way men usually did, the way she'd expected him to. He'd just held her and let it happen.

She heard him sit up. The bed shifted. The sound of clothes being gathered, fabric pulled on — the quiet, careful movements of a man getting dressed in a room that wasn't his. Jordan didn't turn around. She listened. Belt buckle. Zipper. The soft thud of a shoe.

"Jordan."

"Yeah."

A pause. She could feel him standing there, behind her, dressed, looking at her back. "Are you okay?"

She almost laughed. Okay. What a word. What an insufficient, absurd, impossible word for what she was — lying in a bed with sheets that smelled like a man who wasn't her husband, in a house where her dead son's room was twenty feet away, with tears drying on her face and a body that felt like something other than a vessel for carrying grief.

"I don't know," she said. It was the most honest thing she'd said all day.

She heard him move to the door. Open it. Hesitate. "I'll be here," he said. "Whatever you need."

The door closed. His footsteps went down the hallway. The front door opened and shut. The truck started. Pulled away.

Jordan lay in the amber light and listened to the house settle back into its silence — the clock, the furnace, and the quiet of rooms where only one person is breathing. She pulled the sheet up to her chin. She pressed her hands against her face — her own hands, not his — and breathed, and the smell of him was on her fingers, and she held them there, and the counting started again, automatic, involuntary, unstoppable.

The number of hours until Tuesday.

15

The school smelled like disinfectant and floor wax and the warmth of a building full of children. Demian crossed the street with his camera bag over his shoulder, weaving through the chaotic mass of kids and backpacks and parents crouched down zipping coats. He spotted Alex down the block, in front of the playground entrance — Donna beside her, leaning down, pressing three kisses to her daughter's forehead. Donna said something, Alex nodded, and Donna turned and disappeared into the stream of parents heading back to their cars.

Demian continued inside. The reception area was a whirlwind — parents signing in, a teacher holding two lunch boxes that didn't belong to her, staff members greeting students with the practiced brightness of people who did this every morning. Near the front desk, Principal Reynolds stood in conversation with another teacher. Demian waited, hands in his pockets, until the conversation ended.

"Principal Reynolds?" She turned.

"Yes?"

"I'm Demian Ochoa. We spoke on the phone."

"Mr. Ochoa, good morning." She extended her hand. "Thank you for coming in. Let's go to my office."

They walked through the bustling hallways — the squeak of sneakers on linoleum, the slam of lockers, the low roar of a hundred kids in motion — until they reached her office. The walls were covered in student artwork, crayon houses and watercolor suns and a construction paper caterpillar that stretched the full length of one wall. Demian took the chair across from her desk.

"How can I help you?" she asked.

"Well, as you know, I'm the photographer who took the photograph. The one with the firefighter, Alex Kelly, and—"

"Yes."

"It ran in all the papers. The magazines. It's been seen by millions of people at this point."

"I remember it."

"There are many who believe the photo should never have been taken. That it caused more harm than good. I've come to understand that it has especially disturbed the people depicted in it — the firefighter, Alex Kelly, and Mikey Lowe's mother. I'm trying to understand the full impact. Whether the school community has any insight — how the photo affected the students, the families, the recovery process."

Reynolds leaned back in her chair and considered this. "The photo was difficult for a lot of people. Not just the families directly involved. Parents in this community saw that image and saw their own children. It made the bombing — which was already the worst thing any of us had ever been through — feel public in a way that was hard to control. Some parents felt exposed. Others felt it was important that the world saw what happened here." She paused. "I don't think there's a simple answer."

"And the people in the photograph specifically? Have you heard anything?"

"Nothing about the firefighter. But as for Mrs. Lowe — we've heard from other parents that she was deeply disturbed. Though who knows if that's simply from the loss of her son or from the photo itself. If anything, the photo would be a tiny fraction of that woman's pain."

"Of course," Demian agreed.

"As for Alex Kelly—" Reynolds paused. "She was one of my star students at our previous school. Bright, talented, remarkable young girl. But she apparently chose a different school. She doesn't attend here."

Demian's head snapped back. "She doesn't go to this school?"

"No. She went here for a week or two, but later we received transfer papers for her to attend Eastmore Academy."

"But I just saw her outside. With her mother. Five minutes ago."

Reynolds's eyebrows rose. "I can't explain that. Perhaps they were visiting someone. But Alex Kelly is not one of our students."

Demian sat with that. The woman across from him had no reason to lie. And Alex — Alex who'd told him school was "fine," Alex who carried twenty-two pounds of textbooks in a backpack every morning, Alex who said "just got home" at three o'clock every afternoon — wasn't going to this school.

He thanked Reynolds, shook her hand, and walked back through the hallways that smelled like floor wax and disinfectant. He sat in his father's truck in the parking lot for a long time, watching kids file through the entrance, thinking about Alex, a girl with a backpack full of textbooks who was dropped off at a school she didn't attend every morning by a mother who kissed her forehead three times for luck.

The next morning, he was parked across the street by seven-forty.

The February air was cold enough to see his breath, and he kept the truck running for the heat, slumped low in the driver's seat with a coffee from the gas station on the dashboard. Parents arrived in waves — minivans, SUVs, a school bus disgorging kids in puffy coats. Demian watched the entrance and waited.

At eight-oh-five, Donna's car pulled up. Alex got out. The backpack, the hoodie, the jeans. Donna came around the car and they walked to the playground entrance together — the same spot as yesterday, the same choreography. Donna leaned down. Three kisses on the forehead. She said something Demian couldn't hear, and Alex nodded, and Donna turned and walked back to the car.

Demian slid lower in his seat as Donna's car passed. He counted to ten, then looked back at the school entrance. Alex was gone. Not inside the school. Gone — peeled off to the left, around the corner of the building, moving fast. Demian caught the last flash of her backpack before she disappeared behind the gymnasium wall.

He got out of the truck and followed. She moved quickly — not running, but walking with the focused, route-certain pace of someone who'd done this many times. Head down, shoulders set, eyes scanning left and right in quick, automatic sweeps. She cut through a parking lot, crossed a street against the light, turned down a side street lined with older houses. Demian kept half a block behind her, using parked cars for cover, feeling ridiculous — a grown man tailing a thirteen-year-old through a residential neighborhood at eight in the morning.

She walked for ten minutes. Eventually, the houses thinned, and a small park appeared between two rows of homes — a patch of grass with a few benches and a massive oak tree, its bare branches spread against the gray sky. Alex slowed. Scanned the park. Satisfied it was empty, she walked to the base of the oak and sat down, cross-legged, her back against the trunk. She pulled out her sketchpad.

Demian watched from behind a parked van for a moment — watched her settle in, watched her pencil start moving, watched the focus descend over her face like a visor dropping. She was drawing something across the park — a man asleep on a bench, bundled in a coat, his face weathered and slack. She was rendering him with the same precise, observational hand he'd seen in her bedroom and in Chrissy's closet.

He walked toward her. No more hiding. His shoes crunched on the frozen grass and she heard him coming — he saw her shoulders tense, saw the pencil pause — and when he stopped beside her, she tilted her head up and looked at him. Her eyes narrowed. "You following me?"

"This is my usual morning walking route." A sly smile.

"Yeah. Sure."

Demian sat down next to her on the cold ground, his back against the oak. The bark pressed through his jacket. The sleeping man on the bench hadn't moved.

"Shouldn't you be in school?" Demian asked.

"Shouldn't you be at work?"

"I don't have an office job."

"Neither do I."

He looked at her drawing. The sleeping man's face was emerging on the page — every line and crease mapped with an accuracy that was almost clinical. "Excellent work. As usual."

"Thank you."

"Closet-worthy?"

"My work is in all the finer establishments these days," she said, and for a moment she sounded like a kid — playful, light, the mask slipping to reveal someone who still knew how to joke.

They sat in silence for a minute. Alex drew. Demian waited for a moment before saying, "The principal told me you're not enrolled at her school, Alex."

The pencil stopped. "You asked her about me?"

"I went there for background on the story. Your name came up."

"What did she say?"

"That you were one of her best students. And that you never registered."

Alex stared at her sketchpad. The sleeping man stared back from the page, half-finished. "She thinks you enrolled somewhere else," Demian said. "Did you?"

A long pause. Alex's jaw worked — the same tight movement he'd seen when she'd talked about Mikey in the coffee shop. The calculation behind her eyes was almost visible: how much to reveal, how much to protect, which walls to lower and which to keep standing. "No," she said.

"How long?"

"Since September."

Demian let that settle. Five months. Five months of walking to a school she didn't enter, five months of libraries and parks and rooftops, five months of a con so carefully constructed that her own mother didn't know. "Your mom doesn't know."

Alex looked at him. The guard was up — fully, completely, the drawbridge raised. "If you tell her, I'm done talking to you. About anything. Forever." The words were flat and final. Not a threat — a boundary. A line drawn in permanent ink.

"I'm not going to tell her," Demian said.

"Promise me."

"I promise."

She held his gaze, reading him the way she always did. Measuring. Weighing. Deciding whether to trust. Her shoulders released a fraction of an inch, and she went back to drawing.

"I couldn't go back," she said. Her voice was quieter now. "Not to the new school. The kids who were at the old school — the ones who went through it — they're fine. They get it. But the other kids. The ones who weren't there." She shaded a line on the sleeping man's cheek. "I feel their eyes. Their looks. The way they stare or the way they try not to stare, which is worse. I couldn't do it."

"So you just stopped going."

"I'm not stupid about it. I do all the work. I study every day. I read more than I ever did in class." She glanced at him. "My test scores would be higher than anyone in that building if I could turn them in."

Demian believed her. He'd seen her room — the order, the discipline, the immaculate arrangement of a life being managed with ferocious precision. This wasn't a kid who'd given up on school. This was a kid who'd given up on the building. "How do you keep your mom from finding out?"

Alex almost smiled. "I have some secrets I keep to myself."

He let it go. She'd given him more than she'd given anyone — the admission alone was enormous. He wasn't going to push for the mechanics. They sat under the oak tree. The sleeping man on the bench shifted, pulled his coat tighter, settled back into whatever dream he was having. Alex drew his hands — curled, gloveless, tucked under his chin.

"Can I ask you something?" Demian asked.

"You're going to anyway."

"The photograph. My photograph. It's been nominated for the Pulitzer Prize."

Alex's pencil paused. "What's that mean?"

"It means a committee of judges thinks it's one of the most important photographs taken this year. If it wins, there's a ceremony. A luncheon in New York. Speeches. Press coverage." He paused. "And the photograph gets published everywhere again. Every newspaper, every magazine, every website. The whole cycle starts over." Alex sat quiet. "Mrs. Lowe will see her son's face everywhere again. The firefighter will have cameras in his driveway again. And you— "

"When?"

"The ceremony is in May. A couple months."

"Do you want to win?"

Demian looked at the sky through the bare branches. "I used to dream about it. Now I don't for this photo. I know what it will cost the people in the photo. I tried to withdraw it. The AP owns it — they won't let me."

"So, it's going to happen whether you want it to or not."

"Yeah."

Alex set her pencil down. She turned to face him, cross-legged, her knees almost touching his. "You told me at my apartment that you came here to find out if the photo hurt people. And to apologize if it did."

"Yes."

"And I told you it didn't hurt me. Not the way you thought."

"You did."

"But Mrs. Lowe and the fireman — you haven't been able to talk to them."

"No. The firefighter won't return my calls. Mrs. Lowe told me to never contact her again."

Alex thought about this. Her fingers drummed on her sketchpad — a rapid, unconscious rhythm, the same restless energy he'd seen in her at the coffee shop. "You feel guilty," she said. Not a question.

"About all of it. Taking it. Selling it. Winning awards for it. The fact that it exists."

"And you think if the three people in the photo forgive you, the guilt goes away?"

Demian looked at her. "I don't know. Maybe. I think I need to face them. All three. Even if they don't forgive me."

Alex picked up her pencil. Drew a single line on the page — aimless, a stroke that wasn't part of the sleeping man. Then she looked up. "I know what you need," she said. She straightened her back, lifted her chin, and made her voice low and solemn, like a priest at the altar. "You are forgiven, my son." She raised two fingers and crossed the air between them. "You are forgiven for taking that photo. I accept your apology."

Demian stared at her. Then he laughed — a real laugh, the kind that came from somewhere deep and surprised and almost grateful. Alex grinned at him, the full grin, the one that transformed her whole face. "Gracias, Padre," he said.

"There are three people in your photo," Alex said, the grin settling into some-thing more serious. "I'm the first of the three. Now you need the fireman and Mikey's mom."

"Who both want nothing to do with me."

Alex pulled her backpack toward her and rummaged through it. "I know Emily Lowe. Mikey's sister. We went to the same school." Demian felt something shift — a door opening that he hadn't known was there.

"Let me talk to her," Alex said. "To Mrs. Lowe. Not for you — don't make it weird. But I can talk to Emily. I can find a way."

"Alex, you don't have to—"

"I know I don't have to." She pulled her bagged lunch from the backpack. "You want to share? I have a cheese sandwich, a hard-boiled egg, and a water."

"I don't want to take your food."

"I never eat the egg. I used to give it to Denise."

"Denise?"

"Girl from my old school. She's a chump, though." She held out the egg.

Demian took it. "Does that make me a chump too?"

Alex unwrapped her sandwich. "Only time will tell."

16

Tuesday mornings had a shape now. Jordan could feel it the moment she opened her eyes—a specific quality to the air, a lift in the hours ahead that the other six days of the week didn't have. She didn't name it. Naming it would mean looking at it, and looking at it would mean seeing what it was, and she wasn't ready for that. So she just got up. Made her bed. Five smooth strokes across the comforter with the flat of her hand. Counted them without deciding to.

Emily was already in the kitchen, eating toast and scrolling her phone. Twelve years old and self-sufficient in the way that children of broken homes become self-sufficient—not because they want to be but because the alternative is waiting for someone who's too tired to show up.

"Morning," Jordan said.

"Morning." Emily didn't look up. "There's coffee." There was. Emily had made it.

Jordan poured a cup and stood at the counter and watched her daughter eat and felt the familiar undertow of guilt—not the sharp kind, not the kind that takes your breath, but the low-grade kind that lives in the background of every day like tinnitus, always there, ignorable until someone mentions it.

"I'm going to Dad's after school," Emily said. "He's picking me up. I'll be home by eight."

"Eight. Okay." Eight. Six hours more than she needed. Jordan caught herself doing the math—Emily leaves at seven-forty, Ronny arrives at two, leaves by four, that's four hours before Emily comes home—and hated herself for it. For

155

the calculation. For the ease of it. For how quickly the shape of her daughter's schedule had become a variable in an equation that should not exist.

Emily picked up her plate and carried it to the sink. Rinsed it. Set it in the rack. Small, practiced motions—the choreography of a girl who'd learned to clean up after herself because the adults in her life were busy falling apart. She grabbed her backpack from the hook by the door. "You should get out of the house today," Emily said from the doorway. Not a suggestion. A diagnosis. Delivered with the flat authority of a twelve-year-old who'd been watching her mother sit in the same chair for months. "Go somewhere. Do something."

"Maybe."

Emily looked at her—a quick, assessing glance, the kind Jordan used to give her own mother when she was twelve, the look that says I see more than you think I see. Then she pulled the door shut behind her, and the house went quiet, and Jordan was alone with the morning and the math and the six hours she would need to fill, three of which already had a shape.

She cleaned the kitchen. Not because it was dirty but because cleaning gave her hands something to do in the hours between Emily's departure and Ronny's arrival, and hands without a task were hands that counted. She wiped the counters. Washed her coffee mug and set it in the drying rack. Then she took a second mug from the cabinet. The white one. She washed it too, though it was already clean, and set it in the rack beside the others.

She'd been doing this for weeks. Washing his mug on Tuesday morning and setting it out. It was clean because she'd washed it last Tuesday after he left, and it had sat in the cabinet for seven days, untouched, waiting. She washed it again anyway. The ritual mattered more than the hygiene. The washing was preparation. The washing was the first act of a play she performed every Tuesday, and the mug in the drying rack was the set piece that told her the show was real.

She went to the bedroom. Made the bed again. She'd already made it once when she woke up, the five strokes, the automatic smoothing. Now she remade it—pulling the sheets tighter, fluffing the pillows, adjusting the comforter so the fold was even. She stood back and looked at it. A bed made for company. A bed that told on her. If Emily came home early and saw this bed—saw the effort, the precision, and the care that Jordan never applied to bedmaking on any other day of the week — she would know. She wouldn't know what she knew. But she'd know something.

Jordan left the bed as it was. Went to the bathroom. Showered. Stood in front of the mirror and looked at herself—forty-two, thin, the lines around her eyes deeper than they'd been a year ago, her hair still damp, her body still hers but different now, different since Ronny, because being touched by someone changes the way you see the thing they touch. She'd stopped seeing her body as a container for grief. On Tuesdays, for two hours, it became something else.

Something that worked. Something that could feel things other than absence.

She put on clothes that were not pajamas. This was the other tell—the one nobody saw but her. On other days she stayed in sweats until noon, sometimes later, sometimes until Emily came home and found her on the couch in the same clothes she'd slept in, the television murmuring, the day gone without her having participated in it. On Tuesdays she dressed by ten. Nothing remarkable. Jeans. A blouse. But the choosing—the standing in front of the closet, the consideration of one shirt over another—was an act of vanity she hadn't performed for anyone else since Nate left. She chose the blue one. He'd said once, not as a compliment but as an observation, that blue was a good color on her. That was enough. She put on the blue one.

The morning stretched. This was the part she hadn't solved—the hours between ten and two, after the cleaning and the showering and the dressing, when the house was ready and she was ready and Ronny was still four hours away. She'd tried reading. She'd tried television. She'd tried the laptop, scrolling job listings the way she'd been scrolling them for months — medical office assistant, teacher's aide, school bus driver — and closing it before she finished a single posting. She closed the laptop. She'd been an X-ray technician. Before. The word before had become a geologic marker in her mind—a stratum, a fault line, the line between one era and the next. Before-Jordan wore scrubs and packed lunches and argued with Nate about the dishes. After-Jordan washed a man's coffee mug twice on Tuesday mornings and checked her reflection in the microwave door.

At one-thirty she cleaned the kitchen again. Not necessary. She'd cleaned it three hours ago. But the ritual had its own logic, its own sequence, and disrupting the sequence felt dangerous in the way that disrupting her counting felt dangerous—not rationally, not with evidence, but in the part of her brain that had decided, sometime in the months after Mikey, that certain patterns were the only things keeping the world from coming apart.

At one-forty-five, she started the coffee. His was black with Irish creamer. She'd bought four bottles since October. The store brand, not the name brand, because the name brand was a dollar more and she was watching Nate's checks as closely as watching a candle burning down— aware of exactly how much was left, aware that it was getting shorter, aware that the savings behind it were thinning to nothing. And isn't that something—saving a dollar on the creamer you buy for the married man you're sleeping with. The economy of an affair on a budget.

At one-fifty she checked her reflection in the microwave door. The image was dark and slightly distorted—her face stretched, her features smeared—and she preferred it to the bathroom mirror, where the light was honest. In the microwave she looked like someone who might be fine. Someone who had it together. Someone whose Tuesday afternoon was unremarkable.

At two o'clock the truck pulled into the driveway.

She didn't go to the door. She'd learned that going to the door looked eager, and eager was a thing she couldn't afford to be, because eager meant this mattered, and if this mattered losing it would break her, and she'd already been broken enough for one lifetime. So she waited. Let him knock. Counted the seconds between the truck door closing and his knuckles on the wood. Fourteen, usually. Today, eleven. He was walking faster. She didn't know what that meant. She filed that one away.

She opened the door. "Hey."

"Hey."

He came in. He was wearing the gray Henley—the one that fit across his shoulders in a way she'd stopped pretending not to notice. His boots were clean, which meant he'd wiped them before he came, which was a small thing, a nothing thing, except that it meant he'd stood on her porch for a few extra seconds thinking about the mud on his boots and deciding she was worth the effort of cleaning them. She loved him for the boots. She couldn't say that. She couldn't say any version of that.

He sat in his chair. She brought the coffee. He took the mug, the white one, his mug, the one she'd washed twice, and drank without commenting on it. A man drinking coffee in a house where he'd drunk coffee a dozen times. Not noticing a gesture that someone performed for him every week because it had become invisible, which is what all the best and worst things eventually become.

They talked. They always talked first. This was another pattern, another piece of the choreography that had established itself without discussion. Coffee at the table. Conversation about ordinary things—his kids, her house, the Steelers, the weather, the small, deliberate territory of the mundane that kept them, for twenty or thirty minutes, in the world of people who were just friends. Just two people having coffee. Just a firefighter checking on a woman who'd lost her son. Just that. Nothing else. The conversation was the runway, and the bedroom was the destination, and neither of them acknowledged the flight plan.

Today he told her about Danny's basketball game. A tournament. Danny had scored twelve points, which was apparently a lot, and Ronny's face opened up when he talked about it—the pride moving through him like light through a window, warming everything it touched. He talked, and she held two things at once: the genuine pleasure of watching someone she cared about be happy, and the cold knife of envy that she would never sit in bleachers and watch her son do anything.

She kept the knife to herself. She'd gotten good at that.

"You should come to a game sometime," Ronny said, and then heard himself say it, and the sentence died in the air between them. He looked at his coffee. She looked at the window. The idea of Jordan Lowe sitting in a gymnasium watching Ronny Martinez's son play basketball while Ronny's wife sat beside her—the absurdity of it, the impossibility—hung over the table like a cloud.

"Sure," Jordan said. "Maybe." Meaning never. He nodded. Meaning he knew.

The conversation ran out the way it always did—not with silence but with a slowing, a thickening, the words getting heavier and further apart until the space between them was no longer a pause but an invitation. Jordan stood and carried her mug to the sink. Ronny stood and carried his. She washed them both. He dried his hands on the towel hanging from the oven handle. Their hips touched at the counter. He didn't move away. She didn't move away.

She took his hand and led him down the hallway. The bedroom door closed behind them.

She'd stopped locking it—Emily wouldn't be home for hours, and the click of the lock had started to sound like something criminal, and she needed this to not feel criminal, needed it to feel like what it was, which was two people reaching for each other because the alternative was drowning separately.

His hands went to her face first. They always went to her face first. She'd trained him to do that without knowing she was training him—the first time, in the kitchen, she'd pressed his palms to her cheeks, and now it was where he started, every time, his hands framing her face the way they'd held Mikey, and the connection was still there, faint but present, the thread that tied this to that, the original need that had started everything. She closed her eyes and felt his palms and for a moment—one, two, three—she let herself believe she could feel what remained of her son in this man's hands.

Then the moment passed and it was just Ronny. Just his hands. Just the warmth and the calluses and his thumb tracing her cheekbone. And that was enough. It had become enough on its own, separate from the grief, separate from Mikey, separate from the reason this started. Somewhere in the weeks of Tuesdays the need had changed shape. It had started as a mother reaching for the last person who'd held her child. It had become a woman reaching for a man. And that was the thing she couldn't look at. Because if this was about Ronny—about wanting Ronny, about needing Ronny, about building her week around a man who would take off his boots at her door and drink coffee from her mug and put his hands on her face at two o'clock every Tuesday—then it wasn't grief anymore. It was something else. And the something else had a name she wasn't ready to say.

She counted. She always counted. Just to hold on. The counting was the one part of herself that stayed constant, the metronome that didn't stop when everything else shifted. One, two, three, four, five. His shirt over his head. One, two, three, four, five. Her blouse—the blue one, the one she'd chosen for him—folded over the chair. One, two, three, four, five. The weight of him. One, two, three, four, five. Her breath against his neck. The counting didn't interfere. It ran beneath everything like a bass line, steady and involuntary, and if Ronny noticed—if he felt her fingers tapping against his back in groups of five, if he heard her breathing in a rhythm that was too even to be natural—he never said.

Afterward, he lay on his back with one arm behind his head. She lay on her side facing him, her hand on his chest, feeling it rise and fall. The bedroom was quiet. Through the window she could hear a lawnmower—the Hendersons, probably, who mowed every Tuesday like clockwork, whose lawnmower had become the unofficial soundtrack of her afternoons with Ronny, the drone of a two-stroke engine scoring every guilty hour.

"What are you thinking about?" she asked.

"Nothing."

"Liar."

He exhaled through his nose. Not quite a laugh. "I'm thinking about the ceiling."

"The ceiling."

"You've got a crack up there. Runs from the light fixture to the corner. I noticed it the first time."

She looked up. He was right—a hairline fracture in the plaster, barely visible. She'd never seen it. She'd lain in this bed a thousand nights and never once looked at the ceiling with the sort of attention that Ronny brought to it, and the fact that he'd been cataloguing her ceiling while she'd been cataloguing his breathing struck her as funny. She laughed. A real one. Small, surprised, the sound escaping before she could catch it.

"What?" he asked.

"Nothing. I just—I've never noticed the crack."

"You don't look at ceilings. You count things."

The sentence landed softly. No judgment in it. Just an observation—the way you'd say someone bites their nails or taps their foot. He knew about the counting. He'd known for weeks. He never asked her to stop. He never told her it was fine. He just knew, the way he knew that her coffee was two sugars and that the third step on the porch creaked and that she kept Mikey's door closed on Tuesdays because open meant she'd been in there and been in there meant she wasn't okay.

"I should go," he said. He always said it the same way—flat, factual, the voice of a man stating a thing he didn't want to be true. He sat up. The muscles in his back moved as he reached for his shirt on the floor. He dressed the way he undressed—efficiently, without performance, the body of a man who'd spent twenty years in a firehouse where changing clothes was a timed event.

She stayed in bed. This was part of the choreography too—he dressed, she stayed. It gave him the exit without making her watch him walk to the door. She heard him in the bathroom.

Water running. Five seconds. The towel. The zipper on his jacket. His boots in the hallway. He came back to the bedroom door. She looked at him—dressed, boots on, the gray Henley tucked in, his keys in his hand. Back in his life. Assembled. The man who would drive home and kiss his wife and ask about the kids and sit at a dinner table and carry nothing visible of the last two hours except the faint smell of her shampoo, which he'd wash off in the shower before Jeannette got close enough to notice.

"Tuesday?" he said.

"Tuesday."

He left. She heard the front door. The truck starting in the driveway. She lay still and listened to the engine idle—he always sat in the truck for a few minutes before leaving, gathering himself, transitioning between one life and the other. She counted the seconds. One, two, three, four, five. One, two, three, four, five. At four minutes, the engine note changed, and the truck pulled out, and she listened to it go. Down the street. Past the Hendersons.' Past the stop sign where he always paused too long. Gone.

The house settled into its silence. The lawnmower had stopped. Jordan got up and pulled on her clothes—not the blue blouse, which she folded and put back in the closet, but a sweatshirt, the shapeless gray one she wore on the other six days. She stripped the bed. Carried the sheets to the laundry room. Started the washer. Remade the bed with the spare set—the white ones, the everyday ones, the ones that didn't smell like him.

In the kitchen, his mug sat on the counter where he'd left it. She washed it. Dried it. Held it for a moment—the warmth was gone, the ceramic cool and smooth and ordinary. She put it back in the cabinet. Not in the drying rack. The drying rack was for Tuesdays. The cabinet was for the rest of the week. His mug lived in two places depending on the day, and the movement of it—cabinet to rack on Tuesday morning, rack to cabinet on Tuesday afternoon—was the smallest, most private measure of what her life had become.

She made herself a sandwich. Ate it at the table alone. The house was clean. The bed was made. The mug was put away. In four hours Emily would walk through the door smelling like Nate's apartment—that other life, the one happening across town in rooms Jordan had never seen—and there would be homework and dinner and television and the ordinary business of a mother and daughter sharing a house, and none of it would carry any trace of what had happened here this afternoon.

Jordan washed her plate. Dried it. Set it in the rack. Stood at the counter and looked at the kitchen—every surface wiped, every object in its place, the room as neutral and blameless as a hotel room between guests.

Six days. She started counting.

17

—·—

Demian showed up with two cameras and his mother's tamales. Alex waited on the stairs outside her apartment, sketchpad on her knees, drawing something she closed the moment she saw him. She did that—hid her work-in-progress the way other kids hid diaries. The finished product she'd show anyone. The process was private.

"What's in the bag?" she asked, eyeing the camera bag slung over his shoulder.

"A lesson."

"I didn't ask for a lesson."

"You told me you wanted to learn photography. A week ago. In Chrissy's apartment. You said some things you see, you can't get right in a drawing."

Alex looked at him with the expression she used when someone remembered something she'd said and she wasn't sure if that was flattering or dangerous. "I didn't think you were actually listening."

"I'm a journalist. Listening is the job." He set the food on the step beside her and opened the camera bag. Inside were two cameras—his Nikon, the professional body he'd carried through three wars, and the Leica Q2, the smaller one he used for personal work. He took out the Leica and held it up. "This is a Leica. It's what I shoot with when I'm not working."

Alex's eyes locked on it the way they locked on things that interested her—with a sudden, total attention that reminded Demian of a cat spotting a bird. She reached for it. He pulled it back. "Not yet. First, you eat."

"You sound like your mom."

"You've never met my mom."

164

"But she feeds everyone, right? You told me. She sent you here with food the second week."

"Eat the tamales, Alex."

She ate the tamales. They sat on the stairs in the courtyard, the morning cool enough for jackets, the tree casting a lattice of shadow across the concrete below. Alex ate the way she did everything—quickly, efficiently, with the focus of someone who treated meals as a task to be completed rather than an experience to be enjoyed. Demian had noticed this about her. She didn't savor things. She processed them. Eating, walking, talking—everything moved at the speed of a mind that was always three steps ahead of its body.

When she finished, she wiped her hands on her jeans and looked at the Leica again. "Now?"

"Now." He handed it to her. She held it the way people hold cameras for the first time— too tight, both hands gripping like it might leap out of her fingers. The camera looked big against her small hands. She turned it over, studying the body the way she studied everything— methodically, taking inventory. The lens. The dials. The grip worn smooth where Demian's thumb sat. She raised it to her eye without being told. "It's heavy," she said, her right eye pressed to the viewfinder, her left eye closed.

"Keep both eyes open."

She opened the left eye. Frowned. "That's weird. My brain doesn't know which one to use."

"The right eye sees what the camera sees. The left eye sees everything else. You need both. The viewfinder is the frame—it's what you're choosing to keep. But the world outside the frame is where the picture comes from. If you close that eye, you're only seeing the answer. You're missing the question."

Alex lowered the camera and looked at him. "That's pretty good. You practice that?"

"I've been saying it for twenty years. It gets better with repetition."

"Like my drawings."

"Exactly like your drawings."

She raised the camera again. Both eyes open this time. She swept it across the courtyard—the tree, the bike rack, the row of doors—and Demian watched her face as she did it. The concentration. The narrowing. The way her head tilted slightly when something caught her attention, the same tilt he'd seen when she was drawing, the same unconscious adjustment of angle that separated people who looked at things from people who saw them.

"Don't point it at everything," Demian said. "The camera isn't a scanner. It's a decision. Every time you raise it, you're saying this matters more than everything else. So wait. Look first. Let the picture find you."

"How does a picture find you?"

"You'll know it when it happens. Something will catch—a line, a shadow, a person doing something they don't know they're doing. Your eye will snag on it. That's the picture. Everything before that is just looking."

Alex lowered the camera. Looked at the courtyard with her bare eyes. Waited. Demian watched her wait—watched her resist the impulse to pick the camera back up, watched her sit with the looking, which was the hardest thing for a beginner because beginners wanted to shoot everything and the discipline was in the not-shooting. She sat on the steps and scanned the courtyard and Demian could see her brain doing what it always did—cataloguing, filing, assessing—except now she was doing it with a camera in her hands instead of a pencil, and the tool was different but the eye was the same.

A woman came out of a ground-floor apartment carrying a laundry basket. She crossed the courtyard with the basket on her hip, a cigarette in her mouth, her slippers scuffing the concrete. Her bathrobe was open over a t-shirt and shorts and her hair was up in a towel. She stopped at the laundry room door, shifted the basket to free a hand, and reached for the handle. The cigarette dropped from her mouth. She looked down at it. Looked at the basket. Looked at the door. The small, private arithmetic of a woman with too many things and not enough hands. Alex raised the camera. Click.

She lowered it. Looked at the screen. Demian leaned over. The image was there—the woman caught mid-calculation, the cigarette on the ground, the basket on her hip, the hand reaching for the door. It was slightly off-center, the horizon tilted two degrees, the exposure a stop too bright. But the moment was right. The woman's face—the exasperation, the tiny comedy of it, the way she was looking down at the cigarette like it had betrayed her—was exactly the type of thing people walked past without seeing.

"That's it," Demian said.

"It's crooked."

"Crooked is fixable. The moment isn't. You can straighten a horizon. You can't manufacture the face she just made. Alex looked at the image again. Recognition moved across her face. She'd been built for this and not known it until the doing.

"Again," she said.

They walked. That was the lesson—walking. Demian had learned it from a photographer named Velasco in Mexico City, twenty years ago, who'd taken him out on his first day as an intern and said, "Walk until you stop thinking about walking. The best photographs aren't found by people who are looking for them. They're found by people who've walked long enough that the looking becomes automatic and the seeing takes over."

He'd never been able to explain the difference between looking and seeing. Not in words. It was the difference between reading a menu and tasting the food. Between hearing music and feeling it in your chest. Between knowing someone's face and knowing their expression. Looking was inventory. Seeing was understanding. And Alex, he was discovering, had been seeing her entire life without having a word for it.

They went south on Millbrook, past the houses and duplexes that made up Alex's neighborhood—chain-link fences, cracked driveways, yards in various states of care and neglect. Alex carried the Leica at her hip the way Demian carried his—strap around the neck, camera resting against the body, ready but not raised. She'd figured that out without being told. Another thing she'd absorbed from watching him, the way she absorbed everything—silently, completely, without asking permission.

"Stop," Demian said.

She stopped. "What?"

"Look at that porch." He pointed at a house across the street. On the porch, an old man sat in a lawn chair with a cat in his lap. His hand was resting on the cat's back, not petting it, just resting there, and the cat's eyes were half-closed, and the morning light was hitting the porch railing in a way that threw a striped shadow across both of them. "What do you see?"

"A man with a cat."

"What else?"

She looked harder. The tilt of her head. The narrowing. "The shadow on the railing. It looks like bars. Like a cage. But they're not in a cage—they're on a porch."

"What does that make you feel?"

"I don't know. Sad? No. More like... stuck. Like they chose to be there but the shadow makes it look like they can't leave."

"Shoot it."

She raised the camera. Took three frames — fast, shifting her angle between each one, moving two steps to the left to change the relationship between the shadow and the man. She was moving without thinking about moving, her body finding the angle before her mind knew what angle it was looking for. That was instinct. That couldn't be taught.

She checked the screen. Scrolled through the three shots. Stopped on the second one. "This one," she said, and held it up.

Demian looked. The second frame was the one—the shadow cutting across the man and the cat at a diagonal, the man's hand on the cat's back, the cat's eyes almost closed. The composition wasn't perfect. The top of the man's head was cut off. But the image had something that couldn't be learned—a feeling, a weight, the sense that you were seeing a private moment that meant more than its parts.

"Why that one?" he asked. Not because he disagreed. Because he wanted to hear her explain it.

"The first one is too straight. Too obvious. The shadow's just a shadow. The third one—I moved too far and the cat's face is in shadow and you can't see his eyes. The second one has the shadow and the man and the cat all doing different things. The shadow says one thing. The man says something else. The cat doesn't care about either." She looked at him. "That's three stories in one frame. Isn't it?"

Demian stared at her. Just a kid. No training. No education in composition or light or the language of images that he'd spent twenty years learning from Velasco and George and a hundred war zones. And she'd just articulated, in three sentences, the thing that separated a photograph from a picture.

"What?" Alex said. She'd caught him staring.

"Nothing. Keep walking."

They walked. Alex shot a fire hydrant with a vine growing through a crack in its base. She shot a row of mailboxes, each one leaning at a different angle, like a line of tired soldiers. She shot a dog asleep on a porch with its tongue hanging out and one ear flipped inside out. She shot a clothesline where someone had hung a bedsheet next to a child's dress, the scale of the two garments making the dress look impossibly small.

As she worked, he didn't correct her framing or adjust her settings or tell her about the rule of thirds. She'd learn that later, or she wouldn't, and it wouldn't matter, because the rules of composition were tools for people who needed structure, and Alex already had a structure. It was just hers, built from years of drawing and from the way her brain organized visual information into meaning. Teaching her the rules would be like teaching a bird aerodynamics. The bird already knew how to fly. The math would come later if she wanted it.

What he did was ask questions. After every shot: Why that? What caught you? What were you feeling when you pressed the shutter? The questions weren't for him. They were for her—to make her conscious of the thing she was doing unconsciously, to build a bridge between the instinct and the understanding so that the instinct could be summoned instead of waited for.

She answered every question with the same direct, undecorated honesty she brought to everything. The fire hydrant: "The vine looked like it was trying to hold the hydrant together. Like it was the only thing keeping it standing." The mailboxes: "They're all crooked but they're in a line. Like people pretending they have it together." The dog: "His ear is inside out and he doesn't care. That's the funniest thing I've seen all week."

The clothesline she didn't answer. She looked at the image on the screen—the bedsheet and the child's dress, the wind catching them both, the dress so small—and she was quiet for a moment, and Demian understood that this one had touched something she wasn't going to talk about. Chrissy, maybe. Or Mikey. Or just the fact of smallness, the fact that children are small and the world is not, and the distance between those two things is where most of the damage happens.

"That's a good one," she said and put the camera down.

They ate lunch on a bench in the park—the rest of Elena's tamales, which Alex declared the best thing she'd ever eaten and then demanded to know why Demian had been holding out on her. The Leica sat between them on the bench like a shared object, neither his nor hers, both of theirs.

"How many photos did you take today?" Demian asked.

Alex scrolled through the camera. "Twenty-three."

"How many are good?"

She scrolled again. Slower this time, studying each one. "Four. Maybe five."

"That's a good ratio."

"Really?"

"I shoot two hundred frames on a good day and keep ten. Four out of twenty-three is better than most professionals."

"You're just saying that."

"I don't just say things."

She looked at him—the direct, measuring look, the one that could see through flattery and would reject it. She held the look for three seconds before nodding once, the way she nodded when she decided something was true, and went back to scrolling through the images. "Demian?"

"Yeah."

"You know what's different about this?" She held up the camera. "From drawing?"

"Tell me."

"When I draw something, I'm making it. I'm deciding what goes in and what stays out. Every line is a choice. But this—" She turned the Leica over in her hands. "This is faster. The world is already there. I don't have to build it. I just have to find the part that matters and keep it."

"That's exactly what it is."

"It's like drawing at the speed of seeing."

The sentence hit Demian in the chest. Drawing at the speed of seeing. He'd spent twenty years trying to describe what photography was to people who asked, and this kid had nailed it in seven words on her first day holding a camera.

He looked at her—this girl on a park bench with tamale grease on her fingers and a Leica in her lap, who'd been pulled from a bombed building with a brain bleed and had rebuilt herself into something the explosion hadn't planned for. He thought about himself at twelve, in a hospital room in Guadalajara with a disposable camera, taking eleven pictures of a boy who was dying because the camera could hold what his hands couldn't. Different cities. Different tragedies. The same impulse—the need to see, to keep, to make a frame around the things that mattered before they disappeared.

"Can we do this again?" she asked. Not looking at him. Looking at the camera.

"Anytime you want."

"Tomorrow?"

"Tomorrow works."

She handed the Leica back. He took it and felt the warmth of her hands on the body—the heat transferred from her palms to the leather grip, the camera carrying the trace of her the way it carried the trace of every person who'd held it. He slung it around his neck and they walked back toward the apartment complex, the afternoon light going long and golden, their shadows stretched out ahead of them on the sidewalk like two people walking toward something neither of them could see yet.

Tomorrow. And the day after that. And the day after that. He'd teach her what he knew, and she'd show him what she saw, and somewhere in the exchange the thing that George had asked him to keep doing—shoot, don't stop shooting—would start to feel possible again. Not because the guilt was gone. Not because the photograph had stopped mattering. But because a girl on a park bench had looked at his camera and called it drawing at the speed of seeing, and for the first time since the bombing, the speed of seeing felt like something worth keeping up with.

18

Alex leaned against the brick wall across from the school entrance, her backpack at her feet, watching the parking lot fill with the serpentine line of cars that appeared every afternoon at two- forty-five. She'd timed it perfectly — positioned where Emily would see her, close enough to the gate to look natural, far enough from the other parents to avoid questions.

The bell rang. The building exhaled. Kids poured out in a wave — backpacks bouncing, shoes slapping concrete, voices layered into a wall of noise. Alex's eyes moved past clusters of girls, past boys shoving each other, past a teacher holding the door, scanning for the one face she needed.

There. Emily Lowe. Ponytail swinging, walking fast, heading for the faded blue car idling in the second row.

"Emily!"

Emily turned. Recognition — the half-second delay of placing someone from a different context — then a grin. "Alex? Hey!"

"Hey." Alex walked toward her, casual, unhurried. "How've you been?"

"Good. I never see you anymore. Where'd you go?"

"I'm at Eastmoor now. I was just picking something up from the office here."

"Oh. That sucks. I liked having you around."

"Yeah. Can I walk with you?"

Disappointed, Emily replied, "Ah, I'm not walking home. My mom's right there."

"That's cool. Let me say hi to your mom."

They walked toward Jordan's car. Alex's heart was knocking against her ribs, but her face showed nothing. Emily hopped into the back seat. Alex bent to the passenger window. "Hey, Mrs. Lowe."

Jordan looked up from her phone, and what crossed her face wasn't just surprise. Her eyes sharpened — a quick calculation, a door opening that Alex couldn't see through but could feel. "Alex Kelly." Jordan's voice was warm, but there was something underneath it. "It's really good to see you. How are you?"

"I'm good. Head's better."

"How's your mom?"

"Mom's the same."

"I'm glad." Jordan stopped at a word that didn't come. Alex waited.

"Could I get a ride?" Alex said. "I mean — you're sort of in my direction, and my mom's at work, and I could just walk from your place."

"Sure. Of course. Get in."

Alex opened the passenger door.

"Don't you want to sit in back with Emily?"

"I get carsick in the back."

She buckled in. Jordan pulled out of the line. The radio was off. Emily had her earbuds back in. Jordan drove — one hand on the wheel, the other on the center console, her thumb tapping a rhythm against the leather that might have been counting. "Would you want to come hang out with her for a bit? I could make you girls a snack."

Simple. Casual. But Alex heard what was underneath it — the same thing Emily had told her in the bathroom at the school tour day. Emily had said it fast, almost offhand, the way kids say things that are actually enormous: *Just so you know, my mom might ask you stuff. About the bombing. About what you saw. She's been wanting to talk to someone who was there. She won't like, be weird about it, but she might ask.*

"Sure," Alex said. "I'd like that."

So Alex knew. She walked into this car knowing she had something Jordan wanted — a firsthand account, a witness, the girl who'd been lying eight feet from Mikey in the dark. And Jordan didn't know that Alex had her own agenda, her own question sitting in her chest like a stone she'd been carrying since Demian asked her to carry it. Which meant they were both sitting in this car with questions they couldn't ask. Alex almost smiled.

"Ms. Lowe?"

"Hmm?"

But Jordan was gripping the wheel with both hands now, her jaw tight. Alex recognized the look — the look of someone rehearsing words in their head, trying to find the version that wouldn't break them.

"Thanks for having me over," Alex said.

"Of course, sweetheart. It'll be good for Emily. Good for all of us."

They drove the rest of the way in a silence full of things neither of them said.

The house was clean and quiet. Alex noted it: the spotless counter, the single mug in the sink, the unopened mail. A house on pause. Emily was already down the hallway. "Come on, I want to show you something."

Alex followed, past the closed door — Mikey's room. Emily's eyes flicked toward it and away. Quick. Automatic. A scar.

Emily's room was half-organized chaos — clothes on the desk chair, a bookshelf crammed with paperbacks and manga, fairy lights along the headboard, band posters covering one wall. A laptop open on the unmade bed. "Sorry about the mess," Emily said, not sorry at all.

"My room's worse," Alex lied.

Emily flopped onto the bed. "So what's Eastmoor like?"

"Different. Fine."

"Do you miss the old school? Before?"

The question landed differently than it would have from anyone else. Emily didn't mean the building or the cafeteria. She meant the world before — the world where her brother was alive and school was just school and nobody flinched at loud noises. "Sometimes," Alex said. "Do you?"

"I miss normal." Emily pulled at a thread on her comforter. "I miss my friends who went to other schools. And I miss—" She stopped. "I don't know."

"Yeah."

They looked at each other. Two girls separated by a grade and connected by the thing neither of them could talk about with anyone else.

"Want to play something?" Emily nodded at the TV and console on the floor. "Yeah. Let's do it."

They set up in the living room, controllers in hand, side by side on the floor. Emily was good — competitive, talking trash, bumping Alex's shoulder when she scored. Alex found herself laughing. Actually laughing. Not performing, not masking — very amused by this girl who had a quick grin and a mouth on her that would get her in trouble in about two years.

"You're trash at this," Emily said, after beating her for the third time.

"I've never played before."

"That's not an excuse. My grandma could beat you."

"Your grandma sounds cool."

"She is. She lives in Akron. She taught me poker, too."

"Poker? You're twelve."

"And I'd clean you out." Emily grinned.

"Let's play."

Between rounds, Emily glanced toward the kitchen, then back at Alex. Lowered her voice. "She's gonna ask about it."

"Think so?"

"She will. On the way home, probably. She does that — waits until you're in the car so you can't leave." Emily said it matter-of-factly, the wisdom of a kid who'd learned to read her mother the way meteorologists read pressure systems. "Just don't tell her anything bad, okay? She can't handle bad."

"Okay."

Emily picked up her controller. "Ready to lose again?"

"Let's go."

"I'm gonna get a soda. Want one?" Emily asked as she rose.

"Water, if you got it."

"Sure." Emily disappeared into the kitchen and a phone buzzed on the coffee table in front of Alex. She glanced at the lit screen, a name displayed across it. "Ronny Martinez." Alex's breath caught. Not shock — she knew Ronny existed, knew Demian wanted to reach him. But the luck of it — his name, his number, right there on a coffee table in front of her. She grabbed and pocketed the phone as Emily returned with the drinks.

Alex rose. "Gotta use the bathroom."

"Want me to watch you pee?" teased Emily with a laugh.

Alex headed down the hallway, replying, "Hey, you accepted my invitation!" The bathroom door was closed. She reached for the handle and it swung open — Jordan came out, almost colliding with her. Alex jammed the phone behind her back. "Oh! Sorry. I need to use it."

"All yours," Jordan said, stepping aside.

Alex locked the door. Leaned against it. Heart hammering. She swiped the screen — no password. Ronny Martinez, missed call, his number right beneath. She pulled open drawers — toothpaste, floss, cotton balls — until she found an eye pencil. Yanked up her pant leg and wrote the number on her calf in quick, shaky strokes. Checked it twice. Pulled the pant leg down. Put the pencil back. Flushed the empty toilet. Ran the water.

She found Jordan in the kitchen. "Hey. Your phone buzzed. Here." She held it out.

Jordan took it. Glanced at the screen. Jordan's face did something Alex couldn't read — a reaction that closed before it opened, private, whatever it was, a reaction Jordan didn't know anyone was watching. Jordan slipped the phone into her pocket.

"Thank you," she said. "Need me to take you home?"

"Sure."

Alex went to grab her backpack from the living room. Emily was still on the couch, controller in hand. "You leaving?"

"Yeah. My mom'll be home soon."

"Come back. I need someone to destroy at video games."

Alex grinned. "Anytime."

In the car, Emily wasn't with them. The silence had a different texture — heavier, more charged. Alex sat with Ronny's number on her calf and the question she still hadn't asked sitting in her throat like a stone. And she knew what was coming. Emily had called it — *on the way home, probably. She does that.*

Halfway to Alex's neighborhood, Jordan spoke. "Alex?"

"Yeah."

"Could I ask you something?"

Alex looked at her. Jordan's hands were tight on the wheel. Her jaw was working — the small, rhythmic clench of someone fighting back tears.

"It's okay," Alex said. "You can ask me anything."

Jordan opened her mouth. Nothing came out. A tear slid down her cheek. She wiped it with the back of her hand, eyes on the road.

"Is it about Mikey?" Alex asked gently. Jordan nodded. More tears. "You can ask me."

Jordan pulled the car to the curb. Stopped. Put it in park. Reached into the glove box for a tissue, pressed it against her eyes. Her shoulders trembled. Alex sat still. Quiet. Letting her take whatever time she needed. "You know he was found next to me," Alex said. Jordan nodded. "You want to know about that?" Another nod. Alex took a breath. "It was dark. I couldn't move. I didn't know he was there until the firefighter came and moved the concrete off me. His classroom was so far from mine — I don't understand how he ended up there."

Jordan's hands twisted the tissue into a tight spiral. "Did he—" Jordan's voice broke. Tried again. "Did he say anything?"

"No." Alex said it as gently as she could. "I'm sorry. No." Jordan turned away, pressing the tissue to her face.

"You know what I do remember?" Alex said. Jordan turned back. Her eyes were red, her face wet, but she was listening. "Not the explosion. Not the dark or the dust. I remember his shoes. Those little Spider-Man sneakers. The laces were untied."

Jordan's breath caught. Her hand went to her mouth. Alex could see her seeing them — the shoes she'd bought, the shoes she'd tied a thousand mornings, the shoes that were always coming undone because Mikey was always running, always in too much of a hurry to double-knot them. "He was always running," Jordan whispered. "Always in such a hurry to get wherever he was going."

"I think about that a lot," Alex said. "How he was probably running when it happened. Full speed. That's not the worst way — to be in motion. To be going somewhere."

Jordan reached over and took Alex's hand. Their fingers laced together. Alex felt the grip — tight, desperate — and she let her hold on. She understood grip. She understood needing to hold something. Jordan wiped her face. Drew a breath. Steadied.

"I wanted to ask you something, too," Alex said.

"Sure, Alex. What is it?"

"About the photograph. The one of me, Mikey, and the fireman."

Jordan's expression hardened. The grief was still there, but something else moved in front of it — something colder. "I hate that photograph with a passion."

"That's what I wanted to ask about."

Jordan glanced at her. "It affected you, too?"

"At first. I hated it. I hated seeing myself like that — screaming, covered in blood. I didn't want anyone to see me that way." She paused. "But then I kept looking at it. I don't know why. I couldn't stop. It was like — the more I looked at it, the less power it had over me. Or maybe I just got used to it. Like how you stop noticing a scar after a while."

Jordan stared at her. "You got used to it?"

"I don't know if that's the right word. I just... it doesn't scare me anymore. It's just a picture."

Jordan's expression shifted — disbelief, maybe. Or envy. The incomprehension of a woman who couldn't imagine a world where that photograph was just anything.

"For me, it's the last image of my son. The darkest moment of my life, and someone put it on every newspaper and magazine in the country." She wiped her face again. "Why did you ask me that?"

"I wanted to know how you felt about it. If it was the same for you as it was for me."

"It's not the same. It will never be the same for anyone as it is for me."

Alex nodded. She understood. "What do you think of the guy who took it?" Alex asked.

The street was quiet. A dog barked. The afternoon light was fading, shadows stretching across the lawns. Jordan stared through the windshield and said, "I think he's scum."

19

Sunday morning and the Martinez family was running late for Mass the way they always ran late for Mass — which is to say chaotically, loudly, and with at least one missing shoe.

"Dad! Sofia took my good belt!"

"I didn't take it, it was on the bathroom floor!"

"It was on my side of the bathroom floor!"

Ronny stood in front of the bedroom mirror, knotting his tie while Jeannette finished her makeup beside him. He could hear Danny and Sofia's argument escalating down the hall, the familiar crescendo of sibling warfare that would peak in approximately thirty seconds and require intervention.

"Danny, check under your bed," Ronny called. "Sofia, give it back if you have it."

"I don't have it!"

Jeannette caught his eye in the mirror. The look said: your turn. He sighed, gave the tie a final tug, and went to referee.

Twenty minutes later they were in the SUV, Danny sulking in the back with his belt recovered from behind the dresser, Sofia scrolling her phone, Jeannette checking her lipstick in the visor mirror. A normal family on a normal Sunday. The performance of it — the ordinariness, the routine — sat on Ronny's chest like a weight he couldn't name.

The church parking lot was full. They filed in, nodding at familiar faces, sliding into their usual pew — fourth row, left side, close enough to the altar to seem devout, far enough to slip out quickly if Sofia got restless. Ronny had been coming to St. Michael's since he was Danny's age. He'd been a Eucharistic minister for eight years. He knew every crack in the kneelers, every water stain on the ceiling, every face in the congregation.

Which is why the face in the back pew stopped his heart.

Jordan Lowe. Sitting alone in the last row, her hands in her lap, her head slightly bowed. She wore a dark blouse he hadn't seen before and her hair was pulled back and she looked like exactly what she was — a woman in a place she didn't belong, trying to be invisible.

Ronny's throat constricted. He looked away. Looked at the altar, the crucifix, the stained glass window with its fractured light. Looked anywhere but the back pew. Why is she here. This isn't her parish. This isn't even her faith.

The Mass proceeded. Father Brennan's homily was about forgiveness — because of course it was, because God had a sense of humor that bordered on cruelty. Ronny sat and stood and knelt at the appropriate times and said the responses from thirty years of muscle memory and felt Jordan's presence in the back of the church like a heat source, a frequency only he could detect.

When the time came for Communion, he took his position at the altar, accepting the ciborium, and began to distribute. "The Body of Christ." Face after face. Hands cupped, mouths open. "The Body of Christ." The repetition was usually meditative. Today it was mechanical, his eyes scanning the line forming in the center aisle.

Jeannette rose from their pew and joined the line. And behind her, three rows back, Jordan stood.

The sweat broke across Ronny's forehead. His hand trembled — just slightly, just enough that the host wobbled between his fingers. Jordan was standing, and Jeannette was walking toward him, and the distance between his wife and the woman he'd been sleeping with was narrowing with every step, and the church that had been his sanctuary for thirty years was suddenly a trap with stained glass walls.

Jordan stepped into the aisle. Ronny's breath stopped. She turned. Not toward the altar — toward the doors. She slipped out of the pew, walked up the side aisle with her head down, pushed through the heavy oak doors, and was gone. The doors swung shut behind her with a sound that was swallowed by the organ.

"The Body of Christ," Ronny said to the next person in line. His voice didn't shake. His hands were steady. The performance held.

In the parking lot, Danny and Sofia were already arguing about where to eat. Jeannette buckled her seatbelt and said, casually, the way she said things that weren't casual at all: "Jordan Lowe was here today."

Ronny turned the key. The engine caught. "Really?"

"I saw her in the back row when we sat down. She left during Communion."

"Huh." He backed out of the space, checking the mirrors he didn't need to check. "I didn't think she was Catholic."

"Maybe she wanted to see what it's about," Jeannette said. "Can't blame her. After losing a child, people look for things."

"Yeah. Maybe."

Jeannette looked at him. He could feel it — her eyes on the side of his face, reading him the way she'd been reading him for eighteen years. He kept his own eyes on the road. "You should invite her for dinner sometime," Jeannette said. "Her and Emily. It might be good for her."

The sentence landed in Ronny's chest like a fist. His wife — his kind, decent, unsuspecting wife — was suggesting he bring Jordan Lowe to their dinner table. The woman he'd undressed in a bedroom twenty feet from her dead son's room. The woman whose tears he'd felt on his shoulder. The woman who counted everything in fives and kissed him like she was trying to breathe through his mouth.

"Maybe," Ronny said. "I'll mention it."

"Dad, can we go to Dunkin'?" Sofia asked from the back seat. "You promised."

"I promised?"

"Last week. You said if we didn't fight during Mass we could go." Danny snorted. "We fought the entire time before Mass."

"That doesn't count. That was before."

Ronny glanced at Jeannette. She shrugged. He turned toward Dunkin' Donuts and listened to his children argue about flavors and tried to remember what it had felt like, before all of this, to simply be their father on a Sunday morning.

Tuesday. Two-seventeen PM. Jordan opened the door. Ronny stood on the porch, and whatever he was carrying — the church, Jeannette's suggestion, the image of Jordan slipping out through the oak doors — was visible on his face before he said a word.

"Hey," Jordan said.

"Hey." He came in. She'd made coffee. The Irish creamer was on the table. He sat in his chair. She sat in hers. The choreography was the same, but the air between them was different — tighter, charged, the way it felt before a storm when the pressure dropped and everything went still.

He didn't reach for the mug. "Jordan, what were you doing there?"

She'd known he would ask. She'd rehearsed answers all day Monday — I was curious, I was just driving by, I wanted to see the church — and none of them were true, and she was tired of things that weren't true.

"I wanted to see your family," she said. Ronny's jaw tightened. "I'm sorry. I know it was stupid. I know it was dangerous. I just—" She wrapped her hands around her mug, the warmth grounding her. "I don't have a family anymore, Ronny. Not like yours. Nate's gone. Mikey's gone. It's me and Emily in this house, and most days Emily's the one taking care of me, not the other way around." She looked at him. "I wanted to see what you go home to. What normal looks like. I sat in the back and I watched your daughter lean on your shoulder and your son fidget with his tie and your wife hand you a hymnal, and I thought — that's what I used to have. Some version of that. And I don't anymore."

Ronny looked at the table. The creamer. His hands.

"It won't happen again," she said. "I'm not trying to ruin anything."

"I know."

"Did Jeannette—"

"She saw you. She doesn't think anything of it. She said I should invite you for dinner."

Jordan closed her eyes. The kindness of it — the unsuspecting, generous kindness of a woman offering dinner to the person sleeping with her husband — was worse than anger would have been. Anger she could have handled. Kindness was unbearable. "That's nice of her," Jordan managed.

They sat with the coffee cooling between them. Ronny reached across the table and took her hand — the gesture that had started everything, the gesture that was now as automatic as breathing. She laced her fingers through his and held on.

"Something happened," Jordan said. "After you left last time. Alex Kelly came over."

Ronny's hand tightened around hers. "Alex Kelly?"

"She was at Emily's school. She asked for a ride, ended up staying for a while, playing video games with Emily. Then on the drive to take her home, she—" Jordan paused. "She told me about the bombing. About being next to Mikey. About his shoes."

Ronny's face went pale. The color drained from it the way water drains from a sink — slowly, then all at once.

"She remembered his Spider-Man sneakers," Jordan said. "The laces were untied."

Ronny said nothing. His thumb had stopped moving against her fingers. He was perfectly still — the stillness of a man hearing something that touched the thing he carried deepest and most carefully.

"And then she asked me something strange," Jordan said. "She asked what I thought about the photograph. And what I thought about the photographer."

"Why would she ask that?"

"I don't know. It was odd. Like she had a reason but wouldn't say what it was."

"What did you tell her?"

"That I hate the photograph. And that I think the man who took it is scum."

Ronny nodded slowly. His eyes were on their joined hands, but he wasn't seeing them. He was somewhere else — in the rubble, in the dark, in the place where Alex's voice echoed: I think it moved.

"That photographer's been trying to reach me too," Ronny said quietly. "Left messages at the station. The guys turned him away when he showed up."

"What does he want?"

"I don't know. To apologize, maybe. To explain himself." Ronny's jaw worked. "I don't want his apology. I don't want to talk to him. I don't want to look at the man who stood outside with a camera while—" He stopped. The sentence had an ending he couldn't say: while Andrew was dying inside.

Jordan squeezed his hand. The silence held them. After a while, they moved to the bedroom. It was still new enough to feel like a decision, not a routine — Jordan leading him down the hallway, the door closing behind them, the quiet negotiation of buttons and breath. Jordan's eyes stayed open. The ceiling stared back at her while Ronny's weight and his warmth and his guilt pressed against her, and she counted — not because she wanted to, but because the counting was the only thing that made the enormity of what she was feeling manageable.

One, two, three, four, five. One, two, three, four, five. The rhythm of holding on.

Afterward, she lay on her side, facing the window. The tears came — they always came — but softer today. Less like drowning, more like rain.

Ronny sat up behind her. She heard him dressing — the belt, the zipper, the shoe. Then he paused. "Jordan."

"Hmm."

"Your counting. You do it a lot. I've noticed."

She stiffened. Nobody had ever said it out loud before. The counting was hers — private, invisible, the secret machinery that kept her functioning. Having someone name it felt like having someone find a diary she'd hidden under the mattress.

"It's stupid," she whispered.

"Tell me."

She rolled onto her back. Looked at the ceiling. "Five. Everything in fives. Stirring coffee, brushing teeth, steps across a room. Even—" She gestured vaguely at the sheets.

"Why?"

"It calms me down. When everything feels like it's spinning, counting slows it down. Keeps it in order." She wiped her eyes. "If I lose count, everything falls apart. I know that's not true. I know it's in my head. But I can't stop." She wiped her eyes. "I told you it was stupid."

"It's not stupid."

Ronny sat on the edge of the bed. He didn't try to fix it — didn't offer advice or comfort or the useless reassurance that everything would be okay. He just sat there, and his silence said more than words would have.

"Your crying," he said after a while. "It's less today."

Jordan blinked. She hadn't noticed, but now that he said it — the tide that usually swallowed her had pulled back a few inches. Still there. Still heavy. But less. "I guess it is," she said. She didn't know whether to feel relieved or guilty about that.

Ronny stood. Moved to the door. "I'll see you next week?"

"Can you come Friday?"

He paused and calculated — the schedule, the excuse, the lie he'd have to tell Jeannette. "If you need me," he said. The words came out before he understood them. If you need me. Not if I want to. Not I can't wait. The language of a man responding to a call — the same language he'd used for twenty years when the alarm went off and his body moved toward the truck before his mind caught up. He didn't know why he kept coming back to this house. He didn't know why he could be with this woman and not his wife, why his body worked here in this bed with this grief and failed in his own bed with the woman he loved. He only knew that when Jordan asked, the answer came the way it had always come. Yes, I'm coming. Yes, I'll be there. The part of him that wanted to stop, that knew this was wrong, that saw the wreckage he was building with every Tuesday and now every Friday, couldn't override it. She needed him. The mother of the boy he hadn't checked needed him.

"Yeah," she said. "I need you." He nodded and left.

20

His mother answered the door because Demian was in the backyard cleaning his camera, which is what Demian did when he didn't want to think. Elena Ochoa stood in the doorway in her house dress and apron, flour on her hands, and looked at the man on her porch the way she looked at all strangers—with the polite suspicion of a woman who'd spent forty years on the west side of Columbus and knew that men in sport coats didn't knock on doors in this neighborhood to deliver good news.

"Mrs. Ochoa? I'm George Gelson, from the Associated Press. Demian's editor."

Her face blossomed. "Ah, George! Demian talks about you. Please, come in." She held the door open and wiped her hands on her apron. "He's in the back. You want coffee? Something to eat?"

"Coffee would be wonderful."

She led him through the living room. George's eyes did what eyes do in a new place— swept, catalogued, filed. The family photos on the shelf. The ceramic virgin. The baseball glove, cracked and stiff, sitting next to a school picture of a boy who couldn't have been older than ten. George paused at the shelf. Elena saw him looking.

"Miguel," she said. "Demian's brother. He passed when they were boys."

"I'm sorry."

"A long time ago." She said it the way mothers say things that are never a long time ago—with a practiced lightness that fooled no one. "He's out back. Go through the kitchen."

George walked through the small kitchen—the yellow light, the stove with something simmering, the table where four people used to sit and two still did—and pushed open the screen door.

Demian was sitting on the back steps with the Nikon in his lap, working a blower across the lens mount. He looked up. His face went through three things in quick succession—surprise, recognition, and the resignation of a man who'd known this visit was coming and had hoped it wouldn't. "How'd you find me?"

"I worked my way up in the newspaper business, Demian. I can find anyone." George sat down on the steps beside him without being invited. The backyard was small—a patch of grass, a chain-link fence, a shed with a padlock. A neighborhood dog barked somewhere. The afternoon was warm and still. "Your mother's nice."

"She'll feed you whether you want it or not."

"I'm counting on it." George looked at the camera in Demian's lap. "You're cleaning it."

"The dust out here gets into everything."

"This isn't Afghanistan. This is Ohio. There's no dust."

Demian said nothing. He kept working the blower. George studied him for a moment — the slow, methodical motions of a man caring for a tool he wasn't using, the way a retired carpenter polishes a saw he'll never cut with again. The observation sat in George's chest and he filed it alongside the baseball glove on the shelf and the flour on Elena's hands and the small backyard where his best photographer was hiding from the world.

"Your agent has been calling Rachel three times a week," George said. "She's about to change her number. Why aren't you calling him back?"

"He keeps finding me jobs I don't want."

"Some of those jobs are from my office. I've had to give them to other photographers." George let that sit. "What kind of jobs don't you want?"

Demian set down the blower. Looked at the backyard—the fence, the shed, the dog still barking. "Violence. Death."

"It's wartime, Demian. That's all there is right now. And you're good at it."

Demian didn't respond. George waited. He was good at waiting—thirty years in the news business had taught him that silence was the most effective question.

People couldn't stand it. They'd fill it with whatever they were holding if you gave them long enough.

"The photos don't make anything better," Demian said. "They don't stop the wars. They don't save the kids. They just hurt the people in them."

"It's not the photo that's hurting these people, Demian." George's voice was steady. Not unkind, but not soft either—the voice of a man who'd been having this conversation with photographers for decades and knew the difference between a crisis of conscience and a dead end. "It's the bombing that hurt them. It's the loss."

"The photo made the loss public. The mother can't go to the grocery store without seeing her son's face. I did that."

"You documented what happened. That's the job."

"Yeah. That's what I used to tell myself."

The screen door opened. Elena came out with two cups of coffee on a tray, a small plate of pan dulce beside them. She set it on the step between them, touched Demian's shoulder without saying anything, and went back inside. The screen door closed behind her with the soft slap of spring-loaded hinges.

George picked up a coffee. Took a sip. Set it down. "Is whatever you're doing here helping you? I hope it is."

Demian looked at the pan dulce. His mother had arranged the pieces in a circle on the plate, the way she always arranged things—with care, with attention, as if the presentation of bread on a plate were a matter of consequence. He thought about the closet in apartment 210, the drawings arranged in rows, the care of it, the attention.

"Yeah," he said. "I think it is."

George studied him. The backyard was quiet except for the dog and the distant sound of traffic on Sullivant. A lawnmower started somewhere down the block. "Let me tell you something, and I'm saying this as someone who's known you for ten years, not as your editor." He set the coffee down. "You have a gift. I've worked with two hundred photographers and I can count on one hand the ones who see what you see. That's not flattery. That's a fact." Demian waited. "Shoot what you want. Whatever that is—if it's not war, fine. If it's not death, fine.

Shoot this backyard. Shoot your mother's bread. I don't care. You know I'll support you. But don't stop shooting." He said it the way a doctor says take the medication—with the quiet authority of someone who'd seen what happened to people who stopped doing the thing that kept them alive. "The camera's not the problem, Demian. Don't give it up because the rest of it went sideways."

They sat with that. The coffee cooled. The lawnmower droned. A sparrow landed on the fence and sat there, tilting its head, and Demian's hand moved toward the camera in his lap before he caught himself. George saw it. The reflex. The instinct that was still in there, underneath the guilt and the avoidance and the three weeks of cleaning a lens he wasn't using. The photographer's hand reaching for the camera. George saw it and said nothing, but his face eased by a degree, the way a doctor's face shifts when the patient's vitals move in the right direction.

"Now," George said, and his voice shifted—harder, the editor clicking back into place. "The ceremony."

Demian's jaw tightened. "George—"

"We had a deal. You said it. And the prize is not just yours, it's the AP's."

"I know what I said."

"The ceremony is in two weeks. Columbia University. You're expected. The AP is expecting you. Rachel has your travel booked. A tux is being rented in your size because I know you don't own one." George ticked the items off with the efficiency of a man who'd organized a hundred logistics and wasn't going to let this one fall apart. "You'll fly to New York. You'll attend the luncheon. You'll accept the award. You'll make a speech."

"I don't want to make a speech."

"Then say thank you and sit down. But you're going to be there." George picked up a piece of pan dulce and took a bite. Chewed. Swallowed. "This is incredible, by the way. Your mother is a saint."

"Don't change the subject."

"I'm not changing the subject. I'm eating your mother's bread and telling you that you're going to the ceremony because we made a deal and you're a man who keeps his deals." He looked at Demian. "You are, aren't you?"

Demian stared at the backyard. The fence. The shed. The sparrow, gone now, the fence post empty. Two weeks. He could see the ceremony in his mind—the chandeliers, the tablecloths, the applause, the crystal award with his name on it. He could see himself walking to a podium and accepting a prize for an image that a dead boy's mother had called an affront to common decency. He could feel the letter in his pocket—he'd been carrying it for weeks, folded along its original creases, the notebook paper going soft from handling.

"Fine," he said. "I'll go."

"Good."

"But I'm writing my own speech."

George looked at him. The look lasted three seconds—long enough for George to calculate the risk, to weigh the possibility that Demian would stand at a podium in front of three hundred people and say something that would embarrass the AP, against the certainty that trying to control what came out of this man's mouth would only make it worse. "Fine," George said. "Write your speech. But run it by me first."

"No."

"Demian—"

"You said shoot what I want. This is what I want."

George exhaled. It was the exhale of a man who'd just lost a negotiation and knew it and was choosing to lose it gracefully because the alternative was losing his photographer entirely. "Alright," he said. "Your speech. Your words." He picked up another piece of pan dulce. "But if you burn the building down, I'm telling everyone I tried to stop you."

"Fair. I won't embarrass the AP, I promise." They ate Elena's bread and drank the cooling coffee in the small backyard on the west side of Columbus while the lawnmower droned and the dog barked and the afternoon settled into a quiet that only exists in neighborhoods where people have been living the same lives for decades. George asked about Demian's father. Demian told him—the meatpacking plant, the retirement, the truck he'd driven for thirty years and refused to sell. George told Demian about his daughter's wedding, which had happened while Demian was in Kandahar and which Demian had missed entirely.

"She married a dentist," George said. "A dentist. My daughter, who grew up in newsrooms, married a man who looks at teeth for a living."

"Teeth are important."

"Teeth are not news."

Demian almost laughed. It didn't quite arrive—it got to the edge of his mouth and stalled—but it was there, and George saw it, and the worry on his face eased by another degree. Elena came out twice more. Once with more coffee. Once to tell George he was too thin and to take bread home with him. George accepted both with the grace of a man who understood that refusing food from Elena Ochoa was not an option.

When George left, carrying a paper bag of pan dulce and a napkin full of empanadas that Elena had produced from nowhere, Demian walked him to the front door. They stood on the porch.

"Two weeks," George said.

"Two weeks."

"Rachel will send the details."

"Yeah."

George looked at him. Then he did something he'd never done in ten years—he put his hand on Demian's shoulder and left it there. Not a clap or the brief, professional contact of colleagues. A hand, resting, with weight behind it. "Take care of yourself," he said.

"You never say that when I go to a battlefield."

"Because that's where you know what you're doing." George squeezed once and let go. "Like I said, this is a different kind of battlefield."

He walked to his rental car. Demian watched him go—this man who'd hired him at twenty-five and sent him to his first war and called every Sunday for the first month to make sure he was eating, who'd flown from Afghanistan to a porch in Columbus to eat bread and make sure his photographer hadn't disappeared completely. George backed out of the driveway. The rental car turned at the end of the street and was gone.

Demian stood on the porch. Through the screen door he could hear his mother in the kitchen, the clatter of dishes, the radio playing something in Spanish. The same sounds he'd heard his entire childhood. The same house. The same street. The same shelf with Miguel's glove and the school photo and the ceramic virgin that his mother dusted every Sunday without fail.

Two weeks. A ceremony. A speech. His own words.

He went inside, sat at the kitchen table, and started writing.

21

— · —

The letter from the Social Security Administration had arrived that morning. Ronny had opened it standing at the kitchen counter with a cup of coffee going cold beside him, and the sentence that mattered was buried in the second paragraph the way bad news always is — tucked behind procedural language and reference numbers, as if formatting could soften the blow: *...no longer eligible to receive disability benefits effective...*

He'd read it twice before he crumpled it, smoothed it out against his thigh, and set it on the dining room table where it sat now, its creases forming a map of a future he wasn't ready for. The letter meant going back. Going back meant the station, the truck, the gear, the calls. It meant being the man on the news again — Ronny Martinez, the hero of the photograph — and he wasn't that man anymore. He wasn't sure he'd ever been.

Danny and Sofia were at school. Jeannette was at work. The house was weekday-quiet, with the hum of the refrigerator, the tick of the hallway clock, and the occasional creak of the foundation settling. Sounds that used to be background noise and were now the architecture of the cage he'd built around himself.

His knee ached. It always ached when the weather shifted, and today the sky had that gray, low-pressure look that meant rain by evening. He limped to the front window and looked out at the street — the same street, the same parked cars, the same neighbor's dog nosing through the same recycling bin. Nothing changed out there. That was the problem and the comfort.

The knock came at eleven-fourteen. Ronny wasn't expecting anyone. Jeannette would have called. Hal would have called. The guys at the station knew better

196

than to show up unannounced — they'd tried that once, back in October, and Ronny had stood in the doorway with his arms crossed until they left. He opened the door.

A girl stood on his porch. Short chestnut hair, hoodie, jeans, a backpack over one shoulder. She looked up at him with eyes that were steady and clear and carrying something behind them that he couldn't immediately read.

"Hello," she said. "I'm Alex. You saved my life."

The air went out of Ronny's lungs. Not a gasp — more like someone had opened a valve and all the pressure that had been building found a crack to escape through. He gripped the door frame. There she was. Older than the girl in the photograph, obviously. The blood was gone, the screaming mouth closed, the wild terrified eyes calm now and watching him with an intelligence that was almost unsettling in someone her age. But it was her. He'd carried her out of a building. He'd felt her weight against his chest, her blood on his turnout coat, her voice — I think it moved — echoing through every sleepless night since April.

"Hello, Alex-You-Saved-My-Life." The joke came out automatically, the fire-fighter's reflex — deflect with humor, buy time to process. "I'd answer the door more often if I had more visitors like you."

She smirked. Quick. There and gone. "You know who I am?"

"Of course, I know who you are. We were in every newspaper in the country." His hand was still gripping the door frame. He let go. "Are you selling magazines or would you like to come in?"

"I'm not selling magazines."

"Well, then, come in." She stepped past him. "How'd you get here?"

"Bus," she replied as she scanned the room the way she probably scanned every room — quick, cataloguing, the eyes of someone who assessed every space she entered. She took in the crumpled letter on the table, the cold coffee, the couch with its permanent dent from where he sat too many hours, the framed photos on the bookshelf — Danny's little league, Sofia's school picture, the family at Christmas.

"Take a seat," Ronny said. "Anywhere. My wife's at work, kids are at school." He lowered himself into the recliner, his knee protesting, and leaned forward on his elbows. "How come you're not at school..."

"Home schooled."

"Home schooled, eh? So, how'd you find me?"

"I'm a detective."

He laughed — a real laugh, surprised out of him. "Alright, detective. So how've you been? Looks like you recovered great. Your head was hurt, if I remember."

"Yeah. Concussion, some cuts. They did surgery later — subdural something. But I'm good now."

"Good. That's good." He studied her. She was sitting on the couch with her backpack between her feet, composed, her hands resting on her knees. She didn't fidget. Didn't look nervous. She looked like someone who'd come here with a purpose and was taking her time getting to it.

"You were at the school's memorial thingy," Alex said. "I walked right past you. You didn't say anything to me."

The words landed like a small, precise accusation. Ronny flinched. "Oh, I'm sorry. Those things — you know how they are. A lot of people, a lot of noise. I might have seen you, but I was distracted."

"It's okay. I just wasn't sure you knew who I was."

"I knew." He'd known. He'd seen her across the gymnasium, a girl with a scar on her temple and her mother's arm around her shoulders, and he'd wanted to cross the room so badly his feet had actually moved before his brain caught up and stopped them. Because crossing the room meant talking to her. And talking to her meant asking the question. And asking the question meant hearing the answer, and he wasn't ready for either possibility — that she'd confirm it and his guilt would become real, or that she'd deny it and his guilt would have nothing to stand on and would keep standing anyway.

"So how've you been?" Alex asked. "You healed up?"

"Yeah. Knee's still messed up — tore something in there. But it's getting better."

"Then why aren't you back at work?"

He cocked his head. "How do you know I'm not back at work?"

"I told you. I'm a detective."

He grinned at her. Thirteen years old and sitting on his couch asking him the same question Jeannette had been asking for months, the same question Hal had been asking, the same question the letter on the table was asking. Why aren't you back at work?

"Taking a little time," Ronny said.

"That's funny. That's what I say."

"Yeah? You're not back at school yet?"

"Taking a little time."

They looked at each other. The silence between them wasn't uncomfortable. It was the silence of two people who were talking around it. The weather. The school. How her head was healing. She asked about his knee and he told her the same thing he told everyone — getting better, taking it slow — and she nodded in a way that made him think she was doing the same thing he was. Circling. Waiting for the conversation to get to the place they both knew it was going.

"Can I get you something?" Ronny said. "Water? A snack?"

"I'm good. I just wanted to talk to you."

"Yeah. And I've wanted to talk to you, too."

The sentence hung there. Alex's eyes narrowed slightly — not suspicious, but attentive. Reading him.

"We've been through it," she said. "You know. The bombing."

"We have."

"I have a reason for being here," Alex said. "But you go first."

"No, you go first if there's a reason—"

Alex interrrupted, "I insist. I'd rather you go first."

Ronny's heart kicked. He nodded and swallowed. She'd seen it — whatever was sitting behind his eyes, whatever had been sitting there since he opened the door, she'd read it. Just a kid and she could read him like a page. "Alex." He leaned forward. His hands were shaking — he pressed them together between his knees. "Do you remember anything from that day? Anything that wasn't in the news, wasn't in the interviews?"

"I remember some. Not a lot. My head was pretty messed up."

"Do you remember me digging you out? Moving the beam?"

"I remember seeing your face. And being outside. The light was bright and it hurt my eyes. After that it's patchy."

"Do you remember me digging you out and then trying to lift the beam, the first time and saying, 'I'll be right back? I had to go back into the hallway — to look for my partner. I told you to wait for me. Do you remember that?"

Alex's brow furrowed. She shook her head slowly. "You told me to wait?"

"Yeah. And I came right back. A minute. Maybe ninety seconds."

"I don't remember that."

Ronny's voice dropped. He could feel the question rising in his chest — the question he'd carried for months like a stone lodged behind his sternum, pressing against everything, making it hard to breathe and eat and sleep and touch his wife and play with his kids and do anything at all except sit in this recliner and go over it and over it in the dark theater of his mind. "You said something to me," he said. "When I came back. You said something." Alex stared at him. Her composure was still there, but something behind it had shifted — she could feel the weight of what was coming. "Do you remember what you said?"

She thought about it. He watched her think — watched her search through whatever remained of that day in her damaged, healing, young brain. The seconds stretched.

"No," she said. "I don't remember saying anything."

"You pointed to something and said, 'I think it moved.'"

Alex blinked. "I think it moved? What moved?" And there it was. The thing Ronny had feared and hoped for in equal measure — the blankness on her face, the genuine confusion, the girl who'd spoken the five words that had destroyed his life looking at him as if he were speaking a language she'd never heard. She didn't remember. She had no memory of saying it. The only witness to the possibility that Mikey Lowe had been alive during the minute Ronny was gone had no memory of being a witness at all. The rope he'd been pulling for months went slack. Not relief. Not disappointment. The specific, disorienting feeling of pulling against something for so long that its absence has no name.

"Never mind," he said. He forced a smile. "It's nothing. Probably just my imagination playing tricks."

"What moved?" Alex pressed. "What are you talking about?"

"Really. It's nothing. I—" He waved his hand. "My mind plays tricks on me, too. You know how it is."

Alex studied him now with an intensity that made him feel transparent. She didn't believe him. He could see that. But she also seemed to understand — in whatever way a young girl could understand — that he'd just opened a door and immediately closed it, and that pushing it open again would cost more than either of them could afford right now.

"Okay," she said. The word sat between them. Ronny exhaled. Pressed his hands against his face. Dropped them.

"I'm sorry," he said. "I interrupted you. You said you had a reason for being here."

Alex looked at her hands. She was quiet for a moment — the first time he'd seen her hesitate. Whatever she'd come to say, whatever mission had brought her to his door, the weight of what had just happened was sitting on top of it. But she could feel something else too — the debt of the moment. He'd asked her the most important question of his life and she'd had nothing to give him. She owed him something.

"You know the photograph," she said. "Of me and you and Mikey."

"Yeah."

"Did you hear it was nominated for a Pulitzer?"

"I heard."

"The photographer. His name is Demian Ochoa. He's here. In Columbus."

Ronny's jaw tightened. "He's been trying to reach me. The guys at the station turned him away."

"I know. I know him. He's been coming to see me for a while now."

"You know him?"

"Yeah. And before you say anything — just hear me out. That's all I'm asking. Hear me out about him, and then you can decide." Ronny crossed his arms. The posture of a man building a wall. But he didn't say no.

"He's not what you think," Alex said. "I thought he was a vulture, too. Some guy with a camera who got famous off our worst day. But it's not like that. He didn't choose to publish the photo."

"He took it."

"He took it. Yeah. He pressed the button. But after that, it wasn't his anymore. The AP owns it — his bosses. It's in his contract. They submitted it for the Pulitzer, not him. He tried to withdraw the nomination and they told him he couldn't. It's their photo. He just happened to be holding the camera."

Ronny's arms were still crossed, but his expression had softened. Not completely, but the hardness had developed a crack. The crack of a man hearing something that didn't fit the story he'd been telling himself. "He called Mrs. Lowe," Alex continued. "She told him to never speak to her again. He called your station and the guys basically told him the same thing. So he came to Columbus on his own time, his own money, to try to face the people in the photo. He's from Columbus. He's staying at his parents' house in Hilltop. Sleeping in his old bedroom. Driving his dad's truck."

"Why should I care where he's staying?"

"Because he's not sitting in some fancy hotel laughing about his prize. He's a guy who grew up five miles from here. His family is from Guadalajara. His dad works at the meatpacking plant. He lost his brother when he was a kid — leukemia — and that's how he got into photography in the first place. He took pictures of his brother dying in a hospital because it was the only way he knew how to hold onto him."

Ronny's arms loosened. Not uncrossing — loosening. The information was landing in places the wall couldn't reach. "He didn't even mean to take the photo," Alex said. "He wasn't on assignment. He was visiting his parents. He heard the explosion and ran toward it — same thing you did. Same instinct. And when he got there, he saw you coming out of the building and he raised the camera because that's what he's trained to do, the same way you're trained to run into fires. He took one picture. One. And it ruined four lives, including his."

"He stood outside the building with a camera while—" Ronny stopped. The same sentence he could never finish. While Andrew was dying inside.

"He didn't know that was happening. He didn't know anything. He saw a man carrying a boy and a girl standing beside him and he pressed a button. Less than a second. And now he can't sleep and he can't work and he drinks too much and he carries around the guilt of it like—" She stopped herself. Looked at Ronny. At the dent in the couch. At the crumpled letter. At the cold coffee. "Like you do," she said quietly.

The silence stretched. A car passed outside.

"You're both stuck," Alex said. "You're sitting in this house and he's sitting in his parents' house and you're both stuck because of the same picture. Maybe talking to each other unsticks something. Maybe it doesn't. But you won't know unless you try."

Ronny sat back. He ran his hand over his face. This girl — this girl who'd been pinned under a beam and cracked her skull and survived a bombing — was sitting on his couch making a case for the photographer he'd fantasized about punching, and she was doing it with the precision of a lawyer and the directness of a kid who hadn't yet learned to soften things. And she wasn't wrong. He knew she wasn't wrong. He just didn't know how to do anything about it.

"He really tried to give back the nomination?" Ronny asked.

"Went to his editor the morning after he called Mrs. Lowe. Said he didn't want it. Editor said too bad, the AP owns the image, the nomination stands."

"And he came here just to — what? Apologize?"

"I think he came to understand. He knows the photo hurt people. He doesn't know how it hurt them because nobody will talk to him. So he just carries the guilt around and can't put it down." The words landed, and Ronny flinched. Can't put it down. She hadn't meant it as a mirror, but it was one.

"If it was up to him," Alex said, "the photo never would have been published. He told me that. He said if he could take it back, he would. But he can't. So he's trying to do the next thing — face it. Face the people. That's all he's got."

Ronny was quiet for a long time. His thumb traced the arm of the recliner — back and forth, back and forth. "I'll think about it," he said.

"That's what adults say when they mean no."

He almost laughed. "That's what adults say when they mean they'll think about it."

Alex reached into her backpack and pulled out a piece of paper — a torn corner of notebook, a phone number written in pencil. She set it on the coffee table between them. "That's his number. If you change your mind."

Ronny looked at the paper. The numbers sat there, small and quiet and loaded with the possibility of a conversation he'd been avoiding since April. "You came here for him?" Ronny asked. "That's why you came?"

"Partly." She slung the backpack over her shoulder and stood. "And partly because I wanted to meet you when you weren't carrying me out of a building."

Ronny stood too. Recognition moved across her face — not pity. The look of someone who understood what it cost to stand up. "Hey," Ronny said. "You OK getting home? You don't live around here."

"I told you, I took the bus."

"By yourself?"

"I'm thirteen. I take the bus everywhere."

He stopped. Looked at her. "You're really homeschooled?"

"Taking a little time," she said, with the ghost of a smile.

He should have pushed it. Should have said something — you're thirteen, you need to be in school, your mother would want to know. But he was a man who'd been sitting in his house pretending to be on disability while his benefits ran out and his wife went to work and his kids wondered why their father had turned into a ghost, and he didn't have the standing to lecture anyone about avoidance. "Be careful on the bus," he said instead.

"Always am."

She walked to the door. Stopped. Turned back. "Hey. That thing you asked me. What you said I said — I think it moved." Ronny's whole body went still. "I don't remember saying it," Alex said. "But I believe you that I might've. And whatever it means to you — whatever it is that's eating at you about it — I'm sorry I can't help you more. My head was messed up. I was seeing things, probably. You know that, right?"

"Yeah," Ronny said. "I know."

"Okay." She studied him one more moment — the same look she'd given him when she first walked in, steady and old beyond her years. "Take care of yourself, Mr. Martinez."

"Ronny."

"Take care of yourself, Ronny."

The door closed behind her. Ronny stood in the living room, the house settling back into its silence, the crumpled letter on the table and the slip of paper on the coffee table and the cold coffee on the counter. Three objects. Three different versions of a future he wasn't ready for.

He walked to the coffee table. Picked up the piece of notebook paper. Read the number. Set it back down.

Then he picked it up again and put it in his pocket.

22

The taxi dropped him on Broadway and 116th, and Demian stood on the sidewalk looking up at the columns of Low Library like a man looking at something he'd been sentenced to. The building was enormous with white stone and bronze doors. Architecture designed to make a person feel small. It was working.

He straightened his tie. The tux was rented — George had arranged it through Rachel, who'd left it hanging in his hotel room with a note that said Don't wrinkle it. He'd wrinkled it. The jacket pulled across his shoulders, and the pants were half an inch too short, and he looked, he imagined, like exactly what he was — a man who'd spent the last year sleeping in tents trying to pass for someone who belonged in a ballroom. He went in.

The ceremony was upstairs, in a room with chandeliers and white tablecloths and the hum of people who were important and knew it. Demian stepped through the double doors and the sound hit him — glasses, laughter, the low confident murmur of an industry celebrating itself. He scanned the room. Suits. Gowns. Name tags. Everyone holding drinks the way people hold drinks when they want their hands to look occupied.

"The man of the hour."

Demian turned. George was crossing the room toward him — George in a suit that actually fit, his beard trimmed for the occasion, his eyes carrying that mix of pride and wariness that Demian had come to recognize as George's version of affection. "You came all the way from Afghanistan?" Demian asked.

"Wouldn't miss it."

Rachel appeared behind him in a red dress that Demian had never seen before — she only wore business clothes at the bureau. She leaned in close. "Where were you? We thought you might not come. Nice tux, by the way."

"Traffic. Nice dress."

"Thank you." She took his arm and steered him toward the tables. "We saved your seat. Try not to make a scene before dinner."

The table was round, eight seats, and George made introductions that went in one of Demian's ears and out the other. He caught a name — Charlotte, fiction winner — and a face — a woman with sharp eyes and silver earrings who was studying him the way he studied subjects through a viewfinder. "Your photograph has generated quite the conversation," Charlotte said, spearing a cherry tomato from her plate. "How does that feel?"

"Complicated," Demian said.

She waited for more. He didn't give it. After a moment she smiled — the smile of someone who recognized a fellow practitioner of saying less than they meant — and turned to the person on her other side.

George leaned over. "You okay?"

"I'm fine."

"You're not fine. You look like you're about to bolt."

"I'm not going to bolt."

"Good. Because you gave me your word." George held his eyes. "Speech. Prize. Smile. That was the deal."

"I remember the deal."

The fish arrived. Rachel had preordered it. Demian looked at it — a pale fillet on a white plate, garnished with something green, its surface gleaming under the chandelier light. He didn't touch it. His stomach was a fist.

Dr. Eleanor Vance, chair of the Pulitzer Prize photography committee, stepped up to the podium. Demian's photograph projected behind her on the screen. She began, "When we gather to choose the Pulitzer Prize for Photography, we ask ourselves a deceptively simple question: What does it mean to bear witness? What separates a photograph from photojournalism? What elevates an image from documentation to art, from record to revelation? The answer lies in excellence--but excellence of a very particular kind. A winning photograph must possess journalistic integrity. It captures a significant moment, a story with real news value. It advances public understanding of something that matters. It does not turn away from difficult truths. Instead, it pulls us toward them, insists that we see, that we know, that we cannot pretend ignorance. But journalism alone is not enough. The photograph must also demonstrate mastery--technical skill and artistic vision combined. The light must be precisely rendered. The composition must be deliberate. The framing must speak. Every element must work in service of the image's purpose. This is craft at its highest level. This is art."

After a breath and a gaze out to the audience, she continued, "And then there is the matter of the human heart. A winning photograph possesses emotional pow-er. It moves us. It provokes thought. It captures something universal--a moment of consequence, an experience that transcends the particular and speaks to what it means to be alive. It recognizes the dignity of its subject. It honors the moment it documents. The images we choose often document historical significance and social importance. They illuminate conditions and conflicts that demand public awareness. They shed light on injustice, on resilience, on the complexity of human experience. They reveal truths about the world that we need to see--truths about ourselves. But context is everything. A winning photograph is never isolated. It exists within a larger narrative, a body of work that tells a story worth telling. It is journalism of purpose and courage--the kind that requires photographers to place themselves in danger, in discomfort, in the presence of suffering, and to bring back proof that this matters. The Pulitzer Prize for Photography has always recognized work that combines excellence with consequence. Images that change how we see. Photographs that serve the public good. Work that proves that truth, rendered with skill and compassion, has the power to transform us."

Dr. Vance turned to Demian. "Damien Ochoa, your work embodies all of these qualities. Your photography is journalism of the highest order--technically brilliant, emotionally resonant, socially significant, and deeply true. You have shown us something essential about the world, and you have done so with both artistic excellence and human compassion. Please come forward."

The room applauded. Demian stood. The chair scraped against the floor and the sound cut through the clapping like a wrong note. He walked to the podium — thirty feet that felt like a hundred — and the applause continued, and he could feel George's eyes on his back, and Rachel's, and Charlotte's, and the eyes of three hundred strangers who'd seen his photograph and formed opinions about it and about him and were now watching him approach a microphone to say something worthy of the moment.

He gripped the podium. Took out the folded papers from his jacket pocket. Smoothed them flat. His hands were shaking. He could see the tremor in his fingers against the white paper, and he knew the front row could see it too.

He leaned toward the microphone. "Thank you." His voice came out thin. He cleared his throat. "Thank you for this honor. I'm grateful to the committee, to the Associated Press, and to George Gelson, who's been my editor and my conscience for longer than either of us would like to admit."

A small laugh from the room. George, in the front row, didn't laugh. His lips were pressed together. Watching.

Demian looked down at his notes. He'd written the speech in the hotel room at two in the morning, sitting on the edge of the bed in his boxers, writing and crossing out and writing again until the wastebasket was full and the page in front of him was something close to honest.

"Photography freezes a moment," he said. "That's what we're taught. You see something, you press the shutter, and the moment is preserved. It becomes permanent. It belongs to the world." He paused. "What they don't teach you is that the moment doesn't stop. The people in the photograph keep living. Or they don't. And either way, the image you made follows them — into their homes, into their schools, into their grief. It follows them in ways you never intended and can't control."

The room was quiet. Not the comfortable quiet of an audience being entertained. The quiet of people sensing that the script had changed. "I took the Columbus photograph on April fourteenth. I wasn't on assignment. I was visiting my parents. I heard the explosion and I ran toward it because that's what I've been trained to do — run toward the thing everyone else is running from. And when

I got there, I saw a firefighter coming out of the building with a boy in his arms and a girl walking beside him, and I raised my camera and I pressed the shutter. It took less than a second."

He looked up from the notes. He didn't need them for this part. "That firefighter is named Ronny Martinez. He's a good man. He went into a collapsing building to save people, and he tore his knee apart doing it, and he hasn't been back to work since. He told a reporter my photograph destroyed his life. I believe him."

A murmur moved through the room.

Demian pressed on. "The boy in the photograph is Mikey Lowe. He was seven years old. He died in the bombing. His mother, Jordan, wrote me a letter. She said my photograph is the last recorded image of her son. She said she sees his face everywhere — on newsstands, on television, on other kids' phones. She asked me to never contact her again."

George's jaw was tight. Rachel had her hand over her mouth. "The girl in the photograph is Alex Kelly. She's thirteen. She survived, but she had a traumatic brain injury that required surgery. She's the only person in the photograph who agreed to talk to me." Demian stopped.

Swallowed. "She told me she used to pull copies of the photograph out of the trash after her mother threw them away. She said looking at it was like picking a scab — she knew she should stop but she couldn't. She's a little girl and she's addicted to an image of the worst moment of her life. An image I made." The room was completely still.

"I tried to withdraw this nomination. The AP wouldn't allow it. The photograph belongs to them — I signed a contract. So I'm here tonight accepting a prize for a photograph that a firefighter says destroyed his life, that a mother can't escape, and that a young girl hides in her backpack like a secret. And I don't know what to do with that. I don't have a clean answer. I don't think there is one."

He folded the papers. Put them back in his pocket. "I'm not standing up here to tell you that photojournalism is wrong, or that we should stop documenting suffering. I've seen what happens in places where no one is watching. I've seen what disappears when there's no camera. Documentation matters. Truth matters.

But so do the people inside the frame. And I failed to consider them. I thought about the image. I thought about the light, the composition, the moment. I did not think about Ronny Martinez or the Lowe family or Alex Kelly. I thought about the photograph. And I'm sorry."

He stepped back from the podium. The applause that followed was strange — scattered, uncertain, as if the audience wasn't sure whether they were clapping for the speech or for the fact that it was over. Demian walked past the table, past the untouched fish, past George who was looking at him with an expression Demian couldn't read — anger or admiration or both at once, held in the same face the way a photograph holds opposites in the same frame.

He pushed through the double doors into the reception area. Empty. Cocktail tables with abandoned glasses, napkins crumpled on surfaces, half-eaten appetizers on small plates — the whole room looking like Miss Havisham's banquet hall, frozen mid-celebration, waiting for guests who weren't coming back.

He kept walking. Through the lobby, down the stairs, through the bronze doors, and out onto the steps of Low Library. The night air hit him — cold, sharp, smelling of exhaust and wet pavement and something green from the campus trees. The city spread out below him, lit and humming, indifferent to what had just happened inside.

The Pulitzer was in his hand. He didn't remember picking it up — someone must have handed it to him at the podium, or maybe he'd grabbed it from the table on his way out. It was heavier than he'd expected. A small thing, metal and engraving, and it sat in his palm like a question he couldn't answer.

He could leave it on the steps. Set it down on the stone and walk away and let someone find it in the morning. That would be a statement. That would be clean. He didn't. He put it in his jacket pocket. It pressed against his thigh as he descended the steps — a weight he'd carry because carrying it was the only honest thing left. Not as an achievement. Not as validation. As a reminder of what a fraction of a second could do to four lives, including his own.

He walked. Broadway was loud with traffic and pedestrians and the ordinary noise of a city that didn't know or care about Pulitzer luncheons. Demian loosened his tie. Unbuttoned the top button of the rented shirt. Breathed. His phone buzzed in his pocket. George. He let it ring.

It buzzed again. A text this time: That was either the bravest or the stupidest thing I've ever seen you do. Call me when you land. We need to talk about Columbus. Demian read it twice. Put the phone away. Kept walking.

He had a flight back to Columbus in the morning. Alex would want to know what happened. She'd ask him how it went, and he'd tell her, and she'd say something that was too smart for a girl her age, and he'd sit under the oak tree in the park and share her egg and feel, for a few minutes, like the distance between who he was and who he wanted to be had gotten a little smaller.

That was enough. For now, that was enough.

23

Alex was already under the oak tree when Demian arrived at the park, her backpack against the trunk, her sketchpad on her knees. The homeless man was gone — had been for a week now, his bench empty, a flattened cardboard box the only evidence he'd ever been there. Alex was drawing the empty bench.

"Famous photographer returns," she said without looking up.

"Famous subject still skipping school."

"Touche." She set the pencil down. "You get it?"

Demian reached into his jacket pocket and pulled out the Pulitzer medal. He held it out on his open palm. Alex leaned forward, her eyes widening — genuine awe, unguarded in a way she rarely allowed herself to be.

"Wow." She ran her finger over the engraved surface. "That's real."

"It's real."

"Congratulations, Mr. Ochoa."

"Gracias, Señorita Kelly." He closed his hand around it and put it back in his pocket. It sat against his thigh the way it had since Columbia — a weight he'd stopped noticing and couldn't stop feeling.

"Did you thank me in your speech?"

"I did, actually."

Her face whipped toward him. "You really did?"

"I mentioned you by name. Told the whole room about the girl in the photograph."

"Oh God. I'm gonna be famous all over again."

"You might be."

She grinned — quick, bright, then gone. Back to business. "So how was it? The whole thing?"

Demian sat down beside her against the oak tree. The bark pressed into his back. The morning was cool, the park quiet, a jogger passing on the far path. "Strange," he said. "A room full of people celebrating journalism. Chandeliers. Fish I didn't eat. I gave a speech that made my editor want to kill me and walked out before dessert."

"What did you say in the speech?"

"The truth. That the photo hurt the people in it. That I was sorry. That I didn't have a clean answer for any of it."

Alex studied him. "How did they take it?"

"Quietly. my editor, George, texted me after. Said it was either the bravest or the stupidest thing he'd ever seen me do."

"Which one do you think it was?"

"Both." He picked up a twig from the ground and turned it between his fingers. "So. What happened while I was gone?"

Alex pulled her bagged lunch from her backpack — the same lunch every day, cheese sandwich, hard-boiled egg, water bottle. She held out the egg. Demian took it. Their ritual. "I went to see Mrs. Lowe," Alex said.

Demian's hand tightened around the egg. "And?"

"I got into the house. Played video games with Emily — her daughter. She's cool. Talks a lot of trash for a seventh grader." Alex unwrapped her sandwich. "On the drive home, Mrs. Lowe asked me about Mikey. About what I saw in the building. She's been wanting to ask someone who was there. She's never been able to get the words out."

"What did you tell her?"

"What I remember. Which isn't much. I told her about his shoes — the Spider-Man sneakers. That the laces were untied. She cried." Alex took a bite of her sandwich, chewed, swallowed. The matter-of-factness was a shield, and Demian could see the effort behind it. "Then I asked her about you."

"What did she say?"

Alex looked at him. She didn't soften it. "She said she hates the photograph with a passion. And she thinks you're scum."

The word landed in Demian's chest and sat there. He'd expected it. He'd expected worse. But hearing it delivered by Alex eating a cheese sandwich under an oak tree gave it weight — the weight of simple, undeniable truth, spoken without malice or apology.

"Scum," he repeated.

"Her word, not mine. I'm sorry."

"Don't be. She has every right."

"Maybe. But she doesn't know you." Alex took another bite. "She knows the photograph and she knows what it did to her life. She doesn't know the rest."

"The rest doesn't matter to her. And it shouldn't have to."

Alex shrugged. The shrug of someone who disagreed but wasn't going to argue. "What about Martinez?" Demian asked.

Alex's expression shifted behind her eyes. Not the cool, strategic look she'd worn when talking about Jordan. Something more unsettled. "I went to see him."

"You went to his house?"

"Took the bus. Showed up at his door." She picked at the crust of her sandwich. "He recognized me. Invited me in. We talked."

"About the photo?"

"About a lot of things." She paused — a long pause, unusual for Alex, who typically moved through conversations at speed. "He asked me something, Demian. About the day of the bombing. Something specific." Demian waited. "He said that after he pulled me out, he had to go look for his partner. He was gone for about a minute. And when he came back, he said I told him something." She looked at Demian. "He said I told him, 'I think it moved.'"

Demian's brow furrowed. "What moved?"

"I don't know. He wouldn't say. He asked me if I remembered saying it and I don't. I don't remember saying anything. My head was messed up — you know that. But whatever I said, it's been eating him alive. I've never seen an adult look like that. Like everything depended on my answer and I had nothing to give him."

Demian sat with that. He peeled the egg slowly, thinking. "Do you think he's talking about Mrs. Lowe's son?"

Alex was quiet for a moment. "Maybe. I don't know. He shut it down after I said I didn't remember. Changed the subject. But it's the reason he can't go back to work. Whatever happened in that building — whatever I said to him — it broke something in him."

"And you told him about me?"

"Yeah. After." She set the sandwich down. "I told him everything. That the AP owns the photo, not you. That you tried to give back the nomination. That you came here on your own time and your own money. That your brother died and that's how you got into photography. That you heard the explosion and ran toward it the same way he did."

"What did he say?"

"He said he'd think about it. Which is what adults say when they mean no."

"Usually."

"But then I left his number on his coffee table. Your number, I mean. And when I was leaving, I turned back and he was looking at it. He didn't throw it away."

Demian peeled the last of the shell from the egg. He looked at it — smooth, white, ordinary. "That's something."

"It's something." Alex picked her sandwich back up. "So that's where we are. Mrs. Lowe thinks you're scum and won't budge. The firefighter has your number and might call. And you have a Pulitzer in your pocket. Quite a week."

"Quite a week."

They ate in silence for a while. The jogger passed again on the far path. A squirrel investigated the empty bench where the homeless man used to sleep.

"I want to go to Chrissy's apartment," Alex said. "Add to the closet. Want to come?"

"Lead the way."

The apartment building looked the same — brick and iron, twenty units, the courtyard tree finally budding after a long winter. They climbed the stairs to the second floor and Alex took the key from her pocket and unlocked the door to unit 210.

Inside, the dust was thicker. Nobody had been here except Alex — her footprints tracking back and forth from the door to the bedroom, the same path worn into the dust like a desire line through a field.

She went straight to Chrissy's room. Demian followed. She slid the closet doors open, and he stopped. "You've added a lot since I was here."

"Haven't I?" Pride in her voice — quiet pride, the kind that doesn't need an audience but is glad to have one. The closet walls were nearly full now. Drawings layered over drawings, taped in rows, some overlapping. The two girls on the staircase. The birthday cake. New ones — a view from the rooftop, a pigeon on a railing, a woman sleeping on a bus. And in the center of the back wall, mounted carefully with four pieces of tape, the glossy photograph. Demian's photograph. Ronny carrying Mikey, Alex standing beside them, the smoke diffusing the light into something almost golden.

Alex pulled a new drawing from her sketchpad — the empty bench in the park, the one the homeless man had left — and taped it to the inside of the closet door. She stepped back and looked at the whole collection the way a curator looks at a gallery wall. "My mom found the last copy of the photo, by the way," she said, not turning around. "The one you gave me. She threw it out."

Demian reached into his bag. He'd brought one. He'd known she would need it. "Here," he said, holding out a glossy print.

Alex turned. Looked at it. Looked at him. A small, knowing smile. "You already had it ready."

"I know you."

She took it and slid it into her backpack without looking at it — the same quick, practiced motion, the zipper pulled shut. The way someone pockets a pill. He'd seen her do it before. It didn't worry him less the second time.

They sat on the dusty floor across from the open closet, their backs against the wall. The late afternoon light came through the window at a low angle, catching the dust motes suspended in the air.

"He said he's going to rent this place," Alex said.

Demian looked at her. "Who?"

"Dale. The building manager. He came in last time I was here — scared me half to death. He's getting the apartment ready to rent."

"What happens to the closet?"

"I don't know." Her voice was flat. Controlled. But Demian could hear the tremor beneath it — the sound of someone bracing for a loss they couldn't prevent. "I told him I'd pay rent on just the closet. My allowance should cover it. If it doesn't, I'll mow lawns."

"Alex—"

"I know it's stupid. You don't have to say it."

"I wasn't going to say it's stupid."

She pulled her knees to her chest. "It's the only place I still feel close to her. My room has drawings, but it's my room. This is her room. This is where we used to hide in the closet during hide and seek. Where she'd tape my drawings up and we'd pretend it was a museum. Where we'd sit on the floor and eat popsicles and talk about who we were going to marry." She pressed her forehead against her knees. "If someone moves in here, it's over. All of it comes down."

Demian sat beside her and said nothing. He understood. He had a shoebox of negatives in his parents' house — eleven photographs of a dying boy, taken with a disposable camera, never shown to anyone. His own closet. His own shrine.

"Maybe I'll tell the new tenants it's haunted," Alex said into her knees.

"That could work."

"Chrissy rattling hangers in the middle of the night. Creepy noises. Nobody would last a week."

"You have quite the imagination."

She lifted her head. Her eyes were red but dry — Alex didn't cry, or if she did, she didn't let anyone see it. "How long do you think before someone rents it?"

"I don't know. Could be weeks. Could be months."

"Could be tomorrow."

"Could be tomorrow," she agreed as she looked at the closet. The drawings. The photograph. The record of a friendship measured in pencil lines and tape and the stubborn refusal of a young girl to let go of someone the world had already moved on from. "I'll figure something out," she said. The flatness was back — the voice of someone putting the lid on something that hurt too much to leave open. She stood. Brushed the dust from her jeans. "I should get home before my mom sends out a search party."

Demian stood too. Alex stopped at the bedroom doorway and took one last look at the closet — the drawings, the photograph, Chrissy's height measurements penciled on the door jamb. 4'4" — March. She closed the door behind her.

They walked out into the courtyard. The tree was budding — small green knots on the bare branches, the first sign that winter was loosening its grip. A kid on a bicycle circled the concrete below. "Same time tomorrow?" Alex asked.

"If you'll have me."

"Depends. You bringing the lunch? I'm tired of sharing my egg."

Demian laughed. "I'll bring food."

"Good. Bring something Mexican. Your mom's cooking."

"You've never had my mom's cooking."

"Exactly. Fix that."

She climbed the stairs to unit 203, backpack bouncing, and disappeared through the door.

Demian stood in the courtyard and looked up at the building — its twenty doors, its iron staircases, its one empty apartment with a closet full of drawings and a clock ticking on its existence.

He thought about the apartment manager getting it ready to rent. He thought about Alex's drawings coming down off the walls. He thought about a girl sitting on a dusty floor pressing her forehead to her knees, trying to hold onto a friend who'd been measured at four feet four inches in March and would never be measured again.

Demian walked to his father's truck and sat in it without starting the engine. Through the windshield, he could see the building's second-floor walkway—the iron railing, the row of identical doors, the dark window of 210. Behind that window, behind the bedroom door, behind the closet doors, forty or fifty drawings were taped to the walls in rows, and a girl's height was penciled on the door jamb in a hand that would never write anything again. 4'4" — March.

He drove home on autopilot—Sullivant to Fifth to the turn onto his parents' street, the route his body knew without consulting his brain. His mother's kitchen light was on. His father's truck—the other one, the newer one he'd bought in '98—sat in the driveway. Demian pulled in beside it and cut the engine. Sat there.

The house was fifty feet away. Through the front window he could see the shelf in the living room—the one with the family photos, the ceramic virgin, and Miguel's baseball glove, cracked and stiff, sitting next to a school picture of a boy who'd been dead for twenty-one years. His parents hadn't moved the glove. Not once, in twenty-one years. It sat on that shelf the way Alex's drawings covered the walls of a closet in an empty apartment—permanent, untouchable, a thing that stayed because moving it would mean admitting it was over.

Under his childhood bed, in a shoebox held together with a rubber band, were eleven negatives. Photographs of Miguel in his last week. Taken with a disposable camera by a fourteen year old boy who didn't know yet that he'd spend his life behind a lens but who already understood, in some wordless way, that the camera could hold what his hands couldn't. He'd never shown those photographs to anyone. They were his conversation with his brother. His closet. His shrine.

He understood Alex because he was Alex. That was the thing he'd been circling for weeks without landing on it. She wasn't a subject. She wasn't a story. She was the young lady with the disposable camera, grown into a different body in a different city, doing the same thing he'd done—building a place where the dead were allowed to stay.

And Dale was going to rent that apartment. Someone was going to move in, and the closet would be cleared, and the drawings would come down, and the height measurement on the door jamb would be painted over, and Alex would lose the only place where Chrissy still lived.

Demian sat in the truck and stared at his parents' house and thought about the hospital in Guadalajara. The room on the third floor where Miguel had spent his last eleven days. The window that faced the courtyard. The chair where their mother slept. After Miguel died, Demian had gone back to the hospital once—alone, without telling anyone—and stood in the hallway outside that room. The door was closed. Someone else was in it. A different child in the same bed, a different family in the same chairs, and the room had no memory of the boy who'd died there. It had already moved on. The walls had been wiped clean and the sheets had been changed and Miguel's eleven days had been absorbed into the ordinary business of a building that processed grief the way a factory processes raw material—continuously, indifferently, without looking back. He'd stood in that hallway for a long time.

The kitchen light flickered. His mother, moving past the window. Demian took out his phone and opened his banking app. He looked at the balance for a while. Then he closed the app, put the phone in his pocket, and went inside.

The call came at six the next morning. Demian sat at his parents' kitchen table with coffee and the remains of his mother's eggs when his phone buzzed. George's name on the screen. George didn't call at six unless something was moving. "Kandahar," George said. No hello. "Two weeks. Reuters is rotating out and we need a photographer on the ground. The embed's already approved."

Demian set down his fork. Through the kitchen window, the backyard was gray with early light. His father's truck sat in the driveway. The neighbor's dog was barking at something it would never catch.

"Demian. You there?"

"I'm here."

"This is the one. Good unit, good access, six-week rotation. It's yours if you want it."

If you want it. Three months ago that sentence wouldn't have existed. Three months ago George would have said You're going, and Demian would have packed his bag and been on a transport within forty-eight hours, because that was the job and the job was the only thing and the bag was always half-packed anyway. The flak jacket lived in the hall closet. The passport lived in his camera bag. He'd spent fifteen years ready to leave at a moment's notice, and the readiness had been its own kind of home—portable, self-contained, requiring nothing from anyone.

Now there was a girl in this town who was teaching herself to see through a viewfinder. There was a closet full of drawings that existed because he'd written a check. There was a park bench where they ate his mother's tamales and talked about light and shadow and the difference between looking and seeing. There was a life here. Small, unfinished, nothing he could explain to George or put in a file or point to as a reason to say no. But a life. "What's the timeline?" he asked.

"You'd fly out the fourteenth. Kabul first, then south to Kandahar."

The fourteenth. Twelve days. Twelve days to finish what he'd started here, or to admit that what he'd started here wasn't something that finished. "I'll take it," he said. The words came out before the decision was fully made, which was how all his decisions came out—the body committing before the mind could build a case against it. The same reflex that made him raise a camera in a bombed-out school. The same instinct that had carried him through three wars. The muscle that said go, and the man who obeyed it.

"Good," George said. "Rachel will send the details. And Demian?"

"Yeah."

"Shoot what you want out there."

He hung up. His mother's eggs were cold. The coffee was still warm. He sat at the table and thought about what shoot what you want meant in Kandahar, where what there was to shoot was the same thing there had always been—dust and convoys and young men with rifles and the faces of people living inside a war they hadn't started. He'd photographed all of it before. He'd done it well. He'd done it the way he'd been trained—document everything, delete nothing, let the editors decide.

But he'd deleted the dead. He'd sat on a cot in a tent and scrolled through his camera and erased every image of a person who couldn't say no. That was a line he'd crossed, and you couldn't uncross a line. You could only decide which side of it you were going to stand on from now on.

He didn't know which side that was. He knew the old side—the side where the camera captured everything and the photographer felt nothing and the work justified itself because the world needed to see. He knew that side the way he knew his own hands. The new side was less clear. The new side was a girl saying drawing at the speed of seeing, and a mother's letter folded in his pocket, and a closet full of drawings that mattered more than any Pulitzer. The new side didn't have rules yet. It just had a feeling—a pull toward something gentler, something that didn't require suffering to be significant.

He'd figure it out in Kandahar. Or he wouldn't. Either way, he was going. But first he had twelve days. Twelve days with Alex and the Leica and the neighborhood sidewalks where she was learning to find pictures in ordinary things. Twelve days to teach her what he could and to let her teach him what she already had. Twelve days before the bag got packed and the passport came out and the man who'd spent months learning to sit still went back to running toward the thing everyone else ran from.

He washed his plate. Poured another coffee. Went to the hall closet and opened it. The flak jacket hung where he'd left it—dusty, creased, the velcro PRESS patch curling at the edges. He looked at it the way you look at a uniform you used to wear. It still fit. He just wasn't sure it still fit him.

He closed the closet. He'd deal with it later. Right now, Alex was expecting him at the park at ten, and his mother was packing tamales, and there were twelve days left, and he was going to use them.

24

—·—

The cop was young. That was the first thing Alex noticed — younger than she'd expected, with a jaw that looked like he shaved twice a day and still missed spots. He had his hand on her elbow, guiding her across the grass toward the cruiser parked on the access road, and his grip was the grip of someone who'd arrested adults and didn't know how to calibrate for a little girl who weighed ninety-two pounds.

"Watch your head," he said, opening the back door.

Alex ducked. The seat was hard plastic, not cloth, and it smelled like disinfectant and something sour underneath — fear, maybe, or the accumulated sweat of everyone who'd sat here before her. She pulled her seatbelt on.

Through the window, she saw Demian. He was standing exactly where she'd left him — by the bench near the oak tree, a white bakery bag in one hand, two coffees in the other. His mouth was open. Not wide, just slightly — the expression of a man watching something he doesn't know how to process. A girl he'd been eating donuts with five minutes ago, now in the back of a police car.

Alex caught his eyes. She winked. The cruiser pulled away.

The station smelled like old carpet and burnt coffee. They walked her past the front desk — a woman on the phone who didn't look up — down a corridor with fluorescent lights that buzzed at a frequency Alex could feel in her teeth, and into a room that wasn't exactly an interrogation room but wasn't not one either. A table, two chairs, a window with blinds that didn't close all the way. A poster on the wall about community policing that was peeling at one corner.

The young cop — his nameplate said REEVES — sat her down and opened a folder. "Alexandra Kelly."

"Alex."

"Thirteen years old. Address is 1740 Millbrook, apartment 203."

"Yes."

"You're supposed to be enrolled at Whitehall...," he trailed off as he studied the papers. "...or transferred to...Eastmore...but never attended."

"Sounds about right."

"But you haven't been to school in—" He flipped a page. Flipped another. His eyebrows went up. "Seven months?"

"Give or take."

Reeves looked at her. She could see him recalculating — the girl who'd been reading on a park bench at ten a.m. on a Tuesday, who'd shown him a library card as ID, who'd been polite and calm and hadn't run. He'd expected drugs, maybe. A runaway. Not a kid who'd simply decided school wasn't where she needed to be and had gotten away with it for a third of the year.

"Where have you been going?"

"Libraries. Different ones."

"Why?"

Alex shrugged. "They don't ask questions."

Reeves stared at her for a long moment, then closed the folder. "I need to contact your parent or guardian. You want to do it or me?"

"I'll do it."

"You can use your cell. Who you gonna call?" He slid her phone toward her.

"My Dad." Alex picked up the cell, found Demian's contact and dialed. "Hello? Dad?" Alex said. She kept her voice pitched slightly higher — not panicked, not calm, the exact register of a kid who was in trouble and knew it but wasn't going to fall apart. "It's Alex. I got busted for truancy." Silence on the other end. She could hear him breathing. "Said you're my dad."

"Alex—"

"Dad, don't freak out." Louder now, for Reeves, who was watching from the doorway. "I know you're upset. I need you to come down to the Third Precinct on Garfield. Can you do that?"

Another silence until Demian's voice, low and careful, asked, "What are you doing?"

"I know, Dad. I'm sorry. Just come, okay? They won't release me without a parent." She hung up before he could answer.

Reeves was still in the doorway. "That your father?"

"Yes."

"Name?"

"Demian Ochoa."

"Different last name?"

"My mom changed mine."

Reeves wrote it down. He didn't check. Alex filed that — another system that ran on trust and paperwork, another gap you could walk through if you knew where the gaps were. "Can I make one more call?" she asked.

"Who else do you need to call?"

"My aunt."

He sighed. But he left the phone.

Alex clicked on Jordan Lowe's contact. She'd found it on a refrigerator magnet she'd seen in Jordan's kitchen — the one with the pediatrician's number on one side and Jordan's cell on the other, stuck next to a crayon drawing that was probably Emily's but might have been Mikey's. Alex had clocked it. Stored it. The way she stored everything.

It rang four times. Jordan picked up with the voice of a woman who didn't recognize the number and almost hadn't answered. "Hello?"

"Mrs. Lowe? It's Alex. Alex Kelly."

"Alex?" The voice changed — warmer, but immediately concerned. "Are you okay?"

"I'm at the police station. Third Precinct on Garfield. I got picked up for truancy."

"For — what?"

"I haven't been going to school. They caught me. My mom's at work and she's — I don't know how long she'll take. Can you come? They said a guardian would work."

"But, Alex..."

"Please, Mrs. Lowe."

It was the truth. All of it. And her mom was at work, and Jordan was a woman who would come when a kid who'd been lying next to her dead son asked her to come. Alex knew that about her. She'd known it since the car ride, since Jordan had gripped her hand on the curb and held on like Alex was the only rope keeping her from going under.

"I'll be there in fifteen minutes," Jordan said. "Don't worry, sweetheart."

Alex hung up. She sat back in the chair and looked at the community policing poster. In fifteen minutes, Demian Ochoa and Jordan Lowe were going to be in the same building together. Jordan didn't know Demian was coming. Demian didn't know about Jordan. Neither of them knew what Alex had done, and by the time they figured it out, they'd be looking at each other. Alex picked at the edge of the table where the laminate was peeling.

She was scared. Not of the police or the truancy charge or even her mother finding out, though that was going to be bad, that was going to be volcanic. She was scared because she'd set something in motion that she couldn't take back, and the two people she'd called were both broken in ways she couldn't fix from this plastic chair in this fluorescent room, and maybe putting broken people in a room together didn't make them whole. Maybe it just made it more broken.

But she'd been watching them. Demian, who flinched when anyone mentioned the photograph and flew across the world to rent an apartment for a dead girl's closet. Jordan, who counted everything and held onto hands like lifelines.

They needed to be in a room. They needed to see each other as people, not as concepts, not as the photographer and the mother. As Demian and Jordan. Two humans who'd been circling the same explosion for almost a year without ever being in the same orbit. Alex had just corrected the orbit. That's all she'd done.

The laminate peeled off in a strip. She dropped it on the floor. Demian arrived first.

Alex heard him before she saw him — his accented voice at the front desk, measured but tight, asking for Alexandra Kelly. A murmured conversation with the desk sergeant. Then footsteps, and he appeared in the doorway of the room where they'd put her. He was still holding the bakery bag. That detail almost made her laugh — Demian Ochoa, standing in a police station, his face white, his free hand opening and closing at his side, and in the other hand a grease-spotted white bag of donuts from Rosario's because he'd been walking to the park to meet her when the world had gone sideways. He hadn't put them down. He'd driven here with them on the passenger seat. He'd walked through the doors holding them. He was holding them now, like a man who'd forgotten he had hands.

"Hey," Alex said.

Demian set the bag on the table. Slowly, like he was placing evidence. He sat down in the other chair. His knee was bouncing. "You told them I'm your father."

"I did."

"Alex, I can't—"

"They won't release me to a non-family member. I checked."

"You checked?"

"I read the truancy statute online. Section 3319.321. The detaining officer must release the minor to a parent, legal guardian, or custodial family member. I needed a family member. You're the closest thing I've got to one who could get here fast."

Demian stared at her. "Donna is your mother."

"Donna is twenty minutes away and she's going to kill me. I needed time."

"Time for what?"

Alex didn't answer. The desk sergeant appeared — older, heavier, a man named Mulvaney who'd been doing this long enough to have stopped being surprised by anything. He looked at Demian, then at Alex, then at the donuts. "You're the father?"

"I—" Demian started.

"He is," Alex said.

"ID?"

Demian pulled out his wallet. His hands were unsteady. Mulvaney looked at the license, looked at Alex, looked at the different last name. "Ochoa?"

"My mom changed my last name," Alex said again.

Mulvaney looked at Demian. "She's been out of school for seven months, Mr. Ochoa. Forty-seven unexcused absences. That's not a warning — that's a referral to juvenile court. I need you to understand the seriousness of this."

Demian opened his mouth. Alex studied his face — the war between the lie and the truth, the absurdity of being lectured about parental responsibility for a child who wasn't his by a sergeant who had no idea he was sitting across from a Pulitzer Prize–winning photographer who'd met this girl because he'd taken the most controversial photograph in America.

"I understand," Demian said.

"We've contacted the mother. She's on her way."

"Good."

Mulvaney looked at Alex. "This kid," he said to Demian, shaking his head. "Forty-seven absences. I've been doing this eighteen years. I've never seen forty-seven."

"She's—" Demian searched for a word. "Resourceful."

"Yeah." Mulvaney didn't sound impressed. "That's one word for it."

He left. Alex and Demian sat in the room with the buzzing fluorescent lights and the bakery bag and the silence. "Who else did you call?" Demian asked quietly.

"What?"

"You called me. Who else?" Alex looked at the peeling poster. She could feel his eyes on her. "Alex?"

"Mrs. Lowe."

The name landed in the room like something dropped from a height. Demian went still — not the stillness of calm but the stillness of a man who's been hit and hasn't started feeling it yet.

"You called Jordan Lowe."

"Yes."

"Why." It wasn't a question. It was the word 'why' pushed through a closed throat.

"Because you need to meet her."

"Alex, you don't—"

"And she needs to meet you. Not the guy who took the picture. You. She thinks you're scum. She told me that. She looked me in the eye and said 'I think he's scum,' and she meant it, and she's wrong, and the only way she's ever going to know she's wrong is if she sees you."

Demian's hands were flat on the table. His jaw was working. He was staring at a spot on the wall like he was trying to bore through it. "You had no right to do this," he said.

"I know."

"She's going to walk in here and see me and—"

"I know."

"I can't—" He stopped. Pressed his knuckles against his forehead. "I have thought about what I would say to that woman every single day. Every day. And I don't have it. I don't have a single word that's good enough."

"You don't need words. You just need to be here."

"That's not how it works."

"It's exactly how it works. You show up. That's the thing. She's spent months hating a concept. A faceless photographer who ruined her life. She needs to see that you're a person. That you're—" Alex gestured at him, at the donuts, at his shaking hands. "That you're this."

Demian looked at the bakery bag. Then at Alex. Then at the door. "She's going to be here any minute," he said.

"Yeah."

"And you're going to sit here and watch."

"I'm going to be in the other room. Mulvaney's going to bring me back there because they're processing the referral paperwork. You're going to be in the waiting area. She's going to walk in. And whatever happens, happens."

"You planned this." Alex didn't deny it. Demian stood up. He walked to the window and looked through the broken blinds at the parking lot. His back was to her. She could see the tension in his shoulders, the way he was holding himself like a man standing at an edge. "The donuts," he said.

"What?"

"I came here holding donuts. To a police station."

"So, eat one."

He almost laughed. It came out as air escaping from a place that had been sealed too long. Mulvaney appeared in the doorway again. "Mr. Ochoa, I'm going to need you to wait out front while we process the paperwork. Alex, you'll stay here."

Demian looked at her. One last look — the kind a person gives you when they know you've pushed them off a cliff and they haven't decided whether to be grateful or furious. He picked up the donuts and walked out.

The waiting area was a row of plastic chairs bolted to the floor, a water cooler with no cups, and a bulletin board covered in flyers for neighborhood watch programs and a lost cat named Sprinkles. Demian sat in the third chair from the left. He put the bakery bag on the chair beside him. He folded his hands in his lap.

Alex couldn't see him from the room where they'd put her, but she could picture it — Demian sitting very still, the way he sat when he was thinking, the way she'd seen him sit on the park bench when he was working through something that didn't have an answer. He'd be running through everything he'd ever wanted to say to Jordan Lowe. Every version of the apology. Every explanation. And he'd be discarding all of them because none of them were enough, and he knew it, and the knowing was the thing that made him decent.

Six minutes later, the front door opened. Alex heard it — the heavy door, the rush of outside air, then footsteps. Quick. Purposeful. The footsteps of a woman who'd gotten a phone call from a kid in trouble and had driven here without stopping to think about what she was walking into. Jordan's voice at the desk. "I'm here for Alex Kelly. She called me." The desk officer murmured a response. "I'm — she's not my daughter, she's — I'm a family friend. She called me because her mother is at work." More murmuring. Jordan's voice again, tighter: "Can I just see her, please? She's a young girl and she's alone."

Then silence. The silence of a woman turning around in a waiting area and seeing someone she didn't expect. Alex pressed her ear closer to the wall. She couldn't hear words anymore, just the quality of the quiet. A loaded quiet. A quiet that was deciding what to become.

Then Jordan's voice. Not to the desk. Not to Mulvaney. To Demian. "What are you doing here?"

And Demian's voice, barely audible: "She called me too."

Alex waited. She sat in the hard chair in the fluorescent room and picked at the table edge and waited. She couldn't see them and could only hear fragments — voices that rose and fell like a radio drifting in and out of signal.

Jordan: "—of course she did. She's — God, that girl—" Something from Demian. Too low to catch.

Jordan, louder: "No. No. I'm not — I can't—"

She was pacing. Alex could hear it — the shoes on the linoleum, back and forth, the rhythm of a woman who couldn't hold still because holding still meant having the conversation and she wasn't ready to have the conversation.

Demian again, still too low.

Then Jordan, and her voice was different now — stripped, the composure cracking: "You don't get to just — you can't just be sitting here when I—"

She stopped. Started again. "Do you know what that picture—" Stopped.

Alex closed her eyes. She could hear Jordan trying to find the sentence. Trying to grab the words that would tell this man what he'd done to her, and the words kept dissolving because you can't express something that lives in your body, not your brain. The rage wasn't the kind that came with speeches. It was the kind that came with shaking hands and a throat that closed and eyes that burned and a sentence that started four different times and finished none of them.

"I see it every—" Jordan said. A long pause. "Every time I close my eyes, I see—" Nothing until, very quietly, almost a whisper: "That's my son. That's my son in that picture."

Demian said something. One sentence. Alex pressed harder against the wall but couldn't make it out. Whatever it was, it was short, and it wasn't an explanation or a defense. It sounded like — she wasn't sure. Something small. Something that fit in two or three words.

Jordan again: "I can't do this right now. I came here for Alex. I came here because she called me and I— "

Her voice broke. Not dramatically, just the fractured line in a voice that had been held together by will and counting and the mechanical determination to get through one more hour, one more day, one more conversation without falling apart. The fracture opened and closed in the space of a breath.

"I can't do this here," Jordan said. Steadier now. The crack sealed. "Not here. Not like this." Footsteps. The front door opened. The rush of air. The door closed. Alex sat in the chair and breathed.

Mulvaney came back seven minutes later. "Your aunt left," he said. "She's not really my aunt."

He looked at her. He'd stopped being surprised. "I heard. And that's not your dad, is it?"

"No."

A beat. Mulvaney's face did something Alex hadn't seen on a cop before — not anger or judgment, just the exhaustion of a man who'd been outmaneuvered by someone less than half his age and wasn't sure whether to admire it or write it up. "This kid," he said again. To himself this time. "What's your mom's number? I'll call her."

Alex willingly gave it to him. She could hear him call her from the sergeant's desk in the front room. Hanging up, he said, "She's on her way," as he passed by her room.

She called out, "Sergeant Mulvaney?"

He stopped and leaned back into the doorway. "What?"

"Can you ask Mr. Ochoa to go? I don't want my mom to see him here. And when my mom gets here, could you not tell her about the dad thing? Or the aunt?"

"Why?"

"Because she's going to be upset enough. About the school thing. And if she finds out I gave a fake name for my father and called someone else to come get me, it's going to be — it's going to be really bad."

Mulvaney studied her. Whatever he saw — and he'd been reading faces for eighteen years — made him pull out the chair across from her and sit down. "You want to tell me what's actually going on?"

Alex looked at his tired eyes and his duty belt and his coffee-stained tie clip. He was the closest thing to a neutral party she'd seen in months. "I'm trying to help people," she said.

"By being a truant?"

"By getting them in the same room." He waited. "The man out there — the one I called dad — he took a photograph. After the Chestnut Street bombing. The one in the papers of the firefighter carrying the kid. I'm the other kid standing next to him," she said as she attempted to recreate the embarrassingly anguished expression she had that day.

Mulvaney's face changed. Not a lot. A tightening around the eyes, the slight backward pull of recognition.

"The woman who left — the one I called my aunt. She's the mother of the kid the fireman held. The one who died. They needed to meet," Alex said. "And they never would have done it on their own. So I did it for them."

Mulvaney leaned back. He rubbed his face with both hands. "That's—" He stopped.

Rubbed his face again. "I'm not going to say what I think about that because you're underage and I'm an officer of the law. But I'm going to tell you something, and I want you to hear it."

"Okay."

"You can't run people's lives. I know you think you can, because you're smart — you're clearly very smart — but you can't engineer people's feelings. You can put them in a room. You can't make them be okay."

"I know that."

"Do you?" he said aiming his thumb toward the waiting room. "Because that didn't go so well."

Alex picked at the table. The laminate was almost gone in the spot she'd been working on.

"What's your name?" Mulvaney asked. "Your real full name."

"Alexandra Rose Kelly."

"Alexandra Rose Kelly. Were you actually in that bombing?"

She pulled back her hair and showed him the scar — the long seam that ran from behind her left ear to the base of her skull, where they'd put the plate in. The hair had grown back over most of it, but the ridge was there, hard and raised under her fingers.

Mulvaney looked at it. He didn't touch it. "My mom doesn't know about any of this," Alex said. "Not about the man, not about the woman. She doesn't know I was ditching school — she'll learn that when she gets here. But the rest of it, the photograph, the people I've been— She doesn't know."

"And you'd like to keep it that way."

"For now. Yeah."

He stood up. Pushed the chair back in. "I'll keep the contact names out of the report. Parent notification only. But I meant what I said — you can't do this. You're thirteen."

"Fourteen in March."

"Thirteen." He picked up the folder. "Your mother's going to be here in about ten minutes. I'd use that time to think about what you're going to say."

He left. Alex sat in the quiet room and thought about what she was going to say. She thought about her mother's face when she walked through the door — not the anger, which would come later, but the first expression, the one before her mother had time to arrange her features. The raw one. The one that would tell Alex exactly how much damage she'd done.

Seven months of lies. One hundred and twenty-five mornings of kissing her mother goodbye and walking to a bus stop she never took a bus from. Forty-seven days of sitting in libraries across the city while her mother went to work, believing her daughter was in Algebra, English, and Gym class.

One hundred and twenty-five performances so convincing that the school had stopped calling after the third forged parent note — Alex had gotten good at her mother's handwriting, good at the clipped, no-nonsense tone her mother used in written communication, good at the misspellings her mother always made because she'd never been a strong speller and Alex loved her for it, loved the way she wrote *definately* and *occassion* and *sincerly*, and Alex had replicated those misspellings in every forged note because that was the kind of detail that made a lie hold.

And she'd done all of it — the libraries, the branches, the twenty-three different locations she'd rotated through so no single librarian would get suspicious — she'd done it for reasons she could never explain to her mother. Because she needed to read. Because reading was the only thing that made the noise in her head go quiet after the bombing. Because the plate in her skull hummed sometimes, a low vibration that felt like a radio tuned to a frequency just below hearing, and books were the only thing that tuned it out. Because she'd been so afraid of falling behind that she'd put herself so far ahead that school became unbearable — sitting in a seventh-grade classroom learning things she'd already devoured in a library three weeks ago, watching the clock count down minutes she could have spent reading.

The libraries were the one place her brain worked. The one place she felt like herself. The one place the plate stopped humming. But her mother wouldn't hear that. Her mother would hear *my daughter lied to me for seven months.* Alex stared at the door.

Her mother arrived in her work clothes — the blue polo with the dry cleaner's logo, khakis with a crease ironed in, her name tag still clipped to her collar. DONNA. As if anyone needed to be told. She came through the front entrance and Alex heard her from the back room — heard the door, heard the quick words to the desk officer, heard the voice that was trying very hard to sound calm and failing. "I'm Donna Kelly. I got a call about my daughter." Murmuring. "Where is she?"

Mulvaney's voice, even and practiced: "Ms. Kelly, I need to go over some paperwork with you first."

"I want to see my daughter."

"You will. But there are some things you need to understand about the situation."

Alex listened to Mulvaney walk her mother through it. The truancy referral. The forty-seven absences. The forged notes. The library circuit. He was kind about it — kinder than he needed to be — but he was thorough. He laid it all out, and Alex sat in the back room and listened to the silence between each piece of information, the silence of her mother absorbing blow after blow after blow.

Then her mother's voice, and it was the voice Alex had been afraid of. Bewildered. Not angry yet. Just bewildered. A woman standing in the wreckage of something she thought was solid, trying to understand how the foundation had been rotten the whole time without her noticing. "Seven months? She hasn't been to school in seven months?"

"One hundred and twenty-five unexcused absences, Ma'am."

"I drove her — I watched her walk in the school's door—"

"We see this sometimes. The student enters the building and exits through another door. Or walks to school but never enters. We called the school. There were forged notes, Ms. Kelly. In your handwriting."

Silence. "In my—"

"Your daughter is a very intelligent young lady. I don't say that lightly."

Another silence. Longer. The silence of a mother replaying seven months of mornings — the breakfast, the backpack, the goodbye kiss, the have a good day, sweetheart — and rewriting every single one of them. Every morning a lie. Every kiss a performance. Every goodbye the curtain going up on a show she didn't know she was watching.

"Can I see her now?" Her mother's voice was thin. Not loud. Thin. Like something stretched until you could see light through it. Mulvaney brought her back. The door opened, and her mother was there. She stood in the doorway and looked at Alex, and Alex looked back, and the first expression — the one before her mother had time to arrange her features — was exactly what Alex had been afraid of. Not anger. Not disappointment. Those would come. Hurt. Pure, uncut, bottomless hurt. The hurt of a woman who had fought to keep this kid alive — who had sat by a hospital bed for six weeks, who had learned to change surgical dressings, who had held Alex's hand through the nightmares, who had worked double shifts to pay the medical bills the insurance didn't cover, who had put vodka in a cabinet because she was trying, she was trying — and who had just learned that her daughter had looked her in the eyes every morning for seven months and lied.

"Mom."

Donna walked to the chair across from her and sat down. She put her purse on the table. She folded her hands. Her fingers were trembling. "Forty-seven days?" Donna asked.

"Yes."

"You weren't going to school."

"No."

"For seven months?"

"Yes."

"And you — you wrote notes. In my handwriting."

Alex nodded. Donna's face was working — the muscles around her jaw, her eyes, the tendons in her neck. She was trying to hold it together the way people try to hold together in institutional settings, in rooms with fluorescent lights and police officers on the other side of a door. She was trying to be the parent. The adult. The one who handles things.

"Where were you going?" she asked.

"Libraries."

"Libraries."

"Different ones. All over the city."

Donna pressed her hands flat on the table. She stared at them. At the dry skin, the chapped knuckles, the nails she kept short for work. Her mother's hands shook against the table and something Alex hadn't let herself feel during the seven months of forged notes and rotated library branches and perfect performances broke through. Shame. "I'm sorry," Alex said.

"Don't." Her mother held up one hand. "Don't say sorry yet. I'm not — I can't—" She pressed both hands against her eyes. Drew a breath. Let it out. Drew another one.

"Were you safe?" she asked, from behind her hands.

"Yes."

"You weren't — nobody—"

"No. I was reading. I was just reading. In libraries. I kept up with my studies. Just didn't turn anything in."

Donna took her hands away from her eyes. They were red but dry. She looked at Alex with the focus of someone who'd been jolted fully awake after months of sleepwalking — and Alex understood, in that look, that the vodka in the cabinet and the double shifts and the exhaustion that hung on her mother like a second skin had made her blind. Not stupid. Not careless. Blind. The bombing hadn't just cracked Alex's skull. It had cracked everything. It had cracked her mother. And the cracks were the places where things slipped through — forged notes, faked mornings, a daughter who walked out the door every day and disappeared.

"I need you to tell me everything," her mother said. "Right now. Not just the school. Everything."

Alex looked at her mother. At the blue polo and the name tag and the trembling hands and the red eyes. At the woman who'd held her in a hospital bed and whispered you're going to be okay, baby, I promise, while surgeons put a metal plate in her daughter's skull.

She thought about Demian, leaving, probably still holding those donuts. She thought about Jordan, driving somewhere with both hands on the wheel, counting something. She thought about the webs she'd spun — the careful, intricate architecture of secrets and half-truths and strategic omissions that had allowed her to move through the world like a chess piece with no square, touching everyone's board, belonging to no one's game.

"Everything?" Alex asked.

"Everything."

So, Alex told her. Not everything. Not about Demian or Jordan or the photograph or the apartment or the mission she'd given herself to put broken people in rooms together. But she told her about the libraries. About the reading. About the headaches and the humming and the terror that her brain wasn't the same brain anymore. About sitting in a seventh-grade classroom and feeling like she was underwater, watching the other kids through glass, unable to make the distance between herself and normal shrink no matter how hard she tried. About the first day she'd walked into the Millbrook branch instead of school and sat down with a book and felt, for the first time since the bombing, like the noise stopped.

Her mother listened. She didn't interrupt. Her hands flat on the table, her jaw tight, her eyes red. She listened like a woman learning that her daughter had built an entire architecture of deception right in front of her, and she'd mistaken it for normalcy.

When Alex finished, her mother was quiet for a long time. Then she said, "We're going home. And tomorrow, you're going back to school. And we're going to talk about this — really talk about it. Not tonight. Tonight, I can't." She stood up.

"Mom?" Her mother stopped at the door. She didn't turn around. "I love you," Alex said.

Donna's shoulders moved. One small tremor. Then she straightened, opened the door, and walked out to sign whatever needed signing. Alex sat in the chair. The fluorescent light buzzed. The poster peeled. The spot on the table where the laminate had been was rough under her fingers, the bare particleboard exposed, the surface stripped down to what was underneath.

She picked up the bakery bag Demian had left on the bench. Inside: two glazed donuts, slightly crushed. She ate one. It was good. Sweet and heavy and still a little warm.

She ate the other one too.

25

The rain had been falling since morning. Rain that didn't build or fade but simply was, steady and gray, turning the street into a mirror and the gutters into rivers and the windows into something Jordan couldn't stop watching. She'd been standing at the kitchen window for twenty minutes, her coffee going cold on the counter, counting the drops that ran down the glass. Not all of them. She'd given up on all of them. Just the ones that started at the top left corner — counting how long each one took to reach the bottom, measuring the variance, looking for a pattern in something that had no pattern.

It was Tuesday. He was late. He was never late. In seven months of Tuesdays, Ronny Martinez had pulled into her driveway at two o'clock with a predictability that bordered on compulsive — two o'clock, never five after, never ten till, as if the precision of his arrival was the one thing about this arrangement he could control. Jordan had come to depend on that precision. She set her internal clock by it. At one-thirty, she cleaned the kitchen. At one-forty-five, she started the coffee. At one-fifty, she checked her reflection in the microwave door — a ritual she performed without acknowledging it, like crossing yourself when entering a church, whether you believe or not. It was two-seventeen.

She picked up her phone. No messages. No missed calls. She put it down. Picked it up again. Put it down. Her thumb hovered over his name in her contacts — R. MARTINEZ — and didn't press it, because calling would mean asking, and asking would mean admitting that seventeen minutes of absence had opened a hole in her afternoon that she could feel in her sternum.

At two-twenty-three, the truck pulled up. But it didn't pull into the driveway. It stopped at the curb. Engine running. Wipers going. Jordan stood at the window — the dark shape of his truck through the rain, the headlights cutting two blurred lines through the downpour. He didn't get out. He didn't turn the engine off.

The cold arrived before she understood what it meant — in her sternum, then her hands. She knew. She didn't know what she knew, but she knew something, like knowing the weather is turning before the sky changes — a pressure shift, a charge, the animal part of your brain registering a signal your conscious mind hasn't processed yet. As his truck idled at the curb, the cold thing in her chest spread.

Her phone buzzed. Can you come out? Four words. No greeting. No, hey or sorry I'm late.

Four words with a period at the end, and Ronny didn't use periods in texts — he was a comma man, everything running together, thoughts chasing each other the way they did in his head. The period was a wall. The period was the thing that told her.

She put on her shoes. She didn't put on a jacket. She walked to the door and opened it and the rain hit her face. An almost gentle kind of rain that didn't feel like punishment — and she ran across the yard and pulled open the passenger door and climbed in.

The truck smelled like him. Soap and detergent and something under it that was just his skin. The heater was on. The radio was off. The wipers slapped a rhythm she would count later, lying in bed — one, two, one, two — but not now. Now she was looking at his profile, at his hands on the steering wheel, at the knuckles white and the jaw tight and the eyes fixed on nothing, and the cold thing in her chest had a name now and the name was last.

"What's wrong?" she asked. Quietly, like how you speak in hospitals, or in churches, in cars, where something is ending. He didn't answer. She waited. The rain fell. The wipers moved. She could hear his breathing — shallow, controlled, the breathing of a man holding himself together the way you hold a cracked glass, carefully, both hands, knowing any shift could be the one that breaks it. "What is it?" she asked.

He inhaled. His chest rose and fell and his hands stayed on the wheel and he stared through the windshield at the rain and the street and the blurred shapes of mailboxes and parked cars and all the ordinary things that didn't know what was happening inside this truck. "I have to stop coming here," he said.

There it was. The sentence she'd been carrying in the back of her mind for months — the sentence she'd rehearsed receiving, the sentence she'd told herself she was prepared for, the sentence she'd built a wall against so it wouldn't knock her down. And it knocked her down anyway. It went through the wall like the wall was made of paper.

She looked at her hands. They were wet from the rain, folded in her lap, and she could see the tendons and the knuckles and the bones under the skin, and she thought about his hands, the ones on the steering wheel, the ones she'd held every Tuesday for seven months, the ones she'd pressed against her face and kissed and needed and built her week around, and the distance between her hands and his hands was eighteen inches and it might as well have been a canyon.

"Okay," she said. One word. She was proud of it. One clean word that didn't shake, didn't crack, didn't betray the thing that was happening inside her, which was something like a building coming down — not an explosion, not the sharp violence of sudden destruction, but the slow, groaning collapse of a structure that had been compromised from the start, that had never been designed to hold what she'd loaded onto it. "Something happen?" she asked. Neutral. Careful. The voice of a woman conducting an interview about her own demolition.

"It's Jeannette."

Of course it was. Of course it was Jeannette, whose name Jordan had heard a hundred times in this truck and at her kitchen table and in the pauses between conversations, Jeannette who existed in every room Jordan had ever been in with Ronny because that was what a marriage was — a presence that didn't require the person to be physically there, an invisible third body that sat between them at every meal and lay between them in every bed and stood between them in every silence. "I'm going to lose her," Ronny said. "If I don't stop."

Raindrops hit the windshield. The wipers cleared them and they came back. Cleared, came back. She started counting the way her brain always counted, the automatic gear that clicked in when the rest of her was too overwhelmed to function.

"She doesn't know," Ronny said. "She hasn't said anything. But she—" He stopped. His hands came off the steering wheel and fell into his lap. The gesture was strange — Ronny's hands were always doing something, gripping, holding, reaching — and seeing them just lying there, surrendered, was worse than anything he'd said so far. "She looks at me sometimes. When she thinks I'm not paying attention. She looks at me and I can see her trying to figure out what's different. What changed. And I can't—" He pressed his thumb and forefinger against his eyes.

Pinched the bridge of his nose. "I love her," he said. "I need you to know that this isn't — I love her."

"I know you do," Jordan said. And she did. She'd always known it. That was the strange, terrible mercy of the whole arrangement — she'd never doubted his love for Jeannette, had never needed to be the one he loved more, had never competed with a woman she'd never met for a prize she didn't want. What she'd wanted from Ronny Martinez was much simpler and much worse than love. She'd wanted his hands. She'd wanted the warmth. She'd wanted two hours on Tuesday when the silence stopped and the counting paused and she existed as something other than the mother of a dead boy in an empty house. "It doesn't bother me that you love her," Jordan said. "You should love her."

Ronny looked at her. She could feel the weight of his gaze but couldn't meet it — if she met it, the one clean word and the neutral voice and the careful composure would go, and she'd be the woman in the bedroom again, the woman who'd said please, and she couldn't be that woman in this truck on this afternoon because that woman would beg him to stay and she would not beg. "Jordan—"

"Don't," she said. Not harsh. Soft, even. But final. "Don't say whatever you're about to say. I know what this is. I've known what it was from the beginning."

The rain hit the roof. The heater hummed. In the silence, she could hear her own pulse — could actually hear it, the blood moving through her, a sound she'd become aware of during the long nights after Mikey, the nights when the house was so quiet that her own body became audible, an unwelcome companion that wouldn't shut up. "If this goes on," Ronny said, "we're going to—"

"I know."

"It's already—"

"I know."

He exhaled. She could feel the breath — could feel the air move between them, warm, intimate even now, even in the middle of this. That was the cruelty of it. The intimacy didn't stop because the relationship was stopping. The closeness didn't switch off. He was sitting eighteen inches away and she could smell him and hear him breathe and feel the warmth coming off his body and in a few minutes he was going to drive away and she was going to walk back into that house and close the door and stand in the kitchen where his coffee mug still sat in the drying rack — she hadn't moved it, she washed it and set it out every Tuesday morning, ready — and the aloneness would come back. Not gradually or gently. All at once, the way it had come back every Tuesday at four o'clock when he left, except this time it would come and stay.

"All right," she said. She put her hand on the door handle. "I should get back."

His hand shot out and caught her arm. She looked at it. His hand on her forearm. The grip. The warmth through the wet fabric of her sleeve. She looked at his hand on her arm and memorized it. The position of his fingers, the pressure, his thumb pressed against the inside of her wrist where the pulse was. She could feel her heartbeat under his thumb, and she knew he could feel it too.

"Jordan." His voice was rough. "I'm sorry."

"Don't be." She turned back to him and what she saw on his face nearly broke the composure she'd been holding like a plate balanced on a fingertip. He was crying. Not the way men cry in movies — not the single noble tear, not the restrained grimace. He was crying the way men cry when they don't know how to cry — his face working, his jaw flexing, his eyes wet and bewildered, like a man caught in weather he hadn't seen coming.

She hadn't seen him cry before. Not once. Not when he'd told her about the bombing, not when he'd held her in the bedroom, not when she'd pressed his hands to her face and felt them tremble. He was the steady one. The one whose hands didn't shake. And now the hands were shaking. "I'll be okay," she said. The lie came out smooth. She'd been lying about being okay for almost a year, and that muscle was strong.

"Maybe I could still come by," he said. "Or we could meet somewhere. For coffee. Just coffee."

The *'just'* cracked something. *Just* coffee. As if they could subtract the bedroom and the hallway and the Tuesday afternoons and go back to being two people who drank coffee and talked about their kids. As if the shape they'd made together could be unmade and reformed into something smaller, something innocent, something a wife wouldn't need to worry about.

"Maybe," she said. Because she couldn't say no — not yet, not in this truck, not while his hand was on her arm and his thumb was on her pulse and the rain was making the world outside soft and blurred and forgiving. "This is for the best," she said. She didn't know who she was talking to. "We should have never—"

"People meet for a reason," he said. It landed. The sentence landed in her chest the way his hands landed on her cheeks — warm, direct, undeniable. People meet for a reason. He believed that. She could hear it in his voice, the conviction underneath the tears, the voice of a man who went to Mass every Sunday and who sounded, even now, like he meant every word of it. He believed their meeting had meaning. That the bombing and the photograph and the hospital and the firehouse and the kitchen table and the hallway and the bedroom had all been part of something larger than two broken people using each other to survive.

She wanted to believe it too.

She took his hand from her arm. Held it. Turned it palm-up and looked at it — the calluses, the scars, the broad fingers and the thick wrist, the hand that had pulled her son from rubble, the hand that had held her face, the hand that was the center of everything. She pressed it against her cheek. Closed her eyes.

One last time. She let herself have this one last time. The warmth of his palm against her skin. The roughness. The size of it, how it covered her cheek from jaw to temple. She breathed in and the smell of him was there — soap, skin, rain —

and she held the breath, held the hand, held the moment, and behind her closed eyes she counted.

One. Two. Three. Four. Five. She let go. "I'll see you," she said. She opened the door.

The rain hit her face. She ran. The front door. The hallway. The kitchen. She stood at the counter, both hands flat on the surface, her head down, water dripping from her hair onto the countertop. She didn't move. She listened to the truck at the curb. The engine idling. He wasn't leaving. He was sitting there the way he always sat there — four minutes in the cab, gathering himself. She wondered what he was gathering himself for this time. There was no visit ahead of him. Just a curb to pull away from.

The engine note changed. The truck moved. She listened to it go. Down the street, past the Hendersons', past the stop sign where he always paused too long, past the corner, and then it was gone. The sound faded the way all sounds faded in this house — absorbed by the walls, the carpet, the heavy silence that lived in every room like a permanent resident.

Jordan stood at the counter. The water from her hair dripped onto the surface and the drops formed and merged and ran toward the edge. She counted them. One. Two. Three. Four. Five. One. Two. Three. Four. Five.

His coffee mug sat in the drying rack. The white one she'd set out this morning. She picked it up and held it and it was dry and cold and empty and nothing like his hands, nothing at all like his hands. She put it back.

She walked to the hallway. The bedroom door was open. The bed was made — she'd made it this morning, the way she made it every Tuesday morning, the ritual of preparation, the smoothing of sheets and the fluffing of pillows for a visit that included more than coffee and had for weeks now. The bed was made and the pillows were fluffed and the room smelled like nothing because she'd opened the windows last week to air it out after his last visit and the rain had been coming in all morning and she hadn't closed them.

She closed them.

She sat on the edge of the bed. The comforter was damp from the rain. She put her hands in her lap. Her own hands. Small and cold and wet and useless. She looked at them the way she'd looked at his — studying the knuckles, the tendons, the lines in the palms — and they were just hands. Just her hands. Hands that couldn't do what his hands did. Hands that couldn't make the silence stop or the ache ease or the house feel like anything other than a place where she waited for something that was never coming back. Mikey had been the first thing that was never coming back. Nate had been the second. Now Ronny.

She pressed her own palms against her face. Against her cheeks, her temples, the same places where his hands went. She pressed hard, trying to feel what she felt when he did it — the warmth, the connection, the aliveness. But her hands were cold and wet and they smelled like rain, not soap, and the feeling wasn't there. The feeling lived in his hands, not hers. She'd outsourced it. She'd given the most essential part of her survival to another person's body and now that body was driving away in a truck and she was sitting on a damp bed with her own insufficient hands pressed against her own wet face.

The counting started. She didn't start it. It started itself, the way a heart beats — automatic, involuntary, the metronome that had been ticking inside her since the day Mikey died. One. Two. Three. Four. Five.

The rain fell. The house was quiet. Somewhere down the street, a dog barked. In forty-five minutes, Emily would be home from school, and Jordan would need to be in the kitchen, and the coffee mug would need to be put away — not in the drying rack, but in the cabinet, with the other mugs, where it belonged — and her hair would need to be dry and her face would need to be composed and the bed would need to be made again, properly this time, with dry sheets, and there would need to be a snack on the counter and a question about homework and the performance of a mother who was fine, who was managing, who was not sitting on a damp bed in an empty house counting raindrops because the man whose hands she needed had just driven away for the last time.

She had forty-five minutes. She used them.

26

The courtyard of Alex's apartment complex smelled like hot concrete and someone's leftover cooking oil. Demian counted the doors as he walked—101, 102—his footsteps too loud against the tile, the way footsteps always are when you're trying to belong somewhere you don't.

He knocked on 103. The security door rattled in its frame, and behind it the main door opened to reveal a short man with a gut that preceded him like a declaration. He had the look of someone who'd been interrupted from something he hadn't been doing.

"I'm Demian Ochoa. For the apartment."

"Two-ten?"

"Yes."

"Dale." He turned without offering his hand, grabbed a ring of keys from the kitchen counter—at least thirty of them, all unmarked, and Demian wondered how the man ever found the right one. "Follow me."

They climbed the exterior stairs in silence that wasn't quite comfortable. Halfway up, Dale spoke without turning around. "You're that guy I saw you with Alex the other day."

"Yes."

"Reporter?"

"Photojournalist. I have an assignment here in town."

"So, get a hotel."

"It's a year-long assignment."

Dale stopped at the top of the stairs and turned, using the high ground to look down on him. He had small eyes set deep in a weathered face, and they were doing something more than seeing. They were measuring.

"Alex is a good kid," Dale said. Not a statement. A warning. "She went through a lot with that bombing."

"I know."

"Don't make it worse."

"I won't."

"Because we've had enough of you people around here. The cameras, the microphones. All of it." He jabbed a thick finger toward Demian's chest without quite touching it. "I won't rent to you if that's what this is."

"It's not."

Dale held his gaze for another beat, then turned and continued down the walkway. Over his shoulder, he said, quieter now, "I remember carrying her groceries up these stairs when she came home from the hospital. Fourteen years old, bandaged up like something out of a war zone."

They stopped at 210. Dale worked through his keys with the patience of a man who'd done this a thousand times. "You know who lived here before?"

"Alex told me."

"Chrissy Dawson. Sweet kid. Her and Alex were inseparable." He found the key, slid it into the lock. "Made it hell to rent this place after. Nobody wanted it. Not because of ghosts or any of that. Just—" He shook his head. "People don't want to sleep where grief lived. You know what I mean."

"I do."

The door swung open to bare walls and clean carpet that still held the track marks of a vacuum. Two bedrooms, one bath. A home that looked like it had been scrubbed of its history. "Simple. Clean. Wouldn't a single bedroom suit you better? Cheaper."

"I like the space."

"Don't have one available anyway." Dale pulled the key free from the ring with a practiced twist. "Got your Venmo, so we're set. Rent's due on the first. Three days late and I get unpleasant." He held the key out between two fingers. "Where's your stuff?"

"Still being shipped."

"Damn movers." He said it with the resigned authority of a man who'd heard the excuse before and would hear it again. Then he was gone, the door clicking shut behind him.

Demian stood alone in the empty apartment. He crossed to the living room window and looked out across the open courtyard. Door 203 sat directly opposite. Alex's apartment. He could see the edge of a curtain, a sliver of yellow light.

He was parked outside Whitehall Prep by seven, his coffee going cold in the cupholder.

Alex arrived with her mother at quarter to eight. This time Donna didn't leave her at the gate. She walked her daughter all the way to the front doors, one hand on Alex's shoulder, the other clutching her purse strap like a lifeline.

The principal met them at the entrance. She shook Donna's hand, then placed her palm on Alex's back and guided her inside with the practiced ease of an institution reclaiming what it considered its own. Donna stood on the steps for a moment after the door closed, her arms folded tight across her chest, before turning back to her car.

Demian watched all of this from behind his windshield, feeling like a man observing a life he had no right to witness. He thought about leaving. Instead, he sat there until the bell rang—a flat, institutional sound that carried across the parking lot like a verdict.

The text came as he was pulling onto Maple Street. He fished the phone from his pocket at the next red light.

Alex Kelly: Meet me at Franklin Park after school. 3:15. Ronny will be there. He read it twice. Then a third time. He set the phone on the passenger seat and stared at the traffic light until someone behind him honked.

How had she arranged this? And more importantly—why was his first instinct not relief but dread?

In the afternoon light Franklin Park looked different than Demian had remembered. The playground equipment had been repainted since the last time he'd been here—a cheerful blue that seemed to mock the gravity of what he'd come to do. He sat on one of the swings, the chain cold against his palms, the rust leaving orange dust on his skin.

He checked his watch, the one that had been his grandfather's. The crack across the crystal divided the face into two unequal halves, the way that single photograph had divided his life. The hands crept toward 3:15. A dog barked somewhere in the distance, muffled and faraway, as if the whole world existed on the other side of glass.

He spotted her first by the backpack—slung over one shoulder, listing to the left. She walked with the confidence of someone who'd learned that the worst thing that could happen already had.

"Well, well," Demian called out, steadying his voice. "Whitehall's most notorious truant returns to the fold. How's life on the straight and narrow?"

Alex dropped onto the swing beside him and let the momentum carry her. "Oh, you know. Nothing screams rebellion like being personally escorted to homeroom by the principal."

"First day?"

She kicked at the dirt. "Surreal. Like everyone got the memo about me except me. The staring I can handle. It's the whispering. All these people trying to figure out the right face to make when they see me."

"Give it a week. Someone else will do something stupid and you'll be old news."

"From your mouth to God's ears." A beat passed. The swing chains creaked in tandem, a lazy metronome.

"So," Alex said. "How'd it go with Mrs. Lowe? I tried to listen."

Demian winced. "It went about as well as a car wreck. She looked at me like I was the one who planted the bomb." He rubbed the back of his neck. "Can't say I blame her."

Alex's swing slowed. She dragged her toe through the dirt. "Not what I was hoping for."

"That makes two of us." Demian turned to her. "Speaking of things I didn't see coming—how did you get Ronny to agree to this? Last I heard, he wanted to break my jaw."

Something sparked behind Alex's eyes. "I just talked to him. That's all. Sometimes people are ready to hear things they weren't ready to hear before. When we spoke, I could see it. The photo had become this... stand-in for everything he couldn't face about that day. It was easier to hate you than to sit with what actually happened."

Demian studied her—this kid who'd been pulled from rubble and somehow come out the other side with more clarity than anyone twice her age. "You're something else, you know that?"

"Skipping school gives you a lot of time to think."

A truck pulled into the lot. A newer model with dust on the fenders. Alex looked up. "That's him." She was off the swing before Demian could respond, jogging across the grass to meet the car. He watched her greet the man who climbed out—watched the way Ronny unfolded from the driver's seat with the careful stiffness of someone who carried his tension in his shoulders.

Alex walked him over. Ronny kept his hands in his pockets, his jaw set in a way that could have been anger or nerves or both. "Ronny, this is Demian Ochoa."

Demian extended his hand. "Thanks for coming."

Ronny looked at the hand for a half-second before taking it. His grip was firm, brief. "The Pulitzer Prize winner," he said.

Demian's stomach dropped. "Ronny, if I could take it—"

"Easy. I'm messing with you." The grin softened into something more complicated. "I mean, it did mess me up. But I know now it wasn't the photo that did it."

Alex looked between them like a diplomat assessing whether the ceasefire would hold. "I'm going to walk the gardens," she said. "I haven't been here since fifth grade. You two hash it out." She turned down the gravel path without waiting for permission, and Demian understood she was giving them what they needed—space, and the absence of a witness.

They followed at a distance, walking side by side through beds of roses that were past their peak, the petals browning at the edges. For a while neither spoke. The path curved around a low stone wall covered in lichen.

"I didn't think you'd come," Demian said finally.

"Neither did I." Ronny exhaled through his nose. "But that kid—she's got a way of making you look at things you'd rather not."

"She does."

Another silence. The crunch of gravel beneath their shoes. The sweet, almost cloying scent of jasmine from somewhere Demian couldn't see.

"I want to apologize," Demian said. "I never meant for that image to cause the kind of pain it did."

Ronny didn't look at him. "Then why'd you take it?"

Demian ran a hand over his face. He owed this man the truth—the unpolished version, not the one he'd rehearsed. "I wasn't even on assignment. I was in town visiting my family. Heard the explosion from my mother's kitchen—felt it, actually, in the windows. I grabbed my camera the way you grab your keys when you leave the house. It's just what you do."

Ronny stopped walking. He turned to face Demian, and in his eyes was something raw and hard-won. "But why that moment? You could have shot any of us pulling someone out alive. Instead you got me—wrecked, on my knees, holding a child I couldn't save."

Demian shook his head slowly. "That's not how it works. Not for me, anyway. I don't choose moments. I got to the school and I started shooting—everything. The smoke, the trucks, the parents running toward the building, the firefighters running in. You shoot hundreds, sometimes thousands of frames, and you sort it out after. You don't think. You can't think. If you stop to think about what you're actually seeing, you can't do the job." He paused. A muscle worked in his jaw. "I didn't choose that image, Ronny. My editors did. Out of everything I shot that day, that's the one they wanted. And I let them have it. That's the part I can't forgive myself for—not taking the photo, but handing it over without thinking about what it would do to the people inside it."

Ronny didn't say anything for a while. They kept walking. The path looped past a bed of roses that needed deadheading, and Demian focused on that—the brown edges, the spent blooms—because it was easier than looking at the man next to him.

"You want to know something?" Ronny said. "For a long time I hated you. Oh, yeah. I'd see that photo pop up somewhere and it was like getting punched in the chest all over again. And it was easy to put that on you. On the camera. On the newspaper. On everybody except me." He picked a leaf off a low-hanging branch and turned it over in his fingers. "But the picture didn't do anything to me that wasn't already done. It just made it so I couldn't pretend otherwise." Demian started to speak, but Ronny cut him off. "Hold on. I'm not done." He dropped the leaf and shoved his hands back in his pockets. "That photo—I belong in it. I do. Because I made choices that day. Who to go to first, who to pass by. I carried a dead kid out of a building, and I knew while I was carrying him that there might have been a live one behind me. That's what I live with. Your camera didn't put that on me."

They walked a few more steps in silence. Somewhere up ahead, Alex had crouched beside a flower bed, pulling weeds that weren't hers to pull. "I'm sorry," Demian said. It came out plain and small, which was maybe how it should have come out.

"Yeah." Ronny nodded once. "I know you are." He looked at Demian—not with warmth exactly, but without the wall that had been there before. "And I think I'm done being pissed at you for it. Took me long enough."

Demian didn't trust himself to say anything else, so he just walked. Ronny walked beside him. Up ahead, Alex stood and brushed the dirt from her knees, and when she turned and saw them coming, she didn't ask how it went. She just fell into step. The three of them walked the rest of the path together, not saying much, and that was enough.

Ronny left first. A handshake with Demian that lasted a beat longer than either of them expected, a wave to Alex, and then the dust-covered car pulling out of the lot and turning south. They watched it go. "I'll walk you home," Demian said.

They went the long way, cutting through the neighborhood streets where the sidewalks buckled over old tree roots. Alex kicked a bottle cap along the concrete for half a block before losing it in the grass.

"I'm leaving," Demian said. He'd meant to find a better way into it. There wasn't one.

Alex didn't look at him. "Back to work?"

"Yeah. I've done what I can here. I can't undo any of it, and staying won't change that." "What about Jordan?" Alex's brow furrowed. "I can still fix that. Give me more time." "Leave her alone, Alex. She should be allowed to hate me. Let her. Maybe that's the one thing I can actually give her—someone to put it on." He shoved his hands in his pockets. "And I already have an assignment. I leave tomorrow."

That stopped her. "Tomorrow?"

"Tomorrow."

"Just when I finally got a partner in crime." She said it lightly, but the lightness cost her something. He could hear it.

"Where?" she asked.

"Afghanistan."

She looked at him like he'd said the moon. "Doesn't that freak you out?"

"After three wars, it's like riding a bike. That's my fuerte."

"Fuerte?"

"My strength. Like forte. Same word, different language."

She turned the word over like she was testing its weight. "Fuerte. I like that. Art is my fuerte."

"It is," he said. And meant it.

They reached the apartment complex. The courtyard was quiet, the evening light going amber on the stucco walls. Alex slowed near her door, and Demian could feel the goodbye pressing in on them like a change in air pressure.

He reached into his bag and pulled out his Leica. It was the Q2—not the one he used professionally, but the one he'd carried for years on his own time. The leather grip was worn smooth where his thumb sat. He held it out to her.

Alex stared at it. "What are you doing?"

"Take it."

"Demian, I can't take your camera."

"You can, and you're going to." He pressed it into her hands. She took it the way people take things they don't believe they deserve—carefully, like it might burn. "Art is your fuerte. So go make something with it."

Then he reached into his pocket and produced a key. Small, brass, unremarkable. He held it up between two fingers.

"What's that?"

"Apartment 210. It's yours for the year. Paid up." Alex opened her mouth. Closed it. She looked at the key, then at the camera in her hands, then up at the second-floor walkway where 210 sat dark and empty.

"Finish the closet," Demian said. "The one you and Chrissy started. Finish it, and take a photo when it's done. Put it on your wall. So you can both see it."

Alex's chin crumpled. She pressed her lips together hard and looked away, blinking fast. When she looked back, her eyes were wet but she wasn't crying. She wouldn't give him that. "Nobody's ever done anything like this for me."

"Nobody's ever done what you did for me, either."

She closed her fingers around the key. Tight. Like if she held it hard enough it would anchor everything—the camera, the apartment, the conversation in the park, all of it—into something that couldn't be taken back.

"This isn't goodbye, right?" she said. "You'll keep in touch." It wasn't a question. It was a condition.

He thought of all the people he'd photographed over the years. The faces he'd carried with him for a week, a month, then lost to the next assignment and the one after that. He'd never kept in touch with any of them. It was the unspoken rule of the work—you got close enough to see them, then you moved on. But Alex wasn't a subject. She'd never been a subject.

"I'll send you postcards," he said. "Real ones. Not emails. Something you can put on the wall next to the photo."

"And I'll send you updates on the closet. Maybe some shots with this thing." She held up the Leica. "Keep you honest."

He tore a page from the small notebook he kept in his back pocket and wrote down his email. "My email. You already have my cell. Now you can bother me anytime."

She took it, folded it in half, and slid it into her jacket. "Oh, I will."

They stood there a moment, neither of them good at this part. Then Alex stuck out her hand, straightened her back, and put on a voice like a society hostess. "It was very nice meeting you, Señor Ochoa."

He matched it. "Indeed, Señorita Kelly. Indeed."

They shook hands with the formal gravity of heads of state. Then Alex broke, pulled him into a hug that was fiercer than her frame should have allowed. The Leica pressed between them, its hard edge digging into his ribs, and Demian didn't care. He put his arms around her and held on.

"Thank you," she said into his shirt. "For everything."

"Gracias por todo," he said quietly. "For reminding me why I do this."

She let go. Stepped back. Wiped her nose with the back of her hand in a way that undid all the dignity of the handshake. Demian crossed the courtyard toward the stairs. At the bottom, he turned back. Alex was still standing by her door, the camera in one hand, the key in the other. She raised the Leica and pointed it at him.

He heard the shutter click. "You haven't seen the last of me, Ochoa!" she called out. "Not by a long shot!"

He raised a hand. Kept walking. And for the first time in longer than he could remember, the click of a shutter behind him didn't feel like taking something. It felt like being given something back.

27

Ronny sat in the driveway for eleven minutes before he turned the engine off. He knew it was eleven because the dashboard clock read 5:51 when he pulled in and 6:02 when he finally took the key out of the ignition. The station was right there—fifty feet of cracked asphalt between his truck and the bay doors, the same fifty feet he'd crossed a thousand times in twenty-three years, and his hands wouldn't let go of the steering wheel.

It was a Wednesday. He'd chosen Wednesday deliberately. Wednesdays were slow— statistically the lowest call volume of the week at Station 17. Hal had told him that once, years ago, standing at the whiteboard during a shift briefing, tapping the chart with a marker.

Wednesdays are for catching up. Ronny had filed it the way he filed everything Hal said— without knowing he was filing it, without knowing he'd need it someday as a reason to pick one day over another for the hardest thing he'd done since April.

The bay doors were up. He could see the tail end of Engine 17 and the chrome bumper of the ladder truck. The overhead fluorescents were on, that flat institutional light that turned everything the same shade of gray-white. He could hear the hum of the building from here—the compressor, the ventilation, the low electrical drone that had been the background noise of his adult life.

He got out of the truck. The limp felt bad today. Cold mornings made it worse, and this morning was cold. He crossed the parking lot with the hitch in his step that he'd stopped trying to hide.

The bay smelled the same. Diesel and rubber and the metallic tang of the trucks and something underneath all of it that was just the smell of a firehouse—decades of sweat and gear and coffee and the fearless scent of men who spent their lives running toward things other people ran from. Ronny stood inside the bay doors and breathed it in. Something in his chest expanded and contracted at the same time — a muscle remembering a motion it hadn't performed in too long.

Gabe saw him first. He was at the equipment rack, checking SCBA bottles, his massive frame bent over a regulator. He straightened, looked at Ronny, and didn't say anything for a beat until, "Well, look who it is."

"Morning, Gabe."

"You lost?"

"Probably."

Gabe grinned with the same grin he'd had for twenty years—wide and genuine. It made his face look like it was built for no other purpose. But his eyes were doing something his mouth wasn't. His eyes were checking. Measuring. Making sure this was real and not another false start.

Tom came out of the kitchen with a coffee mug in one hand and a newspaper folded under his arm. He stopped when he saw Ronny. Looked at him. Looked at Gabe. Looked back at Ronny.

"Light duty," Ronny said, before anyone could ask. "Ride the truck. Answer calls. That's what Hal said."

"Hal know you're here?"

"I called him last night."

"And?"

"He said Wednesday was good."

Tom nodded. Set the coffee down. Extended his hand. Ronny took it. The grip was firm and brief and said everything that needed saying without a single word wasted on sentiment. "Your gear's in your locker," Tom said. "Same one. Nobody touched it."

Of course nobody had touched it. That was how it worked. A firefighter's locker was his locker until he came back or didn't, and the gear inside it waited with the same patience as the men who'd stored it.

Ronny walked through the bay toward the lockers. Past the engine. Past the ladder truck. Past the tool board where the axes and halligan bars hung in their brackets, each one outlined in tape so you could see at a glance if anything was missing. Past the turnout racks where the bunker gear hung on hooks—coats and pants paired together, boots on the floor beneath them, helmets on the shelf above. Andrew's hook was empty. It had been empty since that April day. Nobody had reassigned it.

Ronny stopped at it. The hook was bare—just a metal curve bolted to the wall, a piece of adhesive tape beneath it with HARRIS written in Sharpie. The tape was yellowing at the edges. Someone had placed a small American flag pin on the shelf where Andrew's helmet used to sit. Ronny touched the pin with his finger. Cool metal. He didn't pick it up. Just touched it, like touching a headstone—not to move it or to take it, just to make contact with the fact of it.

His own locker was three down from Andrew's. He opened it. Everything was there—his turnout coat, his pants, his boots, his helmet with MARTINEZ stenciled across the back. The coat smelled like it always smelled—smoke and Nomex and the faint chemical residue of the last fire he'd worked, which was the school, which was April, which was the building. He pulled the coat off the hook and held it. Fourteen pounds. He used to put it on without thinking. Now the weight of it felt deliberate, significant, like picking up a book you'd been avoiding.

He put it on. The familiar compression across his shoulders. The stiffness of the collar against his neck. The reflective stripes catching the fluorescent light. He pulled up the bunker pants and stepped into the boots and felt the old posture return—the stance of a man wearing sixty pounds of gear, the slight forward lean, the widened base. His body remembered even when his mind resisted.

The helmet was last. He held it in both hands and looked at the shield—EN-GINE 17, the Maltese cross, the number. His number. He put it on. The weight settled onto his head and something settled inside him too—not peace, not readiness, but something closer to resignation. The particular surrender of a man who has run out of reasons not to do the thing he's been afraid of.

"Fits like you never left." Hal was standing in the bay, arms crossed, leaning against the engine the way he leaned against everything—casually, as if the support were optional. He was in his uniform, the captain's bars catching the light. His face was doing the thing it always did when something he'd been working toward finally happened—nothing. No smile, no nod, no visible satisfaction. Just the flat, steady gaze of a man who'd held a door open for fourteen months and had never once considered closing it.

"Feels weird," Ronny said.

"It'll feel weird for a while. Then it'll feel normal. Then it'll feel like the only thing that makes sense." Hal pushed off the engine. "Shift briefing in ten. You're riding the engine. Light duty means you stay outside unless I say otherwise. No interior. No roofs. You hydrant, you assist, you observe. Clear?"

"Clear."

"And Ronny."

"Yeah."

"Welcome back." He said it the way he said everything—without weight, without ceremony. But Ronny heard what was underneath it. Fourteen months of phone calls and porch conversations and a living room intervention and the same two words repeated like a prayer: the door's open. The door's open. The door's open. And now Ronny had walked through it, and Hal's welcome back meant all of it—every conversation, every silence, every patient, stubborn refusal to give up on a man who'd been giving up on himself.

"Thanks, Cap."

The first call came at 9:14. A kitchen fire on Greer Avenue—grease on the stove, smoke showing from the second floor, the neighbor's 911 call audible through the dispatch radio.

Ronny was in the jump seat before the tones finished, his hands finding the buckle and the harness and the chin strap with a muscle memory that fourteen months of absence hadn't erased. The diesel roared beneath him. The bay doors rose. The truck pulled out into the gray morning and the siren split the air. The vibration moved through his chest and his teeth and the bad knee — the diesel doing what it always did, and for a moment—one clear, uncontaminated moment—he was just a firefighter going to a fire. The moment passed, but it had been there.

The kitchen fire was small. Hal put two men inside and Ronny on the hydrant—the assignment he'd been given, the assignment Marcus had been taking voluntarily for over a year. Ronny connected the supply line, charged it, and stood at the engine panel monitoring gauges while the crew worked inside. Smoke pushed from the second-floor window in gray columns that thinned as the water found the fire. He could hear the radio chatter—Gabe calling for more line, Tom confirming the second floor was clear. Familiar language. The shorthand of men doing a job they'd done a thousand times.

Ronny stood at the panel, the smoke thinning, the gauges holding, the crew moving through the building the way crews move through buildings with purpose, with training, with the choreography of men who trusted each other with their lives. He'd been part of that choreography for twenty-three years. Standing outside it, watching it from the hydrant, felt like watching a dance through a window. He was close enough to hear the music. Not close enough to move to it.

The fire was out in twelve minutes. No injuries. The resident—a woman in her sixties, standing on the lawn in a bathrobe and slippers—thanked them four times. Ronny helped with overhaul, pulling ceiling tiles in the kitchen while the crew checked for extension. The work was physical and simple and good. His knee ached. His shoulders remembered the weight. His hands knew what to do.

On the ride back, Gabe clapped him on the shoulder from the seat behind him. Didn't say anything. Just the clap. Ronny nodded.

Marcus sat at the weight bench in the station gym when Ronny found him after lunch. He was doing curls with a focus that seemed less about the exercise and more about having somewhere to put the energy that lived inside him—the restless, contained force of a man who'd been holding something down for fourteen months with nothing but silence and routine.

Ronny sat on the bench across from him and waited. He'd learned a long time ago that Marcus talked when Marcus was ready and not a second before. Pushing him was like pushing a wall—possible in theory, pointless in practice.

Marcus finished his set. Racked the weight. Sat up and wiped his face with a towel.

Looked at Ronny. "First day back," Marcus said.

"Yeah."

"How'd the hydrant feel?"

Ronny almost smiled. "You tell me. You've been working it for a year."

Marcus held his gaze. The gym was empty—just the two of them and the hum of the fluorescent lights and the faint sound of Tom's radio playing country music in the kitchen down the hall. "I took the hydrant because I couldn't go inside," Marcus said. Flat. Direct. The voice of a man stating a fact he'd been carrying alone. "Not can't like physically couldn't. Can't like my body wouldn't let me."

"Since the school?"

"Since I found Andrew." Marcus draped the towel over his neck. "First call after the bombing was a house fire on Inglewood. Nothing special. Routine. Hal sent me in and I made it to the front door and my legs stopped. Just stopped. Like somebody hit a switch. I stood there in full gear with the line charged and I could not make my feet cross that threshold."

Ronny didn't respond. He knew what that felt like—the body overriding the mind, the animal brain slamming the brakes before the conscious brain could argue.

"Hal pulled me off interior the next day. Didn't make a thing of it. Didn't file anything. Just moved me to the hydrant and told the shift it was a rotation."

"That sounds like Hal."

"He's a good captain." A pause. "Better than I deserve."

"Don't do that."

"I'm not doing anything. I'm telling you what happened. I did get over it eventually, but…" Marcus picked up the dumbbell again, turned it over in his hands without lifting it. "You know what I see? When I close my eyes at a doorway? It's not the fire. It's not the smoke. It's Andrew's arms." Ronny's stomach tightened. "He was under the stairwell. On his stomach. And his arms were stretched out in front of him—both of them, straight out, reaching. There was a door six feet ahead of him. A fire door. If he'd gotten through it, he'd have been in the loading dock. He'd have been outside." Marcus's voice didn't waver. It was controlled, metered—the voice of a man who'd told this story to himself so many times it had worn smooth. "Six feet. I measured it later. Went back to the building before they demolished it and I measured the distance from where I found him to that door. Six feet, two inches."

Ronny sat with that. The weight of it. Six feet, two inches. The specificity of a man who needed a number the way Jordan needed her counting—a measurement to contain something that had no edges.

"I carried him out," Marcus said. "Wouldn't let anyone else touch him. Hal tried. I told him no. I carried him through the loading dock and out the back and laid him on the grass before the screams pulled me back into the building. After everything, I saw someone had covered him with a sheet. Thank God someone did that." He set the dumbbell down. "So when I stood at that door that day, I saw his arms. Reaching for a door he didn't make it to. And my legs wouldn't go any further. Counseling has helped me get over it. And Hal."

"I never told you what happened in the building," Ronny said.

"You don't have to."

"Yeah, I do. You told me yours." Marcus looked at him. Waited. Ronny told him. Not the version he'd given Jeannette—measured, controlled, shaped for a wife's ears. And not the version he'd started to give Hal on the porch—partial, guarded, one inch of a door opened and then shut. He told Marcus the whole thing. The hallway. Finding the girl pinned under debris. The boy beside her, a slab of concrete across him. The girl saying I think it moved—meaning the boy's foot, meaning maybe he was alive. Ronny looking at the boy and making a decision in a fraction of a second that had expanded to fill every hour since: he didn't check. He went to find Andrew instead. One minute. Maybe less. He came back. Lifted the slab. The boy was dead. Might have been dead the whole time. Might not have been.

"And that's the minute," Ronny said. "That's what I carry. Not Andrew dying. Not the building. The minute I walked away from a kid who might have been alive because I thought I could find my partner. And I didn't find him. And the kid was dead when I got back. And Andrew was dead under your stairwell. And I was outside getting my picture taken."

The gym held the silence the way a church holds silence—not empty but full, the air dense with something that had been released into it. Quiet for a long time, Marcus said, "You made a call."

"I made the wrong call."

"You made a call. In the dark, with no information, with a building coming down. You made a call and you've been carrying it like you had a choice you didn't have."

"I had a choice. I chose Andrew over the boy."

"The boy was dead or, at least, you thought the boy was dead. You chose to go to someone you thought was alive, your partner. That's training. That's twenty years of training telling you to find your partner. If you'd stayed with the boy and Andrew had been alive in that hallway calling for you—" Marcus stopped. Let the sentence finish itself. "You'd be carrying that instead. You'd be sitting here telling me a different version of the same story."

Ronny stared at the floor. The rubber mats. The scuff marks. The small, meaningless geography of a firehouse gym. "The girl said his foot moved," Ronny said. "The girl lying next to the boy. She was there. She said she saw it."

"Maybe she did. And maybe it was a muscle contraction. Or maybe she was a young girl pinned under rubble with a head injury and she saw what she needed to see." Marcus leaned forward, elbows on his knees. "Ronny. Andrew was under a collapsed stairwell with his arms stretched toward a door. He was trying to get out. He wasn't in that hallway. He wasn't where you went looking for him. Even if you'd spent that minute with the boy, you wouldn't have found Andrew. Andrew was already gone."

The words landed — not like a blow, but like something setting down, something that had been suspended above him for fourteen months, finally making contact with the ground. He'd heard versions of this from Jeannette. From the counselor. From his own rational mind at four in the morning. But hearing it from Marcus—from the man who'd measured six feet and two inches between Andrew's hands and the door he didn't reach—was different. Marcus wasn't guessing. Marcus had been there. Marcus had the measurements.

Marcus stood and picked up the dumbbell. "Nothing fixes it. But carrying it alone is stupid, and you've been stupid long enough."

Ronny looked up at him. Marcus was standing over him with a thirty-pound dumbbell in one hand, his face as flat and unreadable as it had been for fourteen months, except for something around the eyes—a loosening, a release, the face of a man who'd finally said the thing he'd been holding and had found that saying it didn't kill him.

"You're an asshole," Ronny said.

"Yeah." Marcus started another set of curls. "Get back to work."

The second call came at 4:47. A car accident on Broad Street—two vehicles, no entrapment, minor injuries. Ronny rode the engine and worked the scene—directing traffic with Pete while the medics assessed the drivers, then helping push one of the cars to the shoulder when the tow truck was running late. Simple work. Necessary work. Work where your hands do things that help people, and your mind can be quiet for a few minutes.

On the ride back, Ronny sat in the jump seat and watched the city slide past through the narrow window. The same storefronts. The same traffic lights. The same woman pushing a stroller on the same corner he'd watched from this same seat a hundred times. The world doing its ordinary business.

The truck pulled into the bay. The crew climbed down. Gabe headed for the kitchen. Tom started the post-call paperwork. Marcus went to the hydrant rack to repack hose, and Ronny joined him without being asked. They worked in silence, feeding the hose through the rack in practiced folds, the repetitive motion of a task they'd done together a thousand times.

Marcus didn't look at him. Didn't say anything. Just handed him the next section of hose when the first one was racked. Their hands moved in the same rhythm, the same cadence, the way partners' hands move when they've been doing the same work for years. It wasn't a conversation. It was something older than conversation—the language of men working side by side, saying everything they needed to say by showing up and doing the job.

Ronny finished the last fold. Straightened up. "Same time tomorrow?" he asked.

Marcus looked at him. And for the first time in fourteen months, something that was unmistakably a smile—small, brief, gone as fast as it arrived—crossed Marcus's face. "Yeah," he said. "Same time tomorrow."

28

It was a Wednesday. That was new — tracking what day it was, whether it hurt, and how much. Wednesdays had been the worst. The day after the day after Tuesday, when the distance from Ronny was greatest and the distance to the next Tuesday stretched out like a hallway with no end. She'd spent Wednesdays in bed. Or on the couch. Or standing at the kitchen window, counting things that didn't need counting because the counting was the only machinery still running.

Jordan sat at her kitchen table with her laptop open and a warm cup of coffee. That was new. The coffee staying warm meant she was drinking it instead of letting it go cold while she stared at the wall. Small metric. She'd take it.

The Ohio Department of Health website loaded slowly. She'd been on this page before— months ago, in the early days of scrolling job listings and feeling the recoil. She'd clicked on it, read the first paragraph about certification renewal for radiologic technologists, and closed the laptop and gone to bed. That had been a Tuesday, she remembered. The recoil had been partly about the job and partly about the fact that she'd been looking at it during Ronny's hours, as if the job search were a betrayal of the afternoon's purpose.

Ronny's hours didn't exist anymore. The afternoon was hers. All of it. Every minute from Emily's departure to Emily's return—hers to fill or waste or stare through, and for three weeks she'd done all three. But this morning she'd woken up and the laptop was on the counter where she'd left it last night, and instead of moving past it she'd opened it, and instead of scrolling she'd searched, and instead of recoiling she'd read.

The certification had lapsed. Two years. She'd need to complete a renewal course—forty hours of continuing education, available online. There was an exam. There was a fee. The fee was two hundred and fifteen dollars, which was money she didn't have and would have to ask Nate for, which was its own kind of humiliation, but smaller than the humiliation of another month on the couch watching daytime television while her daughter made the coffee.

She picked up the phone. Dialed the number on the screen. It rang. She counted the rings. One, two, three, four—

"Ohio Department of Health, credentialing services."

The counting stopped. Not because she'd decided to stop it but because the voice on the other end required a response, and responding required her to be a person instead of a counter, and for the first time in months, the person won. "Hi. I'm calling about renewing my radiologic technologist certification. It's been lapsed for two years."

"No problem. Can I get your name and license number?"

She gave them. The woman on the phone typed, asked questions, explained the process. Jordan wrote everything down on the back of an envelope—the course name, the website, the exam date, the fee. Her handwriting was steady. She noticed that too. Steady handwriting on a Wednesday afternoon.

"Is there anything else I can help you with?"

"No. Thank you."

She hung up. Looked at the envelope. Forty hours. An exam. Two hundred and fifteen dollars. Steps. Concrete, sequential, finite steps that led to a specific thing—not happiness, not healing, not any of the words the therapist had used and that Jordan had learned to distrust—but a job. A place to go. A reason to put on scrubs and drive somewhere and use her hands for something other than counting.

She'd been an X-ray technician. She'd been good at it. That skill was still in her. Lapsed, like the certification, but not gone. You don't lose the ability to see. You just stop looking. She opened the course website and registered. Name. Address. Payment—she'd call Nate tonight.

Email confirmation. The screen said *Welcome Back*, which was a generic message sent to everyone and meant nothing, and it made her eyes sting anyway.

She was still at the table when Emily came home at three-thirty. The door opened, the backpack hit the floor, the shoes came off—the sounds of her daughter entering the house, the small percussion of a life that happened every day whether Jordan participated in it or not. Emily came into the kitchen and stopped. Looked at her mother. Looked at the laptop. Looked at the envelope with the handwriting and the phone number and the course name. She didn't ask what it was. She didn't say good for you or that's great or any of the encouraging things adults said to other adults when they did something that should have been done months ago. She pulled out the chair across from Jordan and sat down. Took out her homework. Opened her textbook.

They sat at the table together. Jordan on her side with the laptop and the envelope. Emily on hers with the textbook and a pencil. The kitchen was quiet—not the heavy quiet of a house where someone was hiding, but the working quiet of two people doing things beside each other, the silence of a shared space that was being used instead of endured.

Jordan counted the minutes. She couldn't help it. One, two, three, four, five. But the counting felt different today—less like gripping and more like breathing. Less like a cage and more like a rhythm. The metronome was still ticking. It would always tick. Only today it was keeping time for something instead of just keeping time. Emily looked up from her homework. "Mom?"

"Yeah?"

"You look different today."

Jordan almost asked how. Almost asked what Emily saw that was different about a woman sitting at a kitchen table with a laptop. But she didn't, because she knew. She looked different because she was sitting up. Because the coffee was warm. Because the laptop was open to something that wasn't daytime television. Because for the first time in a long time, she was facing the window instead of facing the wall. "Good different or bad different?" Jordan asked.

Emily studied her for a moment. The same assessing look she'd had since she was small—the look of a girl who'd learned early that the adults around her were unreliable and that the only way to know if things were okay was to check for herself. "Good different," Emily said and went back to her homework.

Jordan looked at her daughter. This girl who'd lost her brother and her father and most of her mother and had kept showing up anyway—making coffee, doing homework, sleeping in Mikey's bed in Spider-Man socks that were too small for her feet. This girl who'd told her to get out of the house. Who'd been watching her, waiting, the way you watch a sick person and wait for the fever to break.

The fever hadn't broken. Jordan wasn't sure it ever would. But she'd opened a laptop and made a phone call and written something down, and her daughter had noticed, and the noticing was enough.

Five, five, five, five.

She turned back to the screen and kept going.

The fence had needed painting since before the bombing. Ronny had stared at it from the back porch a hundred times—during Hal's beer that night in January, during the long months of disability, during the mornings when he'd sat outside with his coffee and watched the yard not change while everything inside him did. The paint was peeling in long strips, the wood graying underneath, the whole thing leaning slightly to the left where a post had rotted at the base. It was the type of job that took a Saturday afternoon and a trip to the hardware store. He'd put it off for fourteen months.

He started at the far corner, working the brush into the grain, the paint going on thick and white over the gray. The work was simple and physical and used your hands and freed your mind, which was dangerous for a man whose mind went to the places Ronny's went, but also necessary, because the alternative was never using his hands for anything, and he'd spent enough months doing that.

Danny's old football was still in the bushes near the patio. Ronny had noticed it again this morning and almost picked it up, then didn't. It had been there since before the intervention. It was becoming part of the yard the way the peeling fence had been part of the yard—something you stopped seeing because seeing it meant doing something about it. He'd get to it. After the fence.

The paint can sat on the grass beside him, its lid pried off, the white surface catching the late afternoon light. He dipped the brush. Pulled a long stroke. Another. The fence took the paint like something thirsty, the wood drinking it in, the coverage uneven on the first coat. He'd need two coats. Maybe three on the worst sections. The post that had rotted would need replacing entirely, but that was a different Saturday.

The back door opened. Jeannette came out carrying two beers, the bottles sweating in the warm air. She handed him one without comment and sat on the porch step and watched him work.

He kept painting. She kept watching. The silence between them had changed in the weeks since he'd gone back to the station. It used to be the silence of two people in separate rooms who happened to share a house. Now it was something else—thinner, more careful, the silence of people who were choosing not to say the thing they were both thinking. A negotiated silence. A silence with a shape.

"Looks good," Jeannette said.

"First coat. It'll need another."

"Still. It looks good. Needed doing."

"Yeah. It did."

She took a sip of her beer. He pulled another stroke along the fence. A bird landed on the railing three sections down and watched him with its head tilted, then flew off when the brush got too close.

"A lot of things needed doing," Jeannette said. Ronny's brush stopped. He didn't turn around.

He stood with the wet brush in his hand and the fence in front of him and his wife behind him and the sentence in the middle, and he felt its weight. Present. Just present. A door that she was leaving open without walking through it. An invitation to say something or not say something, with no consequence either way except the truth of it hanging there, acknowledged by both of them.

"Yeah," he said. "They did." He dipped the brush. Kept painting. Jeannette drank her beer. The yard was quiet except for the brush against the wood and the distant sound of Sofia's music coming through her bedroom window. Danny was at practice. The dog next door was, for once, not barking.

Jeannette hadn't asked. She hadn't said Jordan's name or the word affair or any of the things a wife says when she's decided to confront the thing her husband did. She hadn't asked because asking would require an answer, and the answer would require a conversation, and the conversation would require them to decide what to do with it. And Jeannette, who had held this family together for fourteen months with a steadiness that bordered on superhuman, had apparently decided that the family was more important than the conversation. That the marriage could survive the knowing as long as the knowing stayed in the silence where they'd both agreed to keep it.

Ronny understood this. He understood it the way he understood Hal's patience and Marcus's six feet and two inches and Jordan's counting—as a survival mechanism, a structure built around a wound to keep the wound from spreading. Jeannette's structure was the silence. His was painting the fence. Both of them were doing the same thing—covering over the rot with something clean, knowing the rot was still there, knowing one coat wouldn't be enough.

He finished the first section and moved to the next. The paint was smooth on the new wood, streaky on the old. His knee ached from standing but he didn't sit. The work needed doing. He'd put it off long enough.

"Ronny," Jeannette said.

He turned. She was sitting on the step with the beer in her hand, her legs crossed, her hair pulled back in the ponytail she wore on weekends. She looked tired. Not the acute tiredness of a bad night but the chronic kind—the tiredness of a woman who'd been carrying too much for too long and had gotten so used to the weight that she'd forgotten what light felt like. "Yeah?"

"I'm glad you're back at the station."

"Me too."

She looked at him. The look lasted longer than it needed to—long enough to carry everything she wasn't saying, long enough for him to feel it land. Then she nodded. Took another sip. Looked away. "Sofia wants pizza tonight," she said. "You want to call it in or should I?"

"I'll call it in. What does Danny want?"

"The same thing Danny always wants. Pepperoni and an argument about the crust."

Ronny almost smiled. Not quite. But close. The near-smile of a man standing in his backyard with a paintbrush and a beer and a wife who'd chosen the family over the question, and kids who wanted pizza, and a fence that was getting its first coat of paint in two years. He turned back to the fence and kept painting. The white went on clean. The evening settled in around them—the shadows stretching, the air cooling, the sounds of the neighborhood winding down the way neighborhoods do on Saturday evenings, the mowers going quiet, the kids being called inside, the whole world pulling in its edges and getting ready for night.

Behind him, Jeannette sat on the step and finished her beer and didn't leave. She stayed. That was the thing she'd been doing for eighteen years, and the thing she was choosing to keep doing, and the choosing was not simple and not easy and not the same as forgiveness, but it was close enough to build on. Close enough to paint over. Close enough to start.

Ronny dipped the brush. Second section done. The fence was starting to look like something that belonged to people who hadn't given up on it.

He'd need another coat. He'd come back tomorrow.

29

Friday evening. The news played from the kitchen television — the anchor's voice steady and impersonal, the sound Donna left on when she wasn't really watching, just filling the apartment with someone else's problems so the quiet didn't settle in. Donna sat at the kitchen table sorting coupons she'd never use, her reading glasses low on her nose. Alex lay on her stomach on the living room carpet, calculus textbook open to a page of derivatives that had started to blur twenty minutes ago. Sophomore year had brought harder math and longer assignments, and Sunday nights had become the only time the apartment held still long enough to get through them.

"It's Friday night, you know," Donna said, not looking up from her crossword. "That homework's not going anywhere."

"Want to get it over with."

Donna peered over her newspaper. "Need any help? I could—" She squinted at the textbook. "Never mind. That might as well be written in hieroglyphics."

Alex glanced up with a half-smile. "It's just derivatives, Mom."

"Right. 'Just' derivatives." Donna shook her head. "You know what, when you're done with that, I'll quiz you on your Spanish vocab. That I can still do. My high school Spanish isn't completely gone yet."

"Deal."

Alex felt her mother watching her and didn't mind. A year ago, the hovering would have made her skin crawl—the constant checking in, the careful questions, the way Donna looked at her like she might shatter if someone said the wrong thing. But this wasn't that. This was just her mom on the couch with a crossword, offering to quiz her on Spanish, being normal. They'd fought hard for evenings like this. Alex didn't take them for granted. Alex turned back to her homework.

On the television, the newscaster moved from a story about trade negotiations to something about weather in the Midwest. She let the words wash past her until she heard his name...

"*—Pulitzer Prize–winning photojournalist Demian Ochoa was killed yesterday while on assignment for the Associated Press in Afghanistan.*"

Her pencil stopped. Not dropped — stopped, the tip still pressed to the paper, a small gray dot darkening where it held. She turned toward the television slowly. The newscaster's face was composed into the expression they must teach in broadcast school — concerned but not shattered, the face of someone reporting loss that belongs to other people.

"*Ochoa had covered conflicts in Pakistan and Afghanistan since the 1980s and was widely regarded as one of the most important conflict photographers of his generation.*" Images filled the screen. Dusty roads. A woman carrying water through rubble. Children behind razor wire, their fingers laced through the chain link. And then — there it was. The photograph.

A noise came out of Alex's throat that she didn't recognize. Something between a gasp and a word that never formed. She sat up on the carpet and stared at the screen as they cycled through more of Demian's work — images she'd never seen alongside images she knew by heart.

"Oh God," Donna said. She was beside Alex now, kneeling on the carpet. "That was— isn't that—"

"Yes." Alex's voice was flat and far away, like it was coming from the bottom of something. "That's Demian."

Donna reached out and put her hand on Alex's shoulder. She didn't say anything for a moment, and Alex was grateful for that—grateful that her mother had learned, over this long and difficult year, that sometimes the best thing you can offer someone is the weight of your hand and the fact that you're not going anywhere.

"He gave me his camera," Alex said, although she didn't know why that was the thing she said. Of everything Demian had been and done, it was the object that surfaced—the Leica on her nightstand with the worn leather grip, the thing he'd pressed into her hands in the courtyard a year ago.

"I know he did," Donna said, stroking her daughter's hair when the tears came. Not the cinematic kind. They were the ugly, graceless kind, the kind that make your nose run and your chest heave and leave you gasping like you've been held underwater. Alex turned and pressed her face into her mother's sweater, and Donna held her, and neither of them said anything, and the toothpaste commercial gave way to a car commercial and the car commercial gave way to the news again, the world cycling through its indifferent rotations while a girl cried on a carpet in a small apartment for a man who'd given her a camera and a key and the belief that she could see things worth seeing.

When it passed — not ended, because grief doesn't end, it just retreats to a place where you can breathe — Alex pulled back and wiped her face with both hands. The homework lay scattered on the floor. The crossword was facedown on the couch. Everything looked the same and nothing was. "I'm going to bed," she said, standing.

Donna stood too. "Honey, maybe we should — I could call Dr. Harrigan, see if she—"

"I don't need a shrink tonight, Mom. I just need to sleep."

Donna looked at her for a long moment, then nodded. She knew her daughter. She knew when to push and when to step back. This was a step-back. "I'm right here if you need me," she said.

"I know."

Alex changed into pajama pants and an old t-shirt and got into bed. The Leica sat on her nightstand where it always sat, next to a glass of water and a paperback she hadn't finished. She picked the camera up and held it in both hands. It was heavier than you'd expect for its size — Demian had told her that once, the first time she'd held it, and she'd laughed and said it weighed more than her backpack.

She got out of bed and gathered them. Back under the covers, she spread them across the blanket. Mountains in northern Pakistan, the light hitting a ridge in a way that made the snow look purple. A market in Kabul with a man selling bright bolts of fabric, his face half in shadow. A village she couldn't pronounce, where children played soccer in a dirt lot with a ball that had no leather left on it.

On the back of each, in handwriting that leaned hard to the right as if the letters were walking into a wind, Demian had written to her. Not long letters. He wasn't that kind of person. Just a few lines — what he'd seen that day, what he thought she'd find interesting, and always, somewhere in the message, a sentence that told her he believed in what she could become. She read them all. Then she read them again.

She waited until the light under her mother's door went dark. Then she waited another twenty minutes, counting them off on the clock, before slipping out of bed. She put on her robe and slippers, looped the Leica's strap around her neck, and took the brass key from her nightstand drawer.

The courtyard was empty. The air had cooled and smelled like wet concrete — someone on the first floor had been watering their plants. Alex crossed to the stairs and climbed them quietly, her slippers making soft sounds on the steps, the camera bumping gently against her sternum with each one.

The key turned smoothly. The door to 210 opened with a small exhale of stale air, and Alex stepped inside, flipping on lights as she went. The apartment was bare. She'd taken down everything except what mattered most. Chrissy's room. The closet. She opened it and stepped back. Every surface was covered. Drawings on paper taped to the walls, some in crayon, some in colored pencil, some in marker. A garden. A dog with one ear up and one ear down. The view from the apartment window. Faces of people Alex loved, rendered imperfectly but with the kind of attention that makes imperfection irrelevant. It was an explosion of color in a white room, a secret kept between two girls, one of whom was no longer here to keep it.

Alex sat down cross-legged in front of the closet. "Hey, Chrissy," she said. The words came out easy. That was the thing about talking to Chrissy — it had never been hard. Even now. Even like this. "So. I have to tell you something, and you're not going to like it." She picked at a thread on her robe. " Demian died. In Afghanistan. They said it on the news tonight, which is a pretty terrible way to find out, but I guess that's how it works when someone dies on the other side of the world."

She sat quietly for a moment. "If you see him up there — or wherever — be nice to him, okay? He takes some getting used to. He's kind of serious and he doesn't smile enough and he'll talk about cameras until you want to scream. But after a while he grows on you. He grew on me."

She raised the Leica and took a photo of the closet. The flash didn't fire — she'd learned to shoot without it — and in the low light of the bedroom the image would come out warm and slightly soft, the colors muted, the drawings glowing the way things glow in memory. She ran her fingers over the top of the camera. "And Demian — Mr. Ochoa — if you're with her, I hope you can see this." She gestured at the closet with the hand that wasn't holding the camera. "I told you I'd finish it. I sent you a photo last month. I hope you got it. I hope you saw it before—"

Her throat closed. She swallowed, waited, tried again. "I hope you saw it." She sat with that for a while. The apartment was so quiet she could hear the fridge humming in the kitchen. "The lease is up next week. So I have to take everything down." She looked at the drawings. "But that's okay. I was thinking — you can both come to my room. We don't always have to meet here. My room's got better light anyway, and Mom won't care as long as I keep the door closed." She smiled. "It'll be like a new clubhouse. Same members, new location."

She stood, brushed off her robe, and took one more look at the closet — all of it, the whole bright impossible record of a friendship that death hadn't managed to end. "I'll come back tomorrow to take it all down. And then we move. Deal?"

She waited, the way she always waited, giving Chrissy time to answer in whatever way Chrissy answered. "Deal," she said for both of them.

She locked the apartment behind her. Crossed the courtyard. Slipped back into her own apartment, eased the door shut, and got into bed. She put the camera on the nightstand and the postcards in the drawer and pulled the blanket up to her chin.

She fell asleep faster than she expected, and when she dreamed, she dreamed about light.

She woke early. Six-fifteen, the light just starting to come through the blinds in pale strips. Her mother was still asleep — Alex could hear the faint, rhythmic sound of her breathing through the thin wall between their rooms.

She dressed quietly. Jeans, a hoodie, sneakers. She picked up the Leica and looped the strap over her head, settling the camera against her hip the way Demian used to carry it. The weight of it was familiar now, comforting in the way that certain objects become extensions of yourself — a baseball glove, a favorite pen, a tool you've used so often your hand knows its shape without looking.

Outside, the morning was still deciding what it wanted to be. Cool, with a thin haze that would burn off by nine. The street was empty except for a man three blocks down walking a dog that was walking him, the leash taut, both of them committed to different destinations.

Alex walked. Not toward anything. Just walked — without a plan, without a destination, just open to whatever the world put in front of her. A crack in the sidewalk where a dandelion had pushed through. Not a metaphor for resilience or hope or any of the things people would make it mean. Just a dandelion that wanted sun and found a way to get it. She crouched, adjusted the focus until the yellow was sharp and the concrete behind it fell to a soft gray blur. Click.

An old man at a kiosk arranging newspapers into neat stacks, his hands working with the unconscious precision of decades. He didn't look up. He didn't need to. His hands knew where everything went. Click.

A woman with a toddler on one hip and a grocery bag on the other, crossing the street at a half-jog, the kid grabbing at her earring while she blew hair out of her face. Click.

A clothesline strung between two oaks in someone's side yard, the sheets catching the first real light of the morning, billowing out like something trying to take flight. A red sock at the end of the line, twisting in the breeze, the only color in a row of whites. She took her time with this one, waiting for the wind to do something worth catching. When it did — the sheets filling all at once, the sock lifting horizontal — she pressed the shutter and felt it in her chest, the small click that meant she'd seen something and kept it.

She kept walking. Past the houses she'd known all her life, past the corner where the bus stopped, past the vacant lot where someone had dumped a couch that was slowly becoming part of the landscape. She photographed none of these. Demian had taught her that too — not everything deserves a frame. The discipline is in what you don't shoot.

She turned onto Sycamore and her pace slowed without her deciding to slow it. Jordan's house was halfway down the block. White siding, black shutters, a front garden that someone — probably Emily — kept in better shape than the rest of the yard. Alex had walked past this house a hundred times. She had never once walked up to the door. She stopped at the gate. Her hand rested on the latch.

She didn't know exactly what she was going to say. She'd thought about it on the walk over, turned phrases around in her head, tried to rehearse something that would sound right. Nothing did. The truth was too big for a script and too important for improvisation, and the only thing she knew for certain was that she couldn't walk past this house one more time without going in.

She had the camera. She had the postcards in her drawer. She had a photograph of a closet full of drawings. And she had a story that Jordan deserved to hear — not about a photograph or a prize or the man the world had known, but about the man who'd sat on a swing in Franklin Park and waited for a kid who'd been skipping school, and who'd given her a key to an apartment where grief lived, and told her to make something beautiful in it.

She opened the gate. It creaked, the sound sharp in the quiet street, and she walked up the path and knocked.

The wait was long enough for her to consider leaving. Then the door opened. Jordan stood in the doorway in a bathrobe, a coffee mug in one hand, her expression cycling from surprise to confusion to something guarded and unreadable.

"Alex?" A pause. "How've you been?" Alex opened her mouth. Nothing came out. All the words she'd prepared dissolved like sugar in water, and what was left was just her — fifteen years old, standing on a porch, holding a dead man's camera. "Want to see Emily?" Jordan offered, already half-turning toward the stairs.

"No." Alex shook her head. "I came to see you." Jordan's hand tightened on the mug. "Me? What about?"

Alex looked at her. Jordan Lowe, Mikey's mother, who had lost the thing no parent should ever have to name. Who had spent years building a wall out of grief and anger, and who had every right to that wall, every right to the mortar of blame she'd used to hold it together.

Alex touched the camera at her hip. Not for strength — for proof. Proof that she'd been seen by someone who knew how to look, and that the looking had changed her, and that the story of how it happened belonged to the woman standing in front of her.

"Can I come in?" she asked. The moment held. Jordan's eyes moved from Alex's face to the camera and back again. She stepped aside.

Alex walked in.

The End

Greg Morgan is an award-winning film director, producer, screenwriter, and novelist whose work spans two decades of independent filmmaking and four novels of literary fiction. Morgan's literary career began with his acclaimed trilogy Weeper, Collodion, and Sin Eater, published under the series title "Death Shall Have No Dominion." The trilogy weaves together the rich tapestry of 19th-century mourning customs with deeply human stories of love and loss. Morgan's meticulous research into historical practices such as professional mourners (weepers), sin eaters, and early post-mortem photography lends authenticity to this powerful narrative about grief, redemption, and the lengths people will go to maintain connections with those they've lost. The trilogy is available through Amazon and major booksellers worldwide.

Morgan lives on the Banana River in Florida, where he writes fiction and continues to develop projects across film and literature. The Prize is his fourth novel.

Thank you for reading The Prize by Greg Morgan. If you enjoyed this book, please consider leaving a review on Amazon or Goodreads. Reviews mean everything to independent authors, and yours helps other readers find Greg's books.

If you would like to know more about the author, Greg Morgan, please visit greg-morgan.com